A Family Worth Waiting For

AMY ANDREWS

MARGARET BARKER

JOSIE METCALFE

MILLS & BOON

First Published in Great Britain 2018
by Mills & Boon, an imprint of HarperCollins*Publishers*
1 London Bridge Street, London, SE1 9GF

A FAMILY WORTH WAITING FOR © 2018 Harlequin Books S. A.

The Midwife's Miracle Baby © 2005 Amy Andrews
A Very Special Baby © 2005 Margaret Barker
His Unexpected Child © 2005 Josie Metcalfe

ISBN: 978-0-263-26878-2

0818

MIX
Paper from
responsible sources
FSC® C007454

This book is produced from independently certified FSC™ paper to ensure responsible forest management.

For more information visit: www.harpercollins.co.uk/green

Printed and bound in Spain
by CPI, Barcelona

THE MIDWIFE'S MIRACLE BABY

AMY ANDREWS

To Karen, midwife extraordinaire, for helping my
daughter and recently my nephew into the world.
You are a truly special person with a truly special gift.

And to the RBWH Birth Centre for a magnificent job.

CHAPTER ONE

CLAIRE took a deep breath and pushed open the solid oak door. Here we go again, she thought. Six men sat around the matching oak table in the boardroom. Their conversation stopped. It appeared they'd started their departmental meeting without her.

'Ah, Sister West, do join us.' Dr Martin Shaw, St Jude's Obstetric Director, pushed back his cuff and looked at his watch.

Claire felt the scrutiny of six pairs of eyes as she prayed that her legs, which suddenly felt as wooden as the furniture in the opulent room, would move her to the indicated seat.

Anger sparked them to life as she reminded herself she had a job to do. This posse of six thought they could ruin one year of her hard work? Determination flushed her cheeks and glittered in her rich, cinnamon-colored eyes. They really ought to know her better than that by now.

She noted her placement at the head of the table and wondered nervously if they'd reserved it to honour her or interrogate her.

'I don't believe you've met our new consultant,' said Martin. 'Sister West, meet Dr Deane.'

Claire bristled at Martin's formality. They had known each other for years, surely he could use her first name? Claire wouldn't have minded so much if she hadn't been absolutely certain that it was Martin's way of keeping her in her place. You nurse, me doctor.

Unfortunately, only a few years off retirement, he was, like so many doctors of his generation, clinging to the formalities of a bygone era when doctors had been gods and nurses merely their handmaidens.

Well, this is a new millennium, she wanted to yell. Move on or move out of the way. Normally she ignored his irritating habit of using her full nursing title, but Claire was already annoyed that she had to be here at all. Unfortunately the hospital board, in its wisdom, thought she might be able to make a difference.

'Campbell. Please, call me Campbell.'

His rich voice invaded Claire's thoughts, dragging her gaze to him. So, this was the man that had driven the hospital grapevine into overdrive! His reputation with the ladies had preceded him. Apparently he was quite the man!

Claire had been so nervous she hadn't even noticed Campbell Deane. Staring at the newcomer, she couldn't think why. Even seated, she could tell he was tall. Tall and broad-shouldered, his impressive bulk dominating the chair. In fact, dominating the whole table.

And young, too—relatively speaking. She judged him to be in his mid-thirties. At least two decades younger than the other men in the room.

But it wasn't her impression of his size that drew her interest, it was his hair. Thick and longish on top with a tendency to flop in his eyes, and very definitely red. Not carrot red, more subtle and peppered with golden highlights that hinted at a fondness for the beach.

It reminded her of a long forgotten ex-fiancé. OK, so Shane's hair had been a different shade of red. Deeper. But the way it drew her gaze was the same. The way it tempted her to run her fingers through it…the same. Great! As if she needed that distraction right now!

His eyes were green and beneath the faint shadow of stubble at his jaw was skin that had obviously seen its share of boyhood freckles. Although considerably faded now, they afforded a tantalising glimpse of his younger years.

As Claire reached across to shake his proffered hand she felt a tingle of apprehension. Something told her she should avoid all physical contact with this man. Just as she should have with Shane. Some lessons in life were too painful to repeat.

'Claire,' she said automatically, as the warmth of his hand enclosed hers. And then something happened. For the briefest moment as his skin touched hers she felt... energised. Like he'd transferred his warmth into her body, raising her temperature a degree. He smiled at her and his eyes glittered like emeralds in sunshine. She knew he'd felt it, too.

She withdrew her hand abruptly and sat, wiping her still tingling palm on her white uniform. Her mind spun. She didn't need this now. She really didn't.

She needed to focus on her objectives for this meeting. She couldn't afford to be distracted by a man who vaguely reminded her of someone else. She thought about Campbell Deane's reputation in an effort to refocus her thoughts. One ladies' man in her life had been more than enough!

So, he was attractive. But the only thing she needed to know about him now was his opinion on alternative birthing practices. The word was he had a more modern approach, but was it really the case? Would he be as difficult to reach as the others? Would he be old school, too? Would he be an enemy or an ally?

The meeting got back on track and Claire pushed thoughts of Campbell Deane out of her head as she perused the agenda. She grimaced and fought her rising irritation. She was last. Item number ten—Birth Centre. The board may have forced their hand, but this group of men weren't going to smooth the way.

She frowned at her watch and resisted the urge to drum her fingers on the table. They may be able to sit around and chat for hours but she had a job to get back to. Nobody else would do it for her while she sat in this room. Claire didn't have the luxury of registrars and residents. She wasn't asking them for much, just a bit of support.

Claire was aware she was considered radical. She thanked her lucky stars this was the twenty-first century and not medieval times. Back then midwives had been regarded with suspicion and often accused of witchcraft. She had a feeling they would have burnt her at the stake years ago. The thought seemed absurdly funny in such a modern setting and Claire smiled to herself.

She looked up and noticed Campbell Deane staring at her, a small smile playing on his full lips. He winked at her and Claire could sense his interest. She dropped her gaze back to the agenda and decided to ignore him.

It was time to emit her famous 'not interested' vibes. Because she wasn't—absolutely not. And even if she had been, the rekindled memory of Shane and their messy break-up ten years ago served to remind her that men were not part of her life equation. That was the way it had to be and Claire had accepted it a long time ago. She wouldn't let an attractive stranger ruin her focus.

The meeting dragged and Claire's impatience grew. She tapped the foot of her crossed leg lightly on the table leg and didn't care how rude it appeared.

Campbell's persistent gaze was unsettling. She didn't have to look at him to know he was staring. She could feel it. The intensity of his scrutiny was almost a physical caress. She doubted he'd heard any of the discussion. He certainly hadn't contributed.

All Claire could do was continue to pretend he didn't exist. She deliberately kept her eyes averted, staring directly at Martin with what she hoped was rapt attention. She shook her head slightly and the heavy curtain of her dark bob swished forward, obscuring some of her face. It was a move designed to hobble his interest. She had to put him off. She just had to.

Despite this, there seemed to be an energy channelling between them that was hard to ignore. Claire could stand his attention no longer. It was doing strange things to her body. She felt like she'd been for a light run, instead of sitting idly. It was totally ridiculous—she'd just met the man!

'Excuse me, Dr Shaw.' She interrupted him in mid-flow.

'Yes, Sister?' He peered over his glasses at her, obviously startled by her intrusion.

'I'm sorry to interrupt.' Claire knew he was unused to interruption. 'I really can't stay for much longer. Do you think we could discuss the birth centre now?'

She was pushing her luck but Claire didn't really care at this precise moment. She had to get out of this room as soon as possible. Before she did something absurd, like stare right back at Campbell Deane.

'Yes, all right, Sister. You have the floor.'

Claire was relieved to stand and stretch her legs. She took a moment to collect herself. A lot was riding on how she presented her case. It was imperative she hold onto her temper.

'Gentlemen, I think we all know why I'm here. I know that opening up a birth centre here at St Jude's hasn't been popular among the obstetric staff. But the hospital board has approved—'

'That's only because it was raised at a board meeting with no obstetric representative, Sister West…by you, I understand.'

Claire stalled at the polite accusation. She couldn't deny

it. She had deliberately waited for the most opportune moment to present the proposal to the board. Claire had known they'd run with it once the idea had been raised, especially as it was extremely cost-effective for the hospital. Money talked.

'Nevertheless…' she smiled nervously, very aware of Campbell Deane's quiet stare at the periphery of her vision '…this project has taken a lot of work and the centre is virtually ready to open. We've accomplished a lot at a negligible cost to St Jude's. All we need now is for one of you—or more,' she joked, yeah right, 'to agree to provide a referral service for our clients. As part of the protocol we've developed, we need an obstetrician to see our ladies first, assess their level of risk and then refer them to us if they fit our criteria.'

'Sister West, I believe you know how we feel about this issue.'

'Yes, Dr Shaw, but the board feels otherwise.'

'What the board says means nothing if you can't get an obstetrician on your team,' he pointed out, and Claire felt her anger boil at his smugness.

'You forget, Dr Shaw, the reason we're offering this service is consumer pressure. The women of Brisbane want a birth centre.'

'What? So they can give birth hanging from the rafters?'

Claire ignored his sarcasm. The obstetric staff had been sent copies of the birth centre philosophy, including alternative birthing positions. His exaggeration was typical.

'Shouldn't women be allowed to give birth hanging from the rafters, if that's how they feel most comfortable?' she asked with saccharine sweetness.

'And if something goes wrong?'

'That's the beauty of the centre,' she said, clinging to the slender thread of her patience. 'For the very small percentage of women who need it, medical attention is only seconds away. It's the best of both worlds—a home birth in a major hospital. That's all we want. It's not some conspiracy to make an obstetrician get down on his hands and knees to deliver a baby.'

'A most unsuitable position,' tutted one of the other doctors.

'There are other positions much more amenable to giving birth besides the stranded beetle,' Claire snapped. She'd seen too many women forced to give birth lying on their backs. She could feel her patience wearing thinner.

'It's the easiest,' he replied angrily.

'No, it's the most convenient for doctors.' Claire took some deep breaths, trying to rein in her anger. 'Look, gentlemen, some women want natural births with no drugs and no or minimum medical intervention—'

'You have something against medical intervention?'

Campbell Deane's rich voice broke into the debate. She spun and looked at him, surprised that he'd decided to add his two cents' worth. Oh, hell, she thought. He's one of them.

'No. Not if it's necessary.' Her voice sounded weak and flustered, even to her own ears. She cleared her throat, determined to inject the passion this subject always engendered in her. 'I do, however, oppose the medicalisation of what is, after all, a very natural process. Women have been giving birth since time began without the complex equipment and procedures we can't seem to do without today.'

'Women used to die, too.'

'Yes, some women did,' Claire agreed. 'That's why we have obstetricians.'

'I believe St Jude's has a natural birth rate of seventy-five per cent. That's very good, Claire.'

About to launch into another diatribe on her pet subject,

she halted abruptly at the use of her name. Not just that he'd used it but the way he'd said it. It slipped slowly down her back, as if he'd stroked his finger down her spine. She felt her skin feather with goose bumps.

'Ah…yes,' she floundered, trying to collect her thoughts. He smiled at her, an encouraging smile, and she tried not to stare at his mouth as she picked up her train of thought. 'But that still leaves twenty-five per cent of women who are having some form of medical intervention, and half of them are Caesareans.'

'You don't believe in C-sections?' he queried.

'Not unless they're necessary medically.' Claire wanted to scream. Why was it so hard to get through to these people? Campbell Deane might be younger than his colleagues but he seemed to be tarred with the same brush. 'In this day and age women can and should have a choice over how they deliver their babies. They want an elective Caesarean? Fine. An epidural? Fine. Truckloads of drugs? Fine. I just don't think women are given an informed choice. For example, how many of the twelve per cent would have progressed to a C-section if they hadn't had a whole gamut of medical intervention first? We all know it tends to have a spiralling effect. And C-sections done for obstetric convenience only are deplorable.'

'Convenience? Such as?' asked Martin testily.

'Golf games,' she snapped.

To Claire's absolute surprise Campbell threw back his head and laughed. His glorious hair flopped back, the golden highlights catching the afternoon sun streaming through the window behind him.

'I hardly think that's fair comment,' Martin blustered.

Claire knew Martin played off a three handicap. You needed to spend a lot of time on the greens to be *that* good.

'I'm sorry,' said Claire, annoyed at having let her temper sidetrack her from the issue. 'That was uncalled for.'

'I should think so,' Martin muttered.

'You're missing the point,' Claire said, with barely concealed impatience. 'It's all set and ready to go. Whether you agree with it or not, it's a done deal. The birth centre is here to stay. What the board wants, the board gets.'

'I'm sorry, Sister West.' Martin shook his head. 'We've discussed this in great detail. Now, I can't speak for Dr Deane, but I know the rest of us agree that we're not comfortable with such a role. It's a big responsibility. Our medical insurance skyrockets every year as it is.'

Claire looked around the table as all of them, with the exception of Campbell, nodded in agreement.

He remained silent. His stare seemed to be weighing her up. She had known that this meeting wasn't going to be easy, but she'd also been sure she'd be able to sway at least one of St Jude's six obstetricians. It was a board initiative. It had been funded and set up—they couldn't refuse. But they had.

Claire felt the heat of her anger flare and rage inside her. 'Well, thank you, gentlemen,' she said with icy sarcasm, gathering her papers, 'for nothing. I don't have time to stand here and beat my head against a brick wall. I guess we all know where we stand.'

Quelling the urge to glance Campbell Deane's way one last time, Claire turned on her heel and marched out of the room. She knew it was childish but she slammed the door after her for good measure.

'Wow.' Campbell expelled a long whistle, stopping about the same time as the windows stopped rattling. She had been magnificent. Obviously passionate about her cause and ready to do what it took, take on whoever it took to see her plans come to fruition.

Not that he'd actually heard a lot of what she'd been saying. It had been difficult to concentrate when so much of the blood that usually dwelt in his brain had found its way to another part of his anatomy. He hadn't had such an instantaneous response since that time when his eighth-grade maths teacher had bent over to help him and he'd had a glimpse of her lacy bra.

If anything, this time was worse. She hadn't had to flash any underwear, just one impassioned diatribe, and he was almost dizzy from the lack of oxygenated blood to his brain. He noted the other men's laughter and was secretly amused by their relieved expressions. Sister Claire West has left the building!

'She married?' he asked. They laughed again, louder this time. Yep—definitely more relaxed now.

'I don't think you're her type.'

'Too old? Too young? Too obstetrician-like?'

'Too male,' said Martin, and the group laughed again.

The answer confused him momentarily. Campbell felt his hackles rise as realisation dawned.

'It seems she likes to wear comfortable shoes,' someone else said with a snigger, amused at his little joke.

'Oh, I get it.' Campbell's icy voice cut through their little-boy laughter. 'Because she doesn't fall at our feet and fawn all over us, she's a lesbian?'

'So the rumour goes,' agreed another, and grinned conspiratorially.

Campbell thought of his sister Wendy and how rumour and innuendo had dogged her because of her sexual preference. Such archaic attitudes made him angry. It flared in his eyes as the other men laughed, oblivious.

'Knocked back every available doctor in the hospital. A

couple of not so available ones, too.' Martin laughed. 'She was involved with a guy years ago but I know for a fact that she lives with a woman now—Mary. I think that's her name anyway. Shame really. Beautiful girl. Damn good midwife, too. Just doesn't know her place.'

'Well, now, that won't do, will it?' Campbell's voice was caustic.

'I say, old chap,' blustered Martin, the mirth slipping from his face. 'Just a bit of harmless fun.'

'Excuse me, gentlemen,' Campbell said politely. He pushed back his chair and grasped it firmly in case the growing urge to wipe the superior looks off their faces suddenly overwhelmed him. 'I have other business.'

Claire steamed into the deserted staff dining room and made herself a cup of coffee. It was too early for afternoon tea so she had the large room to herself. Good. At least she'd be able to hear as she silently berated herself. In half an hour the noise level in the room wouldn't allow for mental self-flagellation.

She flicked impatiently through her notes as she sipped the hot drink. Neat, concise, calm, reasoned. Absolutely nothing like her performance in the boardroom. She shut the folder in disgust. Try insulting and inciting. She'd blown it! Her agenda had been to flatter a few egos and gently persuade. Instead, she'd gone in with a caustic tongue and a sledgehammer.

Where they would go from here, she really had no idea. It would have to go back to the board and they would have to apply pressure. Claire had no doubt that eventually the obstetricians would have to back down. The board could be an immovable force when it wanted something badly enough. Fortunately, it believed in the birth centre.

But it all meant more time. As if the process hadn't been

slow enough already. This latest development delayed things further. Damn them, Claire thought as she stared into the murky depths of her coffee. Her eyes were a matching colour as she worried her bottom lip.

Unbidden, Campbell Deane's face entered her mind—again. His red-blonde hair, his green eyes, the intensity of his stare. The way he said her name.

'Claire.'

His voice startled her, causing the remainder of her coffee to swish perilously close to spilling into her lap.

'May I sit down?' He gestured to the seat opposite.

Still smarting from what had happened in the boardroom and irked by the way her hands were trembling, Claire wasn't feeling very charitable.

'Something wrong with all the other tables in this joint?'

Despite her deliberate rudeness, he threw back his head and laughed, and Claire was reminded how he had laughed at her golf *faux pas*. She felt her scalp tingle.

'You're not sitting at them.' His laughter sobered to serious contemplation.

Claire felt her breath stop in her throat as their eyes locked and held. Cinnamon brown drowning in sea green. She pulled her gaze away with difficulty.

'It's a free country.' Claire shrugged her slim shoulders. She had to be nonchalant, cool. She couldn't let him see that somehow he'd created a chink in her defences. He mustn't find out.

'I'll do it,' he stated, pulling out the chair and sitting down.

'What?' She eyed him dubiously.

'I'll be the admitting obstetrician.'

Claire's first reaction was to reach over and kiss him. But her ever-present sensible side cautioned her against wild impulses.

'Why?' she asked, trying to keep her bewilderment at this sudden turn of events in check.

'Because the birth centre philosophy is everything I believe in. I'd love to be part of it.'

'Didn't sound that way in the boardroom.'

'I was playing Devil's advocate.' He shrugged. 'I wanted to test your conviction. See how passionate you were about your cause. Very, as it turns out.'

Claire blushed. She'd certainly left nobody in that boardroom in any doubt about how passionate she was about the centre. She regarded him seriously. Dared she hope? Could Campbell Deane be trusted?

'You won't be popular,' she stated.

'I've never really cared for what other people think.'

He shot her such a dazzling smile Claire wanted to reach for her sunglasses. He was flirting, she realised with dismay. Claire had been flirted with enough to recognise the signs. Oh, dear. This wouldn't do at all.

'You're not doing this to…be popular with me?' she asked.

'Would it work?' His green eyes sparkled with humour.

'Definitely not. I don't date.'

'Oh? And why is that?'

'Didn't they tell you about me? About my sexual preference?' Claire watched as Campbell valiantly tried to swallow his mouthful of coffee instead of spluttering it all over her crisp white uniform. 'I'm not stupid, Campbell. I know what people say about me.'

'I guess I didn't expect you to be so open about it,' he mused, facial contortions now under control. 'So, is it true?'

'What do you think?'

'I hope not.'

Claire held her breath. A surge of energy had charged between them again. The surroundings faded away as her gaze locked with his. 'And if I am?' Claire couldn't stop the question tumbling from her lips. She blushed as his gaze zeroed in on her mouth.

'It would break my heart.' His voice was little more than a whisper.

She registered his preposterous statement but still didn't seem to be able to drag her eyes away from his hungry gaze on her mouth.

A burst of raucous laughter heralded the first people arriving for their afternoon tea. Claire quickly pulled herself back, the spell broken. How had she got so near? He seemed to exert some kind of magnetic pull she couldn't resist.

'This is an entirely unprofessional, inappropriate conversation,' she stated briskly, gathering her crockery together and rising to leave.

'Absolutely. I agree,' he said, also rising and falling into step beside her. 'Perhaps we could have a more appropriate conversation another time. Over dinner maybe?'

'I don't do dinner,' she said primly.

'Lunch?'

'No.'

'I suppose breakfast is out then?' he suggested cheekily, and her step faltered at his implication. She stopped before she tripped.

'You're wasting an awful lot of time on someone whose not supposed to be interested in men.'

'I think you are.'

'Really? And how do you know that?'

'The way you looked at me before…we definitely shared a moment back there. No one interested in women would look at a man like you just looked at me.'

'Oh, really? An expert on sexual behaviour, are you?'

'Nah. My sister's a lesbian. Trust me—she's never looked at a man in that way. Ever. Not even as a baby.'

'OK, so I'm heterosexual. Don't tell anyone. I'd hate to ruin my reputation,' she quipped, and walked away.

'So, who's Mary?' he called after her, catching up easily.

'Mary?'

'The woman you're allegedly living with.'

It was Claire's turn to laugh now. The absurdity of it all gave her a fit of the giggles.

'You don't live with a woman called Mary?'

'No, that piece of information is one hundred per cent correct. Mary West. My mother.'

'Ah.' Campbell laughed, seeing the funny side. 'In that case...'

'Look,' she said, stopping again. 'Thank you for your support with the birth centre. I appreciate it more than you can ever know. But...if it's going to come with strings, then you should know, I won't play that game.'

'No strings, Claire. I promise.' He laid his hand on his heart.

She rolled her eyes and continued on her way, walking quickly. To her dismay he continued to keep pace with his long-legged stride.

'Can't a guy just ask a girl out?' he cajoled.

'Like on a date?'

'Yes.'

'I told you already—I don't date.'

'What, never?'

'Now you're catching on.'

'I'm going to keep asking until you say yes.'

'Why?' She stopped abruptly. Exasperation strained her voice.

'Because from the moment I saw you today, I knew you were the only woman for me.'

For a moment she wondered if he'd pulled out a stun gun and shot her with it. She couldn't remember ever being lost for words. 'Don't be ridiculous. You…you've only just met me,' she spluttered.

'Don't you believe in instant attraction? Love at first sight?' he asked. The smile that warmed his face seemed to detract from his crazy statement.

'No,' she croaked emphatically, her feet finally responding to the frantic messages from her brain. Get out of here now. Run like the wind. Campbell Deane was certifiable.

Claire shook her head to clear it as she walked away. Her coal-black bob swayed like a piece of satin around her head as it swished from side to side. If she hadn't heard it with her own two ears, she wouldn't have believed it. Campbell Deane had to be insane. She should have enquired if he'd been taking his medication lately. It was patently obvious that he'd missed a few days.

Worst of all, she was going to have to decline his offer to join the birth centre team. It would do nothing for their fledgling reputation if their admitting obstetrician was as nutty as a fruitcake.

She pushed the button for the lift as Campbell caught up with her.

'I'm scaring you away.'

'You're crazy,' she hissed.

'Only for you.'

'Campbell.' She turned to him, exasperation changing her eyes to a turbid brown. 'This is the most ridiculous conversation I've ever had, but let me set you straight anyway. Whatever fanciful notions you're entertaining, I suggest you forget them immediately. My interest in you is purely professional. I'm grateful to you for coming to the rescue of the birth centre. But even if I were the dating kind, I certainly wouldn't go out with a man who talks like he's just escaped from the loony bin. I also wouldn't date someone who seems to have a bigger reputation than Casanova.'

'Ah.' He smiled, unperturbed. 'You don't strike me as someone who listens to gossip.'

'The whispers about you were pretty loud.'

'Look, sure, I've had my share of relationships.' He shrugged nonchalantly. 'All mutually satisfying and all mutually ended. But I always knew that when I found the one, my Casanova days would be over.'

The one? Yeah right. That sounded familiar. She'd been here before. 'Well, that's great. I hope you find her. But I'll tell you something for nothing—I am not the one. I am not interested. Don't waste your time on me.'

'So you don't feel anything for me, then?' he asked with a completely fake crestfallen look.

'Gratitude.'

'Gratitude?'

'Respect. I respect that you took a chance instead of following the crowd.'

'That won't keep me warm at night, Claire,' he teased.

'Buy an electric blanket,' she quipped, and leapt into the lift, grateful for its timely arrival.

Claire almost screamed when he followed her in. Her heart pounded painfully in her breast. Despite her protestations, she was desperately trying to quash an excited flutter taking hold of her body. His persistence was flattering on a level Claire didn't want to acknowledge. It had been a long time since a man had persevered. The wall she had built around herself was thick with thorny brambles. It took a brave man to even attempt to hack his way through.

'Claire—'

'Shh,' she hissed, desperation taking over. 'Don't talk.'

'It's not going to go away, Claire.'

'How old are you, Campbell?'

'Thirty-five.'

'Too old to be carrying on like a lovesick adolescent.'

'Are you ever too old for that?' he asked quietly.

Claire shut her eyes and sighed deeply. She'd read something in Campbell's eyes. An emotion that was blindingly honest. The lift reached her floor and Claire's relief was palpable. Once again Campbell followed her out.

'Why are you following me?' she muttered, annoyed by his dogged persistence.

'I was hoping for a tour of the birth centre. Surely that's not too much to grant your knight in shining armour?'

Claire suddenly felt churlish. Of course he would want to see it. Now who was being unprofessional? Claire kicked herself for not having offered sooner. It might also have given them something else to talk about. 'It's an excellent idea,' she agreed, shooting him a grateful smile.

Grateful to be back on familiar ground…even if she was walking it with Campbell Deane beside her.

CHAPTER TWO

TRYING to ignore the man walking next to her on the way to the centre was impossible. Damn it all! Why couldn't he be old and fat and balding with bad breath and an even worse toupee? Instead, the man who turned out to be her saviour was as sexy as hell, with hair and green eyes you could fall into. The fact that he also resembled someone who had hurt her badly ten years ago was a whole other distraction.

Claire was very confused. How had this man got under her skin on such short acquaintance? Was it the Shane factor? No. This reaction was completely new. Not even with Shane had she felt so instantly and acutely aware of a man. Whatever the reason, Claire knew it all added up to one thing—danger.

Pushing aside her confusion and the prickle of unease she could feel all the way up her spine, she concentrated on the joy at showing off her 'baby'. Confidence and pride added a spring to her step.

'Here we are,' she announced, as she retrieved a set of keys from her pocket and opened the double swing doors. The sign above said, WELCOME TO ST JUDE'S BIRTH CENTRE. He preceded her and Claire couldn't contain the thrill of excitement that always hit her when she walked through the doors. It was her dream, the culmination of a year's work.

'This place used to be one of the postnatal wards until it was shut down a few years ago. We've taken over the

23

first two bays on either side of the corridor. It's my hope that one day the centre will need the entire ward area.'

'You're ambitious.' He smiled. 'I like that.'

'No, not really,' she continued, 'I just want to see the beds made available. We already have a waiting list. I don't want to see our numbers restricted by space constraints.'

Claire opened the door to the first birthing suite. It was spacious, taking up an entire bay which once would have held six beds. A large, low, queen-sized bed was neatly made up with a bedspread that matched the bright, attractive curtains. Beside it a mobile crib, complete with a warming blanket, was ready to receive a newborn.

There was also a sofa which converted into a double bed and next to it a bar fridge, as well as tea- and coffee-making facilities. Behind it was a bathroom with a shower cubicle and a toilet. Against the far wall was a bathtub. Two trolleys stood against available wall space. They had covers that matched the curtains to disguise their medical purpose. One was for linen and the other carried equipment, which was used at the moment the baby entered the outside world.

Every effort had been made to create a homey atmosphere. It was as far removed from standard hospital accommodation as you could get.

'As you can see, there's plenty of room for whatever support team the couple wishes. The double bed allows for partners to stay with the new mum if they want.'

'What's the policy on siblings?'

'If that's what the parents want, that's fine, as long as there is a support person solely to look after the older child or children.'

He nodded his approval and Claire beamed.

'You planning some water births?' he asked.

Claire laughed. 'Can you see the board agreeing to that?

I thought I did a good enough job getting them to agree to the centre.'

'I've delivered a few. In the right circumstances, it's a wonderful experience.'

Claire was becoming more impressed with Campbell's grasp of modern birth practices. Perhaps he wasn't insane after all. Professionally he seemed completely *compos mentis*.

'Water births would be fantastic, but maybe down the track a bit. One step at a time. I really pushed for the baths. Water is too often overlooked for pain relief. So many women find the warmth and buoyancy an incredible help. The plumbing was the most expensive part of the conversion.'

'It's been really well thought-out. The room looks… peaceful.' He followed up his compliment with a broad grin.

It had been exactly what they had hoped to achieve. So often babies were born into bright, noisy environments. Part of the centre philosophy was to create a peaceful, harmonious atmosphere. Claire soaked up his positive comments like any mother proud of her baby. She felt weak from the full force of his smile.

'The other room is a mirror image of this one,' she said, indicating the closed door. 'Across this side,' she said, walking into the room opposite, 'is our office area.' The room held three desks. 'Two desks for the four midwives and one for our receptionist. And in here…' she opened a large built-in cupboard near the door '…is the resuscitation trolley and other medical equipment in case of emergency. The laughing gas is kept in here also.'

Campbell pulled the trolley out of its alcove. He removed the green cloth that covered the top and checked everything. She watched his large hands run over the array of first-line emergency drugs, the selection of breathing tubes and masks. His long fingers opened the drawers and checked the oxygen and suction hanging off the side of the trolley.

'Everything's here I would ever need in an emergency,' he said approvingly, and Claire felt like she had passed some kind of test.

'The other room is a staffroom-cum-commonroom. We'll use it to eat our lunch or whatever, and clients can use it to make themselves a cuppa while they're waiting to be seen. We're also planning on running our own antenatal classes. This room will be perfect for that.'

It was spacious enough. There was a sink with a jug and coffee and tea things and a microwave near the entry. A round table with four chairs stood nearby. Over by the window were a couple of comfortable lounges. A bookshelf on the wall held a variety of midwifery and birth-related books and journals.

'You've done a great job, Claire.' His easy compliment massaged her ego.

'It wasn't just me. Four of us worked on the project and set the centre up. I was just the one delegated to deal with all the red-tape stuff.' She grimaced and screwed up her nose.

'Because…you're so good at it?'

Claire laughed. 'No. Because it was my idea and that was all the reason they needed to make me do it. You should meet the others in the next few weeks.'

'How about you have dinner with me tonight and fill me in on how you envisage the centre will run?'

Claire wasn't fooled by his innocent smile. Same motive as before, just disguised in a different wrapper. Who was she kidding? If her life were at all normal then she'd have jumped at the chance. He was, after all, a very attractive man. But there was so much about her life that was complicated.

It was far easier to deny herself completely than to suffer the inevitable heartache. That was the mantra she lived by. Despite this, Claire felt a flutter in her chest that was an entirely new experience for her. Why? She hardly knew the man!

'Take a seat.' Claire indicated behind him. 'I'll fill you in now.'

He laughed but pulled up a chair anyway. Claire continued.

'Pregnant women, when they first make contact with the hospital, will be offered our service. If they decide it's for them, they'll have their initial consultation with you. If they're suitable, you'll refer them to us. All their subsequent appointments will be with us. We'll see them every four weeks until twenty-eight weeks, and then every fortnight until thirty-six and then weekly until they deliver. Same as usual. If they haven't delivered by forty weeks then you'll see them again to check everything's OK.'

'Right. I assume it's short stay? How long do they stay after the baby is born?'

'Twenty-four hours generally. Each case will be different, of course. It'll also be influenced by demand. If women wish to stay longer, they'll be transferred to one of the postnatal wards. The hospital's Community Midwifery Service will follow up the women who choose early discharge. Then we see them here again six weeks later.'

'Very good.' He nodded. 'But what about the birth? What pain relief do you offer? What's the procedure if complications develop?'

'We offer gas and pethidine, although we'd prefer to try alternatives first.'

'Such as?'

'Heat, massage, positioning, water. However, if the client wants something stronger, or if complications develop, we transfer them to Labour Ward. We continue to be their midwives and will still deliver their babies, and then they come back to the birth centre afterwards, depending on their level of intervention.'

Campbell continued to fire questions at Claire. She answered them in full.

'One more question, Sister West.' He smiled, his green eyes glittering with mirth.

'Yes?' she replied warily.

'Do you like Thai or would you prefer Indian?'

Claire groaned and rolled her eyes. 'Neither.'

'Italian?'

'I'm not going to go to dinner with you, Campbell. Quit asking.'

'I never quit. My mother says I'm the most stubborn person she knows.'

'Well, I think you've just met your match.'

'I'm not going to go away, Claire. I won't give up.'

'Always get what you want, huh?'

'No, not always. I've just never wanted anything so much before.' Campbell's pager beeped and he whisked it off his belt, frustration marring his handsome face. 'Saved by the bell, Claire West. I've got to go. Labour Ward needs me.'

Claire stood, grateful that he was finally leaving and that she'd be able to breathe properly again. He stood at the same time and suddenly their bodies were a whisper away from touching. She wanted to close the gap so badly, she had to look down to cover the surprising reaction his proximity had caused. Something was wrong—she'd known him for less than two hours! This shouldn't be happening.

'This isn't over.' The low timbre of his voice slid down

her spine as he pressed two fingers beneath her chin and raised her head. 'It's just the beginning.'

She held her breath and stood very still, watching his green eyes glitter with promise. And then he was gone and Claire sagged into the chair, relieved to be alone.

Well, his mother was right. Claire had never met someone so determined. If he pursued her as relentlessly as he had today, how long could she hold out against his resolve? Especially when she knew, deep down, that if the circumstances of her life had been different, she wouldn't have hesitated.

Claire couldn't deny she was attracted to Campbell, and it had been a long time since she'd felt that about a man. It had been a long time since she'd even been with a man. And many had tried. One or two had even been quite persistent. But despite their ardour, she'd been unmoved.

It had been easy to stick to her guns when the men in question had done nothing for her. But Campbell was a real enigma. Could she honestly say she was indifferent to him?

Claire shook herself. It didn't matter. She was still bound by her no-relationship policy and it was one she must adhere to, no matter what artillery he used to try and persuade her.

She might be appealing to him now, but Claire knew from bitter experience that initial attraction waned. She need only think of Shane to be reminded of that. Campbell didn't know it, but she was doing this for his own good.

'Ready for the last patient, Campbell?' Sister Andrea Marshall asked, poking her head around his office door. She'd been nurse in charge of Obstetric Outpatients for the last five years. She had been at St Jude's for as long as Claire, and they had done their midwifery training together.

He stretched and smiled at her, noting her keen interest.

She'd been flirting with him all morning. A month ago he wouldn't have hesitated but, since meeting Claire, all other women had ceased to exist. Still, her interest was flattering to his increasingly deflated ego. A harmless flirtation with a busty blonde was exactly the right medicine.

'Sure, Andrea, send her in,' he said, his mind distracted by the challenge Claire presented.

That she had been avoiding him, and quite successfully too, hadn't escaped his notice. Still, he was prepared to wait. All good things came to those who waited. Didn't they? And with the birth centre officially opened last week, Campbell knew she wouldn't be able to shun him for ever.

Andrea ushered in his patient and handed him the chart.

'Hello, Mrs Craven. I'm Campbell Deane. Congratulations on your pregnancy. Twenty weeks already.' He smiled and shook his patient's hand, noting the area of darkened pigmentation across her face, which was common in pregnancy and caused by hormonal changes.

'Call me Lex, please.'

'So, you're planning on having the baby here at St Jude's,' he said, flicking through the chart.

'Yes, Dr Deane, that's what I wanted to talk to you about.'

'Please, call me Campbell.' He'd never been comfortable with the blind reverence afforded to doctors. His mother had always taught him that respect should be earned. He didn't consider that what he did for a living automatically made him better than the next person. We're all just cogs in a wheel, his mother, a midwife herself, insisted. Besides, his four sisters, three of them nurses and one a GP, were always ready to cut him down to size should he let his position go to his head.

'I got a phone call last week from the receptionist at the

birth centre—I'm in! I'm so excited.' Her dark, wavy hair bounced as she laughed.

Campbell joined her, noting her glow of excitement. 'Well, congratulations again.'

'Thanks. I've really wanted to have my baby there ever since I heard about it.'

'Oh, yes? And why's that?'

'Well, I've read so much about active birth and I really like the philosophy. I've bought and borrowed every book there is on the subject. The whole concept of a birth centre is fantastic. Kind of like a home birth but with medical back-up if you need it.'

'I think we need to put you in charge of advertising.' He laughed. 'You sound like an ideal candidate. Have you thought about how you're going to cope with the pain?'

'I'd like the baby to be in the best possible shape when it arrives, so drug-free is my ultimate aim. I'll try all the alternatives first. But I'm flexible. You hear enough horror labour stories to know it's going to hurt.'

'Good for you. I think flexibility is definitely the key.'

'The receptionist said I needed to see you first and get a referral.'

'That's right, so let's do it. Hop up on the examination bed over there.' Campbell walked to the door and called to Andrea, who was sorting through a mountain of charts. 'Andrea's going to stay while I examine you. Blood pressure first.'

He pulled the cuff down from the wall and quickly took Lex's BP. 'Perfect,' he said, smiling. Next he asked her to slip her skirt down slightly so he could feel her abdomen. 'Sorry, cold hands,' he apologised in advance. What was it with hospitals? The air-conditioning always seemed set at freezing.

Campbell shut his eyes as he gently probed Lex's abdomen, feeling for her burgeoning uterus. He found the top and Andrea handed him a tape measure. He measured the distance from her pubic bone to the where his hand was. Twenty weeks exactly.

'Would you like to hear the baby's heartbeat?' he asked.

'Of course,' she said with a laugh.

Andrea gave him a hand-held Doppler. It was similar in appearance to a transistor radio. He squeezed a daub of gel on Lex's abdomen and turned the machine on. He fiddled with the volume control and turned it down until the noise was less jarring. Manipulating the transducer through the gel, he quickly located the steady *whop, whop, whop* of the baby's heart.

They were all silent as the noise filled the office. Campbell loved this part. The sounds of new life never ceased to amaze him. The miracle of it all. This was why he'd become an obstetrician. He grinned at Lex and saw the shimmer of tears in her eyes.

'What a beautiful noise,' he said.

'One hundred and sixty-four,' said Andrea, who had counted the beats.

'Excellent,' said Campbell, switching off the machine and wiping gel off Lex.

He left Andrea to help her straighten up, walking back to his desk to peruse her chart once more.

'Swabs are negative. Blood tests unremarkable. Haemoglobin good. Any foetal movements yet?'

'I've been feeling fluttering for a couple of weeks now.'

'Good,' he said, writing in the notes. 'Any concerns?'

'Nope.' She shook her head.

'All right, then. You can give the birth centre a ring and organise an appointment for four weeks.'

'Oh, thank you so much, Dr Deane…I mean Campbell. You don't know how much this means to me.' She jumped up and shook his hand vigorously. 'Actually, I think I'll go up there now. I haven't seen it yet and I can make my appointment while I'm there.'

'Good idea,' said Campbell, grateful for this golden opportunity. Look out, Claire West. Here I come. 'I'll walk you there,' he offered.

Lex Craven's excited chatter occupied most of Campbell's attention on the short walk. As they alighted from the lift on the fifth floor, Campbell listened less, becoming tuned into his body's anticipation. He could feel his heart thudding in his chest and echoing in his ears.

His stomach growled, reminding him that it was almost two o'clock and he hadn't had anything to eat since breakfast. Maybe he could persuade Claire to join him for some lunch? Nothing ventured, nothing gained.

He saw her the second he walked through the doors. She had her back to him, talking to a client, and he noticed the easy way she held her body when she didn't know he was around. She was too erect and straight when she talked to him. Like she was afraid that if she relaxed, even for a nanosecond, she might get too close.

He loved how her white uniform fitted her perfectly. It accentuated her lushness, flattering her curves and emphasising her cute derrière. It was a stark contrast to her rich olive skin and her midnight-black bob. Just watching her now, his fingers itched to feel its silky weight.

She turned to usher her very pregnant client to the door and spotted him. He watched with dismay as her clear brown gaze became muddied with caution.

'Campbell,' she said. 'This is a surprise.'

Obviously not a pleasant one, he thought. In fact, looking at her expression, he felt about as welcome as a venomous snake.

'I've bought Lex Craven for a visit. I've just given her a referral.'

Claire had to stop herself from breathing a sigh of relief. He was here professionally. She'd been very busy in the last couple of weeks, which, while tiring, had been advantageous. She'd seen him rarely and when it hadn't been avoidable, her excuses to take her leave had been completely genuine. No matter how brief their contact, she never felt in control of herself around him. He made her feel…clumsy. Claire was terrified of clumsy.

'How wonderful to meet you,' said Claire, greeting their latest client with delight, temporarily forgetting her Campbell-induced anxiety. 'Go on in and make yourself a cuppa,' she said, indicating the commonroom. 'I just need to have a quick word with Campbell.'

Campbell raised his eyebrows as Lex disappeared into the room. She wanted to chat? Was that good?

'Campbell, I'd like you to meet Shirley Miller, one of our clients.'

'A pleasure.' He smiled and shook her hand. He hadn't met her yet so his registrar must have seen her.

'Shirley's thirty-three weeks and her baby has just decided to go breech.'

'Bit of a swimmer, hey?' he joked lightly, and Shirley laughed.

'My other three have been breech until the last four weeks.'

Ah. Fourth child, he thought. That explained her very large tummy. He would have put her closer to term.

'Could you feel the position properly?'

'Pretty sure it's lying frank,' she said.

'Well, you've got a few weeks yet for the baby to turn.'

'Here's hoping,' said Shirley, and held up crossed fingers. 'I so want to have the baby here.'

'We'll cross that bridge if and when we get to it,' he reassured her. 'Did Claire give you some postures you can try at home to encourage the baby to turn?'

'Sure did. I'm going home right now, before the kids get home, to try them out.'

She said her goodbyes and they watched her leave the premises.

'She does understand she'll have to deliver in the labour ward if the baby doesn't turn?'

'Of course, Campbell,' Claire said testily, annoyed at her body's response to his nearness. 'Don't worry. I won't break any of your mates' precious rules.'

'No need to be so touchy,' he teased, his green eyes sparkling. 'I didn't make the rules.'

'I'm sorry,' she said. 'You're right. But one day, Campbell…one day I hope that we'll be able to offer all kinds of births here.'

'Amen to that,' he said, hand on his heart.

'Goodness, I can hear your cronies having apoplexy as we speak.'

He laughed heartily and his red-blonde hair flopped back. 'C'mon, Claire. Even you've got to admit that breech presentation is potentially much more complicated.'

'Potentially, sure. But you and I both know that Martin and his pals automatically think breech equals C-section.'

'You think trial of labour first?'

'Depends on the woman and the presenting part. There are too many variables. You can't treat them all the same, as Martin and co do.'

'They're just scared, Claire. Haven't you ever been scared?'

His question startled her. It was like he had seen right into her soul. Had she? About one thousand per cent more than anyone could know. She'd been scared for the last ten years.

'We…we're…not talking about me,' she stuttered. His astuteness was unsettling.

'Right.' He grinned. 'Shame…I'd much rather talk about you.'

'Me?'

'Us, actually.' Campbell watched as fear and confusion reflected briefly in her eyes before she masked them behind a shutter of wariness.

'Campbell.' She rolled her eyes and took a step away from him. She couldn't think when he was too close. 'I thought you'd given up.'

'Nope. Just haven't been able to track you down much.' He stared pointedly at her and Claire felt her face warm. He knew that she'd been avoiding him.

'I've been very busy,' she said, sounding lame even to her own ears.

'Have you had lunch?'

'No.'

'Let me buy you some. I'm starving.'

'I've brought mine,' she replied stiffly.

'OK. I'll watch. I like to watch.'

Claire stared at him incredulously. Was he serious? His expression was far from it. He looked like raucous laughter was only seconds away. He was winding her up.

She rolled her eyes and smiled grudgingly. 'I'm going to show Lex around.'

'I'll wait for you at your desk.'

'Don't bother. I'm never going to agree to go out with you.'

'We'll see. Never say never.' He grinned and ducked away before she had a chance to protest.

Claire would have screamed out loud if it hadn't been

for Lex in the next room. She wanted to stomp her foot so badly, it itched. Suppressing her childish impulses, she went to join Lex.

She felt herself relax as she gave their new client the grand tour. She answered all Lex's questions and then went back to her desk to make an appointment. She ignored Campbell, who was poking around the office.

'I understand you're offering antenatal classes?' asked Lex.

'That's right. You start them at about twenty-eight weeks. They'll run every Wednesday night for four weeks. Would you like me to book you in?'

'Yes, please.'

Claire retrieved the booking diary from her desk drawer, ignoring a muscled thigh she could see in her peripheral vision as Campbell lounged against her desk. She pencilled Lex and her husband in to start in eight weeks' time.

As Claire bade her goodbye, Campbell joined her. 'See you in four weeks,' said Claire.

'Actually, I might see you tomorrow. I've got my ultra-sound at ten.'

'Oh, what a shame you didn't get an appointment for today. Save you coming back again tomorrow.'

'It was the only one available this week, otherwise it was a couple of weeks' wait. Unfortunately Brian is away until next week so he's going to miss out.'

'Is someone coming with you?' Claire asked, noticing her client's disappointment.

'I really don't have anyone else. No family nearby and we've only just moved to Brisbane so I don't really know anybody yet.'

Claire could feel Lex's sense of isolation and sympa-thised with her. 'Ten o'clock, you say?' She consulted her appointment book. 'I'm free then—would you like some company?'

'Oh, yes, please!' Lex's sigh of relief was audible. 'I really didn't want to go by myself.'

'I'll meet you there at ten tomorrow.'

They watched her leave with a new spring in her step.

'That was a really nice thing to do.' Campbell's low voice intruded into Claire's thoughts.

He'd come closer again. There were only a few milli-metres separating them now. Appreciation sparked in his eyes. Nothing sexual. Just recognition of another person's kind heart.

He had the most expressive eyes Claire had ever seen. If he felt it or thought it, it was right there for the world to see. He'd obviously never had anything to hide. Claire envied him that.

'Nonsense,' she said, moving away. 'Anyone would have done the same thing.'

'No, Claire, they wouldn't.' His voice was serious.

'Goodbye, Campbell.'

Claire turned on her heel and left him standing in the corridor. He smiled at her dismissal but wasn't that easily perturbed. He followed her into the commonroom, catching up with her just as she had opened the fridge door and was rummaging around inside it. Her very appealing bottom was all he could see of her. He lounged in the doorway, allowing his male appreciation full rein. Soon enough she would dash it all with her shrewish tongue.

'Alone at last,' he said from the doorway.

Claire hit her head on a shelf and cursed under her breath. 'Do you mind?' she snapped. 'I thought you'd gone. You scared the living daylights out of me.' She rubbed her head.

'Sorry,' he said, trying to look suitably chastised.

Claire sat at the dining table, ignoring him. She opened her lunchbox as he pulled up a chair opposite.

'Why don't you date, Claire?'

So unexpected was his question that Claire nearly choked on the carrot stick she'd been eating. She coughed and spluttered and Campbell poured her a drink of water from the glass pitcher sitting in the middle of the table.

'Thank you,' she said in a raspy voice, taking a gulp of water. 'Is it so hard to believe that some women don't want to be in a relationship?'

'No, not at all.'

'Well, then, I guess I'm one of them.'

'There's a difference between not wanting to and choosing not to, Claire.'

'Oh, yeah? How?'

'Well, not wanting to indicates lack of interest. Choosing not to is a conscious decision that never allows for the possibility of something happening. It's choosing with your head.'

'Oh, I get it. You think I should choose with my heart.' Sarcasm laced her voice.

'I think you should *listen* to your heart. Don't just ignore it because you decided once upon a time that you weren't going to date.'

'And if I did listen to my heart? What makes you think it'd lead me to you?'

'Ah, that's easy.' He grinned a cheeky, schoolboy grin. 'I'm irresistible.'

'Oh, really.'

'Just ask my mum.'

'Oh, I'm sure to get an unbiased opinion there,' she said sarcastically.

'Hmm, you're right,' he mused thoughtfully, stealing a carrot stick from Claire's lunchbox. 'On second thoughts, ask my sisters. They have absolutely no illusions about me and they *still* think I'm irresistible.'

Campbell grinned again and stole a cherry tomato this time.

'Hey,' she protested feebly, growing weaker at the intimacy of him helping himself to her lunch.

'I'm starving,' he cajoled, and closed his eyes and sighed rapturously as he bit into the ripe, red flesh. 'Hmm. This tomato is delicious. So flavoursome.'

'My father grows them,' she said, distracted by his moan of enjoyment and the slow trickle of juice leaving the corner of his mouth.

Campbell opened his eyes and caught Claire staring. She was watching his chin where he could feel some juice trekking slowly downwards. Her stare was so intense and hungry he couldn't have been more surprised if she'd reached over and unzipped his fly. In fact, she might as well have, from the way his body was reacting.

'Claire, if you're trying to convince me that you don't want me, staring at me like that isn't the way to go about it.'

His words registered on a superficial level only. They didn't penetrate her intense concentration. She knew she shouldn't be looking but the juice drew her gaze like a moth to flame.

'Claire,' he whispered hoarsely.

It was a ragged, desperate sound that succeeded where his words hadn't. She gasped slightly, dragging her eyes away, shocked at her behaviour. It was practically X-rated. Her hand trembled as she passed him a paper napkin and tried to deny how bereft she felt that he was the one wiping the errant juice away and not her.

Oh, God, get a grip. What was the matter with her? Why did this man get to her so much?

'Is it because of him?'

'Him who?' she asked, wary again.

'The man you dated years ago who broke your heart. Or so the story goes.'

'Been snooping, Campbell?'

'No, not at all. It's amazing the stuff people will tell you.'

'Mind your own business,' she snapped, rising to wash her dishes at the sink.

'Oh, come on, Claire,' he persisted. 'If I'm paying the price for his sins, surely I deserve to know why.'

'Campbell!' She let her exasperation show.

'OK. I'll leave you be if you tell me.'

'Yeah, right.'

'I promise. Cross my heart.'

She turned to assess the honesty of his statement. He looked sincere and…it was way too good a deal to pass up. His relentless pursuit was annoying. Really, it was. And pointless. And as difficult as she found even breathing when he was near, she couldn't be with him. They had no future.

'All right.' Her shoulders sagged and she came back and sat at the table. 'We were young. No, correction, I was young. A third-year student nurse. Shane was a resident. We were in love, or at least…I was in love with him. He said he wanted to marry me and then some…stuff happened to do with my family and he…he dumped me.'

Campbell sat in silence as she laid out the bones of something that had obviously been such a big part of her life. Her complete lack of emotion as she gave just the facts spoke volumes about her hurt.

'How old were you?'

'Twenty.'

Campbell covered her hands with his. 'What stuff?'

'It doesn't matter now,' she said quietly, and removed her hands. She wasn't going to tell a virtual stranger things that even now were too painful to think about.

'Shane was a fool.' Campbell's voice held an edge of contempt.

She met his gaze and read the compassion in his emerald depths. Easy to say when he didn't know the half of it.

'No. It hurt for a long time but I think I'd have done the same thing if our situations had been reversed.'

It had been a traumatic chapter in her life. Her mother being diagnosed with Huntington's disease had been a gut-wrenching time. Not to mention the real possibility that the disease could have been inherited by herself. The last thing she had needed had been her fiancé deserting her in her hour of need. But he had.

It'd taken the better part of a year to get over Shane's betrayal. But with the passing of time, Claire had been able to see his side. It had been a tough call for someone in their prime, like Shane, to confront the possibility of his fiancée falling prey to a debilitating genetic illness. The hurt had dissipated but the determination not to make the same mistake with someone else lingered.

'I don't care what it was. If he'd really loved you, he'd have stayed.'

Claire shook her head sadly. Some things were too big, too awful to deal with. She knew that too well. 'You, Dr Deane,' she said, injecting a light teasing quality into her voice, 'are a romantic.'

'Guilty as charged,' he grinned. 'So, how about tonight?'

'Campbell! You promised.'

'Sorry, I lied. I had my fingers crossed behind my back.'

'You tricked me.' She glowered and marched back to the sink.

'You can't give up on men because of one stupid guy. I

won't let you. It's not fair to compare me to him. Give me a chance, I'll prove to you that we're not all the same.'

'Campbell,' she sighed, turning to face him, 'it's not just about Shane. There are other reasons...' Big reasons. 'He just helped to put everything into perspective.'

'I'm never going to give up, Claire. You may as well surrender now.'

'I've been pursued by some determined men, Campbell. I've never surrendered.'

'Honey, trust me. I bring new meaning to determined.'

'Well, bring it on, *honey*. But be prepared to lose.'

The instant her challenge was out Claire wished she could retract it. Damn him. Damn him for goading her into throwing down the gauntlet.

Campbell grinned. He felt an energy zinging through his body and revelled in how good and alive it made him feel. *She* made him feel. His pager beeped and he checked the message. 'Labour Ward. One of my ladies is in. I asked them to page me when she was ready to deliver.'

He walked slowly towards her as he talked, stopping a hand's length away. His gaze captured hers for a long moment.

'I'll be seeing you,' he said quietly, and walked away.

As it turned out, Claire reluctantly made her way to his office a few hours later with a document that required his signature urgently so she could send it off with the last courier run. Martin had been on the phone to her, harassing her about how important it was to have the document on the Minister's desk by close of business.

Internal mail would have been way too slow and the document too urgent and sensitive to trust to this not always reliable service.

Although Claire had resigned herself to doing the job

personally, she approached Campbell's office with a great deal of trepidation, the subtle challenge in his last words resonating in her head.

His door was closed and her hand shook as she knocked softly. Claire found herself wishing he'd left for the day, despite Martin's dire warnings, but his command to enter dashed the fantasy.

'Oh…sorry,' said Claire, taking in the two people sitting on the other side of Campbell's desk. 'I didn't realise you had clients…'

'Claire.' Campbell half stood, pleasure and surprise registering on his face. 'Come in.'

'No. It's OK. I'll come back.'

'No. Don't go. Stay. Actually, you've probably got some advice for Kay and Col.' He pulled up a chair next to the couple and she reluctantly sat down as he introduced her. 'Kay's pregnant with her second baby. They have a little boy who's three and has cystic fibrosis.'

Claire was pleased now for the seat. She couldn't believe what she was hearing. He wanted her to give advice on a genetic illness? He didn't know it, but he couldn't have picked a better person!

Claire's heart went out to the young couple. What terrible things they must have faced over the last three years, and now to have to confront the possibility of their new baby inheriting CF as well.

Every cell in her body rebelled at being part of this conversation. She wanted to get up and run. It was just way too close to home. She felt her heart beating painfully in her chest and was surprised they couldn't hear it in the room.

'Now…where were we?' He turned back to his clients. 'Oh, yes, the options. Well, you're only eight weeks so we can still investigate the baby's CF status with a special test called chorionic villi sampling. I can make an appointment for you right now,' he said, picking up the phone.

'Actually, no, Campbell, that won't be necessary,' said Col. 'We've talked about it and we've decided not to do that.'

'Ah…OK. Can I ask why?'

'We've had all the genetic counselling. We know we have a one in four chance of this baby inheriting CF, and we're OK with that. Obviously we don't wish it for our baby but if it happens, we'll deal with it.'

'Well, sure. It's your choice and you're obviously well informed, but a test at this early stage gives you options.'

'If we tested now and the baby was positive, we wouldn't be doing anything about it, so what's the point? We'll wait for the results of the heel prick after the baby's born, and in the meantime we'll be doing a lot of wishing and hoping and praying,' said Kay.

Claire admired her quiet resolve. It obviously wasn't easy for them. They were holding on tight to each other's hands as if one of them might fall if they let go.

Claire felt a pang and realised she envied their closeness. She gave herself a mental shake. This was crazy! When had this happened? Why would she feel jealous of this couple's relationship? It didn't make sense. But, then, a lot of things had changed since Campbell had entered her life— damn him!

Claire glanced across the desk at the man responsible for awakening feelings and emotions she doubted she'd ever felt before. She wanted to be angry with him but his obvious concern for this couple's plight softened her anger— double damn him!

While Claire understood totally where Kay and Col were coming from and empathised with their plight, she could tell Campbell didn't agree. He was being very professional.

Not pushing. Trying only to keep them as informed as possible. But Claire could read him like a book.

She knew how hard it was for some health professionals, particularly doctors, to take a step back sometimes. If there was a problem, they wanted to fix it or at least investigate it to the hilt in an attempt to fix it. They were healers. Doctors didn't like to sit back and not have the answers.

And then came the question she most dreaded.

'What do you think, Claire?' he asked earnestly, his green eyes begging her to support him.

She swallowed, her throat dry, trying to collect her thoughts on a subject she'd thought about every day for the last ten years.

'I think...' she started slowly, clearing her throat, 'I think...Kay and Col know better than anyone what's at stake, and they've obviously thought about it—a lot. You've done your bit, informing them of their choices, but ultimately the decision is theirs.'

'Campbell, we appreciate what you're trying to say. Really we do, but we've made up our mind.'

'All right, then.' Campbell smiled and stood and shook their hands. Claire stood also. 'It was great talking to you both and I'll see you again in four weeks. But, please, if you have any questions in the meantime, don't hesitate to contact me, OK?'

Claire watched Campbell as he showed his clients out, courteous and professional to the end. But Claire saw dissatisfaction in every line of his body. She knew what he was thinking, she had witnessed it often enough. He felt he had failed.

'Damn it,' he swore softly as he paced over to his window.

'You don't approve,' Claire said, not wanting to hear his

answer. Anything he said next she couldn't fail to take personally. It was too close to home.

'They don't need my approval Claire, I know that. It's just…' He raked his fingers through his glorious hair and turned to face her. 'I think they're going to go ahead and have a baby in the blind hope that it's not inflicted with an awful disease which, in reality, it has a very high chance of inheriting.'

'I don't think they're in denial over the risks, Campbell. I just think they're prepared to roll the dice and go with their lot.'

'What about the child? It's the one that's going to have to live with it.'

Despite understanding his sentiments, Claire could more than see the flip side. The fact that he couldn't irritated her.

'You think people with genetic illnesses can't live normal, fulfilled lives?'

'It's a debilitating lung disease,' he said, exasperation tinging his voice. 'I shouldn't have to tell you that. That child will spend the majority of its life either in hospital, taking meds or having physio and then dying too young.'

'If he or she has it.'

'If they take the test, they'll know. It'll buy them peace of mind.'

Having refused testing herself, Claire understood their reasons. How could knowing you or your child had a genetic disorder give you peace of mind?

'Ignorance can be bliss, Campbell,' said Claire, her voice stilted.

'I'm just saying…if it were me, I'd want to know. If it were me, I would think twice about bringing a child into the world if there was a history of genetic disease.'

And there it was. His statement hit her square in the solar

plexus. They were only words but they could sure wound. She almost staggered from their impact.

Claire knew what he meant, felt exactly the same way. Wasn't that why she had chosen to never have a baby herself? Why she'd even denied herself a relationship, so the temptation to conceive would never be an issue?

But, still, his statement stung. Any flutterings of attraction she may have felt for Campbell she needed to well and truly quash. If he knew the truth, he wouldn't want her. She couldn't bear to be rejected twice.

'But it's not you—is it?' Claire knew it wasn't a decision anyone else could make for you.

'No.' His admission was tinged with regret. He was silent for a moment. 'Anyway,' he said, shaking his head and pushing away from the window, 'You needed something?'

Claire admired his ability to change focus so quickly. She was having trouble processing their conversation. If she took nothing else away when she left the room, at least she knew where she really stood with him, even if he was completely oblivious to the fact.

'Claire?' he prompted, and she looked at him blankly. 'Wait? Maybe you didn't need anything? Maybe you've come to wave the white flag and go out to dinner with me?'

He laughed and she smiled despite the fog clogging her brain. He recovered easily after such a heavy conversation. He was too quick on his feet.

'Sorry, just a signature,' she said, handing him the document.

'Alas,' he mocked as he signed it and gave it back. 'I haven't forgotten your little challenge, Claire. In fact, I look forward to it.'

'You're wasting your time,' she stated, more calmly than she felt, turning on her heel and leaving the room.

She made her way back to the birth centre in a haze of

mixed emotions. Something was happening to her which she couldn't define. It was new and unwelcome and scary and all Campbell Deane's fault!

Before he'd come into her life she'd had clearly defined goals. Establish a birth centre. Make it strong and successful. Offer a real alternative to the women of Brisbane. Suddenly it didn't feel enough. She wanted more.

At least she now knew his views on genetic illness. He'd unwittingly given her the perfect weapon. All she had to do was tell him the truth and watch his interest die. See him run for the hills. Just like Shane.

But she knew she wouldn't. She'd made such a habit of concealing it she doubted she'd even know how to start. She didn't want people to treat her differently. She might have to live with it hanging over her head but she refused to let this disease define her.

It was her deep, dark, family secret. Her business and hers alone. And now, thankfully, a constant reminder to give Campbell Deane a wide berth.

CHAPTER THREE

WHEN Claire arrived at work the next morning a spectacular flower arrangement was waiting for her. 'Let the games begin,' she muttered to herself.

They were absolutely gorgeous. Claire knew they would have cost Campbell a fortune, with exotics like sprigs of wattle, grevillia, bird of paradise and dried rosellas. She fingered the card. Her impulse was to throw it in the bin but curiosity overwhelmed her. That they were from him was a foregone conclusion, but what words had he used to woo her? Romantic? Poetic? Flowery?

She glanced at the bold, black print. A gasp escaped involuntarily. Claire screwed it up and tossed it in her bin as if scalded.

LET THE GAMES BEGIN.

Was the man capable of reading her mind now? She didn't like it that he'd chosen the same words she'd only just thought. She didn't want to be on his wavelength.

Claire reeled in her frantic thoughts. It didn't matter. It wasn't going to happen. And if he thought that flowers would do it then he was sorely mistaken. Ignoring the part of her that loved, adored and appreciated things as beautiful as these flowers, she picked them up and marched them down to Obstetric Outpatients.

She dumped them in Andrea's arms, ignoring her surprise and curiosity. 'This place could do with some nice flowers to make it a little less hospital-like. Shove these in a few vases, will you?'

Andrea was well used to Claire's private life being a

taboo subject so she didn't ask. They had become firm friends over the years despite Claire's reticence over indulging too much personal information. Andrea knew that Shane had hurt her very badly, although Claire had never told her the reason for their break-up.

Before she could change her mind and snatch them back, Claire turned abruptly and left a stunned-looking Andrea in her wake. Mission accomplished, she sat down at her desk to review her day. Her concentration, however, was shot by the lingering scent of wattle.

'Who were the flowers from?' asked Pauline, entering the room and sitting at her desk. She was the centre's receptionist.

'Someone who hasn't got the message yet,' said Claire, her voice shorter and sharper than Pauline deserved.

'What did you do with them?'

'I gave them to Andrea down in Outpatients. It's too clinical-looking down there.'

'Claire,' Pauline said, with all the exasperated patience of someone who was well used to Claire's rejection of men. 'Next time, I'll have them. We could do with some around here, too.' Pauline laughed at Claire's unimpressed look. 'What poor man are you trying to annihilate with your rejection this time?'

'I wouldn't worry about this one. He's got pretty thick skin.'

'Pretty big wallet, too, judging by that bouquet.'

She was right. Claire was beginning to regret her rash action. She had been too hell-bent on getting them as far away from her as possible to think very rationally. All she knew was that she'd desperately wanted to bury her head in them and inhale their bushy fragrance. And if she'd succumbed to that temptation, she doubted she'd have been able to give them away.

And then they'd be sitting here on her desk, a constant reminder of him. He may as well be sitting on her desk because she knew that's all she'd be able to see when she looked at them. His smiling face, his red-blonde hair flopping in his eyes. Eyes that sparkled green and were so easy to read. His impressive physique…

She groaned and shook her head. No. She had done the right thing. Heaven knew, she was thinking about him enough now and the damn flowers were nowhere in sight. Despite her good intentions, too much of her time of late had been taken up by thoughts of Campbell. Her mind just kept wandering there of its own accord!

She made a determined effort to put him from her head and mentally braced herself for the day. She crossed her fingers and hoped that their paths wouldn't cross.

A very expensive bunch of flowers was an impressive opening salvo in this cat-and-mouse game they were playing. It was certainly going to be followed up. Claire braced herself for that also.

At ten o'clock Claire wandered into the radiology department and found Lex Craven sitting there, reading a magazine.

'How are you, Lex? Ready to see your baby?' Claire sat down beside her client.

'I'm so excited. I can't wait. I hope they're not running too late, I'm sure my bladder's going to burst any moment.'

Claire laughed. A full bladder was required for the scan. It provided a clearer picture of the uterus and the baby within it. Patients were told to drink at least a litre of water prior to their appointment. A big ask for many pregnant women.

Luck was on Lex's side when they were ushered in five minutes later. The radiologist, Darren, gave Lex a gown to change into.

'How's that baby of yours coming along, Darren? He must be six months old by now,' Claire asked. She had looked after Darren and his wife in Labour Ward and had delivered their son.

'Six months tomorrow. Impressive recall, Claire.'

Claire laughed. She did seem to have a photographic memory regarding the babies she had delivered. Claire was sure she could remember every baby she'd helped into the world. The moment of birth was so magical that each baby seemed to be indelibly imprinted into her memory bank. And if, occasionally, a birth did slip her mind, she only needed to refer to her scrapbook at home that had a picture and some basic information on all her deliveries. It was quite thick now, boasting over four hundred photos.

Lex rejoined them and climbed up onto the narrow bed. Darren pressed some buttons on the machine while Claire helped prepare Lex, exposing what was necessary and keeping everything else covered. Darren flicked a switch and killed the overhead lights.

'OK. Let's start. Goo first,' he said, squeezing a generous daub of the warmed gel onto Lex's tummy. A bright glow emitted from the screen and three pairs of eyes watched as the white static took form and shape as Darren applied the transducer and a twenty-week-old foetus filled the screen.

Claire took Lex's hand as she glimpsed tears shimmering in her client's eyes. Lex squeezed it gratefully and Claire didn't bother to let go.

'OK, I'm just going to check the placenta first,' he informed Lex, running the transducer around until he found what he was looking for. 'Good position,' he murmured. 'Now, we start from the head and work down. I'll be taking various measurements as I go.'

Darren explained what he was looking at as he went methodically from head to toe. He looked at the brain and took some measurements, satisfying himself that it was the right size. He checked other brain structures and calculated the diameter of the baby's skull.

Next he looked at the face, paying particular attention to the mouth and lips, checking for any abnormality. It was a perfect face. Two eyes, two ears, one nose. He moved down further and found two lungs and then visualised the tiny, beating heart. Satisfied there were four chambers and all associated structures were present, he pressed a button and the room filled with the noise of the baby's strong, regular heartbeat.

'There's the baby's stomach,' Darren informed them, as he moved lower.

'Yeah right. I'll have to take your word for that,' said Lex with a laugh.

Claire knew exactly how she felt. Ultrasound was a specialised field and what was obviously a stomach to Darren looked like a blob of black and white fuzzy nothing to most other people. He found the liver and kidneys as well. The spinal column was thoroughly checked to make sure it was complete.

'All intact,' Darren murmured, as much to himself as to Claire and Lex.

The baby was active during the procedure, allowing them a good view of everything. Ten fingers and toes were all accounted for.

'Do you want to know the sex?' Darren asked.

'Can you tell?'

'Uh-huh.'

Lex looked at Claire questioningly. Claire shrugged non-committally.

'I didn't want to. We discussed it and we wanted it to be a surprise. But…oh, gosh, I can't believe how tempted I am.'

'Yeah, I know what you mean,' said Darren. 'We were tempted, too.'

'No. Don't tell me. Brian will kill me if I found out.'

Darren took some measurements of the baby's thighbone next. He entered the data into his machine. With all the other measurements he'd imput, it would now calculate the growth of the baby, its weight and its precise gestation.

Claire felt tears prick her eyes at the wonder of this developing life, still only half-developed in medical terms but already a fully formed little person being nurtured and protected in the safety of the womb. She felt an ache deep inside, an emptiness that she had suppressed for years, refusing suddenly to be quelled. Watching Lex's baby on the screen, Claire felt a yearning begin and then intensify.

What was the matter with her? Babies had been part of her working life for over a decade. When had they started to get to her like this? At twenty, after her mother's diagnosis, Claire knew she would never allow herself to bring a baby of her own into this world. It had been difficult to come to terms with, but she'd felt she hadn't really had a choice.

Maybe she hadn't taken the appropriate time to grieve? For someone who loved babies as desperately as Claire did, never achieving motherhood was a real loss. Losses needed to be mourned. She should have cried, but she hadn't. She should have railed against the fates, but she hadn't done that either. She'd felt immensely sad but had moved on with her life. Forged a career.

Was she doing it now? Grieving? Was that what was happening to her? And why now? What had happened to trigger it? And then Campbell poked his head in the door and something deep inside her knew it was him. He was responsible for this discontent. She shut her mind to it. She didn't want to go there.

'Here you all are,' he said cheerfully, closing the door behind him, along with the bright outside lights that intruded into the darkened room.

'Campbell,' said Lex, delight in her voice. 'Come and look at my beautiful baby.'

Campbell did as he'd been bidden and admired the ultrasound images, oblivious to Claire's turmoil.

'Beautiful. Absolutely, no doubt.'

Claire raised her head to discover him staring at her. His look immobilised her. Even breathing was difficult when he looked at her with such hunger. Claire blinked rapidly to dispel the moisture that had dewed her eyes. It was too late. He'd seen it. She could see his eyes narrow with concern. Even in the gloom he was very easy to read.

'Looks like you're spot on, Lex,' Darren continued. He was so focused, Claire doubted he'd even registered Campbell's presence. Pity she couldn't say the same for herself. 'Twenty weeks and one day, according to the calculations.'

With the scan over, Darren flicked the lights on and Claire helped Lex down from the narrow bed. She rushed off gratefully to relieve her full bladder. Darren left the room to retrieve the video recording for Lex. Campbell, his back to the wall, watched Claire.

'Clinic smells nice today,' he commented casually. 'Wattle, I believe.'

'Yes, I thought it could do with a few humanising touches.'

He laughed and she ignored him.

'Where will you send tomorrow's flowers?' he asked, amusement in his voice.

'I was hoping you'd get the message today.'

He looked at her with a bemused expression. There

would be flowers tomorrow. And the next day and the day after that…until she surrendered.

'Pauline, our receptionist, has first dibs.'

He laughed harder and Claire was drawn to the way his hair flopped forward, almost in his eyes. He looked so little-boy endearing, she had to quell an urge to ruffle it. He wasn't a boy and this wasn't child's play.

'You can send me flowers from here to Christmas, Campbell, I won't be changing my mind.'

'I thought women liked receiving gifts?'

'Well, I guess that depends on the motive of the sender.'

Lex re-entered the room, out of her gown and looking more like herself.

'Darren's going to leave the recording at the desk,' Claire said.

'Oh, fantastic. Brian was so disappointed he couldn't be here. He's going to be rapt when he sees it. I just hope I remember everything.'

'You'll be fine,' said Claire, waving goodbye. 'See you in a few weeks. Take care. Ring if you have any problems.'

'You know,' Campbell said after the door had closed behind Lex, 'when I first arrived, I could have sworn you looked like you were about to burst into tears. For an awful moment, I thought something must have been wrong with the baby.'

Claire remained silent.

'You looked so…stricken.'

'I did not look stricken,' she snapped. Had she looked that bad? Had it been that obvious?

'Whatever.' He shrugged. 'I mean, I was pleased just to be able to read any sort of emotion in your face.'

'Oh, so I'm cold now?' she asked waspishly.

'No. You're just…guarded. What made you that way, Sister West?'

'Life.'

'Why haven't you got a couple of babies of your own?'

Campbell's question caught her completely off guard. It hit her like a sledgehammer to the heart. She gasped and stared at him, dumbstruck. Had he seen that much? Could he have guessed the cause of her tears?

'Maybe I don't want any.' Her heart pounded loudly, each beat mocking her. Liar. Liar. Liar.

'I don't believe that. C'mon, Claire, you've immersed yourself in babies for years. You don't do that if you're indifferent.'

'Exactly.' She forced a light note into her voice. 'I've witnessed labour first-hand many times. I've seen how much it hurts. I'm not silly.' She smiled a fake smile but Campbell was clearly unconvinced. 'Just because I'm a midwife, that doesn't mean I'd be a good mother.'

'I don't believe that either.'

'Since when is this any of your business, anyway? How would you like it if I asked you such prying questions?'

'Shoot.'

Claire glared at him. Typical. Trust him to call her bluff. Stubborn, exasperating man. 'Fine. Why haven't you had children, Campbell? Or don't you want them either?'

'I can't wait to have kids,' he said and grinned. 'I think I'd be a fantastic dad.'

Claire had to agree with him there. He would make a great dad. She should have known he'd want children. But he wouldn't want her children. Her children with her mutant genes.

'So what are you waiting for?' she asked, trying to keep a bitter edge from her voice.

'Haven't found the right woman yet. Well...' He winked. 'Until now.'

'Argh! Campbell!' She stalked to the door and yanked it

open. The conversation in here was getting too uncomfortable.

'I told you I was obstinate.' Claire caught his words just as the door closed behind her and shut him out of her sight.

Obstinate was a good word, Claire acknowledged after two weeks of floral gifts. Every morning a bunch of flowers, each more exquisite than the last, greeted her. Gorgeous, expensive creations that were increasingly difficult to give away. She did, however, part with every single bloom.

The hospital grapevine was working overtime as Claire went from ward to ward, spreading her floral cheer. Somehow they'd discovered the identity of the man responsible so Claire couldn't even pretend she didn't know him.

'Give in, Claire,' said Andrea from the clinic, as Claire passed her with yet another bouquet.

'Andrea, how long have we known each other?'

'Eleven years.'

'So you know I don't date.' Exasperation tinged her voice.

'Claire, it's been a long time. I know Shane hurt you but surely you're over him by now.'

'Of course I am.' Claire sighed heavily, weary of having to explain her motives. 'But that's the thing—doesn't he remind you of Shane? I mean, if I was going to suddenly start dating again, why would I choose someone who's exactly like my ex?'

'Are you crazy? He's nothing like Shane.'

'They both have red hair and a reputation.'

'And that's where the similarities end. My God, you can't be serious! Shane's reputation was justified. He was superficial, conceited and arrogant. He flirted with everyone, including me. He was a creep! And he wasn't even a very good doctor.'

Claire listened to her friend in silence. 'Why have you never told me any of this?'

'You loved him, Claire. He could do no wrong. What would I have gained from that except maybe a ruined friendship?'

Claire absently sniffed the bouquet in her arms while she digested Andrea's words.

'Look, I've worked with Campbell a lot in Outpatients. I can tell you he has more integrity in his little finger than Shane had in his entire body. And he's a fantastic obstetrician. Don't judge him by Shane's standards. Do yourself a favour…cut him a break.'

'No point,' Claire said, straightening her back and hardening her heart, ignoring the truth in Andrea's words. 'I don't date. No exceptions.'

Andrea's words gave Claire food for thought as she went on her way. Maybe comparing Campbell and Shane had been doing Campbell a disservice. So they both had red hair—a minor superficial physical resemblance. Apart from that, they really were nothing alike.

Claire had to admit Andrea's description of Shane's character was more than accurate and despite keeping her distance from him, Claire knew enough about Campbell to know that his red hair was where his likeness with Shane ended. And he was definitely, no contest, a much better doctor.

But, Claire reminded herself sharply, whether he looked like her ex-fiancé or not was immaterial. There were other reasons to keep her distance. Much more serious ones. The fact that his appearance had stirred up some long forgotten wounds helped make it all the easier to stay away.

If only the rest of the hospital staff would make it just

as easy. Instead, Campbell was fast gaining notoriety throughout St Jude's as the underdog. Claire had become the tyrant! Poor brave Campbell pitted against Big Bad Claire who rebuffed him heartlessly, rejecting his expensive romantic gestures. She'd even heard that one ward was running a sweep on who would win the battle.

Claire detested being the subject of gossip. Heaven knew, she'd spent most of her working life at St Jude's being a curiosity. Who? Claire West? Oh, the one who doesn't date? I hear she's a lesbian. And on and on. Nonetheless, every bunch of flowers hardened her resolve. Let them talk. A relationship with Campbell was out of the question.

Campbell was conspicuous by his absence. But she knew his game. His strategy was to keep a low profile and let his gifts work their magic. He was hoping she'd be so overwhelmed and flattered she'd be begging for a date. Well, she was on to him and it wasn't going to work.

However, when flowers arrived on the Friday of the second week, Claire knew she had to protest. She dialled his room number, knowing he did a clinic at this time.

'Campbell Deane.' His voice was warm and sexy, and Claire gripped the receiver as her heart tripped. How could a voice affect her in such a way?

'Stop it, Campbell. No more flowers.'

'Ready to surrender?'

She could hear the humour in his voice and knew his green eyes would be twinkling. 'No. I've just had enough. I'm running out of vases.'

'That's not what I hear. The rest of the hospital has a vase shortage. In fact, you seem to be the only one with available vases. Maybe you could loan them some of yours.'

'They go in the bin come Monday. Enough.'

'You want me to stop sending flowers?'

'Good. You're catching on.'

'Come and ask me. Face to face.'

'What?' He had to be joking!

'I'll be in my consulting room for another fifteen minutes.'

Claire gawped at the dead phone. He'd hung up! Why, of all the... So he wanted an audience, huh? She rose to her feet. She'd make him sorry he was so damned imperious!

Anger carried her to his office before she realised she'd just done exactly what he wanted. She stormed in without knocking and found him leaning against his desk, facing the door. Waiting for her.

'Six minutes.' He whistled as his gaze fell to the rapid rise and fall of her chest and the way the fabric of her uniform pulled across her breasts. 'I see you took the stairs.'

'It was faster,' she snapped.

'Before you start...' he held up his hands to placate her '...I apologise.' He pushed himself off the desk and walked slowly towards her. As he advanced a step she retreated a step. 'I just wanted to see your face again and I figured...well, if you were steamed up enough...'

Claire bumped against the wall. Campbell halted also. An arm's length separated them. His apology had taken the wind out of her sails.

'I'd forgotten how beautiful you are, Claire. Staying away has been so hard but I thought, well, you know, absence is supposed to make the heart grow fonder.' He stepped closer.

'Campbell.' Desperation tinged her voice. 'Stop this, please.' She pressed her hands against his chest to prevent him from coming any closer.

'You don't want me to send you any more flowers?'

Claire nodded, not quite trusting her voice, which she felt sure would betray her trembling. With Campbell so close, her entire body was quivering. She'd forgotten how magnificent he was in the flesh. *I can't let this happen. I can't.*

'I thought women loved flowers,' he said quietly, staring at her mouth as his head inched closer.

'I...I hate them.' Her voice tripped over the lie.

'Really?' he whispered.

'I do now,' she whispered back, swallowing to moisten her suddenly parched throat. *I can't let this happen.*

The room was silent. All that could be heard was the ticking of the wall clock and the thunder of two galloping heartbeats.

'Kiss me. Kiss me and I'll stop.'

She felt his warm breath on her face as he uttered the outrageous request. Only it didn't seem so outrageous now. In fact, to Claire's ears it seemed like a very sensible suggestion. His lips were so close, she was mesmerised. She couldn't think of one reason why she shouldn't. And she wanted to. Lordy, she wanted to.

He placed his arms against the wall on either side of her head. Her hands were being crushed by his body weight—a completely ineffective barrier—as he inched closer. And suddenly she could bear the suspense no longer. She closed the millimetres that separated their lips and surrendered to the decadence of the moment.

It had been a long time since she'd kissed a man. She expected Campbell to lead and dominate, and he didn't disappoint. He devoured her mouth, plundering its softness, branding hers lips with his own. It wasn't hard or savage, just thorough. It was like this kiss was his sales pitch and he was giving her all he had.

It went on and on, sucking her every breath from her body, shattering the memory of any kiss she'd ever had before this one. They were nothing compared to this. It was blinding and drugging and left her wanting more.

She clung to him, revelling in her sweet surrender. The lyrics of an old country song came to her mind. 'I feel sorry for any one who isn't me tonight.' She'd reached nirvana.

He pulled back and she gasped in a ragged breath. They stilled and he rested his forehead against hers as their breathing settled.

'Claire…?' he murmured in a throaty whisper.

And it brought her crashing back to the real world. She straightened up and he dropped his arms, allowing her some space to move away. She crossed to the window, completely oblivious to the million-dollar view of Brisbane's skyscrapers.

I can't let this happen. I can't. The frantic beating of her heart refused to settle and Claire knew it needed a prod.

'So.' She cleared her throat. Even to her own ears she sounded like a woman who'd just been kissed—breathy and husky. She turned to face him. 'No more flowers, right?'

'You used me,' he accused, laughter in his voice.

Yeah, right. He looked like someone who'd been used and abused, completely against his will. More like the cat that had swallowed the bloody canary.

'You practically sexually harassed me. You deserved it.'

'Good point,' he said, straightening his tie. 'No more flowers. I promise.'

He looked so appealing, standing there all rumpled and obviously affected by their kiss. She had to get out of there before she threw him on his desk and he *could* accuse her of sexual harassment. It had been a long time.

'As if that's worth the paper it's written on,' she quipped, walking past him with her head held high. She didn't look back, just walked straight out of his door and closed it firmly.

Claire spent the weekend in a flurry of activity. The entire house, inside and out, was cleaned. The garden was weeded. Her car was washed. Idle time was her enemy.

The minute she stopped doing something memories of Friday and the kiss would crowd in and then other thoughts and feelings that she couldn't afford to nurture came along, too. She needed to work. She had to work! Anything to stop herself from thinking.

She mustn't entertain fanciful thoughts. Just because he had kissed her like she'd never been kissed before, it was no reason to go and lose her head. There were too many reasons why it wouldn't work.

She fell into bed each night exhausted, hoping for the kind of sleep that was deep and dreamless. But even in sleep he occupied space in her head and she woke each morning tired and cranky and confused. Damn him!

On Monday, a box of sinfully rich chocolate truffles, beautifully gift-wrapped, was waiting for her. Great. Her biggest weakness next to flowers and men with red hair. She groaned and opened the card.

No Flowers. A Promise Is a Promise.

Campbell was again conspicuous by his absence as each day a box of chocolates arrived. She gave them away, too, but did allow herself the odd indulgence from each box. She wasn't weakening, she was just being practical. A person had to eat.

A week passed and Campbell hadn't contacted her. The weekend came and went and Monday morning saw another delivery of chocolates, more heavenly than the last five. Claire knew she should ring him and demand that he stop, but with their kiss and its emotional fallout still fresh in her mind she didn't think she was up to another audience with Campbell.

She knew it was the reason for his silence. He was biding his time until she tired again of his persistence and initiated contact. This time she wasn't going to give him another opportunity to steal a kiss.

Claire put the fact that she'd actually kissed him to one side. He'd probably had it planned all along. The minute she'd walked into his office…probably even before that. She'd bet he'd been plotting how to get a kiss from her.

And despite all the reasons she shouldn't, Claire doubted she could be strong enough to resist a second taste of his lips. Never in all her experience of men had she ever met the like of Campbell. Rationally she knew that starting something wasn't possible or even fair, but she was struggling with an inner resistance that seemed to have sprung from nowhere.

Claire opened the box and absently chose a chocolate, her mind reliving the kiss for the hundredth time. Her phone rang and she was grateful for its intrusion. She'd spent far too much time daydreaming about Campbell lately.

Campbell was smiling as he shut the door. What a great way to end the week and put you in a good mood—delivering a baby. And what a whopper! Four and a half kilos! No wonder the mother, who had endured a long and exhausting labour, had required some suturing. As Campbell strode past the nurses' station the sweet aroma of chocolate wafted out to meet him. His stomach grumbled and he realised it was lunchtime.

He chose a chocolate and popped it into his mouth. He knew they were the ones he'd ordered for Claire this morning. He'd specifically asked for a box of heart-shaped chocolates. Her continual rebuffing was beginning to irk. Especially when he saw his gifts being enjoyed by the entire St Jude's nursing staff. Especially when he couldn't sleep at night from thinking about that kiss.

'Great chocolates, Campbell. Thanks,' said one of the labour ward nurses with a cheeky grin as she chose one and scurried off.

Campbell straightened his tie, took another chocolate and decided it was now or never. He wondered if Claire liked chocolate-flavoured kisses. He had to have more of her sweet lips.

He found her at her desk, writing industriously in a chart. She hadn't heard him so he lounged against the doorframe for a while. The heavy swing of her raven hair obscured her face, so on she wrote, completely oblivious to his presence. He liked being near her. Even with an office and several desks' distance between them, he could feel his body's cells responding. It was hard for him to describe what it was, the feeling was so basic, so elemental. But he liked it.

'You look like you could do with some lunch, Sister West.' He watched as her pen stilled and she slowly peeked out from behind the curtain of her hair. 'Hello, Claire. How are you?'

'Four kilos heavier, thanks to you. Lunch is out—I'm on a diet.'

'So...' he laughed '...you didn't give them all away?'

'I sampled a few,' she said, and turned back to her notes.

Claire allowed her hair to swing forward again. Seeing him so unexpectedly had brought him squarely back into her focus. And in the last few days she'd been doing so well, relegating him to the far reaches of her grey matter. Only her dreams visited him there.

'Lunch, Claire?' Her dismissal amused him.

'Can't do,' she said, not bothering to look away from her notes. 'I'm expecting Shirley Miller any moment.'

'The breech?'

Claire heard the doors to the unit open. 'Perfect timing.' She looked up and grinned. She was careful not to come into contact with Campbell's lounging body as she passed him to greet Shirley. Even just walking nearby, her body responded. It trembled as if they were two magnets, irresistibly drawn to each other.

All thoughts of Campbell fled when Shirley doubled over and clutched her husband's arm.

'What's up, Shirley?' asked Claire, remaining calm. She guided her client into one of the birthing suites, motioning to Campbell to stay where he was.

'I don't know,' she said, straightening. 'I've been having a lot of false labour pains over the past couple of days and some nagging backache. But just now, in the car park, I think I had a couple of contractions.'

'OK,' said Claire. 'Are you all right to lie down while I feel the baby's position?'

'It's still breech. It hasn't turned,' said Shirley as her husband helped her onto the bed.

Claire gently palpated her client's very pregnant abdomen. 'Hmm. You're right. You're, what...thirty-seven weeks now?'

'Yes.'

Claire paused, removing her hands as Shirley had another contraction. She gripped Claire's hand hard as Claire watched the clock to time the contraction. Ninety seconds.

'They're bad, aren't they?'

'Yes.' Shirley grimaced.

'Right. Well, I think we need to get you up to Labour

Ward straight away. I'm sorry but, as I already explained, we can't do a breech birth here.'

'I know. It's all right. Frankly, I just want this baby out. I don't care how or where you do it.'

'OK,' Claire laughed. 'We can do an internal when we get there.' Claire popped her head out the door.

'What's happening?' Campbell asked.

'Still breech but definitely in labour. Grab the wheelchair from the storeroom, will you? You can accompany us up to Labour Ward.'

'Oh, so I do have my uses,' he teased.

'Just get the wheelchair.'

Campbell did as he was asked and entered the room shortly afterwards, pushing the chair just as Claire was helping Shirley off the bed. 'Your chariot, madam,' he said with a flourish, and bowed.

Shirley and her husband laughed. As she turned to sit in the chair, she cried out and her membranes ruptured. Amniotic fluid flooded over the chair and floor.

'Oh, God. I'm sorry,' Shirley apologised.

'It's fine, don't worry,' Claire assured her, grabbing some hospital-issue towels and throwing them onto the puddle on the floor.

Shirley clutched her stomach and her eyes grew wide in alarm.

'What?' asked Campbell.

'It's coming. The baby's coming now!'

Campbell and Claire exchanged the briefest look and sprang into action. They knew that a woman who had been through this three times already could give birth quickly. They also knew that often, when a mother made such an alarming statement, she was spot on.

'Right, Shirley,' said Campbell, his voice calm and confident. 'We're going to need to have a look at what's happening. I know this may be difficult right now, but the most important thing to remember is not to push. OK? You can pant but don't push. Are you comfortable standing? It really is the best position to deliver the baby. It's better to have gravity on our side.'

'This is fine,' Shirley agreed.

'If your husband…?'

'Graham,' Claire supplied.

'Graham could support under your arms and you lean back into him… That's great,' he complimented them as Graham supported his wife perfectly.

Campbell pushed the wheelchair out of the way and got down on his hands and knees on the towels. Claire followed suit.

Shirley was absolutely right. The baby *was* coming. In fact, as Claire removed Shirley's underthings it was evident that it was already there. Adrenaline accelerated her heartbeat as they looked at the baby's bottom and scrotum bulging from the birth canal.

'Delivered any breeches before?' Campbell asked quietly.

'A few, when I worked out west. You?'

'I studied for six months under a French obstetrician who specialised in breech deliveries. I delivered plenty while I was there. So we can do this, OK? Remember the cardinal rule? Hands off the breech.'

'Let's do it.' She smiled and he squeezed her hand.

His confidence buoyed her. The potential for complications increased with a breech presentation. It was good to have an experienced obstetrician by her side.

Claire got up and pulled a trolley close. Campbell grabbed some gloves and pulled them on.

'OK, Shirley, your little boy is going to be here soon.'

'B-boy?'

'Yes, the evidence is hanging free for all to see. I'm just going to have a feel and see where the legs are, OK?'

'Sure,' she panted.

Campbell inserted two fingers and shut his eyes, concentration puckering his brow. 'It's a frank,' he said, removing his hand. A breech in a frank position meant that the legs were jackknifed onto the abdomen—the commonest form of breech.

'You're doing so well, Shirley. At the next contraction, feel free to push with it, OK? We'll see if the legs will come out without any help.'

'Oh, boy, another one—now,' she said, starting to breathe heavily.

'Go with it, Shirley. Big push for me.'

Shirley bellowed loudly as she bore down. The legs slipped out in textbook style and the baby was now visible up to his belly button.

'This baby sure wants out, Shirley,' Campbell joked. 'He's doing all the right things. He's practically delivering himself.'

Campbell pulled a loop of umbilical cord down to give them some slack for when the rest of the body made its appearance. The baby started cycling his legs, slowly inching himself out, obviously determined to be born. The arms and shoulders came out next. The baby was almost completely out now. Only the head remained.

'Wonderful, Shirley,' Claire soothed. 'You're doing really well. The head will be out soon.'

'I'll hold you to that.' A flushed and sweaty-faced Shirley attempted humour.

Campbell was supporting the baby's weight, cupping his bottom. His other hand spanned the tiny chest to slow the delivery while they waited for the next contraction to deliver the head.

Both Claire and Campbell knew that delivering the head was the crucial time and the one most fraught with potential complications. With a normal delivery the head was the first part out, having fully dilated the cervix and vaginal opening to accommodate it. With a breech, the head was the last part to come out, so if full dilatation hadn't occurred, and particularly if the head was large, the baby could get stuck.

Shirley moaned as another pain contracted her uterus. Graham comforted and encouraged her as he took her weight. Campbell continued to support the baby as the back of the head cleared the birth canal. They could see the nape of the neck now. Shirley cried out as her birth outlet slowly stretched to allow the passage of her baby's head.

Campbell supported the baby as it slipped out. He stood and placed the newborn in his mother's arms. Jubilation reigned supreme as the baby wailed lustily. Claire felt hot tears prick her eyes. She let them shine, not caring whether Campbell saw them or not. What a rush! The birth centre's first birth, and a breech! Shirley and Graham stood in the middle of the room, hugging and laughing and crying.

Putting her excitement aside, Claire covered the wet newborn in a warmed blanket and helped Shirley to the bed. The job wasn't finished yet. The cord had stopped pulsing so she clamped it and showed Graham how to cut it. She administered an intramuscular injection of a drug that stimulated uterine contraction, and then she delivered the placenta.

Frivolity, excitement and laughter ebbed and flowed around her as Claire completed her responsibilities. Campbell sat on the bed with the new parents, admiring the latest addition to their family. Claire watched him surreptitiously. It was good to see the grin couldn't be wiped from his face either. It made her own smile even bigger.

A quiet knock at the door interrupted the celebrations. It was Valerie Baines. She was one of the centre's midwives who'd come in especially today to attend a training course. She'd been out to lunch.

'Oh! I leave you alone for an hour and you deliver our very first baby!' she exclaimed.

'A breech, too,' said Claire.

'Such clever people,' she teased, and joined in the excited gathering, cooing at the baby and congratulating everyone.

'This requires a celebration,' Valerie declared half an hour later after the paperwork had been completed and the room put to rights. 'Let's crack open that bottle of champagne we've been keeping for this occasion.' She ran off to get it.

She returned with the chilled bottle and five glasses. They clinked them together and toasted the baby—David John Miller. The newborn slept peacefully in his father's arms. He'd had a tough day, too. They also toasted Claire and Campbell and the birth centre.

'To you.' Campbell raised his glass to Claire as Valerie helped Shirley to the shower, husband in tow.

Claire stroked her finger down the soft red cheek of baby David. 'Ditto.' She smiled and they grinned at each other like idiots. Claire felt the attraction between them treble. She was in real trouble! 'You know Martin is going to have a fit over this, don't you?'

'Let him,' he said and laughed. They toasted that as well.

Claire had to admit that working beside Campbell had been exhilarating. She'd seen another side to the man who had pursued her so persistently. The dedicated doctor. Cool and calm in a situation that would have tested most doctors' mettle. And he wasn't afraid to get on his haunches to deliver a baby. She felt her admiration for him rise and mix with her burgeoning attraction. The champagne must have gone to her head.

Campbell stared at the very different Claire in front of him. Her cheeks glowed and her brown eyes were as tempting as the expensive chocolates he'd been sending her. For once he could read everything in their sweet depths. She wanted him. It was there, as plain as day. He should have plied her with champagne a month ago.

'Have dinner with me tonight.' He held his breath.

'OK.' She grinned. Yup. It had definitely gone to her head.

CHAPTER FOUR

CLAIRE sat beside the bed, holding her mother's bony, frail hand. Her thumb stroked rhythmically over the papery skin. Right here in front of her lay the reason that a relationship with any man was impossible.

The clock in the lounge room chimed seven, breaking into her reverie. Time to go. She leaned forward and gently kissed her mother's cheek. Mary didn't stir.

'I'd better go, Dad,' she said, locating her father in his bedroom, watching the evening news.

'Goodnight, darling.' He smiled his gentle smile. 'Claire...'

'Yes?'

'I don't mean to interfere...but...you know you don't have to come home tonight. I can manage just fine.'

'Dad,' she joked in mock horror. 'You're not suggesting I spend the night with this man on the first date?'

He smiled, a rare occasion of late. 'Seriously, darling, it's been years since you've been on a date. I want you to enjoy yourself for a change.'

'I have to be here in the morning, Dad. She expects me.'

'She's not your responsibility, Claire.'

'Dad...she's my mother.'

'You're young, you're supposed to be selfish and irresponsible. I can manage.'

'I know but...she'll fret if I'm not here.'

'Darling, she probably won't even be aware.' His voice cracked and Claire had to swallow hard.

'She'll know,' Claire insisted. She walked into the room

and kissed him on the head. 'I've got my mobile. Call me if you need to. I mean it, Dad. Anything. See you in the morning.'

Claire pulled out of her driveway, her mind preoccupied with her mother's illness and her father's devotion. He deserves a medal, she thought as she pulled up at the lights. She chewed absently at the inside of her lip, worrying about the future.

She gave herself a mental shake as the car behind her hooted to let her know that the light had turned green. Her thoughts should be on the evening ahead and Campbell. If she was going to worry about anything tonight, it should be him.

He'd wanted to come and pick her up but she had insisted on going to the restaurant independently.

'Is that so you can make a fast getaway?' he had asked.

'Huh! My plan is foiled,' she had quipped, and he had laughed and left it alone.

Not for the first time, she admonished herself for her rash acceptance of his invitation. Once the euphoria from little David's birth had ebbed, her doubts had resurfaced. She'd even attempted to page him and cancel, but he must have already left for the day.

If she had known his home phone number she would have tried him there. But she didn't, so here she was, feeling rather like she was driving to her doom instead of a pleasant evening with a nice man.

Her gaze fell on her mobile phone and she pushed aside the temptation to ring the restaurant and cancel through a third party, like a coward. She also quelled the urge to just drive around for a few hours and then go home.

Stand him up? After he'd hunkered down on his hands and knees in a pool of amniotic fluid and helped her deliver a baby? And not just any baby, but one that a lot of obstetricians would have baulked at delivering. That seemed pretty churlish.

So. She'd go. As a thank you and nothing else. She'd be polite and companionable and beat a hasty retreat as soon as was possible. Easy. Simple.

And if her thoughts turned fanciful, all she need do was picture her mother. Remember her just as she had left her this evening, lying in bed, ravaged by a cruel disease, waiting to die. That should do it.

Claire arrived at the restaurant only a little late. She hadn't really known what to expect. She'd assumed it would be something posh and à la carte. So to find a small Italian joint off the beaten track was a pleasant surprise.

Claire had been unsure what to wear so had decided on a very plain sleeveless linen shift dress with a modest neckline and an even more modest hemline, falling below the knee. She had chosen it because of its simplicity. She hadn't wanted to wear anything too provocative and give Campbell the wrong idea.

If she'd known that the moment she'd slipped it over her head the dress went from simple to sexy, she'd never have worn it. It was the colour. A bright fire-engine red, which complemented her olive skin and accentuated the richness of her black hair. The colour naturally drew attention but, once gained, the vision of her in it was one not easy to forget.

Well, she sure knew how to make an entrance, Campbell thought as two waiters nearly collided in their haste to seat her. She did look ravishing, and Campbell understood the effect she was having on them. But the most important thing was that she was here with him, finally. The wait had been worth it.

A young Latin-looking waiter, the apparent victor between the two, ushered her to the table where Campbell waited. He half rose politely as the waiter pulled her chair out and then spread a starched linen napkin on her lap, lingering a little longer than Campbell felt was appropriate. Victor or not, Campbell was going to break his fingers if he touched Claire again. Anywhere. At all.

Claire could feel Campbell's scrutiny as the waiter fussed and took her drink order. She was pleased to be sitting because Campbell in casual mode was a sight to behold. Having seen him in nothing but suits and ties, it was an unexpected pleasure to find him in faded denim jeans and an open-necked polo shirt, which clung to the firm muscles of his arms and chest.

They regarded each other steadily over a wax-encrusted Chianti bottle complete with flickering candle. Damn! The lingering memory of his devastating kiss swamped her traitorously. Claire could feel her resolve weakening and the internal struggle she had fought with herself from the minute she'd met him seemed less important by candlelight.

'I thought you were going to stand me up,' he said, the candlelight accentuating the blond highlights in his hair.

'So did I.' She smiled and he laughed.

'I'm pleased you didn't.' He raised his water glass. She raised hers and they clinked them together.

'This place is nice. Kind of quaint. Authentic.'

'It's my favourite place to eat out. You can keep all those fancy places with their nouvelle cuisine. Me, I like good hearty food and lots of it. Places that serve you up a teaspoon of food in the middle of a huge plate just don't do it for me. I hope you're not disappointed.'

'On the contrary.' She shrugged her slim shoulders, her bob brushing against them. 'I agree. I can't bear the pretentiousness of those places.'

'So you're not one of these women who just nibble when they go on dates?'

'Absolutely not. If you think I'm going to sit here and pick at a garden salad all night, think again. I'm in the mood for lasagne.'

'Your choice in cuisine is matched only by your choice in clothes,' he complimented her. 'You look amazing tonight. That dress and the candlelight...wow!'

Claire blushed and laughed. Their gazes held and locked. The heat between them could have lit a thousand candles.

The waiter arrived to take their order and Claire released her breath. Campbell ordered lasagne for her and marinara for himself. He also ordered a bottle of red wine, which arrived promptly.

'To the birth centre.' He raised his glass.

'To breech births,' she countered.

'To little Davy,' he agreed, and clinked his glass against hers.

'Thank you for today, Campbell. Your ability and professionalism impressed me. You said you studied in France for a while?'

'Yes. There's an obstetrician there, Henri Busson, he's quite well known.'

'Yes, I've read some of his papers.'

'He has his own private clinic. Women come from all over Europe to give birth there. He really is the leading expert in alternative birthing practices.'

'Alternative birth?' Claire shook her head. 'Is it just me, Campbell, or has the whole world gone completely crazy? Surely things like inductions and Caesareans should be alternative birthing practices? What they call alternative these days is really just natural childbirth. When did it all get so screwed around?'

'I guess when doctors decided to interfere.'

'I'll drink to that.' She smiled and swallowed some of the rich, full-bodied wine.

'You'd get along so well with all my sisters.' His voice was laced with humour.

'All? How many do you have?'

'Four.'

'Wow.' Claire whistled. 'Let me guess. You're the youngest.'

'How did you know that?'

'You've obviously been spoilt and indulged. You certainly don't know how to take no for an answer.'

'Huh,' he snorted. 'You couldn't be further from the truth. More like harangued and henpecked.'

'Yeah, right.' Claire didn't believe a word of it.

'Well, maybe a little indulged. But mostly the h-words,' he answered sheepishly.

'Tell me about your family,' Claire said as the waiter placed their meals in front of them.

'Well…' He picked up his fork. 'My sisters, except for one, are nurses, two of them midwives. The other one's a GP. My mother is also a retired midwife. She's English and was a community midwife over there for many years. I think that's where I get my more modern approach from.'

'And your dad?'

'He died a few years ago. Heart attack.'

'Oh, Campbell.' Claire reached across and touched his hand. 'I'm so sorry.'

Campbell reeled from the look of compassion in her cinnamon eyes. She might be guarded most of the time but, hell, she could certainly be expressive. Something told him she knew a lot about grief. Would she open up to him? Was it worth the risk of seeing the shutters come down when her compassion gave her a whole new appeal?

'What about your family?'

Campbell felt the cool air against his hand as she abruptly removed hers, like a slap in the face. She returned her concentration to her meal and Campbell regretted having opened his mouth.

'Nothing to tell really. Nowhere near as colourful as your lot. Just Mum and Dad and me. Dad took early retirement a couple of years ago…for medical reasons.'

Campbell didn't dare ask about that. From the rigidness of her back he doubted she'd tell him anyway. They ate in silence for a little while, Campbell groping for a way to continue the conversation without her completely freezing him out.

'Have you always lived with them?'

'No. I moved back in a few years ago.' She placed her knife and fork down on her empty plate. 'Mmm, that was delicious.'

Campbell knew when to take a hint. 'Pleased you liked it. We'll have to come here again. Do you like sorbet? It's divine here. Better than anything you'll get in Italy.'

'Sorbet sounds perfect,' she agreed, and watched as he leaned back to beckon the waiter. His shirt pulled slightly out of his waistband. Claire tried really hard not to ogle but the tantalising glimpse of tanned skin gliding over muscle proved too much temptation. It certainly distracted her from the awkwardness she'd felt when he'd been quizzing her about her family and from his comment about them coming back here together.

Campbell placed their dessert order, aware the entire time of Claire's gaze. He felt his heart beat faster in anticipation. He looked at her and she didn't even bother to hide her hungry stare. He wanted her more now than he had since he'd first met her.

'Let's skip dessert,' he suggested softly, their gazes still entwined.

'Too late.' She gestured to the fast-approaching waiter.

'It's never too late.' His gaze didn't waver.

'I'm hungry.'

'So am I.'

Claire had no doubt as the waiter placed their plates before them that Campbell wasn't talking about the sorbet. Their desserts started to melt as their eye contact continued. The air between them grew thick with unspoken desire.

'You no like?' The waiter, completely oblivious to the raging atmosphere, interrupted their silent exchange.

'Oh, I like,' said Campbell, his eyes never leaving Claire's face. 'I like very much.'

Claire smiled at the waiter and rolled her eyes dramatically, assuring him that everything was fine. She picked up her spoon and took a mouthful of the tangy sorbet.

'Mmm, I think you're right. This definitely beats the sorbet I had in the Platz de San Marco in Venice. I didn't think that was possible.'

'Maybe it's the company.'

'Maybe.'

The evening air was balmy as they stepped outside twenty minutes later.

'Why don't you come back to my place for a coffee?' Campbell kept his voice light.

'Oh, Campbell, I don't think that's a very good idea. I've had a lovely evening but I think I should go home.' Claire was surprised at how badly she wanted to go with him. Still, that didn't make it wise.

'No strings, I promise. I've got this great home video of a footling breech I delivered while I was in France. I thought you might be interested.'

'A footling?'

'Ever seen one?'

'No. We just don't deliver them any more.'

'It's fantastic footage,' he coaxed.

'OK,' she agreed slowly, and smiled. Sure, why not? It sounded interesting. Claire knew it was a probably just an excuse to spend more time with her, but she was an adult. Whatever his motive, she was there to watch the video, make some polite conversation and then leave. Nothing was going to happen. She was sure she could keep her hormones in check for an hour or so.

'I'll drive you,' he suggested, holding out his hand.

'No. I'll follow you in my car.'

'I really thought you were going to do a runner,' Campbell told her as he inserted his key into the front door.

'Oh, ye of little faith,' she mocked him playfully as she stepped into his apartment. He switched the lights on then dimmed them to a soft glow. Claire wandered over to the bank of huge floor-to-ceiling glass windows offering a spectacular view of the river and the city skyline.

'Wow! Nice digs,' she complimented him as he clattered around in the kitchen, fixing coffee.

'Yes, I was really lucky to find it,' he said, carrying a tray to the lounge area where the television rested in a beautiful heavy wooden cabinet. He placed the coffee-mugs on a matching low table and indicated for Claire to sit beside him on a double-seater leather lounge chair.

She sat sipping her coffee, watching his jeans pull and strain across his taut bottom as he found the tape and placed it in the machine. She tried not to look but, hell, he was sexy!

He smiled at her as he sat beside her and pushed the play button on the remote. She dragged her gaze from him with difficulty as the screen flickered to life and the low moans of a woman in labour commanded her attention.

For the next fifteen minutes Claire watched, intrigued, as Campbell deftly guided the couple through the birth of their baby. He supplied a low commentary from time to time and when Claire saw the first foot hang free from the birth canal she was totally involved and in awe of Campbell's cool and professionalism.

Despite the risks, the baby was delivered without a hitch and Claire felt tears prick her eyes as the emotional couple embraced Campbell and wept openly. She was touched by his handling of the sentimental moment and somehow wasn't surprised to see his eyes shimmer with tears as he held the newborn he had helped into the world.

'That was beautiful, Campbell,' Claire said, blinking rapidly as the screen went blank.

'It was one of the most incredible experiences of my life,' he admitted quietly.

She stood before she was tempted to turn and look at him. They were a little too close on the lounge for comfort. After witnessing such an emotional scene, Claire didn't trust her reactions.

'Why don't you open the doors and go out onto the deck?' Campbell suggested softly. 'I'll bring us out a drink.'

The fresh air hit Claire's heated skin like an arctic blast. She sucked in deep, cleansing breaths, waiting for her heart rate to settle. She had to get out of here. Seeing Campbell all dewy-eyed with the naked, wet newborn had started Claire's thoughts on a path she didn't want to go down. She had to leave. Now.

He crossed to where she stood on the far corner of the deck, her hands gripping the railing, her back to him. He drew closer until he could feel the nervous heat radiating from her body. He was careful not to touch her, ignoring the urge to pull her against him.

'Port,' he murmured quietly, and watched her shoulders tense as she turned to face him.

'Th-thanks.' OK. One drink and then she'd leave.

Claire sipped at the warm liquid and felt its fiery residue trail a path all the way to her stomach. She looked into the glass, swishing the liquid around and watching it coat the sides of the glass.

He stood beside her, sipping his own drink. Nearly touching. Nearly.

'Claire…' he murmured, his voice deep and throaty. He turned to face her and the breeze enveloped him in her scent. 'God, you smell incredible,' he groaned as he closed the small space separating them and nuzzled her hair. He inhaled the exotic aroma of her shampoo and felt himself tighten.

Claire swallowed as his nuzzling sent the most delicious sensations crawling along her scalp.

'I really must go,' she croaked, desperately trying to fight the fog of desire and sound like she meant it.

'OK,' he whispered, as his lips travelled to the sensitive skin of her neck where he continued to nuzzle up and down the slope of her neck and along the slant of her shoulder as far as the fabric of her dress would allow.

Claire shut her eyes tight and felt herself swaying into Campbell. She wasn't sure if she made it all the way by herself or if he met her halfway. Her thought processes were beginning to blur as her skin broke out in goose-bumps and her abdominal muscles contracted with desire.

She felt the hardness of his erection immediately. Her toes curled as she heard his swift intake of breath. He pressed his lips into her neck just below her ear and gave a groan that conveyed pleasure and pain.

'Don't do that,' she begged passionately. 'I can't do this,' she panted. 'We have to stop.'

Campbell drew back, his chest heaving. 'Are you sure?' he asked, and his eyes conveyed the pure sexual agony he was feeling.

'I shouldn't...'

'But you want to?'

Claire watched, mesmerised, as his lips descended slowly towards hers. He was taking his time, giving her time to back out, but she was rooted to the spot, hypnotised by the magic she knew his lips would unleash.

She sighed softly as his mouth gently touched hers. She needed this kiss like she needed her next breath. She opened her mouth and it was all the encouragement he needed.

Claire matched his ardour, one intoxicating kiss following another. The solid wall of his body pinned Claire back against the railing. He used the position to his advantage, rubbing his pelvis long and hard and slow against hers, placing the most exquisite pressure on the sensitive flesh beneath her dress. She cried out for mercy, sure that she was about to break into a thousand pieces from the pleasure.

'Let's go inside,' he suggested raggedly, sweeping her up into his arms.

Claire wrapped her arms around his neck and kissed him again. Deep, wet, delicious kisses. If she'd been at all aware of her surroundings she would have admired the way Campbell strode through the apartment, blindly navigating his way past furniture and through rooms, not once breaking contact with her lips.

They tumbled onto his bed and Claire felt his hands glide the zip of her dress down. She was suddenly consumed with the urge to be rid of it. She pushed him aside and stood beside the bed. One shrug of her shoulders and the red linen slipped to the floor.

Claire stood before Campbell in her black lacy hipster knickers and black lacy camisole. The two wispy pieces of satin didn't quite meet, her flat midriff bare to his hungry gaze.

Claire thought, rather belatedly, that she should feel shy, standing in front of him practically naked. But when he sat up, perched on the edge of the bed and whistled appreciatively, all she could feel was pride.

'Are you sure about this?'

Claire nodded. Right or wrong, she couldn't deny her body this. His kisses had woken the part of her that had slumbered for too many years.

She crossed her arms in front of her and grasped the fabric of her camisole, about to pull it over her head, when Campbell placed a restraining hand on her arm.

'No,' he stated. 'I want to take them off.'

He pulled her to him, his head level with her stomach, his mouth finding the bare skin of her middle, his tongue dipping into her belly button. His hands pushed under the silky fabric and slowly ascended her ribs, taking the camisole with him.

When they reached her breasts, Claire gasped and clutched his shoulders as he rubbed the already fully aroused nipples. Whoever had said there was a fine line between pleasure and pain had sure known what they were talking about. It was exquisite torture.

His hands left her breasts and in one swift movement he pulled the scrap of material over her head and flung it across the room. Her breasts swung free into his eager palms, quickly replaced by his even more eager mouth.

Claire felt a jolt of desire stab low in her pelvis and radiate further until it tingled between her legs. The friction of her lacy knickers against her engorged flesh was almost too erotic to bear.

Campbell's mouth laved every inch of her breasts, tugging and sucking at the nipples until they were hard and elongated with need. He had turned her body into one giant, exposed nerve, hypersensitive to his every touch. She couldn't think. She couldn't talk. All she was capable of was holding on and groaning monosyllabic primal noises as her body dissolved in a vortex of pleasure.

She didn't even register him pulling her underwear down to her knees until she felt his fingers gently probing the tingling flesh at the apex of her thighs. She cried out loud and clutched at his shoulders when she felt one, then two fingers enter her. He repeated the motion rhythmically as his thumb found the swollen nub it was seeking and moved in sync to the tempo set by his fingers. In, out, round and round.

Claire's head fell back as a maelstrom of sensations stormed through her. Her fingers sliced through his hair, hanging on for dear life as she felt her legs give way. He adjusted his position slightly to support her weight, never breaking his rhythm.

He picked up the pace, her desperate cries urging him on. Her hands imprisoned his head against her breasts as a pressure of intense proportions built rapidly in her core. It spread outwards, its tentacles stretching to all her muscles, tensing them to an almost unbearable rigidity. It paralysed her diaphragm, her breath stuttering out in short hiccupy blasts.

Claire heard herself cry out his name, begging him for

release. And just when she thought she'd explode, it happened. Her spine arched, her head flung back and an animalistic groan escaped from her open, gasping mouth. She clung to Campbell like flotsam in a swirling, cyclone-tossed sea, grateful to him for holding her up and for the pleasure that battered her like torrential rain.

Campbell held on tight as she rode the crest of her climax, his breathing as ragged as hers. He felt her muscles clench against his fingers still buried inside her. He felt each contraction and revelled in the knowledge that he was responsible.

As he held her body, still quivering in the aftermath, he was amazed at how she'd given herself so completely, especially after her earlier reticence.

'Claire?' He eased her away slightly, wanting to look into her eyes. 'Are you OK?' Her flushed face and glazed eyes spoke volumes. She certainly looked OK. More than OK.

Claire moved out of his embrace, stepping out of her not quite removed knickers, and collapsed on the bed, her glazed vision coming to rest on the ceiling. Had what had just happened really happened to her? Even now, minutes later, she could still feel the odd ripple undulate through her muscles deep inside.

'Claire?' Campbell's voice intruded on her musings. She turned her head as he lowered himself back so their faces were level. Their gazes met, her brown eyes still a little glazed. His were greener than green. Irish eyes. So expressive. So green. They screamed meadows and shamrocks.

'Wow,' she whispered, raising her hand to push his fringe back off his forehead.

Campbell laughed, a deep hearty noise. Claire joined

him. It was easier to laugh than to try and wrap her head around what had just transpired.

Gradually their mirth subsided, leaving them staring into each other's eyes again.

'Campbell, I...' Claire groped for the right words to express her wonder.

'Shh,' he ordered quietly, placing his fingers against her ravaged mouth. 'Don't say anything.'

Claire felt a tingle in her lips beneath his fingers and was suddenly aware of her nakedness. The air cooling her skin was the merest of caresses.

Campbell noticed the change in her eyes immediately. The glaze cleared, to be replaced by the flame of rekindled desire. His pulse, which had only just settled, picked up again. His breathing became shallower.

Her lips pressed together, laying a gentle kiss against his fingers. Such a sweet, almost innocent thing for her to do, especially given what had just happened. But his reaction to it was swift and definitely not innocent. His erection, still the same one from the deck, raged against the confines of his zipper, almost bursting free.

'I think you're a bit overdressed, Dr Deane,' she whispered, and Campbell groaned as she vaulted up and straddled him all in one smooth movement.

If he'd thought she'd looked magnificent before, nothing prepared him for this view. Gloriously naked, sitting astride him, her breasts jutting, nipples dark, still engorged from his earlier attentions.

She pressed her hips down onto his denim-clad erection, smiling knowingly. She rubbed herself against him as she threw her head back, revelling in her power.

She leaned closer to him so her mouth was mere millimetres from his, her breasts touching the rough fabric of his shirt. She rubbed them slowly against the material, kissing his mouth simultaneously.

He felt her low moan against his lips as it escaped hers. She lifted her mouth and grinned wickedly at him. He smiled back, wondering what was going on inside her head to give her that smug look. She shifted slightly, presenting a breast to his mouth, just out of reach. Campbell licked his lips, his throat suddenly as dry as the Sahara.

Campbell groaned as Claire slowly, bit by bit, lowered herself into his mouth. He sucked greedily the second he felt her puckered flesh nudge his lips. He missed her sharp intake of breath as his moan of satisfaction rumbled through his head.

She tasted so good it was suddenly too much for Campbell. He grasped her hips and ground them against his erection. He heard her cry out as she continued his action, writhing against him. It felt incredible. Her breast in his mouth and her pelvis rocking into his. He dug his fingers into her buttocks, encouraging her to continue.

'We really must do something about these clothes,' she murmured, as she tugged at the hem of his shirt, yanked it up over his head and flung it across the room, where it joined her camisole.

Campbell found her proximity too hard to ignore as his hands caressed her back and his lips sought the elegant length of her neck. He wanted to taste every inch of her.

'Nuh-uh,' she admonished, wagging her finger at him as she pushed him backwards gently. He reached for her again and she slapped his hand away playfully. Campbell thought he was going to lose his mind. He had to touch her.

'Claire,' he groaned. Campbell wasn't at all sure he could last the distance. He felt ready to erupt at any second.

She opened her eyes and grinned that wicked grin.

'Temptress,' he accused. His voice trembled with desire.

She laughed and pushed herself off him, hushing his complaint. 'Still too many clothes,' she said, and reached for his zipper.

Campbell hastily lifted his hips off the bed, and as she divested him first of the denim and then his cotton underwear. He suppressed the urge to groan out loud as his erection finally sprang free of its cloth prison.

Campbell sat up and tried to drag Claire closer.

'Nuh-uh.' She shook her head and then knelt in front of him, kissing him full and deep and long on the lips. Campbell felt the blood rush through his veins as the heat from the kiss burned a hole in his stomach lining.

'Claire,' he said urgently, pulling her off him to look into her eyes. It was almost his undoing, seeing them drunk with passion, her mouth swollen and moist from kissing him. They stared at each other, their harsh breathing the only noise in the room.

He kissed her again roughly, plundering her mouth. 'I want it to be perfect the first time. I want to be inside you. I want to feel you around me.'

He watched her as she considered his words for a moment.

'OK.'

Campbell fell back on the bed, bringing her with him until she once again straddled him. He clutched her hips and surrendered to the sensation of her lithe naked body lowering itself onto him. Campbell groaned as bit by bit she swallowed his erection into her tight, moist depth.

He heard a corresponding moan and he pulled out and plunged in again just to hear it once more. She didn't disappoint him. Each moan from her enticed him to plunge again, deeper and harder.

Campbell knew he was coming almost from the first time he entered her. He pushed it aside and held it off for as long as possible, but when he heard Claire's escalating cries and felt her begin to contract around him, he knew he was spiralling out of control.

He gripped her thighs, his fingers digging into the tanned skin. His body tensed and then bucked and reared as his climax erupted.

Their cries rose and mingled as their separate orgasms became one.

CHAPTER FIVE

CLAIRE woke at 4.30 to the first signs of the encroaching dawn. Campbell's hand rested, heavy and warm, on her flat stomach. She looked into his face, relaxed in slumber, his hair flopping in his eyes, and remembered how it had looked last night, animated with passion. She suppressed the urge to kiss his, oh so tempting mouth. That would probably wake him, and Claire had to get going.

Her mother would be awake in an hour and it was imperative that she be home. Claire always tried to be there first thing, to attend to her mother's personal needs. It allowed her father, who got up twice a night to change Mary's position, to get as much sleep as possible before he began his long day caring for his wife. It also preserved her dignity—what was left of it.

As she gazed on Campbell's sleeping face, her heart contracted with an emotion too frightening to analyse. Thinking about her mother was just the bucket of cold water she needed to bring her back to reality. Last night had been a mistake. She should have been stronger.

It wasn't fair to become involved with him when she knew that one day she might end up like her mother. She didn't want Campbell to have to go through what her father was now going through—no one should have to.

And what if he didn't want to? Shane had wasted no time in leaving after the bombshell had hit. And he had been in love with her—supposedly. She couldn't bear being rejected like that again.

And what about Campbell's desire to have children and

94

his feelings about bringing children into the world when a genetic illness existed? Her decision to remain childless would deny him the baby he yearned for, and he'd made it quite plain that he wouldn't want one with mutant genes anyway.

No. It was better this way. There were too many reasons they couldn't be together. Claire gently removed his arm and slid out from under the sheet. She gathered her clothes in the semi-gloom and quickly put them on. Campbell didn't stir. It took every ounce of her self-control to walk away.

Campbell knew the instant he woke up that he was alone. Somehow he wasn't surprised. Disappointed was a better word. Being with Claire had been fantastic. Not just the sex. It was about more than that. Snuggling close as they'd drifted off to sleep had somehow seemed natural. Right. It would have been perfect to have woken up and been able to reach out and touch her. Talk to her. Tell her he loved her.

Yes, Campbell thought, rolling onto his back, he loved her. There was no sense denying it or trying to wrap it up any other way. Holding her, kissing her, making love to her last night had cemented his realisation. He had fallen for her hard. He basked in the truth.

But did she love him? Somehow he suspected that it was still too early in their relationship for Claire. So could she, or rather would she, allow herself to love him, too?

The afterglow that he'd woken with was starting to fade as the questions kept coming. How should he proceed? What he wanted to do was make a huge romantic declaration. He loved her and he wanted to share his feelings with her. Hell, he wanted to shout it to the world.

But the sensible part of him urged caution. It had been

a long, hard slog getting her to agree to a date, and that had only eventuated because he'd shamelessly taken advantage of her at a weak moment. Getting her to fall in love with him was a big call.

Campbell acknowledged he was going to have to be patient. Not one of his best traits. But if that's what it required, he was willing to give it a go. He'd woo her slowly, subtly, and before she knew it she'd be declaring her undying love. He needed a plan.

He puzzled over it for a few minutes, formulating a recipe for success. Yes, he mused, it was all about the three Ps. Patience. Persistence. Presence. The last one particularly. It would be important to see her as much as possible. Show her the time of her life, make her see what she'd been missing all these years.

Not just lots of sex, although that'd be nice. No. It was about more than that. It was about having fun together, laughing, talking, sharing. Lovers' stuff. And no pressure. Just always being there until she couldn't recall what life had been like without him. Until she said those three little words.

'Good morning, Shirley,' Claire greeted the new mother as she entered the room.

'Hello, Claire. Goodness, what have you been up to? You're glowing!'

Claire blushed. She felt like she'd been caught with her hand in the cookie jar.

'You should talk.' She grinned at her client. 'I could see your I've-just-had-a-baby glow from the car park.'

Shirley laughed and Claire breathed a sigh of relief that she'd successfully turned the conversation back to Shirley.

'Davy get you up much?'

'A few times,' Shirley confirmed.

'Is he feeding well?' Claire sat on the edge of the bed and stroked the sleeping baby's head.

'Seems to be. He's attached much better than the other three ever did. Maybe I've finally got the hang of it.' She laughed.

'Where's Graham? Didn't he stay?'

'No, he went home with the kids early last night. He'll be back to pick me up around lunchtime. That should be OK, shouldn't it?'

'Don't see why not.' Claire smiled. 'Why don't you put him down and I'll check how you're doing?'

Shirley placed the sleeping baby in his clear plastic crib and lay down on the bed. Claire took her temperature, pulse and blood pressure and then gently palpated Shirley's abdomen.

'Tummy's going down nicely,' Claire confirmed. 'How's your loss?'

'Still heavy,' said Shirley, used to such personal questions.

'Any afterpains?'

'Initially, yes! But Graham got me a hot pack, which helped. They're a bloody nuisance. After all you go through with labour, you'd think that'd be it but, oh, no!'

Claire smiled and agreed with Shirley. Some women, more commonly those who were on their second or subsequent babies, found these pains, caused by the contracting uterus, even worse than labour. Most found them uncomfortable, like heavy period pains, but a few even needed pain relief when they occurred.

'Well, I'll have whoever's on call for Paediatrics come and check little Davy over, and then you should be able to go.'

'What about his day-three heel prick? Will they do that at the clinic?'

'You can, but the hospital has a community midwife service that can do that for you. I'll call them on Monday and they'll come out to your home and do the heel prick there. You'll also be able to talk to them about any concerns.'

Claire left Shirley to shower and pack. She wandered into the kitchen and made herself a cup of tea, her mind completely preoccupied with the events of last night. She took the tea into her office and sat down at her desk, staring absently out the window.

She worried her bottom lip as snippets of their conversation and flashes of their love-making came to her unbidden. It had been a wonderful evening. Perfect in every way. Except for the fact that it should never have happened.

Goodness only knew what Campbell was thinking about it all. Would he assume there was more to come? Would he expect that? She could hardly blame him if he did. What if he thought they were now a couple?

Claire took a sip of her lukewarm tea. Had she really been staring into space that long? She put her cup down and firmly pushed her thoughts aside. She had a lot to do to organise Shirley's and Davy's discharge.

She made a note in her diary for Monday to organise with the community midwifery service a home visit to Shirley. Next, she paged the paediatric registrar covering for the weekend. He answered promptly and agreed to come straight away. Claire collected the paperwork together, writing her own notes and filling in the discharge form.

'Hi, Claire.'

She'd been so preoccupied with her work she hadn't heard the swing doors open. 'Hi, William. I was so pleased when it was you who answered the page.'

Dr William Casey and Claire had known each other for many years. They had a good relationship, which had flourished, despite her rejection of his advances when they'd first met. He was very easygoing and had taken it in his stride.

'Only one more year of this awful shift work and then private practice here I come.'

Claire laughed. William had wanted to be a paediatrician for ever and had been steadily working towards that goal.

'You're not selling out, are you?' she mocked.

'Claire, Claire, Claire,' he tsked. 'You really have problems with the establishment, don't you?'

'Nah. Getting too old for that now.' She laughed.

William stood up straighter in the doorway, his eyes narrowing, speculation causing them to gleam.

'Something's not right,' he mused. 'You look…different.'

'Different?' she enquired, trying not to blush. 'I don't know what you're talking about.'

'Yes, you look like you've just been… Oh, my God! He did it, didn't he? He won. He wore you down. Campbell, the old dog! Well, well, well.'

'Don't be ridiculous, William,' Claire blustered, trying to look affronted.

'Oh, I see. Not going to kiss and tell, huh? Don't worry, Claire, your secret is safe with me.'

'William,' Claire sighed. 'You're the biggest gossip this hospital has ever known.'

'Yeah, you're right. Guess that's bad luck for you.' He laughed at her unimpressed face. 'Got a baby for me?'

Claire was grateful for the change of subject and led him in to Shirley before she succumbed to the urge to throttle him.

A gossip he might be, but a more thorough doctor was hard to find. 'Sorry to disturb you, little mate,' he whispered to the baby as he picked him up out of his cot and unwrapped him.

Davy opened sleep-bleary eyes but didn't look too cranky at the intrusion. Even when William flashed a torch in his eyes, checking for the red reflex of the cornea, he didn't object. William assessed all five reflexes that newborns should have, and then flipped him on his tummy. He visually inspected, as well as physically checked, by running his finger down, Davy's spine to make sure it was complete.

Davy did object when William performed the test for clicky hips. He howled and went a very impressive shade of red as William applied pressure through his little bent knees down into the hip joint.

'Sorry, little mate,' he soothed, rubbing the newborn's tummy as he checked that both testicles were descended.

'Good time for a feed,' said Shirley. 'If you've finished?' she asked.

'Sure,' William agreed. 'Nothing like a full stomach after such a harrowing experience, hey, little man?' William crooned as he handed Davy to his mother.

'Has he passed urine yet?'

'Several times,' Shirley confirmed.

'Any meconium yet?'

'Oh, yes!' Shirley laughed. 'I've saved it for you if you want to check.' She laughed again. Having done this for the fourth time, Shirley knew that black, tarry bowel motions were best left alone.

Mercifully William didn't stay on after he passed little Davy for discharge. He left straight away but did manage a lewd wink at Claire before he shut the door.

She escaped to her office, once again cursing under her breath. Great, it was going to be around the hospital in five minutes flat. Of that Claire had no doubt. By the time

Campbell got to work on Monday it'd be so blown out of proportion they'd be practically married. So much for one night of passion. No one was going to believe that was the extent of it.

Oh, well, Claire decided, rearranging the stuff on her desk, she'd weathered years of St Jude's gossip before. She could do it again. Once people realised that she and Campbell weren't an item, the talk would die down and be completely snuffed out once a juicier titbit came along.

Claire heard Shirley's family arrive and went out to greet them. Graham had brought the other three kids and they were all very excited, jostling to be the first to hold their new baby brother.

While Graham supervised the children, Claire finalised things with Shirley.

'Now, page me if there are any problems. That's what I'm here for—all right?'

'Sure thing,' Shirley agreed, as she signed the discharge papers.

'Here's your appointment for your six-week check,' said Claire, handing the card to her. 'Expect a phone call on Monday about the heel prick. I'll see you in six weeks, but remember—'

'I know, any problems and you'll be the first to know. I promise.'

'Good.' Claire grinned as she accepted Shirley's hug of gratitude.

She saw them out the door. It was quite a noisy goodbye and Claire was still smiling when she shut the door and started on the clean-up in Shirley's room.

Claire was making the bed, her last chore, when she heard the swing doors open.

'Hello. Anyone here?'

Campbell's voice reached out and touched her, even

from the other side of the wall. She groaned inwardly. She wasn't ready to face him just yet. She hadn't had enough time to work out what to say to him.

She knew what had to be said but hadn't anticipated how difficult it would be to face him so soon after having seen him naked. After he'd seen her naked. How could you tell someone that one night of mind-blowing sex was it and expect them to believe you? Because that was what she had to say. There could be no more.

Claire contemplated hiding somewhere, quickly scanning the room for a good position, but discarded the idea just as quickly. How juvenile! Never put off till tomorrow what you could do today. Right? She took a deep breath and went out to him.

'Hi,' she said quietly, coming to a halt in the doorway. She leaned against the doorframe, feeling weak from her reaction to his presence. He was in casual mode again, looking even more delicious than last night, kind of rumpled and content. Damn her weak body! Claire had to grind her shoes into the floor to stop herself running into his arms.

'Hi, yourself.' He smiled.

They stared greedily for the longest time. Campbell moved towards her, reaching out. She very nearly gave in to the temptation. Heaven knew, she wanted to feel his body against hers so badly she ached.

But at the last moment sanity prevailed and she backed away from him into the room. It didn't matter how much her body ached, she had to think with her head. There were things to say.

She crossed back to the bed and picked up the sheet, busying herself. Claire could feel the intensity of his gaze fill the distance between them.

'I missed you this morning.' His quiet voice broke into her activity.

'Help me with this?' She nodded for him to get the other side.

He crossed until he was opposite her. One bed and ten years of baggage between them.

'We need to talk.' Claire fussed, getting the corners just right as she spoke. 'I'm really sorry—'

'Please, don't say you're sorry last night happened.'

'No. Campbell, I don't mean... I'm not sorry about last night. I should be. I shouldn't have let it happen, but...it did and, no, I'm not sorry.'

'Oh, Claire.' Campbell sat down heavily on the half-made bed, a sigh of relief escaping his lips. 'Don't do that to me.'

'What I was going to say,' she said, sitting down on her side, 'was that I'm sorry but the cat is out of the bag. As far as the hospital grapevine goes anyway.'

'Already?' Campbell whistled. 'How did that happen? Were they looking through the keyhole?'

'No.' Claire laughed. 'William Casey came and did the discharge check on little Davy. He guessed.'

'Guessed?'

'Yeah, I know. Crazy, isn't it? He reckoned I looked different and put two and two together.'

'Well, you do have that thoroughly kissed look.'

'I...I do?' Claire pressed a hand to her mouth.

'Very much.'

Claire's eyes dilated as his hungry gaze followed the movement of her hand to her lips. She felt as if a hand had grabbed her insides and was squeezing. She heard the texture of his breathing roughen and felt hers fall into sync.

'It doesn't matter anyway, Claire. Let them talk. Our relationship is our business.'

Claire stood up and moved over to the window. He'd just mentioned the R-word. This was what she had feared would happen. She sensed things would get out of hand if she didn't put a stop to his fanciful thoughts right now. One roll in the hay did not a relationship make. Right?

'It matters to me, Campbell.'

'Why?'

'Because…it was just one night.' She turned to face him. 'We don't have a relationship. Last night was great. But wrong. I'm sorry if us sleeping together led you to believe differently. It shouldn't have happened and it's not going to happen again.'

'How do you know that?'

'Because I'm not going to let it. I seriously don't know what came over me last night, Campbell. But it doesn't negate the reasons I have for not dating or getting involved. They still exist.'

'So, what was last night, then?'

'Last night was a serious error in judgement. A very pleasant one but…I guess I just didn't expect to be so swept away. It's been such a long time for me…'

'So you used me last night?' He stood and paced and Claire didn't need to look at him to know he was angry.

'No. It wasn't like that!'

'No? Seems to me I was a convenient body to ease years of sexual frustration.'

Claire felt wounded by Campbell's unfair judgement of her. She had obviously hurt him, but he knew how to wound her just as effectively.

'Look, we went on a date. I was very attracted to you—'

'I know the feeling.'

'I wasn't thinking about the future. I wasn't thinking at all. We were kissing and one thing led to another and… I was just feeling, Campbell. I wasn't thinking. I never promised you a relationship. I never promised you a happily ever after.'

'Well, pardon me if I assumed certain things while you were half-crazy with lust last night.' His voice was icy.

'Lust, Campbell. Lust. You said it.'

'I didn't think you were that kind of woman.'

Claire's head snapped up as his accusation hit home.

'What? You mean the kind who indiscriminately sleeps with someone and then dumps them the next day? I'm sorry, I forgot that was a man's prerogative.'

Campbell stopped pacing and pushed his hands through his hair. 'I'm sorry,' he said placatingly, rubbing his eyes. 'That was unforgivable. Claire...I just want to be with you. Let me be with you.'

'I don't want to be with you,' she said, turning away from him so he couldn't see the lie reflected in her expression.

'You're a liar.' His voice was calm. Emotionless.

'Just go, Campbell,' she said quietly.

'This isn't over, Claire,' he warned. 'Every time your head hits your pillow, you're going to be thinking about me. About me inside you. I hope it drives you mad. As mad as it's going drive me.'

Claire heard his footsteps retreat and it took all her will-power to stand her ground. Her arms shook with the effort of keeping them firmly planted on the window-sill. She would not call him back. It was better this way.

Later that day, Claire found herself back at the birth centre with another of her clients in labour.

The birth stretched into the night and she paged Barbara Willis, the night-shift midwife, to tell her not to bother coming in as she would stay until her patient had delivered.

Finally around three a.m. the tiny baby boy made its

entry into the world, much to Claire's delight and the mother's relief. Baby Jonathon slept on obliviously as Claire fussed around, settling him into the mobile crib.

The first embers of dawn were glowing in the heavens when Claire finally left St Jude's. She yawned as she pushed open the front door. Two nights with little sleep had really taken their toll. But her work wasn't over yet.

Claire poked her head into her mother's room. She was awake, as Claire knew she would be. 'Hello, Mum,' Claire said softly. She opened the curtains to admit the early morning sunshine. 'How about I read you the paper and then I wash your hair?'

The pump that delivered hourly metered doses of a special nutritional formula into her mother's feeding tube beeped that it was empty, and Claire switched it off. She opened the newspaper that had been on the front lawn and thumbed through it with one hand and stroked her mother's hand with the other. Claire picked out stories she felt would interest her mother…had once interested her anyway.

She looked into her mother's vacant, staring eyes. Who knew what went on inside her head any more? Speech had been difficult for a few years and non-existent for a year now. Did she understand? Claire wanted to believe that she did.

One thing was for sure, seeing her mother like this reinforced her reasons for rejecting Campbell. She'd definitely done the right thing.

Campbell… Would he be awake yet? Would he still be mad with her? Spending time with her mother like this always left her feeling flat. It was like looking into a mirror. She was scared for her mother and anxious of what would become of her father after…

It would have been so nice to go to Campbell, crawl into

bed beside him and have him hold her until all her fears went away. To confide in him.

She shook herself. What was wrong with her? Surely years of denial had annihilated such temptations? Had sleeping with Campbell triggered these feelings? She should have known it'd be more complicated than just two people having sex. Intimacy was never that straightforward—that's why she had avoided it!

She pushed these confusing thoughts aside as she lifted Mary onto the mobile shower chair with ease. Years of nursing had taught her to lift properly and, despite the nightly supplements, her mother had wasted away to practically nothing in the last year.

The *en suite* bathroom had been modified as her mother had become more dependent, so there was ample room for Claire to shower her mother and wash her hair. She chatted as she saw to her hygiene needs, prattling on about baby Jonathon and baby David.

Claire yearned to tell her about Campbell. Confide in her mother as daughters the world over usually did. But something held her back. Telling her mother made it seem like they were involved. And they weren't.

All these thoughts whirred around in Claire's head as she finally collapsed into bed a couple of hours later. Fortunately they weren't enough to halt the pressing need for sleep. She closed her eyes and for the first time in a long time it was not her mother she dreamed about as sleep claimed her. It was Campbell.

CHAPTER SIX

CAMPBELL had no sooner sat down at his desk on Monday morning than the phone rang. It was Martin with a command, poorly disguised as a request, to see him immediately in his office.

Replacing the phone, Campbell decided that Martin could wait until he was good and ready. He'd head up there in a few minutes. He was in no mood to be ordered around, particularly by a pompous fool like Martin.

He drummed his fingers on the desk and then stood abruptly, stalking to the window. He stared with unseeing eyes at the phenomenal view.

Snatches of the incredible experience with Claire on Friday night chased snippets of their argument on Saturday morning around and around his head. So much for the three Ps. If she refused to see him again, his plan would be down the gurgler.

He'd wanted to shake her on Saturday. Grab hold of her arms and shake her until she understood that he loved her and they were wasting precious time, arguing. Time that they could spend loving each other.

Not for the first time, Campbell wished he knew what was eating her. Why did she persist with her no-relationship mantra? Why couldn't she open up to him? Had Shane hurt her that badly? No. She seemed to be way over that—there had to be something more.

He reluctantly made his way up to the executive offices, still deep in thought. The lift opened just as Campbell was coming to an important decision. Whatever her reasons, they were irrelevant. His objective was still the same—to make Claire West his. If one night of passion wasn't enough to sway her, then he'd have to go back to basics again.

He heard the raised voices coming from Martin's office from out in the hallway. He quickened his pace as he realised that one of them belonged to Claire.

Campbell burst through the door just as Martin was saying, 'If it's the last thing I do, I'm going to see that centre shut down.'

'Morning, all,' he said cheerfully, entering the fray.

Martin shot him an irritated look. Claire had murder in her eyes. Her look of relief as she realised it was him was heart-warming. Campbell cautioned himself not to get too caught up by it. She was probably only grateful that his arrival had stopped her from strangling Martin with his own necktie and spending the rest of her life in prison. The cleaner would probably have been given the same treatment.

Hell, she looks tired, he thought. He knew he shouldn't be, but he was secretly pleased that sleep hadn't come easily to her either. Good. He'd hate to think he was the only one suddenly afflicted with insomnia.

'So pleased you could join us.' Martin's sarcastic comment intruded on Campbell's thoughts.

Deciding to let that one slip by, Campbell guessed that calm and reason was definitely lacking in their conversation. Luckily, he was very good at calm and reason.

'Is there a problem here?'

'You could say that,' snorted Martin. 'Were you aware that Sister West delivered a breech baby at the centre on Friday afternoon?'

'Yes.'

'Were you aware that this contravenes the birth centre

protocol? A protocol that Sister West herself implemented?'

'Yes.'

'This is exactly what I feared would happen. Give them some autonomy and she takes it upon herself to risk the life of a mother and her baby, all in the name of natural birth.'

'I don't think that's entirely fair, Martin.' Calm and reason.

'Fair! Fair? How fair would it have been if complications had developed and the baby had died? They would have sued us from here to breakfast-time, and quite rightly, too.'

'The baby didn't die.' Claire tried to keep the exasperation from her voice.

'Lucky.'

'No, not lucky. Educated.'

'Oh…you think you know more than me, Sister West? I've been delivering babies for nearly forty years. Your experience is nothing next to mine.'

'Now, wait a minute—' Campbell interjected.

'Campbell, I don't need you to defend me,' she snapped. 'If Martin could just listen for a minute instead of ranting and raving—'

'I have not ranted or raved,' he blustered.

'Martin, I haven't been able to get a word in edgewise since I got here.'

Martin glared at her and sat down huffily.

'Firstly, I made every attempt to get Shirley to Labour Ward but that baby wanted out. Would you rather she gave birth in the lift or a corridor?'

'I think anything is preferable to delivering it yourself.'

'I am perfectly capable of delivering a breech baby. I've delivered more than my fair share. I assessed the patient and I assessed the risks. I'm a good midwife, Martin. You may have more years than me but it doesn't negate my experience. Quite frankly, I'm insulted that you would think so.'

Campbell sat back and watched Martin squirm. She was doing it again. Making a speech. Just like the first day he had met her. And his body was as predictable as ever. Man, how did she do this to him?

She was standing her ground, stabbing the air with her finger to emphasise her points. Her brown eyes boiled like hot mud pools and her chest rose and fell quickly, sucking in much-needed oxygen for her brain to formulate her next words.

His brain, on the other hand, was suffering from the usual reduction of oxygen as all the blood rushed to another part of his anatomy. Stop this! Rhetoric shouldn't be sexy. Heaven help him.

'Secondly, a complete novice could have delivered that baby. We really did nothing. He all but delivered himself.'

'We?' Martin queried, sitting forward.

'Yes, we. Campbell was at the centre when Shirley arrived.'

'You were there?' Martin demanded.

'I've been trying to tell you that from the minute you hauled me in here,' Claire snapped.

'And is that your assessment?' Martin asked Campbell. 'There was no time to get the patient to Labour Ward?'

Campbell noticed Claire bristling, drawing herself up to launch another verbal attack. 'I absolutely agree with Claire. Little Davy's bottom was well and truly out.'

'Well, if you feel it was an unavoidable situation, I shall just have to trust your judgement.'

'It'd be nice just once to enjoy the same trust.' Claire's icy voice conveyed her displeasure. Campbell caught the irritated look she shot him. Even that wasn't enough to dampen his raging response.

Martin chose to ignore her. 'I want written incident reports on my desk about this by the end of the week from both of you. And I still intend to make a full report to the board.'

'Well, you do what you have to do, Dr Shaw,' Claire said wearily. 'I've got a centre to run.'

Claire was too exhausted to even slam the door after her. Too tired to acknowledge how wonderful it had been to have Campbell on her side. She'd expected to feel awkwardness after their argument on Saturday, but she was honestly too tired to care.

She couldn't remember ever having felt so tired. The adrenaline that had been pumping around her system during their heated discussion had left her feeling even more depleted. All she wanted was to get out of there. She could almost feel her mattress beneath her.

If only it wasn't this morning she so desperately needed sleep. Mary went to respite care until mid-afternoon and her father hosted a regular poker game at his house with some old friends.

Claire knew they wouldn't disturb her. Nothing short of a nuclear explosion would wake her today, but she also knew her father would insist on cancelling. He had so few fun times lately she didn't want him to sacrifice the one thing he looked forward to all week. He'd already sacrificed so much of his life.

She pushed the lift button, trying to work out a solution with a brain shrouded in the heavy fog of fatigue.

'Claire! Hang on.'

The lift pinged and Claire got in, holding the doors open for Campbell.

'Are you OK? You look done in.'

'Too many sleepless nights.' She shrugged dismissively and then blushed when she realised she'd drawn attention to their night together.

'Me, too,' he agreed quietly.

Despite her tiredness, warmth suffused her body. He was so close! If she just shut her eyes and leaned a little, she could rest her head against his chest. His magnificent chest.

'Every time I close my eyes, I think of you and me and Friday night, and then I can't sleep.' His voice was soft and she yearned to fall into it.

Silence filled the space between them. Claire felt herself sway towards him. She despaired at how her body still responded to the pull of his, despite overwhelming exhaustion. So much for awkwardness!

The lift arrived at their floor and the doors opened. Saved by the bell! Wake up, Claire! Damn, this conversation was too hard to have when her energy reserves were at zero. It needed to take a different direction.

'Well, lucky you,' she quipped, striding from the lift. 'At least you've had a chance to get to bed. I've had about two hours' sleep in total. I was at the centre all weekend, delivering babies. I'd just done all the paperwork on my six a.m. delivery and was almost out the door when I was summoned.'

'No wonder you're almost out on your feet!'

'Three days off now. I'm going to sleep like the dead.' She half smiled and stumbled. He caught her arm and steadied her before she fell on her backside.

Campbell resisted the urge to pull her close. She smelt fantastic and the feel of her skin beneath his hands was glorious. They stood stock still while the hubbub of hospital life went on around them. She looked at him through sleep-hazed eyes, her lips parted, strands of her dark hair stuck to her lipstick.

'Can I do something for you?' he asked quietly, brushing the stray hairs from her mouth with one finger.

Yes. Pick me up and carry me away from here to a big nice soft bed somewhere and lie with me. Claire didn't know if lack of sleep was making her delirious, but suddenly a solution to her earlier problem was standing right in front of her.

'Do you mean that?' Some of the fog was clearing from her brain.

'Sure.'

'Are you? I know we didn't exactly part under the best of circumstances the other day…'

'I'm an adult, Claire. I can take it. What do you need?'

'A favour would be great.'

'Anything.'

'No strings?' This time she didn't want him to get the wrong idea.

'Of course!' His insulted look was rather endearing. 'Are you going to be at work all day?'

'Until about five.'

'Can I crash at your place?'

'Uh…sure.' Confusion furrowed his brow. 'Why? I mean, what's wrong with your place?'

'My dad has a poker game at our house every Monday morning. If I'm home, sleeping, he'll be stressing out about being quiet. I don't want to spoil his fun.'

'I knew I loved poker for a reason.' He grinned and fished his keys out of his pocket.

'It's just for five or six hours. I'll be gone by the time you get home.' She was suddenly serious. 'I will be gone, Campbell.'

'I know. I know.'

Claire let herself into Campbell's apartment and rang home straight away. She informed her father of her whereabouts and that she'd be home later in the afternoon. He seemed quite pleased by the arrangement. No doubt, all part of his push to have her get out more.

Zombie-like, Claire got in and out of the shower and quickly towelled herself dry on one of Campbell's fluffy towels. It was kind of bizarre, being here again after all that had happened between them.

She could have picked up the phone and dialled a handful of friends who would have been only too happy to oblige and give her a bed for the day. Why ask Campbell? The one person she should be keeping her distance from?

Because he'd been right there when the idea had come to her. He had been the quickest, easiest and most convenient person to ask. No wasting time, ringing around. Just a quick request and a quick answer. Tired minds didn't always come up with the wisest ideas!

Plus, geographically, his place was the closest. It hadn't even taken her ten minutes to get here. When bone-deep tiredness had you in its grip, a long car trip could end in disaster.

Claire briefly debated where to sleep. Campbell had a guest bedroom, she should use that. But as she stood in his doorway, his king-sized bed beckoned. The bed where she had slept with him only a few nights before. It was unmade, the sheets twisted, the pillows skew. She could almost picture him in it. Maybe if she'd been less tired and had had greater capacity to think rationally, she'd have chosen the guest room, but his bed was just too tempting to ignore.

As her head hit his pillow, she wondered fleetingly at the wisdom of being naked in his bed. But she was going to be out of here before he got home. Besides, she was too tired to move now. And the pillow smelt so-o-o good. It smelt like man. It smelt like Campbell.

*   *   *

For a day that had started out as bleakly as Campbell's, it had improved rapidly. Just the thought of Claire in his bed was enough to keep a smile permanently plastered on his face. Campbell's behaviour was enough, without gossip from William Casey, to confirm to all and sundry at St Jude's that he had indeed made progress with Sister West.

Campbell was sure he even saw money exchange hands on some of his rounds. It seemed his frivolity, along with the idiotic grin that he didn't seem to be able to shift, was enough to declare him the winner. Given that the opposite was true, he knew Claire would be furious, but he was just too damned happy to care at the moment.

He tried really hard all day not to fantasise about her asleep in his bed. And not to speculate about what she was wearing, because that led to images of a naked Claire and he really couldn't concentrate on his job. At all.

And he had to keep reminding himself that she had insisted she wasn't going to be there when he got home. Still, at least he could lie down where she'd been and smell her scent once again. It had started to fade from his sheets.

Campbell had a morning theatre list, which he whistled his way through. It was amazing he didn't accidentally incise something he wasn't supposed to, given how shot his concentration was. Luckily, they were procedures he could perform with his eyes closed.

The last op was a Caesarean for transverse foetal position. This scenario was a no-brainer for Campbell. Babies lying sideways across the uterus couldn't be born any other way. He tugged the wet and slippery baby from the safety of her mother's womb and was pleased to hear the little girl wail heartily at the intrusion.

He held the baby up over the top of the drape so her parents could grab a quick look before a nurse whisked her off to check her over. She returned the precious package to the parents a few minutes later, wrapped up as snug as a bug in a rug. Baby Anne looked very content, Campbell thought as he prepared to close the surgical incision.

He tried to tackle some paperwork at lunchtime but instead daydreamed about Claire and subsequently got nothing much achieved.

His afternoon clinic commenced at two and was filled with the usual antenatal checks. Weight, urine, baby's position, foetal growth and heartbeat.

He'd finished for the day and was signing his name to the last chart when Andrea popped her head in.

'Sorry, Campbell, I've just had a call from Hillary Beetson.'

'Do I know her?' Campbell searched his memory bank unsuccessfully.

'No. She's one of Martin's patients, but everyone has left for the day and you're on call. She's just rung to say she hasn't felt the baby move all day. I told her to come straight up and you could squeeze her in.' She ended with a sweet, pleading look, handing Hillary's chart to him.

'How many weeks?'

'Thirty-six.'

Despite Campbell's urge to make a quick getaway, he knew he had to see this client. 'Let me know when she gets here,' he sighed, thumbing through the chart.

The scenario was common enough. As the pregnancy reached its advanced stages and the foetus grew larger, there was less and less room for the baby to move. Decreased foetal movements were common in the last few weeks and usually meant nothing.

But Campbell also knew that it couldn't be ignored. An intra-uterine death at this late stage was unlikely but it was one of the more sinister possibilities. He pushed fantasies of Claire at home in his bed to one side and focused.

Five minutes later Andrea informed him that his patient had arrived.

'Afternoon, Hillary,' he greeted her confidently, introducing himself.

'Hi,' she said. She looked anxious and Campbell pulled up a chair beside his patient, hoping to allay her fears.

'Andrea tells me you haven't felt the baby move today.'

'That's right, I only realised a little while ago I haven't felt any movements since last night. It's usually so active but I've been so busy today...' she replied softly, obviously worried. 'What does that mean?'

'Nothing usually,' Campbell reassured her, 'there's not a whole lot of room for the baby to move around now, so it's common enough to go for longer than usual without feeling the baby move.'

'Oh. OK. That's a relief,' Hillary exhaled loudly.

'We'll just listen for the heartbeat first and then see if we can't prod it into giving us a kick.'

Hillary got up on the examination bed and Campbell waited while Andrea had squirted some gel on Hillary's bulging abdomen, running the Doppler through it to locate the heartbeat.

Campbell watched Andrea try several spots where the heartbeat was usually found. Nothing. Andrea stopped and palpated the abdomen, locating the baby's head low down in the pelvis, satisfying herself that she was indeed looking in the right places. Silence still greeted her attempts to find the heartbeat.

She turned to Campbell and handed him the transducer. Her eyes said it all. She was worried. Campbell felt the first prickles of impending doom.

'What's happening?' asked Hillary, the worried edge back in her voice. 'Why can't we hear it?'

'They can be tricky to find sometimes,' Campbell said, injecting into his voice a confidence he didn't feel.

He got Andrea to try and stimulate the baby to move while he ran the transducer all over, listening for the *whup, whup, whup* that indicated life. She poked and prodded. Nothing.

Campbell was very concerned now. 'Get someone from Ultrasound up here now,' he told Andrea, his voice calm but his eyes conveying urgency. She left immediately.

'What's wrong?' Hillary asked, raising herself on her elbows, tears gathering in her eyes. 'Why can't you find it?'

'Sometimes the baby's position can make it really hard. Sometimes the mother's heartbeat can confuse things. I want to get an ultrasound. We'll know more after that. It's probably just the baby playing hard to get.' He smiled, trying to reassure her. 'Why don't we ring your partner to come and be with you?'

'I rang Danny already. He should be here soon.'

Danny, Andrea and Darren from Ultrasound all arrived together a couple of minutes later. Campbell explained to Danny what was happening.

'What's the worst-case scenario, Doc?' asked Danny, coming right to the point.

'Let's just get this picture first. I don't want us to get ahead of ourselves.'

Andrea switched out the lights and Darren applied more gel to Hillary's tummy. Danny stood behind the bed, his hands on his wife's shoulders.

The screen flickered and their baby came into view. Darren manipulated the transducer to get a look at the heart. Campbell's worst fears were realised when no heart movement could be detected at all. He stared at the screen silently, willing the heart to move, to beat, but…nothing. The baby was dead.

Campbell felt an overwhelming, crushing sadness for this couple. He was going to have to give them news that would devastate them. Every part of him rebelled at having to be the one to do it. He ran his hands through his hair. Sometimes being a doctor really sucked.

He indicated to Andrea to turn the lights back on. 'Page the social worker,' he whispered to her as she passed him.

'Hillary, Danny,' he said, turning to them. 'I'm sorry to have to tell you this but we've just looked at your baby's heart and it's not beating. I'm sorry, but your baby has died.'

Hillary's face crumpled into a heap as she clutched at her husband's shirt. 'No, no, no,' she wailed. 'My baby, my baby.'

'What do you mean, dead? How can that be? What happened?' Danny demanded, his voice loud with anger and indignation.

'I don't know for sure,' said Campbell quietly. 'I'd like Darren to have a really good look and see if he can find the cause…if that's OK.'

'Do it,' said Danny, Hillary's sobs and cries of denial stimulating his aggression further.

Darren applied the transducer again and did a thorough ultrasound scan, looking for a reason for this tragic intra-uterine death. Hillary's sobs echoed around the room during the procedure.

Darren stopped and pushed a few buttons. 'There's no blood flow through the cord,' he said solemnly. 'There…' He pointed. 'I think that's the problem.'

'Is that a knot in the cord?' asked Campbell.

'I think so—it's kind of hard to tell. Might just be a lump

but, given that there's no flow, I'd say it's probably a true knot. The cord is quite long, which does increase the risk.'

Darren wiped Hillary's belly off and left the room. Andrea returned with Sharon, the social worker, and Campbell introduced her to the grieving couple.

'Did you find anything?' Danny asked, the angry edge to his voice dissipating as reality settled in.

'We think that there's a knot in the cord. We can't be certain until after the baby is born—'

'A knot? How can that happen?' Danny was angry again, his voice incredulous and demanding.

Campbell didn't take offence. The man had just had the rug pulled out from underneath him. Beneath Danny's veneer of aggression was a grief-stricken father. Campbell would feel the same way if it had been him.

'It's very rare but some babies can be so active that they can swim around in the womb and tie a knot in their cord. If it pulls tight enough, it can completely deprive the baby of nutrients from the placenta and they die.'

'I didn't think there was enough room at this stage for that,' said Danny.

'At this stage there isn't. It probably happened weeks ago, and the knot has been pulling tighter and tighter over the last few weeks as the baby grew more and there was less room to move.'

'Oh, God! I should have come in earlier,' sobbed Hillary. 'If only I hadn't been so busy… I should have been paying more attention.' Tears streamed down her face.

'It's not your fault, love,' Danny said gruffly, hugging her close, stroking her hair.

'He's right, Hillary. Cord knots are completely out of anyone's control. It was a freak accident. The baby probably died some time in the night. You did say the last time you felt it move was last night?'

'Yes, it was moving as I drifted off to sleep,' she sniffed.

'You weren't to know. Coming in earlier would have made no difference.'

Hillary's gut-wrenching sobs filled the room again and Campbell allowed them time to vent their grief. His skin puckered with goose-bumps as Hillary's wailing displayed her utter devastation. Campbell's heart went out to them. What did you say in this kind of a situation? He felt so helpless.

'What happens now?' asked Danny, wiping his tears and blowing his nose.

'We induce the pregnancy and Hillary will give birth to the baby. We don't have to rush into this. If you want time to think about everything, we could leave that till the morning.'

'Oh, God.' Hillary broke into loud sobs again.

'I'm so sorry, I wish I could have given you better news,' said Campbell, feeling wretched. 'I'm going to leave you now for a while and let you speak to our social worker. I'm going to be out at the desk if you need me for anything. I'll come and talk to you again after you've finished with Sharon.'

Campbell wandered to the nurses' station and sat down. His heart was heavy with the tragedy that had just unfolded. He'd give anything to not be here right now. To not have met this couple under these dreadful circumstances.

He'd have given anything to be at home with Claire. He needed her more now than he ever had. Just to feel the comfort and solace of her arms, to forget the awfulness of the day in the magic of her lips and the secrets of her body. To be held by the woman he loved.

Campbell used this time to write a thorough report in Hillary's notes. He documented everything from the beginning, including the ultrasound images that Darren had printed out for him. Such a waste, he thought as he signed the chart. So unfair!

'Campbell.' Sharon interrupted his thoughts.

'How are they?' Stupid question.

'No different from before. Devastated. They wanted me to ask you if you would perform a Caesar as soon as possible. Hillary doesn't want to be induced. She was booked for an elective Caesar with Martin anyway. I really think psychologically she wouldn't cope with waiting until the morning. She keeps saying she can't bear the thought of her baby being dead inside her. She wants to be able to hold it.'

'I'll go and talk to them. Thanks, Sharon.'

Campbell approached the room reluctantly. He didn't want to intrude on their grief. It was tragic enough for Hillary and Danny, without being forced to share such a personal time in their lives with people who were basically strangers. Even the intimacy of their grief wasn't sacred.

They looked up when Campbell entered. The soul-destroying cries had dissipated, replaced by expressions of utter disbelief and misery.

'Sharon said you'd like a C-section?'

Hillary nodded, her chin wobbling. 'She can't go through hours of labour to give birth to a dead baby, Doc. She just can't,' pleaded Danny.

'I can't do that, Campbell,' Hillary confirmed, tears coursing down her face.

'I understand,' Campbell reassured them gently. 'Are you sure you don't need more time? There really is no rush.'

'I want to be able to hold my baby,' Hillary cried. 'I don't want to wait. I want it to be over.'

'I'll arrange it immediately. I'll see you in Theatre in about half an hour.'

Andrea rang up to the operating rooms to check the emergency theatre wasn't in use, while Campbell made his way up there. He did so with a heavy heart. This would be no joyous event, like most Caesareans. There would be no lusty wail to bring a tear to the eye. Instead, he would have to pull out a stillborn baby. It was too sad for words.

The operation went without a hitch. Campbell felt profound sadness as he handed the lifeless baby boy to a waiting nurse. He knew they would wash the baby and dress him and have him ready to take to his parents when Hillary got out of Theatre. They would be able to hold their baby at last.

Removing the placenta was interesting as he was able to examine the cord close up. Sure enough, it was a true knot. He's never seen one in all the years he'd been in obstetrics.

Sometimes cords had a lumpy appearance, similar to a knot on a tree-trunk, but this one was a definite knot. He untied it to prove it to himself and so he could be one hundred per cent sure when he saw his client post-op.

Campbell finally got away from the hospital around nine o'clock. He'd stopped in and spent some time with Hillary and Danny. They were lying on the bed together, facing each other, their precious baby boy between them. They were crying and stroking his little face and talking to him as they held each other, and Campbell knew there was no easy way, no quick fix for their grief. They had a hard road ahead.

When Campbell pulled into his parking space he was surprised to find Claire's car still parked there. She was still here? He'd expected her to be long gone. He breathed a sigh of relief. After today he needed to hold her desperately.

Claire was dressing hurriedly when she heard Campbell's key in the lock. 'Oh, hell,' she cursed under her breath.

Why had she slept so long? Now she had no choice but to face him.

She looked at her attire, a pair of Campbell's baggy gym shorts turned over several times at the waist and pulled down low on her hips to anchor them. A flannelette shirt, also Campbell's, with the sleeves rolled up. Even her undies were a pair of Campbell's cotton clingy boxers.

It was either that or get back into her uniform. Yuck! She obviously hadn't thought about a change of clothes in her tired rush this morning.

'Campbell, I'm sorry, I know I'm still here,' gushed Claire, rushing into the lounge room, her attention on buttoning up the flannelette shirt. 'I'll get out of your hair straight away, I promise.'

Job complete, she turned her attention to him. She stopped in her tracks. Oh, lord, she thought, he looked awful. Her awkwardness at being caught still in his apartment and in his clothes diminished instantly.

'What's wrong?' she asked. 'What's happened?'

'Awful day.' He grimaced and ran his fingers through his hair, pushing his floppy fringe back. He walked past her and sat on the lounge, throwing his keys onto the coffee-table.

'How awful?' She sat beside him, not too close, sensing his need to vent his angst.

'I've just delivered a thirty-six-week stillborn baby boy. First true knot in a cord I've ever seen.'

'Oh, Campbell,' Claire gasped quietly, putting her arm around his shoulders. 'That's terrible.'

Claire listened while Campbell filled her in on the details. She absently rubbed his shoulder and caressed his forearm, her head pressed to his in shared sorrow.

'Sometimes I hate my job so much. I just felt so helpless, you know? Life is so bloody unfair.'

'I know,' she soothed quietly. She knew it well.

Campbell pressed his fingers to his temples and supported his face in his hands. Claire stayed silent, hoping her presence was some support.

They worked in a field that had its share of tragedies. Some got to you more than others. She'd been where Campbell was. She wouldn't desert him in his hour of need.

He raised his head and turned to look at her, giving her a small, sad smile that pulled at her heart. She smiled back, acutely aware of his maleness and his proximity. She felt the intensity of his gaze on her mouth and felt herself sway closer.

The sadness in his eyes drew her like a magnet. They called to her. She wanted to erase his pain and help him forget the last few hours. Every part of her knew she shouldn't, but he was hurting and he needed her.

His lips touched hers and she sighed into him. The potent need evident in his kiss forced a moan from deep inside her.

'I need you tonight, Claire. Don't leave.'

The rawness of his request as he cradled her face couldn't be denied. She knew what it felt like to need someone to seek solace in. She stood and followed him to his bedroom.

Their love-making was different this time. The frantic, desperate, bordering-on-obsessive need to mate had lessened. Campbell felt as if they were making love underwater. Slow and languorous, their touch unhurried. More explorative than explosive.

When he entered her she gasped his name and clutched him to her. He revelled in the feeling of connection. He wanted to stay inside her for ever. At least here, sheathed inside her, he finally felt close to her. In the world outside this bed, she never let him close enough.

He moved slowly inside her. She moaned and he felt her tighten around him. He pulled out a little and slowly re-entered. The slightest of movements, the most erotic pressure. Three more agonisingly slow pulses and Campbell could feel his orgasm build. At the same time Claire was raking her nails down his back as she spasmed around him.

The contractions of her climax pushed him over the brink. Then he collapsed on top of her, waiting until their breathing had settled before rolling onto his back.

They lay staring at the ceiling for a few moments. Claire felt her eyelids growing heavy again as post-coital malaise invaded her bones.

'Claire…'

'Shh,' she whispered, turning to rest her head against his shoulder. 'Don't talk. Just sleep.'

Claire woke a couple of hours later. She was alone. Alone with the realisation that she'd done it again. Slept with Campbell after she'd told him it wasn't going to happen.

But lying there with only her thoughts for company she could finally be honest with herself. She'd wanted it to happen. Friday night, last night and for many more nights. She was attracted to him, even more so now she'd seen his vulnerable side. She could fight it or she could run with it and finally have a bit of fun in her life.

She turned on her side, smoothing his pillow and wishing he were there beside her. Would he agree to be her lover? She couldn't do long term. Would he agree to that? One thing was for sure, there would be no misunderstandings this time. A relationship was possible on her terms only.

Her stomach grumbled and Claire realised she hadn't eaten in over twelve hours. She rose and groped around in the dark for something to wear. She found the light to the *en suite* and squinted at the insult to her pupils. A fluffy navy gown hung on a hook near the bath. She slipped into it and was immediately surrounded by soap and aftershave. Very manly.

Leaving the bedroom, Claire went in search of Campbell. They needed to talk and she was starving. She found him sipping a glass of wine on the balcony. A toasted sandwich was in the process of being devoured.

She reached over his shoulder and grabbed one of the cut portions. She sat down opposite him, devouring it instantly.

'Hello, sleepyhead.' He smiled.

'I'm so sorry I fell asleep, Campbell. I should have tried to stay awake. Some support I was!'

He pushed the plate towards her, offering her the last piece. She grabbed it before he could change his mind.

'You helped more than you can know.' Silence stretched between them. 'I'll make you another, shall I?'

'Yes, please.'

'Drink? Wine?'

'Coffee would be nice,' she said, swallowing the last bite.

He rose to go, the light from the lounge framing him. He was dressed in cotton boxers, similar to the ones he'd ripped off her earlier, that clung to his muscular thighs. His unbuttoned shirt flapped in the light breeze, revealing his hard stomach and smooth chest. He truly was magnificent.

Soon the aroma of brewing coffee and toasting bread intruded on Claire's thoughts. Her stomach growled in response and she was most grateful when he plonked a plate of toasted sandwiches in front of her. They ate in silence until the plate was empty.

'We need to talk,' he said, and she nodded.

'You first,' she invited.

'If tonight has taught me one thing, Claire, it's that life

is short. Whether you want to admit it or not, there's something between us that can't be ignored.' Campbell wanted to tell her he loved her, but couldn't bear to make his day worse should she reject him. 'I think we should explore it, see what happens.'

'I agree.'

'You do?' Campbell should have been ecstatic but he was suspicious. It was too easy. 'You mean you want to do more of this?' Campbell hardly dared to breathe lest she change her mind. He couldn't quite believe what he was hearing. She'd just done a complete about-face.

'Yes.' Claire smiled at Campbell's doubtful expression.

'Why the sudden change of heart?' Campbell needed to understand her motives. It still seemed too easy.

'Isn't it a woman's prerogative?'

'Apparently.'

Claire sighed. 'I don't know, Campbell. I only decided just now and I'm making it up as I go along. All I know is that you make me feel good and we're amazing in bed. And I don't want to give that up yet.'

'Yet? Does that mean that a time will come when you will give it up?'

'Yes.'

Campbell pushed back his chair and wandered over to the rail, gazing out over the river. He wanted for ever. Not just for now, or for as long as she wanted. Could he have the kind of relationship she was describing, waiting each day for the axe to fall?

'There's more,' she said, and he gripped the railing tight. 'Some ground rules. No L-word. No marriage proposals. No cohabitation.'

'What's left?' His voice held a bitter edge as he braced himself for her answer. Her cool dismissal of the things he wanted most wounded like barbs tearing his flesh.

'Sex and laughter and fun. Good times, Campbell. I don't know how long for. Let's just take each day as it comes. Oh…and another thing. You have to promise to let me go when the times comes.'

Claire felt dreadful, talking in such a detached manner. But she was trying to be honest. She had to lay her cards on the table now so he knew exactly where he stood. She didn't want to start this thing under false pretences. Well, not too many anyway.

She knew she couldn't have for ever with Campbell— she wouldn't inflict that on anyone. But being with him had been so amazing. As long as they kept their relationship in perspective as a temporary distraction, they could have amazing for a bit longer. Maybe a lot longer.

Campbell was torn. This was a man's dream come true. A relationship based entirely on sex and good times, with no fear of commitment. Before he'd met Claire, it was the kind of situation he would have jumped at.

Except now he wanted all the things she didn't. Could he promise to watch her walk away? To just let her go? Why was she so determined to avoid committing herself? Why? Why? Why?

'Why?' he spun around, facing her. 'Why the rules? What are you so afraid of?'

'Don't ask me why. I won't tell you. My reasons are my reasons. You're just going to have to accept that I have them.'

'Are they good?'

'Yes.'

He eyed her seriously. Claire could tell he was weighing up his options. His fringe flopped down in his eyes and the breeze lifted his shirt flaps aside, revealing tantalising glimpses of his firm torso.

Claire felt desperation invade her body. Now she'd made

up her mind she wanted him to agree very badly. His silence was making her nervous. Worse, she was convinced he was going to turn her down as each silent second dragged on. She had to do something to convince him. She'd never wanted anything this much.

'What do you say, Campbell?' Her voice trembled as she began to untie the belt of her robe, desperation making her bold. 'Do you want me? Want this?' she parted the robe until he could see her nakedness. 'Even if it's only for a little while? Or do we call it quits now?'

Campbell's hungry gaze devoured her body. His response was instantaneous and unable to be hidden in his clinging cotton boxers. He watched her triumphant smile, and he should have resented her for it but he wanted to take her so badly now he couldn't think straight.

He wanted to yank her up off the chair, push her against the bricks and have her against the wall. He wanted to teach her she shouldn't tease, and punish her for closing herself off to his love.

'Claire.' His voice was low and husky. 'That's not playing fair.'

'Say yes, Campbell. You know you want to.'

'You think you can sway me with your body. You think I can't resist you?'

She could see he was angry. He looked brooding and dangerous, and strangely enough it was really turning her on. Her breathing was ragged and her blood roared in her ears. 'Why do you even want to?'

He stalked over to her chair, pulling her up into his arms, grinding her against his straining erection. He was breathing heavily, his hooded eyes piercing her with rabid lust and intense dislike. She accepted the punishing force of his mouth on hers, matching his onslaught.

They pulled apart, chests heaving. Campbell yanked the

robe down and off her arms until she was completely naked in his arms. Their eyes locked in a silent battle of wills.

'Not fair,' he muttered with a brief bruising kiss. And then he picked her up. Striding into the lounge room, he threw her on the couch. He tore his clothes off, joining her on the narrow space, entering her immediately, his kiss silencing her cry of exultation.

He was so riled and so turned on it was hard to know where one emotion started and the other ended. He wanted to punish her for hurting him. He wanted her to feel his pain. He wanted to brand her so she belonged to him, despite what she thought.

Claire welcomed each thrust greedily. She lifted her hips to take him deeper, welcoming the pounding and cried his name as his mouth fastened roughly on her nipple. He sucked hard and grazed his teeth against it until she was ready to faint from the pleasure.

'Look at me!' he demanded.

Claire opened her eyes. Their gazes locked and held even as Campbell's increased pounding rocked her head back and forth. She bit her lip and cried his name as her release swamped her. She fought the natural urge to shut her eyes, wanting Campbell to witness her ecstasy.

Campbell's eyes widened at the wild abandon in hers. It was enough to take him right over the edge. He too fought the urge to close his eyes as his body shuddered and released inside her. He kept them open, sharing the tumult of his orgasm as she had shared hers.

CHAPTER SEVEN

IT SEEMED to take an age for their breathing to return to normal. Campbell lay spent and collapsed on top of Claire, silently berating himself for letting her goad him into such an ardent response. He pushed away, sitting up on the lounge, gathering his wits.

'You won't regret it,' Claire said breathlessly.

'I already do,' he said. Disgust filled his voice as he stalked over to where he had discarded his clothes and put on his underpants.

The smile slipped from her face. 'Campbell?'

'It's no good. I can't do it.' He retrieved his robe and threw it at her.

'Do what?' she asked quietly, catching the robe.

'Have a relationship with you on those terms.'

'What? Sex without commitment?' Claire laughed incredulously, belting the robe. 'Most men I know would jump at the chance.'

'I want more.' His voice was quiet but emphatic.

Claire could feel him slipping away. She'd obviously underestimated his moral fortitude. Now she'd made up her mind, she didn't want him to walk away, but it was important that she was clear with him.

'I'm sorry. I can't give you more.' She took a step towards him but he held up his hands and she stopped.

'I can't live by your stupid rules.'

'That's just your pride talking,' she stated, swallowing a lump.

'No. It's self-respect. You've led me a merry dance,

Claire, but enough is enough. We either agree to an equal relationship on mutual terms or...'

'Or what?' she asked quietly.

'We're finished.'

Campbell left the room and stood in the cool night air on the deck. He clutched the railing, begging the fates to make her see sense. He was taking a gamble. He knew that. But for the first time she'd admitted to wanting a relationship with him—but did she want it as badly as he did?

One thing was for sure, he wasn't going to let her toy with him any longer. Sure, being her plaything would, no doubt, be a thoroughly enjoyable and unforgettable experience, but he loved her and he needed her to give him more of an emotional investment. He'd rather lose her than be with her every day and not be able to tell her how he felt.

Anger and frustration and desperation chased around and around in his head and weighed heavily in his heart. What was taking her so long? The suspense was killing him. He was about to storm back inside and demand a response when he heard the front door open and then click shut. He had his answer.

Days came and went. Weeks passed. Claire hardly noticed. She felt as if she was living in a movie scene where the main character walked along obliviously as the scenery changed behind her, indicating the passage of time.

When she'd left Campbell's apartment that fateful night, it had been with the decision not to look back. Dwelling on what had been or could have been was a recipe for disaster. They'd had some good times. She chose to think of them instead of what she was missing.

Ten years ago, when her mother had been first diagnosed, it would have been easy to fall apart and wallow in self-pity, but she'd chosen not to, focusing on her career instead. She'd decided right from the outset that she wasn't going to let the disease define her, as her mother had done.

No way had she been going to sit around and wait for her genetic lottery ticket to come up. Life was there to be lived, so she'd lived it. She'd travelled and she'd back-packed and she'd nursed in remote locations and had steadily built a career to be proud of. Work had been her salvation. And so it was again.

Irritatingly, Claire found herself once more at the centre of St Jude's rumour mill. She weathered the curious looks and the whispered conversations with polite silence and years of practice, despite its outrageous content. Give the grapevine a juicy titbit and the details, no matter how fanciful, were made up as it went along.

Claire contemplated posting a memo on the notice-board in the foyer, stating that nothing had happened between her and Campbell and that they were only colleagues. Anything to stop the Chinese whispers.

It was difficult enough just being in the same hospital as Campbell. St Jude's was big, but it wasn't that big. Inevitably they ran into each other. At those times they behaved professionally, treating each other with politeness and respect. It was formal and a little strained, but it worked.

They were very careful not to get too close. In fact, Claire was aware of Campbell actually physically distancing himself when necessity required them to be closer than a safe distance. Claire knew she should, too, but was amazed at the degree of difficulty of such a simple task.

Just as hard was having to talk to him about a patient or a related matter while her mind was elsewhere. Like in bed with him naked and inside her. It was cold comfort but Claire knew she had done the right thing. The only thing.

He wanted long term and she could only give short term. As much as her body yearned for him, she was a time bomb he couldn't handle.

And then there was the gossip about all the dating he'd been doing. Apparently leopards didn't change their spots, and Campbell had returned to his old ways.

Claire didn't want to admit how much it hurt. After all, he was a free agent. Besides, she knew that listening to gossip or, worse, actually believing it was stupid. It had, no doubt, been blown completely out of proportion. However, the rumours persisted.

In an effort to scrub Claire from his mind, Campbell also threw himself into his work. Still, even one month on, it was difficult to forget when everywhere he went and everything he did at St Jude's reminded him of Claire.

His ultimatum and her subsequent rejection still felt like a raw, gaping wound. His mind kept on replaying it like an old movie projector stuck in a rut.

He was moody and distracted and even snappy on a couple of occasions. It wasn't anybody's fault but he was taking it out on whoever was unfortunate enough to cross his path. It was so unlike him yet he didn't seem to be able to stop.

His concentration was shot, particularly in the operating theatre, which made him annoyed. Consequently he was demanding and picky and ruining his status among the theatre staff who were already jaded from one too many prima donna surgeons.

Trying to distract himself with a bevy of beautiful, available women wasn't working either. His heart and mind really weren't in it, and that wasn't fair to them. He made up his mind to cease all such behaviour forthwith! There was only one woman he wanted.

He just hadn't bargained on how hard it would be to act normally around her. So hard, in fact, he avoided it like the plague. But when you worked in the same building and your professional lives crossed paths frequently, coming face to face was inevitable.

Campbell had to actually physically move back in her presence. She was too tempting when they were unavoidably thrown together. Her scent was so familiar to him, so addictive he had to suppress the urge to lean in and inhale along the curve of her neck where he knew she smelt the sweetest.

He missed that smell. It had dissipated quite quickly from his bed and his unit, and damn it all—he wanted it back!

A week later, Claire's phone rang and she picked it up. It was Casualty.

'Claire, we need you here. We have a patient of yours who's arriving in about two minutes in premature labour.'

'Who?' Claire heard alarm bells ringing in her head.

'Lex Craven.'

'She's twenty-eight weeks, isn't she?'

'That's right. I've already paged Campbell.'

'I'm coming now.'

Claire hurried down to Casualty, her mind running through all contingencies. The odds for premature babies had improved dramatically with modern drugs and supportive respiratory measures, but twenty-eight weeks...that was quite early. Where prematurity was concerned, the longer the gestation the better the baby's chances.

A lot was going to depend on the size of the baby and the maturity of its lungs. Hopefully it wouldn't come to that. They might be able to stop the labour if it wasn't too far advanced, or at least delay it a little to allow the administration of steroids to help mature the baby's lungs.

Claire was so focused on achieving a good outcome for Lex and her baby, the thought of having to work closely with Campbell was completely secondary. The most important thing was they put aside their awkwardness and act as a team. They were both professional enough for that.

She arrived slightly out of breath, adrenaline energising her blood in anticipation. The Casualty department was bedlam.

'Claire.' The nurse who emerged from behind the curtains of the obstetric cubicle greeted her, handing her a gown as she washed her hands. 'Campbell's just arrived. It's a madhouse here. There's an arrest in cubicle two and the neonatal team are dealing with an emergency in Theatre. They've been paged and will get here as soon as they can. It's just you and Campbell for the moment.' She gave a lewd wink and Claire rolled her eyes. 'The minute anyone becomes available I'll send them your way.' She scurried away, pushing a pole laden with pumps.

When Claire entered the cubicle, Campbell was hooking Lex up to the CTG machine to monitor the baby's heart rate. Lex was hysterical—crying, moaning and writhing around on the narrow trolley.

'I can't have the baby now,' she cried. 'It's too early. Please, please,' she begged them. 'I don't want my baby to die.'

Brian was trying his best to calm and comfort his wife, but Campbell's relief at seeing her was palpable and Claire didn't need to ask to assess what he needed first.

'Lex,' Claire said loudly, to cut through the woman's hysteria.

'Claire… Oh, Claire. My baby, please, my baby.' She burst into renewed tears.

'Lex.' Claire gripped her hand firmly. 'I know this is a worrying time for you, but it's very, very important that you calm down.'

'But my waters broke. I'm bleeding and it's too early,' she sobbed.

'I know, but we won't know anything for sure until we've checked you out. It's imperative you stay still so Campbell can assess how the baby's doing. Now, take some deep breaths and calm down. Come on,' she encouraged, demonstrating how she wanted it done. 'Breathe with me.'

Lex started to relax a little, which allowed Campbell to get a good trace of the baby's heart rate.

'One hundred,' he said quietly, but loud enough for Claire to hear. A little slow.

'Shall I get a speculum?' she volunteered, swapping the hand-holding job with Campbell.

'Lex,' he said, 'I need to check and see if you're dilated at all. Your membranes have ruptured so this baby obviously wants out, whether we like it or not. The only choice now is whether to let you deliver normally or to section you, and that will depend on your dilatation.'

'But it's too early for the baby to be here,' she sobbed.

'Obviously I wish the baby was further along, but the choice is no longer ours. Don't worry, Claire and I are here.' He shot a reassuring smile at Lex.

Claire handed him a speculum to allow him visual access to Lex's cervix. 'You want me to give her this?' she asked, holding up the empty ampoule of steroids she had already prepared in a syringe.

'You read my mind,' he said, his brow puckered in concentration as he removed the speculum and felt the amount of dilatation with his fingers. 'Fully dilated.' He grimaced as Claire injected the steroids into Lex's leg. This would hopefully have some effect on maturing the baby's lungs.

Ideally, two doses were given before the premmie baby was born, but they obviously weren't going to have enough time.

Lex groaned as a contraction swamped her body, and Claire noted the baby's heart dip into the sixties. She glanced at Campbell and his eyes mirrored her concern.

'Oh, no! I need to push!' Lex cried, alarm causing more tears to fall.

'Lex, you're fully dilated.' Campbell's calm voice took control of the situation. 'I want you to push, go with it. Push.'

Lex face reddened as she pushed down with all her might. When the contraction eased she said, 'What about a Caesarean?'

'Not enough time. This baby will be out quicker than I can section you. Now, I'm not going to lie to you. The baby does seem to be showing some signs of distress so the quicker you can push it out, the better.'

Lex started to cry again, working herself up very quickly. Claire had to get Lex to settle and focus if they were going to get the baby out quickly.

'Lex, we're here. Trust us. Stay calm and push on the next contraction.'

With Claire's soothing, Lex settled again and Claire encouraged her to channel her anxiety into the pushing. Five minutes later a tiny baby girl slid safely into Claire's waiting hands.

Thankfully another nurse arrived just at that moment to tend to Lex, which freed Claire to help Campbell resuscitate the small and as yet silent neonate.

'Doesn't look very big. Eight hundred grams if we're lucky,' Claire said in a low voice, placing the baby in the specialised resuscitation cot, complete with overhead warmer and removable sides for easy emergency access.

'She's barely breathing.' Adrenaline pounded through Claire's system as her trembling hands hooked the baby up to the monitor. 'Heart rate fifty.'

Claire's fingers worked rapidly administering gentle chest compressions as Campbell fitted a mask attached to a bag over the baby's face, enabling him to give respiratory support to the baby's feeble attempts at breathing.

'I'll need to intubate,' he stated, grabbing a thin curved plastic tube handed to him by a member of the neonatal team, who had burst through the curtain seconds ago.

Campbell felt adrenaline charge into his system, kicking his heart rate up and honing his concentration. His hand shook and he took a deep breath. He would not lose another baby.

Claire continued working as he quickly passed the tube down the baby's throat and into her lungs. Campbell exhaled the breath he'd been holding, but there was still too much to do to dwell on the success of the tricky procedure.

'Adrenaline,' he said, as he attached the breathing tube to the bag and puffed one hundred per cent oxygen into the little lungs.

Campbell quickly disconnected the bag again so adrenaline could be squirted down the breathing tube directly into the lungs. Claire watched the monitor as the heart rate accelerated to one hundred and eighty.

The collective sigh of relief could be heard outside the curtain as people started to relax, knowing that they had brought the tiny baby back from the brink. The first hurdle had been passed.

'Her lungs are very stiff,' Campbell commented to the neonatologist, who was dialling up settings on a portable ventilator. 'She'll need high pressure.'

Claire let the neonatal team take over and went back to

her patient who was inconsolable, desperately needing to know what was happening with her baby.

'Is she OK?' asked Brian.

'We've managed to secure her airway and get her heart to beat faster,' Claire confirmed cautiously.

'That's good, right?' asked Lex, an edge of hysteria in her voice.

Claire looked at Lex's and Brian's desperate faces, hungry for good news. She knew all they wanted was any scrap of positivity she could give them. It was a difficult line to walk. The compassionate nurse and human being in her wanted to help allay their fears and assure them everything would be OK.

But in reality she knew that the combined effects of their baby's prematurity, her weight and the high pressure needed to ventilate her were not good signs. As much as she wanted to, she couldn't give them false hope.

'She's over this initial hurdle. They're taking her to the neonatal intensive care unit. Her progress from now on will all depend on how her little lungs cope. Luckily, we have some very good drugs to help her in that department.'

'So she's not out of the woods yet,' Lex sniffed.

'No. In fact, she's quite critical.' Claire softened her voice to ease the blow. It had to be said. There was no point trying to put a positive spin on it when Claire knew the baby's chances were slim.

Lex began to cry again and Brian hugged her to him. Claire stood by silently, holding Lex's hand, giving them time to express their grief.

'But premmie babies do really well these days, right?' asked Brian. His face begged her to agree.

'Yes, some of them do really well,' she confirmed gently. Claire didn't have the heart to go into any more detail. She'd tried to prepare them for what the neonatologist would say, but she didn't want them to give up all hope. 'Why don't we get you sorted and you can both go up and see her?'

'Really? We'll be able to see her this soon?'

'Absolutely!'

Lex and Brian were cheered by this prospect and Claire spent the next hour dealing with routine post-delivery matters. Campbell had gone to the NICU with the baby and Claire was too busy to dwell on the heart-stopping events that had just taken place.

Brian pushed his wife in a wheelchair to see their daughter, with Claire tagging along. On their arrival at the unit they were put in a comfortable lounge area and told the doctor would come and talk to them. Claire waited with them—she couldn't leave them now.

Campbell found them there a few minutes later. Claire's heart sank at the grim look on his face.

'Campbell.' Lex's voice lifted at his arrival, 'What's happening? Is she all right?'

'It's touch and go,' he said quietly, pulling up a chair to sit close to them.

Lex's face crumpled and Campbell took her hand, rubbing it soothingly.

'The neonatologist will be here to speak to you soon. I just thought you might like an update.'

'Claire said she's critical. Is that right?' Brian's voice wobbled with emotion.

Campbell looked at Claire and smiled sadly at her worried face. He was glad she was there. Glad for Lex and Brian, who were going to need a lot of emotional support, and glad for him, too. Her presence helped make his words easier to say. Knowing she was there to support him as well as them was comforting. Giving people bad news was never easy. Having someone you knew and trusted by your side was a godsend.

'Yes, Brian. Your baby is critical. She's needing one hundred per cent oxygen and special drugs to support her blood pressure. Her lungs are very hard to ventilate, they're very stiff. The machine that is breathing for her has to deliver her breaths under great pressure to even get them into her lungs. I won't lie to you. Her outlook isn't good.'

Claire closed her eyes, feeling dreadful for Lex and Brian and thankful that she didn't have to deliver such devastating news herself. She looked at Campbell. His face was as grim as the news he'd just imparted.

She felt a tug in the region of her heart. He hadn't had a very good run. He'd worked wonders today under great pressure but she wondered if he felt a sense of *déjà vu*. Having witnessed at first hand how affected he had been by Hillary's baby only weeks ago, she worried how he'd be if he lost this baby, too.

'What are her odds?' Brian asked gruffly.

'We'll be doing everything in our power to get her through this, Brian. But she's nearly on maximum support now so I'd say her chances are quite slim. I don't like to give percentages, the neonatologist will probably go through that with you, but she's so tiny. That's her biggest disadvantage at the moment.'

'How tiny?' asked Lex, realising that she knew almost nothing about her little girl—not even how much she weighed.

'Eight hundred and fifty grams.'

Claire's heart went out to Campbell as his words sank heavily into the silence that followed. No further words were necessary to impart the seriousness of her size. One thousand grams was the magic number for premmie babies. Those weighing less often didn't have good outcomes.

How could a baby so small ever survive? Even with the medical technology they had today? It would be a miracle. But, Claire reminded herself, miracles can and did occur in intensive care units all the time.

'Maybe we should think about getting her christened,' Brian said quietly to his wife, tears glistening in his eyes. Lex's shoulders shrugged up and down as she sobbed into her husband's shoulder.

Claire and Campbell sat in silence while the couple's grief echoed around the room. Claire felt helpless. What could you say to make things better? Nothing. All she could do was be there for them.

'Would you say a prayer with us, Campbell? Claire?' asked Brian quietly, lifting his head.

Campbell wasn't a religious man but he knew that people's faith could help them through extremely traumatic situations. Who was he to argue with that? Whatever helped Lex and Brian cope was worth a try.

They all joined hands and bowed their heads.

Claire was conscious of Campbell's hand engulfing hers and of their shoulders rubbing lightly together. The circle was intense and intimate and she felt a connection with Campbell she hadn't felt before. It suddenly seemed right to be here by his side.

Claire felt her heart thudding in her chest as a realisation began to dawn. This feeling of intensity and connection—she knew what it was. It was love.

Suddenly it was clear. She'd been in love with him all along and hadn't known it. Claire suppressed a groan. What a completely inappropriate time to have such an epiphany!

'Amen,' whispered Brian.

Amen, thought Claire.

A nurse entering the room broke the mood and startled Claire out of her introspection.

'I'm sorry we've taken so long to get to you, Mr and Mrs Craven. My name's Leah. I'm looking after your baby today. Julie MacDonald, the neonatologist, will speak to you both shortly. Would you like to come and see your daughter first?'

Leah spoke to the new parents on the way to the bedside about all the machines and tubes and monitors they would be seeing. She knew it was often devastating for parents to see their intensely monitored baby for the first time.

Claire and Campbell tagged behind slightly. It was hard for Claire to concentrate now. She was trying to come to grips with her revelation and act normally at the same time. A difficult thing to do when the man in question was so close she could feel the heat radiating from his body.

'She's so tiny,' Lex whispered, a tear running down her face as they watched the fragile little girl through the clear plastic of the isolette. Tubes and lines crisscrossed her practically transparent body. There didn't seem to be an area of skin that had escaped being covered by one thing or another.

'What's her name?' Claire enquired.

'Charlotte. After Charlotte Brontë. *Jane Eyre* is my favourite book,' replied Lex, her voice flat, her hand pressed to the plastic.

'It's a beautiful name,' said Claire, squeezing Lex's shoulder.

Julie MacDonald arrived and Claire withdrew, knowing that Lex and Brian were in good hands. She gave assurances she'd call back later when the new parents had digested some of the information. Claire arranged with Leah to page her should the baby's condition change for the worse.

Now all the drama was over Claire needed to be alone.

She had to get away from Campbell's presence to think. A lot had happened today. Professionally and personally.

Her hands trembled as she walked back to the birth centre. What kind of a fool had she been? She'd honestly thought she could deny love from her life. She'd thought that if she didn't allow a man into her life and didn't allow herself to think about it, or talk about it then it couldn't possibly happen. She'd been wrong. Love didn't work like that. You didn't get to choose where love was concerned.

She realised now that those feelings and emotions that had puzzled her so much after she'd met him, the ones she'd never experienced before, had been the first stirrings of her love for him. Her feelings for Shane had been puppy love in comparison.

She sat at her desk and cradled her head in her hands. Watching Campbell in action today, his compassion and gentleness with Lex and Brian, the way he'd empathised with them—that had done it. That had been the clincher.

She'd already witnessed his brilliant professional skills in highly stressful situations. She knew he was an excellent practitioner. But to see him connect and take the time to be with grieving people—that was special.

His involvement with Hillary and Danny and their baby was a perfect example. He cared. He got involved. Too many doctors departed after bad news and left it to the nurse to do the comforting. Not Campbell, and, heaven help her, she loved him for it.

Claire groaned and gave herself a mental shake. She swivelled in her chair so she could look out the window. It didn't matter anyway. That she loved him was immaterial. The facts of her life were still the same. Nothing could come of it.

So she'd just have to get over it. Yes, it was going to take time, but she'd acknowledged it, hadn't she? Surely that was the first step. She couldn't be with him, so pining was pointless. Besides, she never pined. Never. She got on with life. She did that really well.

Claire rose and wandered into the staffroom to get a cup of coffee, still not quite believing these strange new feelings. She should be happy—wasn't that how women in love felt? But it was hard to be excited about unwanted feelings.

OK, she loved him and, short of leaving St Jude's she was going to see a lot of him. So she had to sort out a way to handle it. They had to work together and they had to find a way to get back to their previous ease. This stiff formality since their split was awful.

Today they had worked together like old times. They had worked as a team for Charlotte. All their baggage had been left outside the curtain and they'd got on with the job.

She shouldn't be surprised. Their recent history not with-standing, he'd always been a pleasure to work with. He treated her as an equal, he was polite, funny, considerate and willing to listen and integrate her opinions and ideas. Claire realised suddenly she missed that dynamic.

It had disintegrated of late, replaced with awkwardness and formality. OK, she'd have to keep her love a secret, but she could do that if it meant they could return to their old professional relationship. If they couldn't be lovers, maybe they could be friends? Surely they were grown-up enough for that?

A knock on her door brought her out of her reverie. She glanced up. It was Campbell. Looking at him standing in her doorway, Claire marvelled at how it had taken her so long to get it. Her love was so obvious to her now.

She noticed his strained demeanour was back in place.

'Just checking in to see if you were OK...you know, after everything that happened today?'

Claire was touched by his consideration, even if it was

a little stiff. This was why she loved him. He cared and he was thoughtful.

'I'm fine.' She smiled, her voice husky. 'A little shaky still...'

'Yes...me, too,' he admitted, and gave her a ghost of a smile in return.

'Any update on Charlotte?'

'No. Still not looking good. They haven't been able to wind any of her ventilation back.'

He sounded so civil Claire could bear it no longer. She rose and took some steps towards him, but stopped when she saw him straighten and take a step back.

'Look, Campbell, I know this past month has been difficult...but we're both adults. I miss our professional relationship—the way it used to be. The way it was today. Can't we put what happened behind us and just be friends?'

She held her breath. All of a sudden she needed this more than anything. Maybe his friendship would be the perfect antidote for her love?

He regarded her seriously. Was the woman mad?

'Friends? Claire, I don't know if I could ever just be your friend.'

'OK. Maybe we can't be bosom buddies, but surely we can be friendly at least?'

'I think for some men and women, especially ones with history, being friends is...difficult.'

'But why, Campbell? Why does it have to be that way?' She took a couple steps closer, beseeching him.

'Because.' He pushed his floppy fringe out of his eyes impatiently. Hell! Was he going to have to spell it out?

'Because why?' Desperation tinged her voice. It would be such a relief to put their awkwardness behind them.

Obviously he was going to *have* to spell it out. 'Because whenever I see you I want to make love to you,' he said, trying to keep the exasperation from his voice. Was she that clueless?

The admission seemed to be wrenched from deep within him and Claire figured it hadn't been an easy thing to admit. She swallowed convulsively, his words melting her insides and calling to her love. It rose in her and threatened to spill out. No! She must stay focused.

'I know it'll be…strange at first, but it'll soon seem more natural. We just need a bit of practice. I'm tired of us being tense around each other. Everyone notices, you know. The gossipmongers are having a field day. If people can see that we're fine with each other, they'll leave us alone and gossip about something else instead. Aren't you sick of the speculation?'

'Yes,' he agreed wearily, rubbing his eyes. The scrutiny was a little wearying. To be able to act normally would be a nice change—or as near normal as was possible for ex-lovers. 'OK,' he conceded. 'I'd be willing to give it a go if you are.'

'Good. Oh, that's great. Thanks, Campbell. I feel so relieved,' Claire prattled, desperately wanting to go and hug him but rooted to the spot. A little too early in their friendship for that.

Campbell shook his head as he made his way back to his office. Friends? It was never going to work. How could he have a platonic relationship with the woman he loved? Every time he saw her he wanted to push her against a wall and have his way with her!

Her professionalism at the birth and resuscitation of Charlotte and her continued empathy, compassion and unspoken support of him today had only served to deepen his love.

Something told him he was going to suck at being friends.

CHAPTER EIGHT

A WEEK later Campbell had to concede that maybe he'd been wrong. The birth centre had been very busy all week, which had necessitated a lot of contact with Claire. Their pact to be friendly seemed to be working. They were both more relaxed and their professional relationship seemed to be getting back on track.

Of course, he was still as horny as hell at the very sight or smell of her, but as far as he knew no one had ever died from it and her friendly, easier way with him compensated to a degree. And then, of course, there were always cold showers. Campbell had never been cleaner in his life!

He whistled as he made his way over to the centre to check on a client who had delivered in the night. Claire was on day shift so he was bound to run into her. Maybe if he didn't push it, friendship could blossom into something more?

Claire was beaming when she bumped into Campbell.

'You look as if you've won a million dollars.'

'Better.' She grinned. 'Sometimes, Campbell, I love this job so much I just want to burst with it. You know?'

'Sure.' Campbell kept his smile in place and tried not to flinch at the ease with which she used the word 'love'. So it wasn't that she couldn't say it—she'd just never associated it with him. 'What happened?' he asked, following Claire to her desk.

'I helped your client with a breastfeeding issue. It never ceases to amaze me that human beings are born with the ability to bear young and then nurture them. I love watching mothers feeding their babies. It's truly wonderful.'

'Yep. It's a beautiful thing,' he agreed quietly. Images of Claire with a baby at her breast rocked him. His baby.

Friends. Friends. Just friends, he chanted to himself. Yep! Sucking at the being friends thing!

Oblivious to his inner turmoil, Claire stood to retrieve a file. A wave of dizziness hit her and she grabbed hold of the desk for fear she would faint. Nausea rolled through her gut. She sat down again quickly.

'Claire? Claire, are you OK? You're as white as a sheet.' He crouched beside her chair.

'I'm fine... I just feel a little light-headed,' she admitted in a small voice, fanning herself as a surge of heat washed over her.

'You don't look fine,' he said gruffly, grabbing her legs and dumping them up onto her desk.

'I'm sure it's just because I haven't eaten anything since breakfast,' she replied shakily, some vigour returning to her voice as she felt the blood rush back to her head.

'I'll get you a glass of cordial,' he said, leaving her side briefly before returning.

'Thanks.' She smiled gratefully. She reached for the water with a shaky hand, feeling the cool glass against the pads of her fingers before it slipped and smashed to the floor at his feet.

Claire sat up in horror, watching vacantly as the water pooled around their shoes. How clumsy!

Barbara bustled in to investigate the sound of breaking glass. 'Not again, Claire,' she tutted, after checking that Claire was OK. 'That's two glasses in as many days! You've been a bit of a butterfingers lately,' she teased, helping Campbell mop up the water.

'No, I'm not,' Claire denied absently, her thoughts still foggy.

'Oh, yeah? What about that tray of instruments you dropped in Theatre the other day during that Caesarean? Goodness, forgetful as well. Anyone would think you were pregnant,' she quipped, as she left the room with a soaked towel.

Claire stilled as she felt the beginnings of fear settle in her stomach. Pregnant…or worse. Barbara was right, she had been a bit absent-minded of late. She could feel herself tremble and a wave of nausea assailed her again. Clumsy as well. Oh, God. Please, no.

'Claire? Hey, Claire! What's wrong? You look terrible. She was only joking about the pregnant thing.'

Campbell was shaking her gently by the upper arms. She couldn't move. Couldn't speak. Fear paralysed her and kept her mute.

'I'm going to be sick,' she whispered, finally managing to speak and move her legs. She dashed to the toilet, her hand clamped over her mouth.

She retched and retched. Once the nausea had passed, Claire pulled the toilet lid down and sat. She was pale and shaken.

'Claire? Are you all right?'

Claire heard the concerned note in Campbell's otherwise gruff voice.

'I'm…I'm fine,' she answered, standing on wooden legs and flushing the toilet.

Campbell helped her out, assessing her pallor.

'I'm fine.' She raised her hand to fend him off and smiled weakly. 'I'll just throw some water on my face and I'll feel better.'

He watched as she splashed water on her face and neck. He handed her a towel.

'Better?' he asked gently, brushing her damp fringe with his long finger.

Claire nodded and allowed him to pull her close. She sank against him gratefully, ignoring the guilt she felt at breaching their new pact of friendship. She longed to stay in his embrace but knew it wasn't healthy for either of them. She broke away and walked on wobbly legs back to her desk.

She sat down, thankful that her head had now stopped spinning. Unfortunately, her mind had taken over. Was it possible that the first symptoms of her mother's disease, one she had a fifty per cent chance of inheriting, were emerging?

Clumsiness and forgetfulness. The hallmarks of Huntington's. Claire tried to keep the panic at bay and think logically. Was it possible to have had these symptoms for long and not realised it?

Ever since her split with Campbell she'd kept herself busy with her work in an attempt to ignore the emotional fallout. Nothing had mattered but her career and the birth centre.

She dismissed the possibility of pregnancy out of hand. They'd used contraception, it wasn't possible. For goodness' sake, they'd only had sex a few times! Although it was slightly preferable to the alternative, Claire had to admit that neither of them were great choices.

'I'll get you something to eat.' Campbell interrupted her swirling thoughts. His pager beeped and he pulled it impatiently off his belt.

'It's OK, Campbell. You go.' Claire assured him. She needed time to think without him being right there in front of her. She'd never been more scared in all her life and she didn't want that to be the catalyst to confess all to

Campbell. 'I'll sit for a bit and then I'll ask Barbara to get me something to eat.'

He hesitated. His pager beeped again.

'I mean it,' she insisted. 'I feel much better now.'

'I'm going to ring you later to check on you,' he threatened lightly.

She smiled weakly and watched him walk away, a sense of foreboding sitting like a lead weight in her stomach.

The week went from bad to worse. Not only did Claire have to contend with the growing fear that she had inherited her mother's disease, but the mere thought of it made her physically ill. Every time she thought about it, and that was practically always, she had to rush to the toilet. Nausea and vomiting were now her constant companions.

She tried hard to remember if her mother had suffered from nausea when she'd first become symptomatic. If she had, Claire couldn't recall it and Mary was in no position to confirm or deny it. She could ask her father, but there was no need to alarm him yet.

What she wouldn't give to have Campbell with her now. To be able to lean on him, tell him everything. The whole sorry story, including her love. Maybe things wouldn't be so scary and uncertain with him by her side.

A few days later she was sitting at her desk, trying to concentrate on the water-birth protocols she'd begun shortly after her break-up with Campbell. It had seemed like a good idea at the time, partly because she really wanted to see it come to fruition but mostly because she knew it'd occupy a lot of time. But try as she may, they just couldn't hold her attention today.

She was staring blankly, her mind going over and over the same things that had been fermenting there for days now. When her eyes refocused she realised she was staring at a big red ring around one of the dates on her desk calendar.

That was the day her period had been due. Tuesday the twelfth. Weeks ago! She was as regular as clockwork every twenty-eight days. Never missed. She sat up straighter.

She counted back and double-checked. How could she have not realised that she'd missed a period? OK, so she'd deliberately shut out everything other than work and her responsibilities at home but this was ridiculous.

It was probably nothing to worry about. To say she'd been under a lot of stress recently was a gross understatement. Just because nothing had ever affected her cycle before, it didn't mean that it couldn't. Trying to come to grips with a potential terminal illness would certainly do it!

The next morning, Claire had to admit that being pregnant was a real possibility. She'd risen early as usual to assist with her mother's care, and had to make a detour to the toilet before she could begin anything.

She felt a brief lifting of her spirits at the thought that the nausea might be related to pregnancy and not the disease. But that didn't account for her forgetfulness and clumsiness. Although most pregnant women she knew did complain of poor memory. So maybe...

As Claire parked her car at St Jude's a few hours later, she knew she had to find out.

'Barbara, I need you to take some blood from me.'

'OK. Sure. Everything OK?'

'No, not really. I think you were right. I might be pregnant after all.'

Claire was most grateful to Barbara who sympathised but didn't pry. She felt absurdly close to tears as Barbara assured her that the secret was safe with her.

The needle stung as Barbara slid it easily into the vein

at the crook of Claire's elbow. The syringe filled with dark red blood. She took off five mils and handed it to Claire.

'Thanks.' Claire plunged the needle into the top of a vacuum-sealed blood tube and watched as the blood was sucked from the syringe into the tube.

Barbara filled out the slip for the lab, writing 'Beta HCG' in the test-required box.

Beta HCG, the pregnancy hormone, responsible for the entire gamut of symptoms described by pregnant women the world over. It became detectable in the blood and urine at a very early stage.

To complete the form she needed to fill in the requesting doctor box. Barbara hesitated over this one. She pursed her lips and firmly put down Campbell's name, hoping that she'd done the right thing. She placed the blood sample and the form in a path bag and sent them off to the lab.

Thankfully Claire had a busy day of appointments and meetings. It wasn't until just before she was due to go home that she could check the computer for her results.

It took a few minutes to get into the screen she required. And there it was, blinking in bright green. POSITIVE.

Everyone had gone off for the day so Claire felt no embarrassment as she burst into tears. Life just wasn't fair. As if it wasn't bad enough that she'd convinced herself she'd inherited Huntington's disease. Now, apparently, she was pregnant. Her two worst nightmares had just come true.

How Claire got through the next few days, she really couldn't recall afterwards. She was pregnant. Pregnant with Campbell's child. And also, whether she wanted to face it or not, she had to confront the very real possibility of having Huntington's. A disease she could pass on to her baby.

A baby. Something Claire had always wanted, more than she could have articulated. Something she had known she could never have. But she was having one now, and she could think of nothing else.

Mercifully Campbell was away at the moment, attending a three-day conference in Melbourne. Not seeing him had given her the space she needed to look at their situation clearly.

She probably had Huntington's disease. Worse, she was pregnant with a baby that could also have the same illness. His beliefs about genetic disorders still rang in her ears, and her belief that she couldn't burden someone she loved with a potential invalid still stood. It was more important than ever that she keep her distance.

Claire kept turning over and over in her mind what she was going to do. All she really wanted to do was revel in the life growing inside her and daydream about happily-ever-afters. But there were decisions to be made.

How could she bring a child into the world with her family history? She'd hardly be protecting it if, by giving birth to it, she was exposing it to the same awful genetic lottery that she'd lived with for too many years.

At least Claire had had twenty carefree years before the axe had fallen. This little one would live every day of its life under a cloud. Sure, plenty of children lived under worse uncertainties, but this was her child. Claire knew she wasn't capable of giving her baby life knowing she could also be passing on a death sentence.

But was she? She had never been tested. There hadn't even been a test available when her mother had first been diagnosed, and after extensive genetic counselling, she'd decided not to bother. Not knowing was preferable to being told you were positive. As she had told Campbell, ignorance was bliss.

But she could no longer just think of herself. If she had the disease, her baby had a fifty per cent chance of inheriting it as well. Was that something she wanted to inflict on her baby? How could she live with herself if she'd passed it on?

Claire knew she was going to have to have the predictive test that had become available in the last few years. But knowing it and liking it were two different things.

Thinking positively helped. If she took the test and it was negative, then her and the baby were going to be OK and she could allow herself to love Campbell—if he still wanted her after all she'd put him through. Yes, she had to focus on love. Love for her baby and love for Campbell. It would get her through what had to be done.

She'd never been more terrified in her life!

The next day Campbell caught a taxi to St Jude's straight from the airport. He wanted to tackle the mountain of paperwork that would be waiting for him and, if he was honest, he wanted to see Claire.

He'd really missed her the last few days. OK, so their relationship wasn't exactly what he wanted, but they seemed to be moving into a comfortable friendship and he was surprised how much he'd missed that.

He removed his jacket and sat at his desk, pulling his bulging intray towards him. He opened the yellow internal mail envelope on the top of the pile and several lab forms fell out. He thumbed through them distractedly.

Campbell always insisted on looking at his own results. It was a double-check system that occasionally picked up abnormalities that had been missed or not reported to him, usually through communication breakdowns and human fallibility.

Nothing seemed out of the ordinary. Just the usual hotchpotch of pregnancy tests, blood counts and electrolyte studies. The last one was a pregnancy test. It was fairly unremarkable in itself, except for the name. Claire West. He sat perfectly still for a few seconds. Surely not? Claire? His Claire?

His heart started to beat a little faster. He looked at the date. It had been done four days ago. He took a deep breath to calm his suddenly raging thoughts. Could it be her? Her name was fairly common. There were probably hundreds of Claire Wests in Brisbane. There was no patient identification number either. Intriguing.

His hand shook as he dialled the number for the lab. He needed to investigate fully before he jumped to any conclusions. He rang off a few minutes later, having ascertained that the blood bearing Claire's name on that day had been logged as having come from the birth centre.

Pregnancy tests weren't usually sent from the centre. There was no need to perform one as the clients were obviously pregnant or they wouldn't have been cleared to attend.

Campbell felt a tremor slither through him. Claire was pregnant. She was going to have his baby. He stood up, trying to quell his growing excitement. Suddenly he wanted to jump for joy. He snatched the pathology form and shoved it into his jacket pocket. If he hurried he might catch her before she left for the day.

He had to see her and reassure her that everything would be OK. He'd be there for her and his child. She could stop running away from relationships. Whatever it was, they could work it out for the sake of the baby. They'd get married and live happily ever after.

Valerie informed him she'd just left and if he hurried he might catch her in the car park. He didn't need telling twice and he rushed out of St Jude's as fast as he could.

Campbell spotted Claire's head disappearing into her car as he arrived at the staff car park. He yelled out but she didn't hear. He bolted to his own car, deciding to follow her until she stopped and got out.

Traffic was always heavy at this time of the afternoon in and around the hospital, and Campbell found himself four or five cars behind. As they travelled further into suburbia, the cars thinned out and he was directly behind her for the last five minutes of the journey.

He drummed his fingers impatiently on the steering-wheel, waiting for her to look in her rear-view mirror so he could alert her to his presence. She must have been deep in thought as she never looked once.

She drove into a driveway in a pleasant suburban street. He parked out front and was undoing his seat belt when his mobile phone rang. He wanted to switch it off but answered it anyway. It was one of the midwives in Labour Ward, ringing about a private patient.

It took ten minutes to deal with the problem. He hung up eagerly and was knocking on Claire's front door in a matter of seconds.

A tall, grey-haired man answered. Campbell assumed him to be Claire's father and was struck by how old and tired he looked. Claire had told him he was sixty-four, but Campbell would have put his age somewhere in the seventies.

'Hello. Mr West? I'm Campbell Deane.' He held out his hand and the older man shook it. Campbell was surprised by the strength of his grip.

'So you're Campbell,' he said in a voice as firm as his handshake. 'I'm Ray, Ray West. Pleased to meet you.'

Ray ushered Campbell into the lounge. 'Is Claire expecting you?'

Campbell could tell that Ray was unused to meeting any of Claire's men friends. 'No.'

'I don't mean to pry, Dr Deane, but Claire did say you

weren't seeing each other any more. I don't know if she'll be too keen to see you.'

'Tell her it's important. Please.'

Ray left to talk to Claire while Campbell waited. He returned quickly.

'I'm sorry, Dr Deane. She doesn't want to see you. I'm afraid my daughter does have a rather large stubborn streak.'

'Yes, I'm well acquainted with that streak. Please, call me Campbell.'

'Well, Campbell, I think it's high time somebody came along and made her see that isolating herself from life isn't the answer. I admire your persistence.'

'Thank you. I fear I'm not out of the woods yet.' Campbell smiled.

He felt the older man's scrutiny and sensed Ray was trying to get his measure.

'Well, that's why I'm off to get the paper. That's a good long walk, about an hour. I expect you to use that time well. She's in the end bedroom.'

Campbell shut his eyes, unable to believe his good luck. Claire's father was on his side. He was grateful to Ray for his support—he needed as much as he could get.

Still, he approached the end door with a degree of trepidation. What he did and said now could make all the difference. Campbell felt the gravity of the situation weighing him down.

He raised his hand to knock and then hesitated. If he gave her the option, she'd no doubt deny him entry. She might even lock the door. He needed to speak to her face to face. Best not to alert her. Forewarned was, after all, forearmed.

He pushed the door open. Claire was in the middle of hanging a feedbag, winding it through a pump. It was obvious she hadn't been expecting him. Her expression went from startled to surprised and then, as her father's betrayal sank in, angry.

Campbell wasn't prepared for what he saw in the room. He stopped short, taking in the sight of Claire and the frail older woman in the bed. What was going on here? He didn't seem to be able to process his visual signals. Who was the woman? Was this her mother?

Claire cursed her father silently. She didn't want Campbell here. Now he was going to ask a whole host of questions she didn't want to answer just yet. She'd wanted to keep her mother's condition a secret, at least until after the test.

'Do, please, come in.'

Campbell didn't miss the anger, thinly veiled by sarcasm. 'I'm sorry, Claire…I didn't realise. Your father said you were in here. I assumed it was your bedroom.'

'I told Dad I didn't want to see you.'

'Yes, he told me. Then he went out to get the paper and told me where you were. I think he approves of me.'

Campbell's gaze returned to the occupant of the bed. She looked very frail, her papery skin stretched taut over her bones. She lay staring blankly into space. Campbell noticed drool pooling at the corner of her mouth.

It had to be Claire's mother. Despite the ravages of an obviously debilitating disease, the likeness was striking. Campbell's professional guess was a terminal illness of some kind. Probably cancer.

'Aren't you going to introduce me?'

'Campbell Deane, this is my mother, Mary West.'

'Pleased to meet you, Mrs West.' Campbell raised his voice slightly.

Mary didn't move. She didn't blink or acknowledge his

presence in any way. She continued to stare blankly at nothing in particular.

'I need to talk to you, Claire.' Campbell's request was gentle. He saw her mouth thin and knew she was still angry with him.

Claire finished hanging the feed set and turned on the pump. 'I'm going outside for a while, Mum.' She stroked her mother's hair as she spoke. 'I'm going to talk to Campbell, I'll be back shortly. We haven't read the paper yet.' Claire pressed a kiss against her mother's forehead.

Campbell followed her out of the room and into the lounge. She walked to the window, keeping her back to him.

'How long has she got?' Campbell watched as she stiffened slightly then sighed and pressed her forehead to the glass.

'The GP thinks months.'

'Oh, Claire, I'm so sorry.' He went to her and put his arms around her, pulling her into him. 'All this time you've been dealing with your mum's illness alone. Why didn't you tell me? Everything's so much clearer now. I've been making these demands…and all the time your mum's been dying.'

'My mother has nothing to do with our break-up. No, actually, that's not true. She has everything to do with it, just not the way you think.'

Campbell tried not to feel dismay at the flatness in her voice. He put his hand in his jacket pocket, desperately searching for a way to reach her. His fingers came into contact with the crumpled piece of paper he had hastily shoved there earlier. It felt like a message coming from his unborn child.

He handed her the lab report. She took it and read it without blinking.

'You're pregnant.'

'Yes.'

'With my baby.'

'Yes.'

Campbell wanted to swing her up in his arms and whoop for joy. 'What are we going to do about it?'

'*We're* going to do nothing. I haven't made up my mind yet. There are some…things I need to clarify first.'

Campbell heard the don't-mess-with-me edge to her voice. 'Don't you want the baby?' He tried not to sound as disbelieving and desperate as he felt.

Claire shut her eyes, wishing it were that simple. Tears suddenly threatened. She loved him so much.

'Because I do, Claire. I do. I'm the father. I have rights, too.'

Claire felt as if she'd been holding herself erect for days now. Ever since the pregnancy had been confirmed. She had to be strong. She had to be. There were so many decisions still to make.

'I'd hate to trample on your rights, Campbell, but trust me—' sarcasm laced her voice '—it just isn't that simple.'

'Sure it is. You either love this baby or you don't.'

'You think I don't love this baby?' Claire felt the tears gather and was stung by his words.

'I don't know, Claire. I don't understand any of this.'

'Come with me,' she snapped, and marched down the hallway, flinging her mother's door open. 'Look at her, Campbell. Look at her.' Tears streamed unchecked down her face. 'What's your diagnosis?'

'I don't know. I assumed it was cancer.'

Claire's brittle laugh echoed around the room.

'Cancer? Oh, Campbell, cancer would be so simple. No, my mother has Huntington's disease.'

Claire watched through her tears as realisation dawned

on the face of the man she loved. 'That's right, Campbell, take a good look. This could be me in ten or twenty years. It could be our child. You want me to inflict this on our baby, because I sure as hell don't. So don't tell me I don't love this child.'

She ran from the room, sobbing, brushing past a stunned Campbell. He stood stock-still, trying to analyse the information she'd just thrown at him. He searched his grey matter for what he could remember about Huntington's.

It was a degenerative disease of the central nervous system. It slowly renders the sufferers incapable of normal body functions leading to premature death. And it was genetic.

So Claire could have inherited it. And so could the baby.

CHAPTER NINE

THINGS were starting to make sense now, Campbell thought as he took some time to sort through the jumble of thoughts spinning around in his head. Bits of the crazy puzzle were falling into place. This was what it had been about all along. This was why she'd pushed him away.

When he joined her a few minutes later she was sitting in a chair, her eyes red and puffy. She looked so miserable he ached to hold her. But now was not the time for that. It was finally time to clear the air.

'Are you telling me you also have it?'

'Not so cut and dried, is it?'

'You think I'm going to run away because of this? You think I'm going to dump you because of this, like Shane did? I'm not him, Claire.'

'You told me to my face that you would think twice about bringing a child into this world if there was a history of genetic illness. Well, that's exactly what's happened here, Campbell. So pardon me if I got the impression that you wouldn't be interested.'

'Just because I said I'd think twice, it doesn't mean I'd abandon you because it's happened. That CF couple planned their second baby knowing full well the possible consequences. This is different. It was an accident.'

'Is it different because of that or different because it's you?'

'Claire, look, all that matters to me right now is our baby. And you. I love you. That's all that matters—we'll deal with the rest together. I know we can make this work.'

He loved her. Those three little words slammed right into her solar plexus. Her heart wanted to take flight and soar— he loved her. She wanted to go to him and tell him she loved him, too, but she held back.

She couldn't confide her love until after the test. If it was negative, she could rejoice in his love and share hers in return. If it was positive, he must never know how she felt.

Claire didn't want to burden him with an invalid and watch his love turn to sympathy and pity. They would always have to have a relationship because of their child, but she would never allow him to be an intimate part of her life if it turned out she had the disease.

'You have no idea,' she said quietly, shaking her head, quashing the elation she'd felt at his declaration.

'Explain it to me, then. I am a doctor.' She rose from the chair, still shaking her head.

'It's got nothing to do with the extent of your medical knowledge. It's to do with the reality of the disease. In ten years I've watched my father become an old man. I've seen his heart break little by little and I know, I just know, that somewhere inside the shell that is now my mother she's seen it, too. I don't want that to be us. I don't want it to be you. Why do you think I've pushed you away all this time?'

'So you've had the predictive test?'

'No.'

'What do you mean—no?' Campbell could hardly believe his ears.

Claire sighed. 'It's not so easy, Campbell. Mum was diagnosed ten years ago, and from that moment on I lost my mother. She gave up. Just took to her bed and waited to die. I was so determined that wasn't going to be me. I refuse to let this disease define me, as my mother has. I'd rather not know than live my life under a death sentence.'

'A simple blood test, Claire, that's all it takes.'

'I know that, Campbell. You think I don't know that? It sounds so simple but the reality is terrifying. What if it's positive?'

'What if it's negative?'

'It's all right for you. You've got what you wanted.'

'What do I want, Claire?' he asked softly.

'You've got me in a position where you have a hold over me. You probably planned this all along. You probably used defective condoms.'

Campbell laughed. It felt good to get some relief from the intensity of their conversation.

'This isn't a joke for me. This is my life.'

'I love you, Claire, and I understand you're scared.'

'Scared?' His love and reassurance soothed the hysteria that threatened. 'I'm terrified, Campbell. Do you know what it's like to live day by day with this hanging over your head? Every time you drop something or forget something, you wonder, Is this it? Do I have it? And then having to watch as it ravages your mother, wondering all the time if this is going to be me.'

'So get tested. Stop the guesswork.'

'Relax, Campbell. I'm seeing my geneticist in a few days—I've already made the appointment. I know I have to take the test for the baby's sake. I know that. I'm just…still in a state of shock about the pregnancy and I'm scared. I think I'm already experiencing some symptoms of Huntington's.'

Campbell felt fear clutch his heart. Claire was scared and he wanted to comfort and support her through this. But how could he do that when he was so terrified himself? Frightened for Claire and for the baby. He loved her and he just couldn't bear the thought of the woman he loved going through such mental anguish.

'If you test positive—' Campbell's voice shook '—then we can have the baby tested.'

'And if it's positive?' Claire shuddered at the thought.

'Claire, this disease isn't like CF. Its onset doesn't start until later, right? So…medicine, genetics, is moving ahead in leaps and bounds. If the baby carries the gene, it'll be, what…another thirty, forty years before it's symptomatic, right? By then they'll be able to selectively remove genes that cause diseases. They've already mapped DNA, it's only a matter of time before genetic illnesses are obliterated.'

Too late for her, though. Claire shook her head, quashing the self-pity as quickly as it had appeared. He had a point. She felt a ray of hope rising inside her. Claire used her hands to swipe the tears from her face.

Genetic advances were happening daily. In the future it would be acknowledged that this period in medicine had been second only to the era when penicillin had been discovered.

'You're right.' She smiled a watery smile.

'I know.' He grinned and they laughed despite the circumstances.

'I love you, Claire. No…' He held up his hand and her interruption died on her lips. 'I know it's not reciprocated. I know there's too much stuff happening in your life at the moment to think about loving me back, but I need you to know how I feel. I'm telling you because I want you to draw strength and determination from my love. Let it make you stronger to face the next few days and weeks and whatever they hold. Just lean on me.'

Claire felt tears well in her eyes again at the sweetness and sincerity of his words. He was right. With his love behind her, she could face anything. She could face the future and fight for herself and her baby if she needed to.

He was, of course, wrong about his love not being reciprocated, but Claire knew it was wise to keep her own counsel. Her life suddenly felt in limbo, dependent on the results of a blood test. Would she be a winner or loser in this cruel genetic lottery?

Three days later, Claire and Campbell sat in the waiting room of Dr Robyn Laidley. Claire battled waves of nausea. Was it morning sickness or extreme nervousness? Claire hadn't been able to stomach breakfast. In fact, food had lost all its appeal over the last few days. Eating was something that was purely functional—she forced herself to do it for the sake of the baby.

Campbell shifted in his chair and smiled at her. She looked away and he squeezed her hands, knowing she was nervous and wanting to comfort her. They felt cold and he instinctively rubbed them between his.

The phone buzzed and the receptionist answered it, murmuring quietly.

'Claire West,' she announced in a clear voice, standing to direct the way.

Campbell and Claire took the indicated seats in the large, modern room and waited in silence for a few minutes. The door behind the desk opened.

'Claire.' Dr Laidley greeted her as she entered. 'It's been a long time.'

'Hello, Robyn.'

It may have been ten years, but the geneticist who had played such a pivotal part in Claire's life all those years ago looked exactly the same.

She'd forgotten how tall the doctor was, almost Amazonian in stature, with softly curled red hair only now showing the signs that she had entered the fifth decade of her life. She wore fashionable glasses that made her appear even younger.

'You must be Dr Deane.' Her eyes twinkled as she extended her hand.

'Campbell,' he said, shaking her hand. 'Don't tell me hospital gossip reaches all the way down here.'

'No, not really.' She laughed. 'I have my sources.'

Campbell's laughter grated on Claire's already stretched nerves. She knew they were just being friendly but she wanted to yell at them to shut up. It didn't seem right to laugh in this office where she'd only ever heard bad news.

'I'm a little surprised to see you, Claire.' Robyn got down to business. 'Last time I saw you, you were adamant I wouldn't be seeing you again.'

'To be honest, I'd really rather not be here, but…my circumstances have changed.'

'Oh? How so? Are you experiencing symptoms?'

'I…could be…' Actually admitting the possibility out loud to Robyn was terrifying.

'I get the feeling there's more,' Robyn prompted.

Claire couldn't speak. Weren't symptoms enough? How could she tell Robyn about the baby when she'd stood in this very office years before and insisted she'd never burden a child with her mutant genes?

'Claire is pregnant,' Campbell stated.

'Ah…I see.' Robyn removed her glasses and placed one earpiece between her teeth, sucking thoughtfully. 'So, your symptoms have been…?'

'Oh…um…some clumsiness, forgetfulness.'

'For how long?'

'A month, maybe a little longer.' Claire's brow creased, trying to concentrate on the facts.

'And you're how many weeks pregnant?'

'Nine.'

Claire could practically see the brain cells working behind the geneticist's eyes. They were busily forming impressions, gathering data and analysing it.

'So these might not be symptoms at all, at least not of the disease?'

'I suppose…' said Claire, sounding unconvinced.

'It could just be the pregnancy. You both must know plenty of women who complain of an appalling memory when they're expecting. That hormonal haze is a killer.'

'Very common,' Campbell agreed.

'So. You want to be tested.'

'No.'

'Claire?' Confusion furrowed Robyn's brow.

'I'm here to have the test, yes. But do I want to take it? No. Not one iota.'

Robyn peered over her glasses at the two of them. Campbell felt her shrewd gaze weighing him up and wondered what she was thinking. Was she thinking what a sorry pair they were? Why two people, supposedly in a relationship and about to have a child, looked so damned miserable?

'Campbell wants you to take the test,' she stated.

Neither of them spoke, and Campbell felt his misery intensify. Great. Now Robyn was going to think him some kind of ogre.

'You do know, Campbell, that the implications of this test are potentially quite awful for Claire? She needs to be emotionally prepared as much as possible before she consents to this.'

'Robyn.' Campbell half sighed, half groaned. 'I'm well aware of that. And, believe me, if this was just about her and me, I wouldn't be pushing. Good Lord,' he said, raking his hand through his hair, pushing his floppy fringe away, 'I don't care about the bloody test! I love Claire, disease or no disease.' Frustration welled inside him and added a husky quality to his voice. 'But there's another person involved now—my child.'

Robyn was quiet again, tapping her glasses against her pursed lips. The silence stretched between them. 'Why don't I start right from the beginning? We'll get a family history from both of you and I can work out a pedigree, and from there we can assess the risks to your baby.'

'That's kind of pointless, isn't it, Robyn?' Claire stated quietly. 'I mean, if I have the gene then my baby has a fifty per cent chance of inheriting it, too. That's right, isn't it?'

'Yes,' Robyn admitted, 'but now we can do special tests and actually find out the baby's status. You'd be much better equipped with that kind of information to make decisions. There have been some interesting advances in this area in the past decade.'

'Can they cure it yet?'

'No.'

'Well, that's the only advance that matters to me.'

'Maybe some more counselling will prepare you better should you carry the gene.'

'Can you ever really be prepared for that?'

Robyn was savvy enough to know a rhetorical question when it came her way. She stayed silent.

'Frankly,' Claire sighed, 'I think it'll be a relief. As much as I've tried to ignore it, deny it—it's there. It's always there. I've lived my life refusing to let this disease define me, but I think it's time to stop driving myself crazy with what-ifs. And I need to know for the baby's sake. Yes, Campbell really wants me to take the test. But I need to know, too. I need to be prepared.'

'Yes,' Robyn said after a short while, 'I think you're right. Very sensible. I'll write out the lab form.'

Claire watched as Robyn scribbled on a piece of paper. She suddenly felt better than she had in weeks. She felt like she was taking control of her life again. OK, the result was in the lap of the gods, but as she squeezed the hand of the man beside her she knew his love would help her through.

'Now, some things have changed since I last saw you. As a consequence of the Huntington gene being isolated in 1993, we can now do direct gene testing.'

'I've been reading up on this. You look for a repeat in the DNA sequence, right?' said Campbell.

'Yes, we identify the fourth chromosome and look for a series of repeated units of information known as CAG repeats. We all have these, but in the general population you find less than twenty-nine CAG repeats. In affected individuals the CAG repeats number between forty and fifty-five, sometimes higher.'

'What if you have more than twenty-nine but less than forty?' asked Claire.

'Well, that falls into a grey area. I can tell you that people with twenty-nine to thirty-five CAG repeats have never been documented with the disease.'

'So,' said Claire, wanting to clarify the technical information, 'it all depends on how many of these CAG repeats I have. Right?'

'Right.'

'How long until the test results come back?' she asked.

'Two weeks. We'll make an appointment for you in a fortnight and we can discuss the results.'

'Can't you just ring me with them?'

'No. If they come back with elevated CAG repeats, I want to be able to tell you face to face. It's not the kind of information I want to give you over the phone.'

'I don't think I can wait two weeks,' Claire said.

'That's understandable,' Robyn agreed. 'But that's the way it is. Look…I know it's easy for me to say, but try and use these next two weeks thinking positively. And you need to take better care of yourself, Claire. I'm sorry to say this but you look like hell.'

Robyn was right, Claire decided, assessing her features critically in the mirror above the handbasin in the public toilets on the way to the laboratory. She smiled at herself and winced at how wan she looked. She did look like hell!

Campbell accompanied her to the lab for her blood test. Claire thought he was probably escorting her to prevent her from bolting than for any other reason, but she was grateful for his presence anyway. Whatever his motive.

As the needle pierced her skin Claire felt her doubts and fears return. What if she had the gene? How would she cope with the awful knowledge that she had a terminal degenerative illness?

Campbell saw the fear in her eyes and tried to imagine how terrible it must be confronting the reality of Huntington's. He couldn't. It must be too awful for words. He loved her more at this moment than he ever had, his heart swelling with pride. This was extreme bravery. He squeezed her hand and she clutched his harder.

'You don't have it,' he said, looking into her panicky eyes.

'How do you know?' she whispered, wanting to believe him, wishing she possessed his assuredness.

'I just do.'

'I wish I could be so sure.' Her voice trembled.

'Positive. We have to be positive.'

Claire nodded, not trusting her voice as she held the cotton ball over the puncture site in the crook of her arm. The nurse fixed it with surgical tape.

Campbell drove Claire home, reciting his positive-thinking mantra while she tried to ignore her dread and the motion of the car and concentrate on not throwing up.

'I've been thinking,' he said as he turned off the engine, 'Robyn has a point about looking after yourself. You do look… Well, you've looked better.'

'Gee, thanks,' she said, feeling less queasy now the car was stationary.

'Maybe you should take the next couple weeks off work. Eat, sleep and pamper yourself a bit. Come and stay with me. I'll treat you like a queen.'

It sounded like bliss. A fortnight being cocooned in his love and attention. But she couldn't allow such intimacy yet. She didn't trust herself not to blurt out her feelings, and she was determined to keep them secret at all costs. She needed him to keep thinking she didn't love him because once she told him, there would be no going back.

'I appreciate your concern.' She smiled gratefully. 'But I'll go mad if I'm not occupied. I really need work to keep my mind off the test. I promise I'll take care of myself…really. And there's Mum to consider…'

'All right, then. I don't agree with you but I understand.'

He smiled at her and ran his index finger down her cheek. Silence filled the car as their gazes locked. He placed his hand on her flat stomach. Claire felt her insides contract followed by a flare of sexual desire. It had been a while since they had been intimate. The sudden need to feel him deep inside her shook her to the core.

'Promise me you'll look after yourself and my baby,' he said huskily.

'I promise,' she said, and crossed her heart.

Campbell found the next two weeks interminable. They dragged by, and he could only imagine how much worse it must be for Claire. He ran into her quite a lot at work, and was cheered by how much better she was looking.

No one could accuse her of having that glow that so many pregnant women had but she looked healthy. She was laughing more and she seemed to be eating almost every time he saw her.

Campbell was saddened that he was denied access to her changing body. He desperately wanted to see the differences in her shape as his baby grew inside her. It wasn't anything sexual, more primal. This was his baby and he wanted to be there to see her stomach blossom and her breasts become fuller and feel the first stirring of foetal movement. Staying away was the hardest thing he'd ever had to do.

He refused to think about the results in any other than a positive way. He couldn't explain why he felt so certain, he just did. And the times his thoughts did wander down the negative track, he knew it wouldn't matter to him. You love for better or worse, right? In sickness and in health?

All he knew was that he wanted to be with her and their baby. The test results would decide his fate, too. They both had a lot riding on them.

It was Friday. The appointment with Robyn Laidley was on Monday. Claire, who had managed quite well to keep herself busy this last fortnight, just couldn't distract her mind from the imminent results.

She took a phone call from Brian Craven, updating her on baby Charlotte's progress. She'd had the breathing tube removed yesterday and had done well overnight. Charlotte had really turned the corner. Claire decided to go up and see her. At least it would be a distraction—a happy one at that.

Campbell was there when she arrived, holding the baby

and blowing raspberries on her tiny fingers. Claire instinctively cradled her still flat stomach. He would be a terrific father.

'Claire,' said Lex. 'Come and hold our precious girl.'

Claire joined the circle, acutely aware of Campbell's intimate stare. She held out her arms for Campbell to place Charlotte in them. Their gazes locked, a heat rising between them. Claire moistened her dry lips and watched Campbell's eyes dilate with desire.

'Hasn't she grown?' Lex chatted away obliviously.

Claire had trouble focusing her attention on the baby. Seeing Campbell reminded her of the desperation she felt about her situation. Worse than that, it seemed to be pushing them together. She should be discouraging this sudden heat between them, but Monday loomed large and he was the only other person who knew what she was going through.

'I actually managed to try a breastfeed with her this morning. She's amazed everyone. She's our little fighter,' gushed the proud mother.

Claire smiled and nodded and mumbled the odd appropriate reply, but as wonderful as baby Charlotte's progress was she was tuned into a different wavelength.

Campbell and Claire left together, chatting inanely about Charlotte. They got into the lift, and their conversation petered out. They stood side by side, close but not touching.

'Come back to my house for the weekend.' Campbell spoke into the silence.

'OK,' she agreed.

They smiled at each other, and he took her hand and pressed a kiss on her palm. The look in her eyes told Claire he was about to slam her against the wall and ravage her. She felt her breath quicken in anticipation, but the lift pinged and the doors open and people crowded in.

Claire couldn't explain it. She just had to see Campbell. As much as she knew she should stay away, he was the only person who understood. She had the weekend off and she couldn't bear the thought of having all that time on her hands. She needed to forget everything this weekend, and two days in his company would be a very pleasant distraction.

Claire's father was pleased when she rang him to inform him of her plans. He'd sensed she was struggling with something but had tactfully decided not to push. He knew his daughter would tell him when the time was right. He was relieved that she was getting out of the house for a while. She'd given up too much of her life helping him with Mary.

Claire and Campbell travelled in his car to the apartment in silence. Their thoughts were separate but similar. They both knew that destiny was running their lives and there was nothing they could do to stop it. The sense of impending fate hung over them like a thundercloud. They needed each other to navigate a way through the next couple of days.

Campbell pushed the door open and pulled Claire into the room and into his arms.

'I'm sorry. I tried to stay away,' he whispered, and he held her and murmured words of love. He felt so helpless. What did you say to someone who was facing demons few people faced? All he could offer her was the solace of his embrace, as she had offered hers when he had needed it. He hoped it was enough for this moment.

She pulled back a little so she could see his face.

'Me, too. I'm sorry. I'm not being fair to you...'

'Shh. It doesn't matter. I love you. I've always loved

you.' He brushed a strand of hair from her forehead and kissed her there gently.

'I know,' she whispered. 'I wish it was enough.'

'It is, Claire. It is.'

She shut her eyes and let herself believe it for a moment, but deep down she knew. If the blood test revealed that she had the gene, love just wasn't going to cut it. She'd push him so far away, drive him if necessary, that he'd never be able to get back. Never want to. She wouldn't have the man she loved sacrifice his life for her, like her father had done for her mother. She loved Campbell too much to put him through that ordeal.

But those were issues they'd be tackling soon enough. This weekend was about distraction. What would be on Monday would be.

Claire kissed him and it *was* enough for now. More than enough. She felt the reaction shudder through his body and pressed herself closer to him. She needed to be closer to him than she'd ever been.

They tore at each other's clothes, rushing, stumbling, fumbling towards the bed. Finally naked, they fell onto the bed and into each other. Claire was impatient for his touch and felt tears spill from her eyes as he buried himself in her and cried out her name. Yes. This was where he belonged. Where she belonged.

Claire wanted to freeze this moment in time and stay like this for eternity…part of each other. Connected. Not just physically but spiritually. Bodies and souls joined.

But the rhythm began to take over, pounding through her head and throbbing in her veins. The primal tempo of physical bonding that could not be denied, like an itch you just had to scratch. Claire revelled in it, welcomed each thrust, urged him deeper until she wasn't sure where her cries ended and his began.

* * *

Claire slept peacefully for the first night in weeks. The usual elusive fragments of dreams about babies and test results, which haunted her, waking her in a cold sweat, were blissfully absent. If only for that, the night was worth it.

They woke late on Saturday morning. The familiar nausea assailed her the second she opened her eyes. Claire remembered they hadn't eaten last night as she ran her hand over her stomach and pleaded with the baby to give her a break. It was no use, it was only a matter of time.

Campbell rolled towards her, snuggling into her side. 'Hmm,' he murmured, nuzzling her ear.

'Ugh!' she muttered, dashing from the bed into the *en suite*, retching into the toilet.

'Oh, Claire!' Campbell squatted beside her and rubbed her back. 'Are you all right? What can I do?'

'Strong, black tea. Two sugars,' she croaked. 'Dry toast—' She broke off as another wave of nausea caused her to retch again.

Claire stayed clinging to the toilet for a few minutes until she was sure the nausea had passed. She emptied her bladder, brushed her teeth and walked weakly back to bed.

Campbell arrived with a tray as she was pulling the sheet over herself. He passed her the steaming mug of tea and she sipped it gratefully between mouthfuls of toast. After she'd eaten the breakfast, Campbell took the tray and she lay back down on her side beneath the sheet.

He joined her in bed, curling around her, spoon-fashion. They lay in silence for a while.

'Claire?'

'Hmm?'

'About Monday.'

'No. No plans. We'll get the result then we'll go from

there.' Claire didn't want to argue this weekend and she certainly didn't want to be reminded about Monday.

A phone ringing cut off any potential conversation, and Claire realised it was her mobile. She dug around in her handbag for it.

'Hello?' Claire lay back against Campbell, his lips nuzzled her neck.

'Claire?'

'Speaking.'

'This is Robyn. Robyn Laidley.'

Claire's heart skipped a beat. She lifted herself up on her elbow, displacing Campbell.

'What's wrong?' she asked ominously.

'Nothing, nothing. Honestly. It's just that…well, I came into the office today to catch up on some paperwork and your results are here.'

'Oh?' Claire was sure her heart had now actually stopped.

'I know I don't usually ring but…it's twenty-two, Claire. Twenty-two.'

'Twenty-two,' Claire repeated.

'Twenty-two CAG repeats. You don't have the gene, Claire.'

'Twenty-two,' she repeated again.

'Yes, you don't have the gene!'

'I don't.'

'No.'

'So…the baby?'

'Doesn't either.'

Claire felt tears course down her cheeks. She was free. She didn't have Huntington's. Her baby didn't either. She was really free. Robyn continued to speak but Claire took none of it in. She was free.

'What's the matter? Who is it?' Campbell sat up, concern

creasing his brow as Claire dropped the phone in her lap. 'What about the baby?' he asked.

'You want to know what my favourite number is, Campbell?' Claire grinned a silly juvenile grin and her heart sang as she kissed him. 'Twenty-two. I'm going to get a new number plate for my car with twenty-two on it.'

'I don't understand. Twenty-two?' he said, wiping the tears flowing thick and fast down her face.

'That was Robyn. Twenty-two.'

Claire watched as realisation dawned on his face.

'CAG repeats? Are we talking about CAG repeats?'

'I don't have it, Campbell,' she said. 'I don't have Huntington's.'

She threw herself into his arms, feeling lighter and giddier and younger than she had in years. She wanted to dash out into the street and yell it to the world.

'So the baby...' he said, pushing her away slightly by the hips.

'Our beautiful baby doesn't have it either. Oh, Campbell, isn't it wonderful?'

'It's the best news ever,' he agreed, kissing her again. 'I love you, I love you, I love you,' he said, dropping kisses all over her face.

'You couldn't possibly love me as much as I love you,' she said between kisses.

He stilled and cradled her face in his hands, suddenly serious.

'You...you do?'

'Of course, you silly man. I think I've always loved you. I just didn't realise it and then when I did realise I couldn't tell you...not till I knew the result anyway. I would never have admitted it if I'd been positive. I love you too much to burden you with an invalid.'

'When will you get it through your head,' he growled

and kissed her nose, 'that I don't care about that? I've never cared about it. When you love someone, it's in sickness and in health.'

'I know that, but I still would never have allowed it.'

'I would have worn you down. You'd have been so sick of the sight of me you'd have given in just to shut me up.'

She laughed and they hugged and kissed again, passion escalating from their joy.

'No. Stop,' said Campbell, extricating himself and leaping out of bed. He started to dress.

'Why?' She pouted at him.

'We're going to go and buy you the biggest, most expensive ring we can find. We're getting married. As soon as possible. No arguments.'

'As if I could argue with you, you obstinate man.' Claire laughed and rose from the bed, going straight into his arms.

'I love you, Claire West.'

'I love you, Campbell Deane.'

'Let's get hitched.'

And they did.

EPILOGUE

CLAIRE and Campbell stared down at their sleeping new-born daughter. Baby Mary was blissfully unaware of their rapt attention.

'I wish Mum could have seen her,' she whispered. Mary had died three months before.

'She knows,' he said, pulling her close.

They stood and stared at their daughter, lost in their own thoughts.

'I can't imagine life without her. Can you?' asked Campbell.

'Absolutely not,' said Claire, stroking Mary's cheek.

'Just think, if I hadn't been so persistent, so—'

'Obstinate. Stubborn. Infuriating. Single-minded,' Claire interrupted, a smile on her face.

'Yes.' He laughed. 'All those things. Mary wouldn't be here today.'

'Yeah right,' Claire snorted. 'She'd be here all right— just a bit later, that's all. I know you well enough to know you'd have never given up.'

A knock at the door interrupted their conversation.

'I'll go,' he whispered, and kissed Claire's cheek. He signed for a rectangular package addressed to Claire.

'It's for you,' he said, as she joined him.

Claire knew what it was just from the shape, and eagerly tore open the cardboard to reveal her brand-new personal-ised number plates.

The word TWENTY-TWO gleamed up at her in shiny red letters. Claire laughed and showed Campbell. He grinned at her.

'C'mon, baby,' he said, 'let's go put them on.'

A VERY SPECIAL BABY

MARGARET BARKER

CHAPTER ONE

'SO, HAVE you decided if we can have a baby sister like Céline's got, Mummy?'

Debbie handed her daughter a croissant as she considered the question that little Emma had first asked when she'd got in from her day at school last night. She was desperately wishing that she'd dealt with it immediately instead of being deliberately vague and changing the subject. Difficult subjects never got any easier if you shelved them. She should have learnt that lesson by now. Why hadn't she simply told the truth to her enquiring six-year-old?

Which was? Well, darling, Daddy walked out on us four years ago, and that put an end to Mummy's dream of having a large family. That's what she should have said. That would obviously have been too brutal for her little daughter. But it would have been the truth.

Paul had put paid to Debbie's long-cherished dream. But she'd have to wrap it up a bit and make the truth presentable. Even though Paul was a two-timing, not to be trusted individual, he was Emma's biological father and Debbie had made a point of never trying to influence the way her daughter thought about him.

Debbie picked up the milk bottle and topped up Emma's glass. 'Well, you see, it's like this, darling—'

'Mummy! You're pouring milk on the table!'

'Sorry!'

Debbie reached for a cloth. Anybody watching her now would think the child more capable than the mother. And to think that in half an hour's time she would be dealing with matters of life and death in Urgences, the accident and emergency department at the nearby Hôpital de la plage. But at least she'd had training before she'd qualified as a doctor, whereas she'd had absolutely no training to qualify her for her role as a single working mum. Apart from the example her super-efficient mother had set her. Somehow Debbie felt she would never be able to be as completely objective as her mother had been.

She put the milk bottle back in the fridge and rinsed out the cloth, keeping one eye on Emma to make sure she didn't drop apricot jam on her clean blouse. All she had to say now to Emma was that it would be impossible for Mummy to give her a baby sister because mummies needed daddies to make babies. Just say that and Emma would go off to school happy—well, not exactly happy but at least she would know the truth about the situation.

Returning to the table, Debbie reflected that Emma couldn't possibly realise how her innocent childish question had upset her last night. She didn't need to know that Debbie had lain awake half the night longing for a solution to the problem. At almost thirty years old she could hear the sound of her biological clock ticking away, and she desperately wanted another baby. She wanted Emma to have a sister or brother. She'd tried to shelve the idea but when Emma had brought up the subject it had touched a raw nerve.

Supposing, just supposing…would it be possible to have another baby without the hassle of a relationship? She didn't want a man! Never again! Not after Paul! But supposing…

Emma wriggled in her seat. 'Have you thought yet,

Mummy? You're taking a long time. Céline's got a lovely little sister and she didn't cost anything 'cos I asked her. She said her mummy just growed it in her tummy. I'd help you to look after it. And they don't eat much, do they?'

Debbie smiled as she stroked Emma's long blonde hair, making a mental note that it needed cutting again.

'You're quite right, babies don't eat much when they're small. Mummies do grow babies in their tummies but they need a daddy to help them to make the baby in the first place.'

'Why?'

Enquiring blue eyes stared up at her.

'Well, the daddy has to plant a seed in the mummy so that the baby will grow in her tummy.'

'You mean like when I helped you dig the garden and we put those grass seeds in and then we got some grass?'

'Something like that. Well, not exactly... Emma, it's quite complicated for a six-year-old to understand so I think we should talk about it when we've got more time. We have to leave in a few minutes. I've got to drive you to school and then go on to the hospital and—'

'I don't want another daddy 'cos I've got one, haven't I? And although I never see him, I've got his photo in my bedroom and he sends me lovely presents on my birthdays and at Christmas, doesn't he?'

Debbie reached forward and gave her daughter a hug. She smelled of fromage frais and croissants and there was a sticky patch of apricot jam on one side of her hair.

'Yes, Daddy loves you, darling,' Debbie said, trying hard to remain loyal to the image that Emma had of her father. 'Come on, let's go to the bathroom and get you cleaned up ready for school.'

'Can I wear my new jacket?'

'Of course you can. You're big enough to take care of your clothes now, aren't you?'

Debbie felt relieved that Emma had stopped asking awkward questions. Allowing her to wear the new jacket they'd bought in Le Touquet at the weekend would be a distraction. But as she supervised Emma's brushing of her teeth in the bathroom she found her mind dwelling on their conversation. One thing that had come out of it was that Emma didn't want another daddy. Well, that was definitely the end of it, then! Not that she'd ever considered the possibility of forming a long-term relationship with another man. Paul had put her off for life!

Leaving Emma at the door to her classroom, Debbie was once again relieved to find that her daughter ran towards her little French friends, chattering away to them as if she'd been born in France instead of London. But she'd made a point of speaking French to Emma when she was small just as her own French father had done with her when she'd spent time with him. It had been English at school and home with her mother, and French with her father and his family.

'*Au revoir, Maman!*' Emma trilled, turning to give a final wave.

'*Au revoir, chérie.*'

As Debbie drove along the coastal road that led to the Hôpital de la plage, she found herself relaxing again. No more difficult questions for a while! She loved this early morning drive along this stretch of the coast, with the sea dashing against the cliffs below her and on the other side of the road the picturesque green and brown, gently sloping hills. With the lovely April weather they'd been enjoying recently, the sheer beauty of this part of France always put her in a good mood and ready to start the day.

And she loved her work. Accident and Emergency departments here in France were much the same as in England. You never knew what was going to happen from one day to the next. It was challenging, exhilarating, sometimes exhausting but always very satisfying. Except when they lost a patient. Then you had to pick yourself up and try to remain detached. Keep a tight rein on your emotions. Over the years of her medical training and during her time as a qualified doctor she'd tried to learn how to do that. But sometimes she broke down—although never in front of the patients.

She waited until she got home. When Emma was asleep she would soak in the bath and have a quiet weep, at the same time telling herself there was nothing she could have done about it. She always wished she'd inherited her mother's tough personality. She'd never known her surgical consultant mother to worry about anything. She'd had to face up to the fact that basically she was a softie and there was nothing she could do about it. Her father had told her she took after him in personality. He was a softie, too, but he kept it well hidden, especially when he was performing a last-ditch, difficult operation to try to save a life which seemed doomed from the start.

And she'd inherited her father's dark hair. As a child she often wished she'd got her mother's blonde hair. When she'd been in her early teens she'd bought some blonde hair dye and given it a try. It had been a disaster, never to be repeated. And the streaky blonde hair had taken ages to grow out. Her own daughter had inherited the previously desired hair from her grandmother, reinforced by Paul's fair hair.

Driving down the hill towards St Martin sur mer, Debbie could see the whole bay spread out in front of her. The undulating sand-hills spilling down onto the beach and behind them the hotels, shops and houses. The hospital nestled at the bottom of the hill connected by a dual carriageway road to the nearby motorway. An ambulance was being driven at speed round the roundabout. Debbie held back, following it through the wide hospital gates before turning into the staff car park.

She squeezed into a space next to the one reserved for the consultant of Accident and Emergency. Climbing out, she was careful to hold onto her door so as not to scratch the flash car parked next to hers. Metallic silver, long sleek bonnet, sporty-looking thing it was. It was obvious that dear old Jacques Chantier had now retired. What a sweetie he'd been! So helpful when she'd first arrived here two years ago. A real warmhearted family man. She couldn't have wished for a better boss to get her started in the French system. She'd been sorry to say goodbye to him yesterday.

Walking across to the entrance marked Urgences, she wondered fleetingly what the new consultant would be like. If he was anything like his car, he would be the exact opposite of Jacques! Jacques had driven the same old car for years, even though with his salary he could well have afforded a new one. She wasn't sure she was keen to meet this flash new consultant, but as long as he was good at his job she didn't care what he was like.

Glancing across at the hospital forecourt, she noticed a couple of patients being stretchered into Urgences from the ambulance she'd followed from the roundabout. Almost immediately a second ambulance arrived, followed closely by a third. She quickened her pace.

Closing the door of her locker, she unfolded the freshly laundered white coat and pulled it on, slinging her stethoscope round her neck.

'*Venez ici, vite, vite, docteur!*' called an imperious voice as soon as she arrived in the main reception area of Urgences.

She hurried across to the cubicle where the voice had demanded she arrive as soon as possible. A tall dark-haired man was securing an injured leg on a backslab. The white-faced patient lay motionless on the couch, seemingly barely conscious.

Debbie, not recognising the doctor attending him but noting the aura of authority surrounding him, surmised this had to be the new consultant. As he straightened up his white coat swung open, revealing an expensive-looking grey sharkskin jacket. The matching trousers were immaculately pressed. Not the usual run-of-the-mill, throw-on-the-first-thing-that-comes-to-hand-in-the-morning doctor she was accustomed to working with.

'Dehydration setting in, Doctor,' the new consultant told her tersely. 'Put in a line and get some dextrose into him. *Vite, vite!*'

Debbie reached for the sterile IV pack before beginning to ease back the patient's sleeve. She could see immediately that the forearm was swollen, and from the unnatural angle at which it was lying she deduced there was a fracture. Carefully she cut through the patient's shirtsleeve. He remained motionless as she worked, his eyes closed. At least he didn't appear to be in pain.

'We'll need a splint on here and an X-ray of the forearm,' Debbie said quietly in French, finding it perfectly natural to revert to her second language as she moved to the other side of the patient to fix up the IV. 'I'll see to that when I've got the dextrose flowing into the other arm. Has the patient been sedated?'

'The paramedics gave him some pethidine at the scene of the crash. I've arranged for him to go to Theatre as soon as he's been X-rayed. There's some internal damage, possibly the spleen...definitely something in the abdominal area. Haven't had time to do a full examination, as you can tell.'

'Do we know what happened?' Debbie said as she adjusted the flow of dextrose.

'Crash on the autoroute. Several cars and a lorry piled up. They're bringing in the casualties now. This man arrived first so I was able to see him quickly. I was told another doctor would be arriving soon, but I expected you would be here much sooner.'

Cool grey eyes surveyed her. 'I'm Marcel De Lange.'

'Debbie Sabatier.'

'Do you always arrive so late, Dr Sabatier?'

Debbie continued to fix the splint on the injured arm. Be polite was her motto when she was annoyed. She cleared her throat and began to speak in her best, much-practised Parisian accent that her father had told her would never fail to impress her seniors in the medical profession.

'I was actually early. I work set hours from nine till five.'

'How convenient for you.'

Debbie moved round the bed, taking care to give a wide berth to the consultant, who was still bending over their patient.

'It's written into my contract. You see, I have a child so I wouldn't want to work more hours.'

'Dr De Lange!'

A nurse poked her head around the door. 'Can you come and look at this patient, please, as soon as you've finished here?'

'*Oui, j'arrive tout de suite.*'

Marcel went over to the sink to wash his hands. 'I'll leave you to it, Dr Sabatier. Here are the patient's notes. He's still semi-conscious so we'd better have an X-ray of the skull. The name on the driving licence in his pocket is Bernard Dubois.'

As Marcel went out of the cubicle, the patient opened his eyes. 'What's happening now?'

Debbie leaned over her patient and smiled as she replied in French in a more friendly tone than she'd used with the difficult consultant. 'Good to hear you speaking at last. Can you tell me your name?'

'Bernard Dubois. What are my chances, Doctor?'

Debbie tried to reassure her patient, telling him that everything was under control and that he was going to be taken to X-Ray shortly. 'After we've decided what injuries you've sustained we'll—'

'You'll take me to Theatre. I know. I was listening to you and the other doctor talking, but I felt so sleepy I didn't want to be part of it. You seem to know what you're doing so I trust you, Doctor.'

Debbie smiled. 'Thanks.'

The patient gave a wan smile. 'Haven't much option, have I? Where do you come from, Doctor?'

'Good question. I lived most of my early life in London, but having a French father, I've also spent a lot of time in France.'

'Ah, that accounts for the touch of a foreign accent on certain words. I thought maybe you were French Canadian or perhaps Belgian.'

'No, I'm half English, half French.'

'So which country do you prefer to—?' The patient broke off, wincing with pain. 'My stomach feels like a herd of elephants have been stampeding over it. I heard the other doctor saying there's some abdominal damage.'

'We can't really tell until we've X-rayed you.'

'And opened me up. Oh, don't worry, I know the drill. I started medical school when I was eighteen. Flunked out at twenty-two. Couldn't stand the pace and being treated like a stupid schoolboy by the consultants. That was two years ago. I drive a lorry now and there's no hassle—but no prospects either. Ah, well, from what I've seen today I think I made the right career move. Wouldn't want all the aggro you doctors have to take. But I sometimes wish...'

'Dr Sabatier!'

Sister Marie Bezier hurried in and grabbed Debbie's arm. 'Dr De Lange needs you urgently. I'll stay with your patient.'

'How urgently?' Debbie asked, intent on fixing the arm splint before she left. She sometimes found that Marie was prone to exaggeration and Debbie always preferred to put the patient first.

'One of the casualties from the motorway crash is in labour. De Lange is furious that Obstetrics haven't taken her immediately. I think things are going to be different now we've got a dynamic consultant in charge. I'll finish that splint for you.'

Debbie downed tools and headed for the door. 'Thanks, Marie. I agree with you that things will never be the same again. We'll all wish dear old Jacques was back with us.'

'Oh, I don't know,' Marie said. 'Marcel De Lange is

such a handsome man, I don't mind how bossy he is. I like a man who's masterful. I've seen all the nurses drooling over him already.'

'Not interested,' Debbie said as she hurried away to find Marcel. She would be studiously professional and polite with him. But the less she saw of him the better. Handsome self-centred men were all the same. She should know! She'd been married to one of that difficult-to-live-with species.

She found him in a nearby cubicle, leaning over a heavily pregnant woman obviously sedated or anaesthetised but completely motionless, her eyes closed.

'*Enfin!* At last!' he said as she went into the cubicle. 'I've alerted the obstetrics team.'

He lowered his voice. 'In the obstetrics department, they're currently delivering several babies simultaneously apparently, including two sets of twins. How on earth they can—*Mon Dieu*…we can't wait any longer! Our patient has already signed a consent form for a Caesarean, should it be necessary. I've given her an epidural so she's not feeling any pain. Just look at the monitor!'

Marcel took Debbie to one side. 'Did you note the foetal distress?'

Debbie nodded. 'If we don't act quickly that baby will be—'

'Exactly! Scrub up quickly, Doctor. We can't risk losing that baby. Nurse, sterile gowns, please. Gloves, mask…'

Debbie had never prepared herself so quickly for a Caesarean section. She was standing on the other side of the treatment couch from Marcel De Lange, gowned, masked, gloved and ready in two minutes flat.

The nurse was swabbing the patient's abdomen in

preparation for surgery. She moved back as the consultant took his place and leaned over the patient.

'Have you any sensation below the waist, Sidonie?' he asked their patient.

'None whatsoever, Doctor. You go ahead and get my baby out, please.'

'You're a good patient. OK. Let's go ahead. Scalpel, Doctor...'

Marcel was holding out his hand, his eyes firmly fixed on the patient's enlarged abdomen. 'Come on, come on...'

Debbie handed over the sterile instrument.

Without hesitation he sliced through the skin, cutting into the abdominal tissue, skilfully negotiating the quickest way through to the uterus.

'Hold this muscle back with your retractors, Dr Sabatier. More retraction here! Yes, I can see now...'

Debbie breathed a sigh of relief as she watched him working. Knowing very little about him except that he was a consultant in emergency procedures, she'd worried that he might have only basic knowledge of obstetrics.

'You've done this before, haven't you?' she asked quietly, as she watched him slicing through the uterine wall.

'You didn't think I would endanger the patient if I hadn't, did you?' he snapped back.

'Sorry, I didn't mean—'

'Swab! Stem the blood flow. Over there, not here! That section where—'

'Sorry!' She leaned across.

'And stop saying sorry! Until I've got this... Ah!' He breathed a long sigh of relief as he lifted the baby through the uterine wall and out through the abdomen, handing its slippery body to Debbie, before commencing to suture the internal abdominal tissue.

As the baby was brought under the bright lights away from the warm dark comfort of its mother's womb, it gave a loud squawk of annoyance. Debbie smiled as she wrapped the squirming infant in a dressing sheet.

'You little darling,' she cooed in English. 'You don't like our bright noisy world, do you? Shall I put you back in your nest?'

Marcel continued to suture the uterine and surrounding abdominal tissue as he began to speak in perfectly correct but heavily accented English. 'You'd better not put him back, Doctor. Not after all the trouble we've gone to.'

So the man actually had a sense of humour! 'Dr De Lange says you've got to stay here, darling,' she whispered.

She gave the tiny infant to his mother for a brief cuddle. 'You've got a beautiful baby boy. I'm just going to clean him up a bit and then bring him back to you.'

She moved away to begin the postnatal checks, placing the baby boy on a sterile sheet as she began by clearing his nostrils to ensure a clear airway. As she worked she talked quietly to him in French, loving every second of being able to handle this tiny precious infant.

Marcel looked up as he finished the external suturing.

'When you're ready, Doctor,' he said, reverting to rapid French again. 'Sidonie, would you like to hold him again before we do any more postnatal checks?'

The happy mother held out her arms for her baby.

'There you go, Sidonie,' Debbie said. 'Your beautiful little boy. He weighs three kilos and he's perfectly formed.'

Debbie handed over the newborn, making sure that the mother was strong enough to hold him in her arms for longer than a few seconds.

The mother's eyes were wet with tears as she hugged her baby son close to her breast. 'He's beautiful. Robert wanted a son. I didn't mind so long as our baby was healthy.'

Debbie turned away. She could feel tears pricking in her own eyes as she watched the young mother with her much-loved son. Oh, how she would love another baby! But it wasn't to be, so she'd better get used to the idea and stop wishing for the moon.

Unknown to Debbie, Marcel was watching her display of emotion. For an instant he felt unnerved by what he saw. Had he been too harsh with this English doctor? Was that why she was looking so upset? She was undoubtedly a very capable doctor. She'd been an asset to him as he'd worked to deliver the baby.

The door opened and a tall young doctor arrived. 'We can take your patient to Obstetrics now, Dr De Lange so…'

The young man's voice trailed away. 'Ah, I see the baby's here already. We hadn't realised the birth was imminent or we…'

Marcel took the young doctor on one side and spoke quietly. 'The baby was in great distress. Without an immediate Caesarean we would have lost him. It's fortunate I'm an experienced surgeon who's worked in obstetrics otherwise…'

He spread his hands as if to emphasise how grave the danger would have been.

'I'll arrange to have Sidonie and her baby transferred to your care now, Doctor,' Marcel continued with steely calm. 'But I will be monitoring the progress of these patients. She is to stay in the preliminary obstetrics ward next door until I'm satisfied that she is ready to go to the main obstetrics ward.'

'Yes, sir. I will explain this to my consultant as soon as—'

'You do that.'

Marcel turned away from the nervous young doctor and smiled down at his patient. 'We're going to have you transferred now to the preliminary obstetrics ward.'

Sidonie put out her hand and placed it on Marcel's arm. 'Will you come in and see us, Doctor? You've been so good to me. I don't know what I would have done without you.'

'Of course I will. You'll be right next door.'

'I shouldn't really have been driving, with the baby due next week. But I wanted to see my mother today and…well, when that car pulled out in front of me I thought that was the end! Have you phoned my husband?'

'He's on his way back from Paris,' the consultant said gently. 'Now, try to relax, Sidonie. I'll come in and see you later.'

He turned to look at Debbie. 'That's one good thing about this hospital. The preliminary units attached to Urgences are a great asset. It does mean we can liaise with the medical staff who take over from us. That way we can follow their initial progress before they're taken to the bigger wards.'

'Is that the only good thing about this hospital?' Debbie asked, recognising Marcel's undertones of discontent.

He raised an eyebrow as he looked down at her. 'I hope there are more good points, but at the moment I've yet to discover them.'

'Doctor for cubicle four!' called one of the nurses. 'As quick as you can make it...please!'

It was several hours before all the casualties of the motorway crash had been taken care of. Six patients had been transferred to the preliminary wards and two were still in Theatre, Bernard Dubois being one of them.

On the instructions of Marcel, Debbie had kept in touch with Theatre and given the consultant a continuous report on Bernard's progress.

'The prognosis seems promising,' she told Marcel as she put her last written report on the desk in the consultant's office situated at the side of Urgences.

Marcel looked up from his desk. He'd only just sat down for the first time for several hours and the mound of paperwork looked uninviting to say the least. He was a hands-on doctor and disliked the inevitable paperwork.

He stood up. 'I'll deal with that later when I've found where my secretary is hiding.'

'She works in your consulting rooms next to the outpatients department where you see patients and their relatives who've asked for a consultation with you.'

'Well, she'll have to come and work here.'

Marcel picked up the most recent report Debbie had placed on his desk, running his eyes down the page. 'I'm glad Bernard is surviving well in Theatre. Complicated case. When we have orthopaedic injuries combined with abdominal injuries it's never easy for the medical staff or the patient. Please, continue to keep me informed of Bernard's progress.'

She hesitated. 'I'm afraid I'm off duty now...well, since ten minutes ago. My little girl will be waiting for me at home, you see.'

'Ah, yes, I'd forgotten you have a family. Well, run along, then. Don't keep them all waiting.'

As she went out of the door she heard him call her back. 'Debbie! I may call you Debbie, may I?' He was speaking in his charmingly accented English again.

'Of course, if I can call you Marcel.'

He smiled. 'That goes without saying,' he continued in English.

Debbie smiled back. The ice was beginning to thaw. The great man was human after all! She'd begun to think he was as human as a machine.

Encouraged by his more relaxed tone, she decided to ask the question she hadn't dared ask before. 'Where did you learn to speak English, Marcel?'

'I worked for a year in an English hospital.' He hesitated. 'And I was married to an English woman for a couple of years.'

The smile had vanished from his face. It was as if the shutters had been pulled down to obscure the sunshine. Debbie sensed that their short friendly chat was over. She turned.

'*A demain.* See you tomorrow, Debbie,' he said as she moved away.

'*A demain*, Marcel.'

As he watched Debbie go, he was wondering again if he'd been too harsh with her. He was always strict with his staff at the beginning of a new job where he was in charge. It was essential to show everybody that he wouldn't allow his exacting standards to slip. But Debbie had probably found him particularly difficult.

He didn't want to alienate her. She was an excellent doctor. And as a family woman she didn't pose a threat. Married women were strictly off limits to him. He couldn't deny that he'd found her attractive, but after the trauma of Lisa's betrayal and his acrimonious divorce he was extremely wary of attractive women.

Her shoulder-length dark hair, which she'd coiled up before putting it into her theatre cap, looked soft and silky. And he couldn't help noticing the fluid movement of her body as she made her way through Urgences. Beneath that white coat she had a slim sexy figure...

No! He checked his train of thought. As a married woman she was out of bounds to him so he'd better continue with the professional stance he'd set up.

But there was no harm in being a bit more friendly than he had been. A bit of friendliness couldn't possibly lead anywhere. And he sensed that Debbie would be fun to get to know—but only as a friend. He was used to ignoring his natural emotional responses since Lisa had deceived him. Life had become much easier since he'd given up on deep feelings. No woman would ever hurt him again as Lisa had. The emotional wounds were healing but the scars remained.

Debbie quickened her step, somehow sensing that the new consultant was watching her. The brief thaw in their relations had allowed her a glimpse of the real man. Beneath that façade of superiority he was probably a warm-blooded individual. She wondered why his two-year marriage had ended. His wife may have died. He'd certainly looked sad when he spoke about the marriage.

She tried hard to put him out of her mind as she headed for the medical staff locker room, but something about him had gripped her imagination. She'd found him demanding to work with, but she admired his skills and judgement of a case. He was without doubt an excellent doctor and sometimes people who excelled in their profession could be very exacting. They expected high standards. That wouldn't be a problem for her. She aspired always to do the best she could.

Maybe she would learn to enjoy working with Marcel, she thought as she slammed the locker shut and turned the key. Walking out to her car, she found herself hoping that Marcel wouldn't be so exacting tomorrow. All work and no play. She'd like him to lighten up a little during the day. Smile more perhaps? Yes, he had a fabulous smile. When he'd smiled just now it had transformed his undoubtedly handsome face.

She'd noticed his dazzling white teeth positively shining between his lips. She opened the car door and climbed in, still thinking about that smile. Inserting the key into the ignition, she remembered in particular his lips. Wide, luscious, sexy... Ah, now, that was where she really must call a halt to thinking about Marcel De Lange. It was enough that she'd discovered he was human, without endowing him with attributes she didn't want to know about.

Emma rushed out through the door as soon as Debbie pulled into the short semi-circular drive in front of their little house.

'Mummy, Mummy, Francoise has made some *pomme frites* for my supper. Come and have some with me.'

Debbie hugged her daughter. As they went into the house together Debbie was thinking what a treasure Francoise had turned out to be. She lived in the village and had been acting as part-time mother's help for Debbie ever since she'd moved there two years ago. A widow in her early fifties, her own children had grown up and she seemed to enjoy looking after Emma, meeting the school bus in the village to bring her home and looking after her until Debbie arrived. She would babysit if Debbie went out or was called in to work on a major emergency at the hospital.

Automatically, Debbie and Emma reverted to French as they went into the kitchen because Francoise spoke very little English.

'*Bonsoir*, Debbie.' Francoise turned round from the sink, wiping her hands down her apron. '*Ça va?*'

'*Oui, ça va bien.* I'm fine, thank you. *Et vous*, Francoise?'

'I've had a good day. And Emma has been helping me to prepare supper. *Voulez-vous du jambon avec les pommes frites?*'

Debbie said ham and chips would be lovely. Francoise was only supposed to make supper for Emma, but she usually made far too much for one small child. If Debbie was hungry, as she was today, not having had time to take a lunch-break, an early supper was most welcome. Especially placed on the kitchen table as Francoise was doing now.

There was a huge bowl of *pommes frites*, a large serving dish of ham and a bowl of salad.

'May I toss the salad, *Maman*?' Emma asked, picking up the large wooden salad servers.

'Of course you may. I'll hold the bowl. Francoise, are you sure you won't join us? Let me get another plate.'

'No, I've got to get back. My son's coming round to fix some shelves for me this evening. *Bon appetit!*'

'*Merci,*' Debbie said, one hand holding the salad bowl and the other holding the back of Emma's sweater as she stood on the kitchen chair, leaning over the table.

Emma and Debbie said their goodbyes to Francoise as she left them. As soon as she'd gone they both reverted to English again.

'I'm glad you're home, Mummy,' Emma said as she sank back onto her chair, placing the servers back in the well-tossed salad and wiping a smear of vinaigrette down one side of her chubby cheek. 'I wish my daddy would come to supper some time. Why doesn't he come to see us?'

Here we go again! Debbie swallowed a chip and looked across the table at her daughter.

'Daddy lives a long way across the sea in America. He's a very busy man and he can't get away from his work at the hospital.'

'But he still loves me, doesn't he?'

'Of course he does, darling.'

'Well, that's OK then.' Emma chewed her chips happily. 'We don't need to get another daddy, do we?'

'No, we don't.'

Absolutely not! Meeting Marcel De Lange and observing his arrogance had somehow reminded her of the first time she'd met Paul. They were similar types. She couldn't imagine ever being persuaded into thinking Marcel would be a warm-hearted man.

And yet there was something dangerously and undeniably attractive about him. Some aspect of his personality that she didn't want to dwell on. Good thing she was only interested in him from a professional point of view. Although, if she was honest, if she hadn't promised herself she would never get hurt again, she wouldn't mind spending some time with him. But a man like that could reduce her to an emotional wreck just as Paul had done.

Sometimes she really felt she'd recovered emotionally from the way he'd behaved and then something would happen to remind her and she'd find herself back at square one. No, she wasn't going down that road again ever!

'Can I have some more *pommes frites*, Mummy?'

Debbie smiled as she picked up the serving spoon. Emma was all she needed...except she'd love another baby. But for that she needed a man...

CHAPTER TWO

AFTER working with Marcel for a couple of weeks, Debbie found she was becoming more relaxed with him. As she flicked through the notes that had landed up on her desk in her tiny office near the end of the main reception area, she realised that the feeling of apprehension that had haunted her for the first couple of days since the consultant's arrival had vanished.

It had also helped that Marcel seemed more relaxed when he was working. Maybe he'd been as nervous as the rest of them when he'd first arrived and had been putting on an act to show them all he meant business. Well, whatever the reason, he was much more approachable now, thank goodness!

She had to reread the letter she'd been skimming because her thoughts had been elsewhere. She looked up as somebody tapped on her door before coming in. She could feel an unwelcome heightening of the colour in her cheeks as she saw the man she'd been thinking about standing in front of her desk.

He put his hands on the desk and leaned forward. 'I'm having a house-warming party tomorrow night. I wondered if you and your husband would like to join us.'

'A house-warming?'

Marcel raised an eyebrow at her surprised tone of voice. 'And what's so strange about that? It's my way of getting to know my medical colleagues better than it's possible when we're all working together.'

So he was mellowing! 'Yes, it sounds like an excellent idea.' She cleared her throat. 'I wouldn't bring my husband if I were able to come. We're divorced. My ex-husband lives in America so as a single parent it's difficult for me to get out in the evenings.'

Marcel chose to ignore the uplifting of his spirits when he heard Debbie say she was divorced. He'd already enquired about her marital status but wanted to make quite sure he hadn't been misinformed. He was trying to convince himself that, although he was intrigued by Debbie and would like to get to know her, he could handle and ignore any emotional feelings that might threaten to complicate their friendship.

She was an interesting woman, an intelligent and experienced colleague, and he would value her friendship—nothing more, apart from the fact that she was very easy on the eye.

Watching her arrive through the main door of Urgences this morning, he hadn't been able to help noticing the way her slim hips had moved beneath her well-fitting trouser suit. She'd looked very competent, ready to deal with any emergency, but delightfully feminine and sexy at the same time. He admired her as a woman—a very feminine, attractive woman—but he was sure he could keep his instinctive desires under control.

He switched from French to English. 'Ah, so we're both in the same boat, as you English say. I'm divorced, too.'

Debbie looked across her desk into the cool grey eyes, but Marcel was giving nothing away. Neither was she. She made a point of remaining emotionally detached when she told people she was divorced. She didn't want anyone to know how she'd felt as if her heart had been ripped out when she'd discovered Paul's treachery.

'I don't go out much in the evenings,' she said quietly. 'Thanks for the invitation, but I'm sorry—I can't come.'

Marcel shifted his hands so that he could perch on the end of Debbie's desk.

'You mean you have a previous engagement?'

It was obvious she hadn't by the guilty look on her face, but he wanted to hear what she would say. Debbie was a woman who wasn't accustomed to lie, so different to Lisa who had got lying and deceit down to a fine art before their divorce.

Debbie hesitated, wondering whether to say she already had a social arrangement and that would be the end of it. She wouldn't feel comfortable doing that but on the other hand…

'Why do I get the impression you don't want to come?' Marcel said as he waited for her reply.

'Well, I'd need to get a babysitter for Emma and—'

'Is that a problem? Don't you ever go out by yourself?'

'Of course I do! I come to the hospital, don't I?'

'All work and no play makes…'

She looked down at her papers, unable to stand the eye contact with this devastatingly handsome and very persistent man.

'Yes, I know. Well, I used to get out more, but lately…'

'It's only a gathering of people from Urgences, not a ball. Eight o'clock till eleven. Come as you are. Dress code optional. The people on call will probably be back in the hospital by eleven and those who've been working since dawn will be falling asleep. My place is just around the corner a little way up the hill, so it's very convenient for those who are on call to nip back.'

'Well...'

'How old is your daughter?' Marcel said, with an air of exasperation.

Debbie smiled. 'Emma's six.'

'No problem with a babysitter, then. I'm sure you can arrange it...if you want to.' He stood up. 'I just think it would be a good idea to get as many of my staff who are working together in a social situation. Now that I know what you're all like professionally, I'd like to get to know everybody in a relaxed atmosphere.'

'So you've decided we're all OK professionally, then?'

'I didn't say that. I'm still reserving judgement on some members of staff.'

'Are you reserving judgement on me, Marcel?'

As he smiled down at her, Debbie felt a distinct quickening of her pulse. Probably just an illusion, but a wide sexy smile like that would have been her undoing at one time. Since Paul had taught her the danger of becoming emotionally involved only to be disillusioned, she hadn't allowed herself to give in to her natural emotional responses.

'I'm particularly reserving judgement on you, Debbie.'

She repressed a shiver as she listened to his deep gravelly voice. Was she imagining it or had Marcel implied a *double entendre* in that last statement?

He turned away and headed for the door. 'You're needed in X-Ray, Debbie. The nurse who took your patient there would like further instructions for when his X-ray is completed.'

'I'm on my way.'

smashed up the tibia and fibula in my leg, the radius and ulna in my arm, not to mention four ribs, I think I might make a good sympathetic orthopaedic surgeon.'

'It's possible,' Marcel said. 'What's happened to your old medical books?'

Bernard gave a sheepish grin. 'I made a funeral pyre when I quit medical school and burned them all so I couldn't change my mind.'

Marcel smiled. 'I felt like doing that during my training but I'm glad I didn't. I'll find you some books you might find useful. Now, let's look at the latest report on the ultrasound scan of your abdomen.'

Marcel fixed the film of the scan into the light-box on the wall. 'We decided the spleen was viable in spite of the damage, and I think we were right. There is obvious regeneration already. Good! As you know, Bernard, we thought about doing a splenectomy but we gambled that with a young fit man like you we might get away with more conservative treatment. And we did. So don't let us down now. Do everything we tell you. Oh, and keep reading the textbooks on orthopaedics when I give them to you. Maybe I'll spring a test on you one of these days.'

Bernard laughed. 'Marcel, you're a slave-driver.'

'I know, but it will keep you out of mischief.'

'What mischief could I possibly get up to in here? No girls—apart from Debbie—and she's happily married.'

'No, I'm not,' Debbie said, regretting immediately how she'd set the record straight. 'That is to say, I'm divorced, but I'm as good as married because I'm totally devoted to my daughter and intend to spend the rest of my life as a single mother.'

'How boring!' Bernard said. 'You're much too young

and attractive to stay single. Marcel, tell Debbie to snap out of it and start living a little.'

Marcel shrugged. 'Debbie is very independent. I've been trying to get her to come to my house-warming party tomorrow but it's one excuse after another so...'

'Oh, Debbie, it's only a party!' Bernard said.

'OK, I'll come! If I can get a babysitter.'

Both Marcel and Bernard groaned. 'Excuses, excuses, excuses...'

'No it's not. Anyway, we're going to have to move you to the main orthopaedic ward, Bernard. I'm going to arrange that now with the orthopaedic firm.'

'That will be a good move for your future career,' Marcel said. 'If you ask a lot of questions you'll gain valuable experience while you're waiting for your bones to heal.'

Bernard frowned. 'I don't want to leave here but so long as you two come in and see me now and again, I'll be happy.'

As soon as she got home, Debbie asked Francoise about babysitting for Marcel's house-warming party. Francoise was delighted to be asked.

'It's ages since I sat in for you during the evening, Debbie. I was only saying to my daughter yesterday that you don't get out enough. I know you're out at the hospital all day but that's work. And Emma will be OK with me, darling, won't you?'

Emma smiled. 'Will you give me another cookery lesson, Francoise?'

'*Eh bien, chérie, Maman* isn't going out until half past seven so you will already be in bed, won't you?'

'Francoise, it will be Friday night. No school on Saturday so I can stay up late.'

Emma looked at Debbie. 'I can stay up late at the weekend, can't I? You always let me, *Maman*.'

Debbie looked at the other woman who was nodding her assent. Francoise loved spending time with Emma. It reminded her of the days when she'd been so important to her two sons and two daughters. Now that they were independent she found she very much missed the enthusiasm and innocence of young children. And the generous wages that Debbie insisted on paying her for looking after Emma were an added bonus.

Debbie put an arm around her daughter's shoulders. 'OK, you can stay up late, but you must go to bed as soon as Francoise asks you to.'

'Bien sûr, Maman!'

The next evening Debbie was plunged into indecision as to what she should wear. It had to be something casual but nothing inappropriate. She wanted to look cool, as if she went out into Le Touquet every night and spent her weekends in Paris. In the end she chose the expensive designer jeans she'd splashed out on when she'd been in Paris, visiting her father and his family the previous summer.

Louise, her father's wife, who was the epitome of Parisian chic, had told her the jeans accentuated her slim figure. If she teamed them with her new floaty chiffon blouse, the outfit would hopefully look like something from the fashion page in the women's magazine she'd bought last Saturday.

Why she was getting so nervous or making such an effort she couldn't imagine. It had nothing to do with Marcel, of course! she thought as she carefully applied her make-up and then wiped it all off so she could redo it.

Downstairs, she could hear Francoise and Emma chattering in French and laughing as they put out the ingredients for the *tarte aux pommes* they were going to make. Marcel had been quite right when he'd accused her of making an excuse so that she wouldn't have to go to his house-warming party. There was nothing to be afraid of.

Except herself! Her own fear of relaxing again in a party situation. Of admitting to herself that it was time she got a life of her own and stopped pretending that being a single mum was the only kind of emotion she required to stay happy. OK, maybe she would relax her rules a bit tonight, but only slightly. Nobody—and especially somebody like Marcel—was ever going to break through her emotional barrier again.

As she pulled a jacket over her floaty blouse and headed for the door, she told herself she was fully prepared for an enjoyable evening. Friendship, that was all she needed. All she would allow herself if she wanted to prevent ever being disillusioned again.

Downstairs, she hugged Emma and thanked Francoise for all her help.

Francoise lifted her hands from the large mixing bowl. 'Now, you enjoy yourself, Debbie. And don't hurry back. Jérome will wait for you if you're not ready when he gets there.'

'You're sure I'm not imposing on your son by…'

Francoise smiled as she dusted some flour from her hands. 'It was my idea wasn't it? No, not too much water in the pastry, Emma…*doucement, ma chérie. Oui, c'est ca. Parfait!*'

Debbie felt decidedly redundant as Francoise began walking to the front door with her.

'There's Jérome now. He enjoys a drive out in the

evenings in his uncle's car. He never touches alcohol but I know you doctors enjoy a glass of wine when you're off duty. And quite right, too, after all the horrors you have to deal with during the day. So let your hair down, Debbie, and enjoy yourself. And don't worry about Emma because it's a real joy for me to have her to myself for the evening.'

Jérome was climbing out of the car and coming round to open the passenger door. The idea of being chauffeured there and back had been entirely Francoise's idea, but Debbie had insisted she must pay full taxi rates for the privilege. She knew that Jérome didn't earn very much over at his uncle's farm on the edge of the village. It was a family arrangement whereby the nephew got his board and lodgings and a small wage in exchange for help with the cows, pigs and general farm maintenance.

'*Bonsoir*, Debbie,' Jérome said.

'*Bonsoir*, Jérome.'

Debbie climbed into the front passenger seat, settling herself against the ancient leather.

They chatted about the unseasonally warm early May weather as they drove along the coast road and then the conversation dried up. Debbie was happy simply to look out over the moonlit sea. She wound down her window so that she could imagine the salty scent of the waves below her. When the hot summer weather really arrived, she would take Emma swimming. Last year she'd taught her to swim during the hot summer months, but the water had been too cold during the winter and she'd rarely got around to taking her to the swimming pool in St Martin sur mer.

'That's the house up there above the hospital,' she told Jérome as they approached the roundabout.

'Nice house. Expensive,' Jérome said. 'Your boss is he, this man?'

'Yes, he's the medical consultant in Urgences.'

'Married, is he?' Jérome asked as he drove into the semi-circular drive.

'I believe he's divorced or something,' Debbie said in a vague tone, anxious to get off the subject of Marcel.

'Could be worth getting to know,' Jérome said dryly as he cast his eye over the large stone house, illuminated as if for a *son et lumière* performance.

'You should know by now I'm not the least bit interested in men,' Debbie said as she climbed out of the car.

Jérome grinned. 'Maybe you should be. Now, you take your time, Debbie. I'm going over to see my girlfriend in Montreuil sur mer, but I'll come back in good time. Eleven o'clock you said, didn't you? Sure you don't want to make it twelve. I don't mind.'

'Eleven will be fine, thank you.'

'Debbie! Come in!' Marcel greeted her as she stepped into the spacious entrance hall.

A Mozart concerto was playing softly in the background. The hall was crowded with colleagues talking noisily and laughing loudly.

'It's just like a normal day in Urgences without the patients,' Marcel said. 'Let me take your jacket. Come through to the kitchen for a drink.'

'Lovely blouse!' Marie said, as Debbie passed her in the terracotta-tiled corridor leading to the kitchen.

'Thanks. I couldn't decide what to wear so…'

'Oh, you always look good in whatever you're wearing. Wish I had your figure.'

Debbie began to relax. She'd made good friends since

she'd started working in Urgences. There was no reason why she shouldn't count Marcel as one of them. There was no need for her to regard him with suspicion. And yet she always found she was holding herself in check whenever she was with him.

But as he handed her a glass of champagne in the kitchen she had to admit she found him attractive in a dangerous sort of way. Perhaps the danger she felt at approaching this friendship helped to heighten the sense of adventure she experienced whenever she was with him.

He was such a vibrant character. He intrigued her with his air of mystery. Well, whatever it was, she was going to enjoy herself this evening. Looking around the huge farmhouse-type kitchen, she reckoned there must be about twenty people crammed in there. She'd worked with all of them at one time or another, which made for an easygoing atmosphere.

A small pretty nurse, newly arrived in the department, approached them.

'Marcel, I wanted to ask you about that patient who came in this afternoon. The lady with the—'

'Sorry Veronique, no talking shop tonight. Come and see me tomorrow morning. Would you like another glass of champagne?'

Veronique smiled a dazzling smile as she accepted. She hadn't really wanted to ask about the patient but thought it would be a good way of getting herself noticed by her highly desirable boss.

Debbie wandered through into the sitting room where another crowd had gathered. Somebody had changed the music to a lively more up-to-date piece they could dance to. Debbie wasn't sure what it was but it was certainly getting people onto their feet. Some were making a valiant attempt to dance gracefully while others seemed to enjoy making fools of themselves occasionally, laughing at the same time as they all enjoyed the relaxation from their busy working lives.

She recognised Pierre Lamentier, the usually straight-faced obstetrics consultant, jacket flung over a chair, smiling happily as he danced vigorously with a junior midwife.

Debbie danced for a while with various colleagues until she excused herself, saying she needed a break. It was at that point that she realised she was looking around in the hope of seeing what Marcel was up to. She could see him now, in the centre of an admiring group as he recounted some story which had them all in fits of laughter.

She turned away, thinking this was a good time for some refreshment from the cold buffet that Marcel had told her about. In the impressive high-ceilinged dining room she helped herself to the cold meats and salad set out on a large round table in the centre of the room. She chatted with a couple of nurses from Urgences as they sat together until they were ready to go back and join the others.

She paused as she was leaving the dining room, turning back to have one last glimpse of the magnificent sea view. The lights from the town illuminated the seashore and she could see myriad twinkling lights shining from the boats moored close to shore. Such a beautiful house! She was enjoying the relative calm here in the dining room but it was time to go back and mingle with the other guests.

'Ah, there you are!' Marcel said as he walked through the door.

'I was just admiring the view. You've got a superb situation here.'

He smiled down at her. 'I love living near the sea.'

'So do I.'

Marcel was so close now she could smell the scent of his aftershave. Something distinctively attractive in a very masculine kind of way.

'Everything OK at home when you left? Not worried about your babysitter, are you?'

'Oh, Francoise is an absolute treasure. I don't know what I'd do without her.'

'And she didn't mind putting in the overtime?'

'Quite the reverse. She loves to come in the evening whenever I...'

Her voice trailed away as she watched the amused smile on Marcel's face.

'So, your original excuse about getting a babysitter was...'

She felt her colour rising. 'OK, yes, I freely admit it was an excuse. But when you've been badly let down and have gone through an acrimonious divorce, you tend to keep yourself to yourself.'

She looked up into Marcel's concerned eyes and saw real sympathy there. She couldn't think why she was saying all this to him.

'I'm sorry, I don't know why I'm telling you this in the middle of your party. You should be mixing with your guests, not listening to my problems.'

He put a hand on her arm and smiled down at her. 'Believe me, I know exactly what you mean. I've been in the same situation myself. You feel as if you'll never be able to face social situations again, don't you?'

She nodded, still mesmerised by the sympathetic expression in Marcel's grey eyes. 'Somehow I didn't think you were a fellow sufferer. You always seem so together.'

He laughed and the tense atmosphere was dispelled. 'I'm a good actor. Sometimes I think I've missed my vocation. Let me top up your glass, Debbie.'

He was reaching for a bottle from a nearby table. 'Are you driving?'

'No, I've got a friend picking me up at eleven.'

'Alors, encore de champagne pour madame?'

'Mais oui, s'il vous plaît.' She realised she needed something to stop her emotions from churning when she was close to Marcel.

'I'm glad you helped yourself to the buffet,' Marcel said as he poured her champagne. 'Everybody's having supper when they feel like it. Those on call had an early supper so they wouldn't miss out if there's an emergency.'

He paused. 'Are you coming back into the sitting room now?'

He put a hand under her arm. She enjoyed the feeling of being escorted by her host. That's all he was. The host politely escorting one of his guests, she told herself as they went back into the noisy sitting room.

She watched Marcel as he set off round the room carrying a couple of bottles, topping up glasses as he went. There was champagne for the lucky ones who weren't driving or on call, and fizzy water or fruit juice for the rest.

Debbie struck up a conversation with a group of colleagues and soon found she was enjoying being in such a relaxed atmosphere. It was the first time since her divorce that she'd begun to feel as if her old self was returning. But she realised that the best part of the evening was when she'd been with Marcel. She'd accepted that he was only playing the dutiful host, as he did with everyone else, but it made her feel special.

Just before eleven she went across the room to speak to him. 'I'd better get my jacket. My lift will be here soon,' she told him.

His eyes flickered. 'Pity you can't stay longer.'

'That would have been nice but...'

'I know, you want to get back to your daughter. Oh, well, perhaps we could have a drink together some time soon.'

'I'd like that,' she said, toning down the eagerness she felt at the prospect. Her mobile rang. 'It's Jérome, my driver. I wonder what he wants.'

'Perhaps he's been delayed,' Marcel said, hoping that this would be the case.

Debbie listened to Jérome apologising that he was going to have to mend a flat tyre so he would be a bit late. As she cut the connection she looked up at Marcel.

'Is there a problem?' he asked.

'Jérome's car has a flat tyre. He's been out to see his girlfriend in Montreuil sur mer and is coming back over the hill. He says it shouldn't take long to mend. I'd better phone Francoise to say we'll be late.'

'Excuse me a moment. Got to say goodbye to a few people.' Marcel drifted off.

As Debbie phoned Francoise, she could see that most people were already leaving. Some colleagues had been called back to the hospital, others, tired from a busy day's work, were heading home.

'Francoise, *c'est* Debbie.' Quickly, she explained the problem, assuring her that there was nothing to worry about.

Francoise said she was falling asleep on the sofa. Did Debbie mind if she went upstairs to sleep in the guest bedroom? She would be near Emma's room if the little girl needed anything.

Debbie said of course she didn't mind. It was a good idea. As she cut the connection, she wished she'd suggested it earlier. Francoise had stayed the night sometimes before when Debbie had occasionally been called in for an emergency situation at the hospital.

Marcel returned and looked at her enquiringly. 'Everything OK at home?'

'Yes. Francoise is going to spend the night with us as she sometimes does.'

'That's nice. So you can stay as long as it takes for your driver to get here.'

She swallowed hard. 'Oh, Jérome will turn up as soon as he's mended that puncture.'

'Well, make yourself at home while I see everybody off.'

She sank down on the sofa, suddenly getting that nervous feeling again. Marcel was obviously being very polite to her. He didn't seem at all put out by the fact that one of his guests was going to be hanging around after everyone else had gone. In fact, he seemed positively pleased. Maybe he was! The thought made her pulse race. She mustn't allow herself to think of Marcel as anybody other than a friend. That was the way she was going to play it with him. Because she knew deep down she fancied him rotten! And that was where the problem lay.

'They've all gone.'

At the sound of Marcel's voice Debbie opened her eyes. She was leaning back against the soft cushions and he was sitting at the other end of the sofa.

She rubbed her eyes. 'I must have fallen asleep. What time is it?'

'Half past eleven. I've brought you some coffee to revive you.'

'Thanks.'

She took the thin porcelain cup from his hands. As their hands touched she felt a shiver of desire running down her spine and knew she was in a dangerous situation, the sort of situation she'd avoided for a long time and should have avoided now.

The most sensible course of action would have been to tell Jérome she would call a taxi. Why hadn't she done that? But, looking across the length of the sofa at the handsome man who was watching her with an enigmatic expression, she couldn't help feeling glad that she'd stayed.

CHAPTER THREE

DEBBIE took a sip of her coffee to steady her nerves. 'Jérome's taking a long time mending that puncture. I think I'll ring him and see how he's getting on. I could always take a taxi.'

Marcel moved along the sofa and put out his hand towards her. 'No, don't do that. It gives us a chance to talk…get to know each other, doesn't it? We're always rushing around when we're at the hospital.'

Debbie took a deep breath. It was so wonderful to be here in this peaceful house with a man who was becoming very important to her—too important, if she was honest with herself. He was sitting much closer to her now, his hand resting lightly on the back of the sofa behind her. So far she'd managed to hold her emotions in check. But, then, so far nothing had happened between them. And nothing of significance ever would if she could convince herself that she simply enjoyed counting Marcel amongst her friends.

She looked across at him now, quelling the mounting excitement at being so close to him.

'I feel I'm beginning to get to know you already, Marcel. I have to say, I found you a bit…how shall I put this?…difficult to work with on your first day in charge of Urgences. You seemed impossible to please.'

'And were you trying to please me?'

She suppressed a shiver at the intimate nuances in his deep sexy voice. Oh, this was so wicked, actually flirting with a man again! Dangerous, but delicious. But

46

being absolutely sure of how far she would go, she knew she could handle her emotions, didn't she?

She was about to find out. 'Maybe I was trying to please you…maybe I wasn't. I just thought you were a bit of a tyrant.'

Marcel exploded with laughter. It was a rich dark sound that reverberated around the high-ceilinged room.

'What's so funny?'

'You are, Debbie. Thinking of me as a tyrant. Well, at least my plan worked.'

'Ah, so you were putting on an act?'

'Believe me, I was playing to the gallery that day! I always do that when I take over a department. Show the staff who's boss so that they know what to expect if they're ever tempted to step out of line. When I became medical director of Urgences in my hospital in Paris, I did exactly the same. And it meant I was rarely disappointed in my staff. I had a brilliant team. I never thought I would ever leave them.'

'What made you leave Paris?'

His enthusiastic expression changed as his face clouded over. 'After my divorce I wanted a complete break. Everywhere in Paris I was reminded of the happy times Lisa and I had enjoyed together before…' He broke off.

Debbie reached out and touched the side of his cheek. He put his hand against hers and held it there for a few seconds before placing her hand to his lips. She could feel the warmth of his lips as gently he kissed the back of her hand before releasing it and looking into her eyes.

'Were you very much in love?' Debbie asked gently, trying not to show the emotions he'd aroused by the touch of his lips.

He nodded. 'I worshipped Lisa…until I discovered

that the goddess I'd placed on a pedestal wasn't to be trusted. But you don't want to hear all this. You've had problems of your own so...'

'Please, go on.'

He leaned back against the sofa and closed his eyes as if to imagine more clearly the day when his illusions had been completely shattered.

'Lisa was a talented artist—still is a talented artist—but I prefer to think of her in the past tense. Hopefully, we will never meet again. She came out to Paris after she'd graduated from art school in England. When I first met her she had a small two-room apartment in Montmartre. One room was her studio, one her bedroom. We had a whirlwind romance and married after a few months.'

'It must have been very romantic.'

He opened his eyes, still looking up at the ceiling. 'It was.'

Debbie tried to quell the feeling of jealousy at the thought of Marcel having a romantic past. It was a stupid emotion she was feeling, completely irrational.

'Lisa kept on her apartment after we were married. She told me her father gave her a generous allowance. Every day she used to go off to Montmartre, ostensibly to paint. Looking back, I should have checked out what was happening but I was hopelessly in love with her and didn't question her fidelity. I was also terribly busy at the hospital.'

'Did you go to see her working in her studio?'

He shook his head. 'I couldn't understand why she asked me not to arrive without phoning first. And she actively discouraged me from visiting her during the time she was there. She said it would interrupt her creative flow...and I believed her.'

'So what actually did Lisa…?'

'She was entertaining her lover…or rather lovers. I believe she had at least two during the two years we were married.'

Debbie drew in her breath. 'How did you find out?'

'I was asked to take over from a professor of surgery at a residential conference on the outskirts of Paris. The professor had suffered a heart attack and I got an urgent call, asking me if I could take over immediately. I phoned Lisa at the studio but her phone was switched off. I decided to drive out to see her on my way to the conference. I parked in a little side street close to the apartment and…'

He stood up as his voice threatened to become too faint to continue. Walking over to the window, he looked out over the dark, brooding sea, the white caps of the waves illuminated by the lights from the shore. He realised he'd never told anybody the awful details of the day his dreams had been shattered. He'd kept it bottled up inside himself, saying that he couldn't bear to dwell on it. But Debbie was having such a calming effect on him he wanted to continue.

His natural instinct was to trust her not to repeat the story among his colleagues, but he knew he could never trust any woman ever again. He'd felt he could trust Lisa and look how wrong he'd been! The little voice of caution was telling him to be careful.

He turned round and walked back towards Debbie, taking strength from the concerned, sympathetic expression in her beautiful eyes. Surely he couldn't be wrong in wanting to take her into his confidence? Yes, he wanted to tell Debbie the whole story.

He took a deep breath. 'The studio door was open. I walked through and knocked on the door of her bedroom. After a few seconds a man opened the door, leaving it slightly ajar so he could peep out. But through the narrow gap I could see my wife reclining on the bed in a…very provocative pose.'

The dreadful memories were too poignant. He cleared his throat before continuing. 'I'll make it brief,' he said hoarsely. 'It transpired that her lover had expected me to be the delivery boy from the nearby wine bar bringing their order, otherwise he wouldn't have opened the door.'

Marcel took a deep breath. 'I'm glad he did open the door.'

'You're glad?'

'I'm glad now! It's always best to know the truth. But at the time I was furious. I forced my way in, intending to beat the pulp out of the man. My wife screamed at me to stop. Her lover didn't know she was married. He meant nothing to her and…'

Marcel put his head in his hands, breathing deeply with a loud rasping sound. Debbie waited for him to continue, not daring to stem the flow of his heartbreaking revelations. When he finally resumed his story he seemed calmer, more in control. He raised his head and looked directly at her.

'It was at that point I realised I'd never really known my wife. My sanity returned and I found I could review the situation realistically. Without a doubt it was over between us. I told Lisa I never wanted to see her again. She was still pleading with me as I walked out of her life. As soon as I could, I contacted my lawyer and instructed him to begin divorce proceedings.'

He sank down on the sofa beside her. 'I've never told anyone the whole painful story so I'd appreciate it if you keep it to yourself.'

'That goes without saying. I'm exactly the same about not wanting everyone to pity me. When I found out that Paul was deceiving me I contacted my solicitor and left everything to him. The big problem was how to explain to my two-year-old daughter.'

'Yes, it must be difficult when you have a child.' He leaned against the cushions, one arm gently resting on the back of the sofa behind her.

'Difficult and yet...' He paused. 'And yet I regret not being able to have a family. Coming from a large, warm family myself, I always intended to have children...but now I've accepted that it won't happen.'

'Why won't it happen?'

He looked surprised that she needed to ask. 'Because I'll never marry again.'

'Neither will I,' Debbie said firmly. She hesitated. 'But I can't stop wanting another child. I tell myself it's simply my hormones, my biological clock ticking away, but I can't stop that deep yearning inside me. I know I'd love to have another child.'

'Would you?'

His expressive voice was husky, full of sympathy but infinitely sexy as he turned towards her, putting both hands on the sides of her arms and drawing her closer until he was holding her in a gentle embrace, looking down at her with an expression of deep tenderness.

For one brief mad moment she thought how wonderful it would be to have a baby with this perfect hunk of a man! She knew he would be tantalisingly virile, impossible to resist... What was she thinking? She must never get herself into a situation where she couldn't resist a man, however desirable he might seem at the time. She was in charge of her emotions and wouldn't

let herself get carried away with wild fantasies.
Decisively, she eased herself away from Marcel.

He smiled. 'I'm sorry. I was only trying to be sympathetic.'

She looked across at him. 'I'm just not used to being
alone with a man, that's all. It's been so long since I
felt a man's arms round me and...actually, I was enjoying it too much,' she finished in a breathless rush.

'Too much? What do you mean?'

'I don't intend to ever get myself in a position where
I'm not in charge again. Because losing yourself to a
person means that...'

She broke off, unable to control her turbulent emotions. Unable to prevent herself, she moved towards him
and touched his face, looking into his eyes and wanting
to drown herself in all the tenderness she could see
there.

'Marcel...would you just hold me like that again?'
she whispered.

She didn't care if she was making a complete fool of
herself. She simply wanted to experience the excitement
of being in Marcel's arms, but only briefly and it
wouldn't mean anything to either of them.

Gently he drew her into his embrace again. Only this
time his arms were firmly around her. He looked down
at her questioningly. She returned his gaze, her lips
parted in hopeful anticipation, her mind completely
closed to all warning signals from her conscience. She
was flirting, tempting him, positively longing for what
might happen.

He lowered his head towards her, she closed her eyes
as his lips began to tease hers. She knew she couldn't
escape her desire for him to kiss her. But still his lips
only teased her. She pressed herself harder against his

strong muscular chest as she felt his mouth steady on hers. His kiss deepened and she could feel she was losing all control of the situation. She wanted more, much more…but she didn't want the regrets that would come if she allowed herself to follow her heart.

With a swift determined move she pulled herself away and leaned back against the cushions, cautiously looking across at Marcel.

'You temptress!' he said in a husky voice. 'You were irresistible, Debbie.'

'I never intended to…'

'I know. We both understand each other, don't we? We're both trying to come to terms with life after divorce and the fact that we'll never commit ourselves again. But it's possible to have a little fun without being too serious about it, don't you think?'

Debbie smiled. 'It depends what you mean by fun. The trouble with me having fun is that I find it hard to stop.'

Marcel laughed. 'That sounds promising!'

Debbie laughed with him. So far so good! They'd managed to keep a light-hearted ambience and dismissed any suspicion that their deeply moving kiss had meant anything. Because it hadn't, had it? Not much!

'But I'm completely determined not to have another serious relationship,' Debbie said firmly.

'So am I!'

Their eyes met. Debbie had no idea what Marcel was thinking but she was already weighing up the possibilities of a light-hearted, no-strings romance.

'But not having a serious relationship means that I've got to come to terms with never having another baby,' Debbie said wistfully. 'You've managed to do that, haven't you?'

'Not really. What I say about accepting it and how I feel about the situation are two completely different ideas. If there was some way that—'

He broke off as the sound of the door chimes echoed through the room. 'That must be your driver.'

He stood up, putting out both hands to draw her to her feet. For a moment he held her in a loose embrace, before his lips came down on hers. She surrendered herself to the deliciously erotic vibes that were running through her body as their lips blended sensually together.

The doorbell chimed again. Debbie drew herself away and looked up into Marcel's eyes.

'Thank you for a wonderful evening, Marcel.'

'You must come here again…let's make it soon.'

She felt a shiver of sensual anticipation running down her spine. 'I'd like that very much.'

The small nagging voice of reason was trying to get through to her confused brain. 'I…er…I'll have to check my diary.'

Marcel grinned. 'Ah, yes, and then you'll have to find a babysitter and all the other excuses you like trotting out.'

She smiled. 'Am I so transparent?'

'You certainly are. But I understand where you're coming from and I respect you for it.'

He put a hand in the small of her back and led her out into the hall, before opening the door to Jérome.

Jérome began by apologising for keeping Debbie waiting. The spare tyre had also had a puncture, which his uncle had meant to ask him to repair but had forgotten to, and so…

Debbie found she wasn't really listening. She was simply wishing she could stay longer with Marcel, yet knowing that she would be treading on dangerous ground if...and when...she returned here.

Marcel watched the car driving out on to the main road before closing the door. He leaned against it and closed his eyes. What an evening this had been. Especially the final part where he'd been alone with Debbie. Ah, Debbie, the beautiful woman he'd been attracted to the first time he'd seen her. But that was his problem. Making instant judgements about someone. Not stopping to think where it might lead if he let himself get carried away...as he had done with Lisa, who'd been nothing like he'd first imagined.

But if he kept his feelings towards Debbie light-hearted and easygoing, no harm would come of it to either of them.

He began to move through the ground floor of the house, switching off lights, leaving the party clutter for his admirable *femme de ménage* to sort out when she came in to clean in the morning. Upstairs, he showered before lying down between the cool sheets, his thoughts still on Debbie. He couldn't stop thinking about her!

And even as he tried to get her out of his mind so he could go to sleep, the thought came to him that they could solve a great dilemma between them. Debbie wanted another baby. He'd tried to convince himself that he would be content not to father a child, but deep down the longing was still there. So if they both wanted a child and yet they didn't want a committed relationship, would it be possible for them to make a baby without becoming emotionally involved?

It would be fun trying! No, he told himself. With that sort of attitude he was doomed to failure. He had to look upon it in a medical way, as a clinical exercise so that their emotions remained under control. And they would have to agree that after the baby was conceived they would draw up a plan that made it quite clear where the boundaries of their relationship lay.

It would be important that the needs of the child were put first. Good parenting, even though the parents weren't committed to each other, was of paramount importance.

He ran his fingers through his hair as he realised the idea was infinitely too complicated. *Mon Dieu!* It would be impossible to take Debbie to bed and keep his true emotions under control! Just thinking about it was making him feel that if she were here with him now... No, he must stop that dangerous train of thought!

And what would Debbie think about all this? She would never agree. She would think he was mad. He'd better try to put it right out of his mind and get some sleep.

Debbie unlocked her front door. The house was aglow with lights but that was only Francoise making sure she wouldn't have to come back to a dark, unwelcoming house. What a treasure she was, Debbie thought as she went around switching off all the lights except those in the hall, on the stairs and in the kitchen. In the kitchen she opened the fridge and took out a carton of orange juice before sitting down at the table. Usually, at the end of the day she went straight up to her room and fell asleep almost as soon as her head touched the pillow.

She knew it was going to be difficult to stop thinking about the events of tonight. The party. Meeting up with her colleagues in a social situation which hadn't proved to be at all difficult, even though she'd been secretly dreading it. She'd now crossed the threshold and become a member of the post-divorce survivors' club! But the end of the evening, being alone with Marcel had been... She took a drink of her juice as she felt a frisson of excitement running through her.

Being alone with Marcel had been wonderful! Just having him all to herself, hearing the sad tale of his own disastrous marriage—something akin to her own. But she wasn't going to dwell on that tonight, not when she felt so fired up with excitement, so looking forward to the future again. And that was something she hadn't done for a long time! One day at a time had been her philosophy for so long. But, although the future stretched ahead of her in an exciting sort of way, she knew she could be heading for disaster if she allowed herself to make the same mistake again.

She mustn't allow herself to fall in love with Marcel! She must fight these strong feelings of attraction. She remembered how she'd looked across the sofa at him when they'd been discussing how they both wanted a child and... She swallowed hard. A child, a baby. She'd love another baby and as she'd looked at Marcel she'd allowed herself to fantasise about how marvellous it would be if he was the father of her baby!

She closed her eyes and for a few seconds let herself dwell on the idea. He would make the perfect father of her baby, quite apart from the fact that the act of conception would be... She shivered as she felt a deep erotic longing to be in Marcel's arms at this very moment! No, she had to stop wishing for the moon. Because if the dream of having Marcel as her baby's father came true—which it couldn't possibly, but if by some stretch of the imagination it did come true!—that would mean commitment, and neither of them wanted that.

She simply wanted a child who would be loved by her and its father for the whole of its life. Her own parents had managed to defy convention and make it work so that she'd always felt loved and wanted. So it could work if...

'I thought I heard you come in, Debbie.' Francoise walked into the kitchen, wearing the old dressing-gown she kept at the house for the times she stayed over. 'You look happy, so it was obviously a good evening.'

Debbie looked up, trying to come down to earth and think clearly again. 'Yes, it was a lovely party.'

'I hope Jérome's puncture didn't spoil the end of it for you.'

'No, no, it...' Debbie took a deep breath as she realised her voice was going all dreamy again. Get a grip, woman! 'Jérome got there as soon as he could and he's an excellent driver. I always feel so safe with him.'

Francoise smiled. 'Good. I'm glad all went well.'

'How was Emma?'

'Fine, she's a little angel! Would you like me to make you some hot chocolate?'

'*Non, merci*, Francoise. I'd better get some sleep. Busy day tomorrow—or rather today! Thanks for looking after Emma. I must go to bed now.'

She stood up and took her glass over to the sink, staring out dreamily at the moonlit garden before turning round and heading for the stairs. '*A demain*. I'll see you in the morning...'

Meeting up with Marcel the next morning in Urgences was a strange experience for Debbie. Standing next to him, studying the X-rays of a badly smashed leg, she was trying very hard to return to her former, professional, unemotional self. But it wasn't easy.

Think of the patient, she told herself. Remember the patient is going through a life-shattering experience and he needs all your sympathy. Marcel doesn't need anything from you except your professional judgement.

Marcel was pointing out the most badly injured area of the leg. 'This section will need pinning. Will you alert the orthopaedics team that early surgery is advisable—as in *aussi vite que possible*? As quickly as possible?'

Debbie nodded as she heard the urgent tone of Marcel's voice. She'd learned that he couldn't stand inefficiency and found it difficult to control his impatience.

'I'll see to it right away, Marcel,' she told him.

He smiled down at her and for an instant she basked in the warmth of his genuine smile before she moved away to set the wheels in motion for an early operation on their patient.

'Marcel! *Venez ici, immediatement, s'il vous plaît!*' Sister Marie's usually calm voice held a hint of panic as she got Marcel to follow her out of the cubicle to deal with the latest emergency.

It took only minutes for Debbie to alert the orthopaedic team and reassure her patient that he would be taken to Theatre for expert attention as soon as possible. Her patient, a holidaymaker from England, had been given painkillers but he was still in a highly distressed state after falling down a cliff higher up the coast.

'You're in good hands,' she told her patient gently. 'The orthopaedic team is excellent. The consultant will be here in a couple of minutes to explain what he's going to do and then—'

'Has anybody phoned my wife? I lost my mobile up there on the cliffs and—'

'I called her as soon as you came in. She's on her way. Ah, here's the orthopaedic consultant. Would you like me to act as interpreter or—?'

'Thank you, Doctor,' Fabien Arnaud said. 'I speak English to my patient. No problem. Besides, Marcel is asking for you to help him with this newly arrived emergency people.'

Debbie smiled down at her patient and squeezed his hand. 'I'll see you later, Mike.'

For a moment her patient clung to her hand before letting her go with a quiet, 'Thank you, Doctor.'

Marcel was in the treatment room, bending over an apparently lifeless patient, connected to resuscitation apparatus. Two members of the cardiac team were at the other side of the bed, trying desperately to restart the man's heart.

Marcel looked up as she went in, and she saw the desperation and frustration in his eyes.

'Take care of the boy and his mother,' he said quietly, his disconsolate voice showing how this difficult case was affecting him. 'My patient here swam out to save his son who'd got into difficulty in the waves. The boy was revived by the ambulance crew but...'

He raised his hands in a typically Gallic gesture, denoting his despair at the futility of trying to revive their patient who'd reacted as any devoted father would have when he'd realised his son was in danger.

Marcel turned back to his lifeless patient and looked across at the cardiac team. 'Let's try one more time.'

From the looks on the two doctors' faces it was obvious they felt they'd reached the end of all their resuscitation possibilities, but they complied with Marcel's instructions.

Debbie moved across the room to the couch where a

small boy of about eight was propped up against a pillow. His eyes widened with alarm as Debbie approached.

'*Mon père? Papa?* How is he?'

Debbie made an instant decision to take the boy into another cubicle. The chances of resuscitating the boy's father were extremely remote and she didn't want the boy to be there when the team decided they couldn't do any more.

Quietly she asked the boy his name.

'*Je m'appelle* Pierre.'

'*Je m'appelle* Debbie.'

'*Et mon papa*, Debbie...?'

'The doctors are doing everything they can, Pierre, but they need to be alone with your papa for the moment. So I'm going to take you to another cubicle so I can give you more attention.'

Quickly she called a porter so that they could move, and accompanied the boy to a nearby cubicle.

Carefully she began to check if Pierre had suffered any injuries. The boy lay still, his eyes staring up at the ceiling as she made a thorough examination.

There was a deep gash in his arm where the waves had buffeted him against some rocks.

'I'm going to put some stitches in your arm, Pierre,' she said gently. 'This cut will heal more easily if I do that so I'm going to make your arm feel cold around that area so that—'

'Is my papa going to die?' the boy whispered.

Debbie swallowed hard as she looked down at the frightened child. The boy was eight. She must answer as truthfully as she could. Thank goodness she had no problem with her French, she thought as she carefully answered the difficult question.

'Your father was very ill when the paramedics got him out of the sea. They were able to save you because you hadn't swallowed as much water as your papa. We are still hoping that we can save him.'

There was a loud scream from the outer reception area. 'No, he can't be dead. I won't believe it. I won't! What about my boy? Where's Pierre?'

The boy's eyes registered panic. He pulled himself up and grabbed hold of Debbie's white coat. 'That's my mother's voice. What did she say out there? She will be so cross with me for swimming too far out. She told me to—'

A woman rushed inside their cubicle and leaned over the boy, putting her arms around him.

'Pierre. Oh, my precious boy! You're alive! But your papa…'

The grieving mother stopped as she realised she had to become strong again for the sake of her son.

Debbie put her arm around the mother's trembling shoulders. The woman raised her tear-streaked face to her. 'Does my boy know that…?'

'You're going to tell me that Papa has died, aren't you, Maman?' Pierre said quietly.

For a moment he remained solemn and in control of himself, looking very grown-up. Then his little face crumpled and he clung to his mother. 'I'm sorry I swam too far out. I'm sorry Papa swam out to get me. I'm sorry…'

'You're a good boy, Pierre,' his mother said softly. 'I might have lost you. Be a brave boy now. Papa would want you to be brave.'

'I'm going to be brave.' Pierre looked up at Debbie. 'Do you want to stitch my cut now, Debbie?'

Debbie swallowed the lump in her throat as she prepared the local anaesthetic. Poor child, having to come to terms with the death of his father. He was being the big brave boy at the moment, but as she stitched up the long cut in his arm she was planning her next move in caring for him. She would admit him to one of the preliminary care units and have him monitored by one of the specialist care nurses throughout the forty-eight hours of his stay.

Pierre's mother had been joined by her sister, an older, very capable woman, who had arrived to give moral support. Debbie was relieved that the grieving woman wasn't alone as she went away to cope with the necessary formalities that followed the death of a patient.

As Debbie finished writing out a report of the patients she'd cared for during the day, her usual sense of achievement was tinged with sadness over the death of Pierre's father. She sat back against her chair and stared at the computer screen for a moment as she dealt with the surge of emotion you weren't supposed to allow yourself to dwell on if you were going to be an objective, composed doctor.

'I thought I'd find you here, Debbie.'

She looked up as Marcel walked in. 'I'm technically off duty but I needed to finish this report before I go. Pierre's father was your patient but I need to mention the effect his death had on the boy. I want to make sure that the staff in the preliminary unit are going to spend a lot of time with him. For one thing, he feels guilty that he was the one who caused his father to swim out. And guilt when you're only eight years old is difficult to handle.'

Marcel eased himself down onto the corner of her

desk. 'Guilt at any age is difficult to handle. Don't worry, he's being carefully monitored and counselled by paediatric specialists. At least he's physically fit and he has a beautiful piece of embroidery on his arm.'

Debbie smiled as she felt her spirits lifting again.

'That's better, Debbie! It's good to see a smile on your face. I knew you'd be sad about losing a patient. So am I because I was still hoping for a miracle even at the very end when the others had given up.'

He shrugged his broad shoulders. 'But I'm always an optimist. I hate defeat.'

He leaned across the desk and put one finger under her chin, tilting it up towards him. 'So, as we've both been defeated today, I thought we needed cheering up. Why don't you come back to my place for supper tonight? You can phone that wonderful lady who takes care of your daughter when you're not there and tell her you—'

'I can't!' The touch of Marcel's finger on her face had been deliciously sensual. She couldn't cope with anything more...at the moment.

He gave a deep sigh. 'Why did I know that would be your answer?'

'I can't leave Emma two nights in succession, can I?'

He gave her a wicked grin. 'Are you asking me or telling me?'

'Well, I'm simply saying that, as a mother, I ought to—'

'Ah, the guilt thing!' He grinned. 'Are you worrying that your daughter will suffer if you're not with her tonight or...?'

'Tonight!' she echoed. 'I'm not planning to stay the night!'

Marcel stood up and came around the back of her

chair, placing an arm around her shoulders. 'Who said anything about staying the night?' he said in a soft, seductive voice.

'I got confused with my French,' she countered.

He drew her to her feet so that she was effectively in his embrace as she looked up at him. 'Then let's speak English this evening when you come for supper.'

She could feel her heart beating loudly and she was sure that Marcel would be able to feel the thumping as he held her against his thin cotton shirt.

'I'd like to come to supper but—'

'Then you must come! Your daughter will enjoy another evening of being spoilt and the lady who helps you...'

'Francoise.'

'Francoise will be overjoyed to have her little treasure all to herself again. Make the call now.'

Debbie smiled as she tried to ignore the boring voice of reason that was nagging her. 'I think you just talked me into it.'

She felt her heart churning with excitement as she picked up the phone. What was she letting herself in for?

'Francoise? *C'est* Debbie. *Est-ce-que c'est possible que...* Do you think you could possibly...?'

CHAPTER FOUR

DEBBIE looked across the kitchen table at Marcel. 'Where did you learn to cook like this?'

Marcel smiled as he placed the casserole of *poulet grand-mère* in front of her so she could help herself.

'I learned to cook at home in Paris. My mother was a paediatrician in charge of the medical care of the schoolchildren in a large arrondissement in Paris. She worked extremely hard and she was often late home. We all learned to cook so that most of the dinner would be ready by the time she got home. My father was a surgeon so he often didn't arrive until late.'

'Did you have any domestic help?'

'There was a *femme de ménage* who came in a couple of days a week to clean. Our grandmother lived with us and she ensured that the domestic work was organised. She also taught all of us to cook from the moment we could stir a spoon in a bowl so that we could help her in the evenings when she was tired.'

'How many brothers and sisters did you have?'

'I was the youngest of three boys and two girls.'

Debbie sighed. 'Sounds idyllic!'

Marcel laughed. 'It was far from idyllic at times! But it's the sort of family life I always wanted for myself if...' His voice trailed away.

'Me, too,' Debbie said quietly, laying down her fork. 'I was an only child and I intended to have lots of children. But Paul put paid to that.'

'Paul was your husband?'

Debbie nodded. 'For three years. When Emma was two I discovered he'd had a series of affairs—two or three, actually. I never did find out how many. When I accidentally overheard one of the nurses talking to a colleague about the affair going on between my husband and a young nurse, that was when my illusions about Paul were shattered. It was only a matter of time before various colleagues enlightened me after I'd told them I was planning to divorce him.'

'Same scenario as my own disastrous marriage,' Marcel commented in a sympathetic voice. 'Any regrets now?'

'Only that I married the wrong man and didn't get the family I wanted,' she said quietly. 'I adore my wonderful daughter but I never intended her to be an only child.'

'I can imagine how you feel.'

He hesitated. Now wasn't the time to broach the subject that had been uppermost in his mind since they'd been alone together after his party. Perhaps later...or perhaps not! Looking across the table at his lovely companion, he didn't want anything to spoil the evening. When they'd spent more time together he would be able to evaluate the possibilities of his mad idea.

He deliberately steered the conversation onto neutral subjects, so that they were soon discussing books they'd recently read, music they liked to listen to, places they'd travelled to or intended to go to at some time in the future.

'At least, with only one child it will be easier for me to travel,' Debbie said. 'My mother took me everywhere with her when I was small. She always had a busy schedule but she made time for me, somehow fitting in her surgical training and working her way up to becoming a consultant surgeon. And she always made sure the two of us had great holidays together.'

'So where was your father?' Marcel asked, as he placed fruit and cheese on the table.

'Ah, that's a long story.' Debbie picked up an apple and began to peel it as she started to explain her background. 'You see, my parents never married. They met in London when my French surgeon father came over to the medical school where my mother was a final-year student. They had a whirlwind romance lasting several months during which my father used to come over to London as often as he could get away from his work in Paris.'

'Sounds very romantic.'

'My father told me it was. My mother rarely spoke about it, only to tell me that just after she'd finished her final exams she discovered she was pregnant. My father wanted them to get married. My mother said she didn't want the commitment of marriage. She wanted to keep her independence. They discussed what was best for the baby she was carrying and my father insisted that his child should know he was the father.'

'Very wise,' Marcel commented, as he felt his interest growing in the details of Debbie's background. 'Did your father make any other stipulations?'

'Oh, Mum said they both had a rational discussion about what was going to happen in the future. My father was to be part of my life but at a distance. In other words, the emotional bond he'd shared with my mother was to end.'

'Sounds complicated.'

'Oh, it wasn't! I had a great childhood. My father was always there when I needed him. I didn't feel I missed out on anything—except having brothers and sisters. After my father married and had two daughters, I enjoyed being with them when I went over to Paris. But they were much younger than me. It's only in recent years that my stepsisters and I have grown closer.'

'Seems like your parents found the perfect solution,' Marcel said, deciding that he would, after all, be able to put forward his idea. Maybe his plan wasn't as mad as he'd first feared.

'And what sort of relationship do your parents enjoy now?'

Debbie hesitated before she could find her voice again. It still hurt. 'My mother died in a skiing accident when I was at medical school.'

'I'm so sorry. I wouldn't have asked if...'

'That's OK. I should be over it by now, but my mother had been the centre of my life while I was growing up and...and I found it hard to come to terms with. That's when my father asked me to go and live with his family in Paris. I regarded it as my home during my holidays from medical school, but after I qualified I found my own place in London.'

He stood up. 'Let's have our coffee in the sitting room. You go through, Debbie. I'll bring the cafetière as soon as it's ready.'

'Let me help with the dishes...'

'That's OK. I'll stack the dishwasher later. Go and make yourself comfortable.'

He switched on the coffee-grinder and conversation was no longer possible. Debbie got the impression she wasn't wanted in the kitchen any more. Marcel appeared deep in thought as he set out crockery on a tray. She made her way to the sitting room and walked over to admire the view over the sea as she had done the previous evening.

As Marcel spooned the ground coffee beans into the cafetière he found it hard to contain his mounting excitement. Debbie's parents had made it work. They'd successfully had a child together who hadn't suffered because they hadn't been committed to each other. So it could be possible. But they would both have to agree.

Debbie turned round from the window as she heard Marcel arriving with the coffee.

'Such a beautiful view! I love watching the lights on the ships moored close to the shore.'

Marcel placed the tray on a small table beside the sofa before walking over to join Debbie at the window. As casually as possible, he put an arm around her shoulders, drawing her gently against him. He waited to feel her body stiffen with rejection but instead she seemed to be relaxing.

'I often stand here in the evenings,' he began, his voice husky, feeling more than a little disturbed at their closeness to each other. 'Just watching the dark sea, occasionally following the path of an illuminated boat. It's a good way of winding down after a stressful day. It feels even better this evening.'

Debbie looked up at him, her eyes searching his expressive face. He was gazing down at her with real tenderness. She realised that she was longing for him to take her in his arms. One little kiss, that was all it would take to...

As he lowered his head and kissed her, oh, so gently on the lips it was almost as if he'd been reading her thoughts. She parted her lips to savour the moment, knowing that her feelings must have been blatantly obvious. But Marcel was already pulling himself away.

'Come and have some coffee.'

As Marcel took hold of Debbie's hand and led her

over to the sofa, he was thinking that he had to tread carefully this evening. If he was to put forward his plan for them to have a baby together, he must hold onto his emotions. Debbie would never agree if she thought he was angling for a permanent emotional bond between them.

He hadn't been able to resist her just now, but he would have to learn how to be more emotionally objective if the plan was to succeed. She'd looked so beguiling as she'd gazed up at him. He loved her clear blue eyes, the gentle curve of her inviting mouth. Simply looking at her when they were alone turned him on.

Debbie sank down against the cushions. On the one hand she was relieved that their kiss had been a spur-of-the-moment action, but on the other hand she knew that she'd wanted more. Her whole body was crying out to be loved by Marcel. She took a couple of deep breaths to calm herself.

Marcel was placing a small porcelain coffee cup on the table beside her. He sat down at the other end of the sofa. They looked at each other over the expanse of cushions stacked between them.

Marcel cleared his throat. 'I'm deliberately sitting at this end of the sofa because I've got a plan to put forward to you and I want to be totally objective about it... No, don't look so worried. I simply want to... Oh, this is going to be so difficult to put into words...'

'Sounds intriguing.' Her heart began to beat faster.

'We've talked before about the fact that we'd both love to have a child but don't want to have a committed relationship.'

'We have.' Her heart was absolutely thumping now. Was Marcel going to suggest that they come to some arrangement between them? The thought of Marcel being the father of her child was a magic idea. She could see him in her mind's eye holding their baby, sitting beside her bedside, holding her hand…

She checked her thoughts. The scenario she'd just imagined could never happen…or could it?

'I think I know what you're going to say,' she blurted out, unable to contain herself.

'You do?' He seemed relieved.

'Is it something to do with what I was telling you earlier…about me having a father figure in my life who didn't live with my mother?'

Marcel smiled. 'It could be just that. And as we're speaking English, you've got the advantage over me. So why don't you tell me what you think my plan might be?'

She moved into the centre of the sofa. Marcel moved closer and casually put his arm along the back of the sofa. He felt a sense of relief flooding through him. Maybe Debbie was already thinking along the same lines.

'I think because we both want a baby…' Debbie began carefully. 'Because it's what we both want, you're wondering if it wouldn't be possible to produce one between us.'

'That sounds very cold and clinical but…'

'Oh, but it would have to be!'

Even as she said that, Debbie knew it would be impossible to remain totally detached during the act of conception. If one small kiss threw her emotions into turmoil, what would a long session in bed with Marcel do to her?

'I think we would find it extremely difficult to remain emotionally detached during the act of conception,'

Marcel said. 'Let's look at the facts. We both want a baby but we don't want commitment. We both want the baby to have a father figure who's there for our baby when needed. Am I correct?'

Debbie nodded. 'That's about the sum of it.'

Marcel stood up and began pacing the room. 'Your parents achieved that and you had a happy childhood. They were able to live independent lives. I don't think the mood they were in during the act of conception made any difference whatsoever. They were able to conceive in the normal way and then continue to remain uncommitted to each other while being committed to the child.'

He was standing by the window again, one hand on the window-sill, turning sideways to look at Debbie.

Debbie stood up and joined him at the window, deliberately standing a few paces away as she tried to remain totally objective.

'The two situations are different. My parents were having a whirlwind romance when I was conceived. I don't suppose they were planning to have a baby. I don't imagine either of them was looking too far into the future. But we know exactly what we want in our future lives, don't we?'

Marcel drew closer and placed his hands on her shoulders. 'Do we?' he said softly.

He knew he should be trying to make sure their discussion continued in an emotionally detached manner, but it was impossible for him to remain cold and clinical when he was anywhere near Debbie.

Debbie was finding the touch of his hands undermining her resolve. She looked up into his eyes, unnerved even more by his expression of real tenderness. 'We both want a baby. We both want to be loving parents, committed to the baby but not to each other. And that's why we would have to be careful during the act of conception not to become too…er…too…'

Marcel gave her a rakish grin. 'Too what, Debbie?'

'Oh, Marcel, don't tease me! You know perfectly well what I mean.'

'Too loving towards each other?'

She swallowed hard. 'Something like that, only…'

'What you mean is that we mustn't fall in love,' he said breathily.

'Exactly!'

'Well, then, if I sign a paper to say I promise not to fall in love while I'm making you pregnant will you…?'

They were both laughing now as he drew her into his arms, nuzzling his lips against her hair.

Debbie was revelling in the feel of his arms around her. She loved the fact that the tension between them had eased. But as far as not falling in love with this wonderful man was concerned, she just knew it would be impossible. She'd fallen too far already.

'It's not going to work, is it?' she whispered.

'We'll make it work,' he said, his voice serious again. 'Because it's what we both want. And even if we do get carried away while we're making love…sorry… trying to conceive a child, we'll be able to come down to earth afterwards and go out into the real world as independent, uncommitted people. Don't you think?'

He was looking down at her with that same tender look that had taken away her resolve earlier. His question still hung in the air. She decided to treat herself to one small kiss again to see if she could remain emotionally detached. She raised her lips towards his.

He smiled as he brought his lips down on hers. His

kiss deepened. Debbie could feel her treacherous body responding. She'd already proved what she'd planned to find out. It would be impossible to make love with Marcel and remain detached. But Marcel thought there would be no problem if they were to lose themselves for a while…a heavenly time together it would be…and then simply walk away and continue with their every-day lives. But…

Her body was responding too much now but, oh, it was the most delicious feeling. She moulded herself against Marcel's strong, virile, muscular body. His hands were caressing her face, her neck, gently begin-ning to tease her breasts… She was beginning to lose control…

She pulled away, panting with suppressed frustration as she gazed up at him indecisively. More than anything else she wanted him to sweep her away to his bedroom where they would make wonderful love, and she wouldn't give any thought to the future.

Gently, he caressed the side of her cheek. 'We could always have a rehearsal, couldn't we?'

There was nothing she would have liked bet-ter…which was why she'd better call a halt now while she was still in control.

'Marcel, I'm still not sure it would work. Let me have some time to think about it.'

'Of course. Take all the time you need.'

'I'll phone for a taxi,' she said quickly, before she could change her mind. 'Jérome took me in this morn-ing because my car's being serviced. I told him I'd get a taxi back when—'

'I'll drive you home.' His voice was masterful, seri-ous, brooking no argument.

'There's no need, really.'

He ignored her protest. 'I'll get your jacket.'

They were both quiet in the car, each deep in their own thoughts. Marcel was disappointed that they hadn't resolved anything that evening, but he was still optimistic that Debbie would come round to his way of thinking. A child was what they both wanted. And even if they both got carried away at the conception—which they doubtless would!—they could try hard to redress the balance afterwards. Or could they?

Just sitting beside Debbie now, the intimate scent of her perfume teasing his nostrils, the close proximity of her sexy, alluring body... He checked his thoughts as he almost groaned aloud. Did she have any idea of the effect she was having on him? He was feeling decidedly uncomfortable as he tried to control his body, which was aching for fulfilment.

'Our house is around the next corner, at the end of the street through the village... Yes, there it is, the one with the lights on. Can't think why all the lights are on so late.'

As Marcel pulled the car into the drive, the door opened. Francoise stood framed in the doorway, peering out into the darkness.

'C'est toi, Debbie?'

'Oui, c'est moi, Francoise. Qu'est-ce qu'il y a?'

Debbie got out of the car. Marcel followed close behind her.

'It's Emma,' Francoise said in a worried tone. 'I was just going to phone you on your mobile but I couldn't leave her. She cut her leg on the corner of the kitchen cabinet and...'

Debbie and Marcel moved quickly into the house. Francoise continued to tell them the details as they hurried through into the kitchen.

'Just a few minutes ago Emma came downstairs and asked if she could have a hot chocolate drink. I said I would make it in a few minutes, as soon as the television programme ended. She went into the kitchen, climbed up to the cupboard, lost her balance and fell.'

'Mummy!' Emma was sitting on a chair, her bandaged leg stretched out across another chair. 'I'm sorry I climbed up. I was just trying to help Francoise and—'

'That's OK, darling. Let's take a look and see what's happened here.'

Debbie began unwrapping the bandage that Francoise had carefully applied. Francoise stood to one side, trembling with the shock of coping with an injured Emma.

Marcel leaned across to look at the wound. It was better than he'd feared, but it was deep enough to require suturing.

'I'll get my medical bag and we'll soon have this cut fixed,' Debbie said, moving swiftly out of the kitchen.

Marcel knelt down at the little girl's side while he held a section of the bandage over the cut to staunch the flow of blood.

'Could have been worse, Emma,' he said in a reassuring voice.

Emma regarded the unknown man solemnly. 'Who are you?'

'I'm Marcel. I work at the hospital with your mummy.'

'You speak good English.'

'Thank you.'

'But you're French really, aren't you?'

'I am indeed.'

'I thought so. I can always tell. French people speaking English make it sound funny.'

Marcel smiled as he thought what an engaging little girl Emma was. A pleasure to talk to.

'What do you mean?' he asked.

Emma grinned. 'Well, you know, like…' She exaggerated a French accent superimposed on an English phrase.

Marcel laughed. 'That was very good. Does that sound like me?'

'No, your English is quite good really.'

'Praise indeed! Ah, here's Mummy.'

As she came back into the kitchen Debbie witnessed the touching scene of Marcel getting to know Emma. She needn't have worried about leaving them together. The two of them were getting on like a house on fire.

Marcel leaned to one side so that Debbie could begin tending the wound. He removed the portion of bandage he'd been holding and they conferred.

'It needs a couple of stitches, maybe three, to hold the edges together,' Debbie said as she swabbed the site of the wound with antiseptic.

'Will it hurt when you stitch me, Mummy? You stitched my teddy bear and he didn't cry, but I think I might…'

Big tears loomed in Emma's eyes and began to spill down her pale cheeks. 'I'm trying to be brave but…'

'Would you like me to give you a magic numbing potion?' Marcel asked. 'You won't feel a thing after one tiny little prick from the needle at the end of my syringe.'

'Is it really magic?'

Debbie flashed him a grateful look. Dealing in a detached way with her own child was always stressful. She stepped aside so that Marcel could select a sterile syringe for the local anaesthetic from Debbie's bag.

'It's a kind of magic,' Marcel explained as he prepared the syringe. 'It's medicine really, but it works like magic. Now, this is the tiny prick you're going to feel. Imagine it's a fly that's settled on your leg and it's tickling you.'

Emma smiled. 'I felt it tickling me. Was that it?'

'That's it. All I've got to do now is pretend you're a teddy bear and sew you up in the bit that you can't feel any more.'

Watching Marcel expertly suturing Emma's cut, Debbie felt a lump in her throat. He was being so kind and caring with her daughter. He would make a wonderful father. And he actually wanted to father her child! What could be more fantastic? Except that the sort of contract she would want wouldn't be the cold clinical kind. The walk-away-afterwards-and-remain-detached kind.

She would want the whole works, the complete scenario, Marcel holding her hand when she went into labour, Marcel at the bedside, Marcel beside her all through the baby's childhood. So what was she going to do about it?

'There you go. Good as new!' Marcel stood back as if to admire his handiwork.

'Thank you, Marcel,' Debbie said.

Francoise came forward. She'd stopped trembling and was smiling with relief. 'I'm so glad you came home when you did, Debbie.' She turned to look at Marcel. 'And you're a doctor, too.'

'Marcel De Lange.' He shook hands with Francoise, who was clearly charmed to meet him.

'I'll make that drink of hot chocolate now for you, Emma,' Francoise said.

'No, I'll make it,' Debbie said. 'You must be tired, Francoise. Do you want to stay the night or…?'

'I'd better get home. I'm going on an early shopping trip tomorrow morning to Le Touquet with my sister.'

'You must let me drive you home, Francoise,' Marcel said.

'I only live at the end of the street,' Francoise said.

'It's on my way,' Marcel said. 'Goodnight, Emma. Goodnight, Debbie.' He smiled. 'You'd better stay with the patient so I'll see myself out.'

'Thanks for the stitching,' Emma said. 'I can't wait to show it to my friends at school.'

Marcel turned at the kitchen door. 'I'll see you tomorrow, Debbie.'

She smiled. Nobody looking at the two of them making their civilised goodbyes would guess that they'd just had a most important discussion that hadn't been resolved.

'Mummy, I don't think I want any hot chocolate now,' Emma said. 'I only asked for it so I could come downstairs for a while. Francoise is so kind. She always says yes when I want a drink. But what I really want now is to go to bed because I'm falling asleep.'

Debbie hoisted her daughter over her shoulder and carried her up the stairs. In a matter of minutes, as she sat at her daughter's bedside reading one of her favourite stories, she saw Emma's eyes drooping. Her breathing changed into the soft sounds of childish slumber.

Debbie put out the bedside light, leaving on the small night-light in the corner of the room before going along to the bathroom. She shed her clothes and climbed into the bath for a long soak. Although she was tired she knew that it would be difficult to sleep while her mind was so active with thoughts of Marcel's plan.

She poured more bath foam in and lay back amongst the bubbles. Mmm...this was blissful. It would be even more blissful if Marcel were here with her. This old bath was big enough for two. Now, wouldn't that be a wonderful experience, a sort of prelude to going to her bed and making love? No, making a baby would be the object of their love-making but it would still be an act of love, whatever she tried to call it.

She knew she wanted more than anything to make a baby with Marcel. The conception itself would be blissful! But it was the aftermath that was completely uncharted territory. How could she possibly walk away from Marcel when they'd made love together? Because it would be making love, on her part anyway. She couldn't speak for Marcel, but from the vibes he'd been putting out tonight she doubted that remaining cool and clinical would be uppermost in his mind.

There was no solution to that problem. Perhaps she should put off giving Marcel an answer for a few days. Yes, that's what she would do. A little procrastination never hurt anybody. Especially when the question under consideration was one of life-changing propensities.

Driving home, Marcel pulled to the side of the road and switched off the engine. His mind was in a whirl. He'd thought Debbie was about to agree to his idea, but then she'd got scared about it.

He looked out through the windscreen. There was a full moon tonight, the landscape lit up almost like daylight. At the bottom of the hill the sea sparkled with shafts of moonlight on the foam-flecked waves.

It hadn't helped that he'd frightened Debbie away by

coming on too strong. But it was so difficult to react in any other way when he found her so attractive, so vibrant, so sexy, so…

No, he told himself. He had to remain more detached next time. If there was a next time. She would probably give a resounding no to his plan and that would be the end of what had promised to be a beautiful friendship. Until Debbie gave him an answer he would remain friendly but would refrain from anything more. In fact, he wouldn't bring up the subject again until she did.

As he restarted the engine he prayed that Debbie wouldn't take too long deciding what she wanted to do.

CHAPTER FIVE

FOR the next few days, Debbie was surprised to find that Marcel didn't refer to their discussion about creating a baby together. Neither did he suggest they get together to review the situation. He was polite and professional when they worked together in the hospital but gave no hint of what had passed between them.

At least it gave her some more time to think about what she wanted to do. Perhaps he'd completely gone off the idea. He hadn't suggested they see each other in their off-duty time either. Perhaps, like her, he realised the baby plan would be an irrevocable and therefore dangerous step to take.

At the end of a week she decided that she would have to be the one to broach the subject, even though she knew that nothing had changed as far as she was concerned. She realised that she wouldn't be able to control her emotions during the act of conceiving a baby. And returning to a companiable friendship afterwards would be impossible. She didn't want to lose Marcel's friendship, so what was she to do?

As she walked across the main reception area of Urgences she decided she would have to bring up the subject today. It would have to be this evening because they were both on duty all day.

There was a lot of screaming going on from a patient who was being wheeled in. She hurried over to investigate. A middle-aged woman was clinging to her grey-haired husband's hand as he held onto the stretcher with the other. He was trying to comfort his wife but the screams were getting louder.

'I can't bear the pain... *Je ne peux plus supporter...* Oh, ooh...'

'*C'est ma femme Béatrice, docteur.* I brought her in as soon as I could,' the man said anxiously. 'She collapsed at home. Just lay there on the sofa, screaming. She's got this terrible pain in her stomach. It goes right through to her back.'

Debbie had instructed the porter who was wheeling the trolley to bring the patient into the treatment room. Together they heaved the exceptionally heavy woman onto the examination couch. The patient seemed to calm herself temporarily as she looked up at Debbie.

Debbie took a tissue and mopped her patient's brow. 'How old are you, Béatrice?' she asked quietly.

'*J'ai quarante sept ans*, forty-seven. *Mon Dieu*, it's coming again. That awful pain. I can't bear it. I can't... Oh, aagh...'

Debbie pulled back the blanket that was covering her patient. The woman had an excess of flesh all over her body but the abdomen was particularly distended. Debbie put her hand over the abdomen and felt the unmistakable rippling of a strong muscular contraction. The immediate diagnosis was obvious.

'When did you have your last period, Béatrice?' Debbie asked as the contraction died down.

'Oh, I don't know. Ages ago. I'm in the menopause, Doctor.'

Debbie knew her diagnosis was going to come as a shock! She prepared herself to be very gentle with her patient when she explained what was happening.

'I'm just going to examine you down below,' she said

as she manoeuvred her patient into a lithotomy position with her legs wide apart.

The worried husband turned white and said he didn't feel well. He was going to go outside for a cigarette but he would come back as soon as he felt better.

Debbie became aware that Marcel had come in and was now standing at the other side of the examination couch.

'It sounded like you might need some help,' he said. 'This looks to me as if we...'

Debbie raised her head from examining her patient.

'Imminent delivery,' she said quietly. 'Fully dilated cervix.'

Marcel was already scrubbing his hands at the sink.

'What are you doing?' Béatrice called out. 'What's the matter with me?'

'You're in labour, Béatrice,' Debbie said calmly, as she wheeled over the Entonox machine and adjusted the painkilling flow of gas and air through the mask. 'You're having a baby.'

'I can't be! I told you, I'm in the menopause. I'm a grandmother, for heaven's sake... Ooh, it's coming again, Doctor, Doctor...'

Béatrice grabbed Debbie's hand.

'Breathe into this mask, Béatrice. Deep breaths. That's the way. This will help the pain. You can hold it yourself like this...'

Marcel was now bending over the patient. Gowned and gloved, he was examining the birth canal. He looked up briefly at Debbie and nodded.

'Yes, cervix fully dilated. The head is now crowning. Don't let Béatrice push. Hold off...it's crucial to hold off until the head...'

He was quiet for a few seconds as he investigated further.

'The cord is round the baby's neck,' Marcel told Debbie in a calm voice that only she could hear. 'I'm going to unhook it... I'm nearly there... Yes! It's OK now. Béatrice can push on the next contraction.'

Debbie breathed a sigh of relief. The main danger was over. Bearing in mind that her patient was in her late forties, there could be further complications but the birth was going smoothly for the moment. As the tiny infant emerged, slipping easily into Marcel's hands, it gave a loud cry.

'Nothing wrong with baby's lungs,' Marcel said, as he cut the cord and wrapped the vociferous baby in a dressing towel. He looked across at Debbie. Their eyes met and locked in a long, meaningful gaze.

'It's a girl,' he said huskily. 'Béatrice has a perfect little baby girl. Isn't that wonderful?'

Debbie swallowed the lump in her throat. 'Yes, I agree.'

She knew without a shadow of a doubt that she had to go ahead with their plan. She desperately wanted to have a baby. She wanted to have Marcel's baby.

'You do? You agree to...?'

It was a poignant, momentous, private moment between the two of them. It was as if there was nobody else in the room. In that instant they'd both acknowledged that they wanted to have a baby together, whatever the problems that might lie ahead.

Marcel was holding the baby close as he moved towards her. Gently he put the child in Debbie's arms. It was as if they were signing the agreement, saying to each other, One day soon, we'll get together and...

Their hands briefly touched as she took the baby into

her arms, holding her close. She was quieter now, but her little fists were waving in the air. The whole of her tiny body was vibrant with life. Try as she may, Debbie couldn't stop a lone tear from trickling down her cheek, though whether it was from happiness or longing she couldn't imagine.

'When you've finished drooling over the baby,' Marcel whispered in English, 'you'd better see if Béatrice has recovered enough to hold her.'

Their patient was lying very still with her eyes closed. The gas and air she'd been breathing had made her drowsy and confused.

'Would you like to hold your baby girl, Béatrice?' Debbie asked.

The new mother opened her eyes to focus on the tiny infant in the doctor's arms. She felt very confused. There had been a lot of pain. She'd breathed in that gassy stuff and now she just wanted to sleep. Was that really her baby? She'd felt the other doctor poking around down there, but she hadn't believed it was happening to her. She would wake up soon and find it had all been a dream.

The door opened and in came Béatrice's husband.

'Mon Dieu! C'est pas possible! Le bébé…?'

Marcel sat the man down on a chair. His previous pallor had deepened and taken on a greenish shade.

'Yes, it's your baby,' Debbie said gently, as she helped Béatrice to hold the infant in her arms. 'You've got a perfect little girl.'

'Frédéric, come and have a look at our daughter,' Béatrice said weakly, as the memories of what the doctor had told her came flooding back. The doctor wouldn't make up a story like that, would she? 'She's a little miracle.'

The astounded husband put his arm round his wife's shoulders as he leaned down to kiss the tiny infant on the top of her downy head.

Marcel drew Debbie to one side. 'All babies are miracles,' he whispered softly. 'But it would be a miracle if you would take the first step. Did you really mean you...?'

Debbie looked up into his eyes. 'Yes. I agree,' she whispered. 'I made up my mind just now when I saw that darling little girl arriving. I want us to have a baby together. I want Emma to have a brother or sister. I don't know how it will work out in the future but...'

Marcel put one finger against her lips. 'Shh,' he murmured. 'We'll work it out together.'

Debbie nodded. 'Of course we will.' She turned to look at the happy new mother and father, now perfectly reconciled to the idea of becoming parents again. 'I'd better start the postnatal checks.'

'I've always wanted a girl. We've got a son of twenty-six and three grandsons,' Frédéric told Debbie proudly as she took the baby from Béatrice. 'So this little girl is going to make history in our family.'

'She's already made history by arriving unexpectedly like she did,' Béatrice said, running a hand through her damp, greying hair. 'I've no idea where she came from.'

Frédéric grinned. 'Oh, I have. It was after that party your sister gave when—'

'Frédéric! Don't embarrass me!' Béatrice giggled. 'What I mean is, I had no idea I was pregnant. It wasn't a bit like when I had Jean-Pierre, although it's so long ago I suppose I must have forgotten about it. What I do remember is that with Jean-Pierre I was in labour for...'

Debbie continued to check out the new baby as Béatrice reminisced with her husband. She was feeling elated at having made the momentous decision. She wasn't going to change her mind now.

A couple of nurses arrived from Obstetrics. Marcel had already contacted the consultant in charge of that department to give him a full report of the situation.

As soon as Béatrice and her family had been transferred, Debbie went along to her small office at the other end of Urgences. She needed to write a brief report and check her messages before she resumed work. The emergency area was relatively quiet. The staff were coping with the patients already there, and unless there was some major disaster the day would be routine.

She switched on the small electric hotplate in the corner of her office, put water and coffee in her little cafetière and settled down to deal with her messages while she waited for the coffee to brew.

'Do I smell coffee?' Marcel pushed open the door, walked in and sat down on the only other chair in the room.

Debbie smiled and swivelled her chair around from the computer. 'You must have the most amazing sense of smell if you can detect coffee from the emergency area.'

Marcel grinned. 'I saw you slipping away and I hoped you'd be switching on your high-tech coffee-machine.'

'You mean low-tech,' Debbie said as she rushed across to the ancient contraption, which had begun to boil over. 'I keep meaning to buy myself an electric kettle and some instant coffee.'

'In France?' Marcel look scandalised. 'Where do you think you are? England?'

Debbie laughed. 'No comment.'

She placed two small cups on the small table near the desk.

'Coffee's good,' Marcel remarked as he took a tentative sip. 'But I didn't come here only for a cup of coffee. I came to make sure that you really have agreed and won't change your mind.'

'No.'

'*Non?*'

'No, I won't change my mind. Yes, I've agreed…but we need to talk about…'

Marcel put down his coffee-cup. It rattled in the saucer as he thumped his hand on the edge of the desk.

'*Non*, the time for talking is over,' he said forcefully. 'We need to act now, before we think up any more reasons why we shouldn't go ahead. Let's be totally positive and objective about this. When we have achieved a pregnancy, then is the time to draw up rules about the baby's future. Better we get started, and the sooner the better! How about tonight, my place?'

Debbie swallowed hard. She'd only seen Marcel as forceful as this when he was working on a difficult emergency case. Being masterful, taking charge of a situation always suited him. So she would simply go along with what he suggested for the first part of their plan. But tonight?

'Tonight? I'm afraid tonight's out of the question.'

'Why? What excuse have you dreamed up now?'

'It's not an excuse! I need to make proper arrangements with Francoise. I'll have to make sure it's convenient for her to stay the night.'

'Francoise doesn't have to stay the night. I can drive you home afterwards.'

'But I thought it might be better if I stay the whole night.'

As soon as she'd said it, she knew it had been a mistake. It was only supposed to be a conception assignment, not a full-blown romance.

Marcel gave her a rakish grin. 'But you were the one who was keen to walk away and restart your normal life as soon as possible after the event, weren't you?'

She coloured. 'Well, in case I feel tired or… Marcel, you're supposed to be helping me stick to my resolve, not…'

'Darling, I'm sorry.' He sprang to his feet and leaned over her chair, his hands on the arms so that she couldn't escape. 'I was only teasing you. I'd planned all along to keep you with me all night. We don't want to rush things.'

He bent his head and kissed her gently on the lips before pulling himself to his full height.

He'd never called her 'darling' before. They were speaking English and his sexily husky French accent seemed to make the endearment sound particularly provocative. It crossed her mind that he must have called his wife 'darling' and she felt a pang of jealousy shooting through her.

She stood up. 'On the practical side. I'll check my menstrual calendar and work out when I'll be at my most fertile.'

'*Absolument!*' Marcel said with a whimsical smile on his face. 'After all, we don't want to waste time having to repeat our pregnancy assignments too many times before you become pregnant, do we?'

Debbie smiled as she sensed the implications of his remark. 'Marcel, you're wicked!'

'I know!' He drew her against him, holding her very close as he kissed her, this time more sensually.

She could feel her body reacting, feel the beating of

his heart against her white coat. She was wearing nothing but bra and pants underneath as it was a hot day, and she was feeling decidedly turned on by the closeness of his muscular body.

Marcel's pager vibrated against her from the breast pocket of his shirt. She jumped back.

Marcel groaned. 'This had better be important.' He hurried over to the door. 'Set up the time for the first assignment and I'll prepare the place.'

It was a whole week before her plans were finalised. She'd got the most fertile date written into her diary. She'd approached Francoise about staying the night, saying that she was going to spend the night with a friend who lived near the hospital.

Francoise, discreet as always, refrained from asking who the friend might be. If she had her suspicions, she didn't voice them. She was secretly hoping it might be that handsome doctor who'd called in and stitched up Emma's leg, but she would wait until she was told.

Debbie asked if Francoise would see Emma safely onto the school bus in the morning. Emma had started going on the bus at her own request as most of her friends did so. It made them feel more grown-up. Debbie explained that her mobile would be switched on.

Francoise agreed to everything.

When Debbie phoned Marcel to ask if the date was convenient, he said that he would move heaven and earth to fall in with her plans. She was the most important person in the equation because she would have to change her lifestyle during her pregnancy, whereas he would only have to be in at the conception.

Debbie said she had no intention of changing her lifestyle during her pregnancy. She would work until the very last minute. Pregnancy wasn't an illness. She was fit and healthy and it wouldn't make any difference. An argument ensued during which it almost seemed as if they might call the whole thing off.

At that point Marcel agreed that Debbie should decide what was best for her during her pregnancy. He ended the phone call amicably but determined to get his own way.

He was actually planning to become as involved with the pregnancy as Debbie would allow. He would have to ensure that she didn't become overtired. She had a tendency to keep going long after she should have downed tools and taken a rest.

And as for working until the last moment, the very idea appalled him! He was sure that he could persuade Debbie to see the reasoning behind his argument that she should take things easier when her pregnancy became more advanced.

On the evening of their so-called pregnancy assignment they both left the hospital together and drove up the hill in Marcel's car to his house. Marcel had told his *femme de ménage* that he was having a guest to stay the night and had asked that she prepare the guest room and also put clean sheets on his bed.

As Debbie walked into the house, she could feel butterflies churning around in the pit of her stomach. Marcel had suggested they have supper first. Debbie wasn't sure she could eat anything but decided to put on a show of normality. She sensed that they were both trying to pretend that it was perfectly normal to get together with the sole purpose of producing a child. And also…this was the most difficult bit!… to remain emotionally detached from the reproductive act. Impossible!

They had a light supper in the kitchen. Marcel

whisked up an omelette, Debbie tossed a salad. Marcel uncorked a bottle of claret.

'I laid this down for a special occasion,' he said as he poured some wine into her glass.

As Debbie raised the glass she could smell the delicious bouquet so typical of the Bordeaux region.

'Mmm, I love claret,' she said. 'The first red wine I was allowed as a young girl when I was taken by my father to a château near Bordeaux. My father allowed me a small taste from his glass. He told me it was a very good wine, so it always makes me nostalgic when I drink this type of wine.'

Marcel put down his fork. 'Nostalgic for the family life you enjoyed in spite of your parents not being together?'

She smiled. 'Yes, in some ways I had the best of both worlds, a doting father and an ever-present, dedicated mother.'

He leaned across the table and took hold of her hand. 'Our child will want for nothing. Our child will be loved by both of us.'

The touch of his hands sent a frisson of excitement running through her. Tonight...very soon now...she was going to lie in Marcel's arms. They were going to make love...all night if they wanted to...

Marcel caressed the palm of her hand. 'What are you smiling about?

'Was I smiling? I think it's because I'm happy. Because at last I may be able to begin the process of having another child,' she said quickly.

Marcel came around the table and drew her to her feet. 'Let's have our dessert later. I'll bring it up to bed...afterwards.'

He was holding her against him, his lips teasing hers.

She parted her lips and savoured his kiss, a kiss that was only the precursor of what was to come.

She sighed as he lifted her in his arms.

'Marcel, this is too romantic,' she whispered against his neck. 'Weren't we supposed to be trying to be unemotional?'

'Not good for the baby we're going to make. It's got to be conceived in love.' Marcel said huskily as he carried her out into the hall. 'For tonight we must pretend we're young lovers making love, without any thought of the future. And if we happen to have a baby…well, that will be a bonus, my darling.'

She relaxed against him as he carried her up the staircase into his bedroom. She'd dreamed of this moment. Already she'd abandoned all idea of putting any kind of restraint on her love-making. She was going to savour every magical moment…

At first when she opened her eyes she couldn't remember where she was. There was moonlight shining through the open casement window and the faint scent of roses from a garden. And then the wonderful memories came flooding back. She turned her head on the pillow and saw Marcel's dark hair close to hers.

He was still asleep, his breathing steady, a half-smile on his face. He looked as relaxed and happy as she herself felt. Mmm… She stretched out her legs beneath the sheet and twiddled her toes. She was still tingling from the ecstatic vibes of their love-making.

Marcel must have covered her with the sheet afterwards because she remembered quite clearly the sheet and quilt being tossed to the floor. What a wonderful lover he was! She'd never known such ecstasy. She remembered how he'd teased her, caressed her, explored every part of her body in the most tantalising way until she'd longed for him to take her completely so that she could experience the final fulfilment of their love-making.

When he'd first entered her, she'd cried out at the sheer joy of coupling with him, feeling him move inside her, throbbingly vibrant. And when she'd climaxed she'd cried out at the absolute heavenly ecstasy that had flooded through her entire body.

Marcel was stirring beside her now. She turned to look at him again and he opened his eyes. His mouth, his luscious sexy lips, those lips that had driven her to distraction during the night, now curved into a slow sensual smile.

He drew himself up onto one elbow, hovering above her, his eyes full of a deep tenderness she'd never seen before.

'You were sensational,' he whispered in English. 'Even if we don't have a baby, it was fun trying. No, it was more than fun. It was…'

He bent his head and kissed her, his lips as light as a feather. She felt her body stirring in response again. His kiss deepened. She sighed. Once more she was completely fluid, liquid, boneless, moving as one with her wonderful sexy lover, timeless, out of this world…no tomorrow…only today…

The early morning sun had drifted over the window-sill by the time Debbie woke again. Marcel stirred beside her and put out his hand to cradle hers.

She glanced at the clock. 'Time to get up, I think.' She was trying very hard to come down to earth. She was already longing for Marcel to take her in his arms again, but the longer she lingered here the more difficult it would be to pick up the threads of her everyday life.

'Don't go! I'll bring some coffee. We can spare ourselves a few more minutes of pretence.'

She hadn't the strength to argue. Debbie lay still, watching Marcel getting out of bed, shrugging himself into a white towelling dressing-gown. His muscular body was honed to perfection. She knew he worked out at the gym but she hadn't realised just how perfectly formed his fantastic, virile body was. She suppressed a sigh. The pretence that they were young lovers simply enjoying making love with each other was over. They had to get back to the real world and forget that they'd spent the night together.

She climbed out of bed and made for the bathroom. Stepping into the shower, she turned it on full so that the warm water cascaded over her. She had to get back to some sense of normality.

As she stepped out of the shower and reached for a white fluffy towel, she knew it wasn't going to be easy to put the events of the night from her mind. This was the point at which she had to walk away and go back to her everyday life as if nothing had happened. But something *had* happened. She was deeply, irrevocably in love, and there wasn't a thing she could do about it.

As for whether she was pregnant or not, she now had mixed feelings about that. That had been the object of them getting together initially. The reason for two very independent, uncommitted people to make a pact. One half of her was hoping that she was already pregnant, the other half hoped that they would need a further excuse to spend the night together.

'Coffee's ready!' Marcel called from the bedroom.

A second white towelling dressing-gown had been

placed on a stool near the shower. Debbie put it on. It was a woman's dressing-gown, a perfect fit for her. She felt another pang of jealousy. How many more females would wear this gown after her? She had no hold on Marcel. Only her child would have the privilege of being important to him.

Marcel was pouring the coffee as she walked back into the bedroom. He looked up and smiled.

'I'm glad you found the dressing-gown. You look stunning this morning.'

He was sitting in an armchair pulled close to a small table by the window. He stood up and pulled another chair close beside him.

'Come and join me.' He held out his arms and drew her against him. She tried to remain calm and composed but she could feel her body beneath the robe reacting to the nearness of this wonderful man.

'You're trembling,' he whispered, holding his lips against her cheek.

'It's the early morning chill.'

He pulled away and made to close the windows.

'No, don't do that. I love the scent of the roses from the garden. June is always a great month for roses. I remember as a child how my father always had roses in his garden during the summer...'

She chattered on about her childhood as Marcel poured the coffee. She was feeling totally confused now by her churning emotions, and she always chattered when she was nervous. She became silent again, losing herself in her disturbing thoughts about the future.

It was such an unnatural situation and for the moment she couldn't think how she was going to handle it. She'd thought she would be able to regain her senses easily, but she'd been mistaken. She realised that what she really wanted now was to cancel the whole idea that having a baby together was part of a contract, with set rules about caring for the child but no provision made for a loving relationship between the parents.

She wanted to change the contract. To rewrite the whole idea they'd dreamed up together and make everything much simpler…if marriage and family could ever be called simple! Looking across the small table at Marcel, she thought that it would never be simple but it would be the most wonderful life she could imagine.

How she'd changed! It was Marcel who had changed her. She couldn't imagine he would ever do anything deceitful. But wasn't that what she'd imagined about Paul until she realised she'd been taken in? Maybe the idea of being uncommitted really was the safest way of living. Definitely the safest, but was safety worth missing out on so much love?

Marcel placed a large breakfast cup of coffee in front of her. 'Would you like a croissant? They're fresh from the *boulangerie* delivery van. They always stop at the house in the mornings to see if I want a baguette or some croissants.'

'I'd love a croissant.' She broke into the crispy outer layer and added a teaspoonful of apricot jam.

'This is so civilised, having breakfast with you, Debbie.'

'Civilised?'

'Yes, we'll always be civilised when we meet in the future after our baby is born. That's what we planned, wasn't it?'

Debbie swallowed a morsel of the delicious croissant. 'Yes, we've got to look ahead at how we'll handle our lives,' she said carefully.

Marcel topped up her coffee-cup. 'Oh, it won't be a

problem. We're already getting back into our everyday selves, aren't we? You on one side of the table, me on the other, having our breakfast, discussing the roses and…'

He broke off and stretched his hand across the table to take hold of hers. He knew he was deluding himself. He didn't know how it was for Debbie, but he was finding it increasingly difficult! After their wonderful night of ecstasy when they'd lived the dream of being young lovers to perfection. But they'd agreed that neither of them wanted to commit to a real relationship, and for Debbie's sake he was going to honour their original plan.

Now, while they were both tingling with the aftermath of their love-making, wasn't the time to say that his ideas on the subject of their relationship were changing radically.

He stood up. 'I'll bring the car round to the front of the house. When you're ready we—'

'I'll be ready in ten minutes,' she said briskly, as she began loading the crockery onto a tray.

Their game of make-believe was over…until the next time. If they needed to meet for a next time, she thought as she stacked the cups. She couldn't help hoping this wasn't the last time she would spend the night with Marcel.

CHAPTER SIX

As THE days passed by and the date when her period was due drew nearer, Debbie found she was on tenterhooks. She had mixed feelings about the possibility that she might be pregnant. The ultimate dream of having a second child had to be weighed against the fact that she would no longer have an excuse to spend another wonderful night with Marcel.

For the first few days after their night together, Marcel had seemed to be making it quite clear that he was sticking to their plan. At the hospital he was ultra-professional with her. Occasionally he would slip down to her office for a coffee and a chat, mostly about work, but he hadn't suggested they meet outside the hospital so she'd come to terms with the fact that this was what her future held. A platonic friendship with her baby's father.

The joy of having another baby would be infinite. If only she hadn't agreed not to fall in love with the baby's father!

And then one morning when she arrived in Urgences there was a message in Reception to say that Marcel wanted to see her in his office as soon as she arrived.

'What's the problem?' she asked as she sat down in the chair beside his desk.

He switched off his computer. 'The weather,' he said, standing up and coming round to her side of the desk. 'We're well into the summer and we haven't made the most of it. Look at that glorious sunshine!'

He waved his arm towards the window.

'Yes, it's lovely out there but we're on duty so—'

'No, we're not. Everything's quiet this morning so I've cleared our work schedules. You and I are off duty unless we get an urgent call that the rest of the medical staff can't handle.'

Debbie's eyes widened. 'What brought this on?'

'I'm giving my staff in Urgences an extra day off duty when the weather is good. I suggested to the board of directors that it would be good for morale. Everybody is getting fed up with being inside when the weather is so glorious. The chairman thought it would be an excellent idea and asked me to arrange it. We'll all take our off-duty days at different times, of course, but providing the department is well staffed and that we agree to return should an emergency arise, there will be no problem.'

'Sounds good to me. So the two of us are to start the scheme today, are we?'

She was trying to sound calm about it, but the fact that Marcel had included her in his day off duty was encouraging. Did it mean the two of them might have a life beside the baby plan?

'I'm going to take you on a tour of the coast till we reach a good beach for swimming. Then we'll have lunch in a small restaurant I know, returning here later this afternoon to check that everything's running smoothly.'

'I wish you'd phoned me about this. I haven't got anything to wear for swimming.'

'I only got the OK from the board of directors a few minutes ago so you would have left home by then. No problem. We'll drive into Le Touquet on our way and pick up a swimsuit at one of the shops. I've got some beach towels in my cupboard here at the hospital so we're all set.'

'You've thought of everything.' She smiled. 'I like the idea of buying a new swimsuit. I've been meaning to buy a new bikini all through the summer but I never got around to it. Last weekend on the beach with Emma I realised the fabric of the one I was wearing was completely washed out with the effect of the sea water.'

'Can Emma swim?'

'Oh, yes!' Debbie said proudly. 'She's getting really good at it.'

'Pity she's at school or we could have taken her with us. I'd like to get to know your daughter. After all, I'll probably see her quite often if we succeed in having a baby.'

Debbie had a moment of anxiety. 'We'll have to be careful about that. Emma said she didn't want another daddy. Even though she never sees her own father, she believes that he loves her and that nobody could take his place. Your visits will probably also make her wonder even more about why her own father doesn't come and visit.'

Marcel placed a finger under Debbie's chin, raising her face so that she had to look him in the eye.

'We'll be extremely careful and, believe me, Debbie, I would never try to take Emma's father's place. She has treasured ideas about her father and I hope nothing will ever shatter them. I'll be her friend if she wants me to be.' He hesitated. 'I feel so impatient to know if we've already been successful.'

Debbie smiled up at him. 'So do I. My period's due at the weekend. I'll let you know if it arrives.'

'If it doesn't, we'll have to try again,' he said huskily. She felt a stirring of desire as he moved closer.

'It was a wonderful night we spent together, Debbie.'

It was the first time he'd alluded to what had passed between them. Since arriving back at the hospital on the morning after their night together, she'd almost imagined she'd dreamed the whole experience. But, yes, it had truly happened and it had been wonderful. Too wonderful! She hadn't meant to be so moved. She'd thought she could handle her emotions better than she was doing.

'So, let's get going,' she said, quickly, anxious not to give way to her feelings.

Marcel drove into Le Touquet and parked in a large car park beside the beach. They had a coffee in a small bar sitting on the terrace overlooking the sea. The sun was streaming down on them and Marcel adjusted the parasol that shaded their table. Although it was only the middle of the morning Debbie was surprised to see that the beach was crowded with holidaymakers.

'It's the height of the season,' Marcel said. 'We'll find a quieter beach for our swim.'

She put down her coffee-cup and began to unwrap one of the tiny ginger biscuits that had arrived with the coffee. 'After I've bought my bikini.'

'You must let me buy it for you. It's an early birthday present. Your birthday's in September, isn't it?'

She looked surprised. 'You've been checking up on me.'

'It was on the curriculum vitae you sent in when you started work at the hospital. It's your thirtieth birthday, isn't it?'

'Don't remind me!'

'You're still very young. I'm thirty-eight already.'

'Yes, but you're a man!'

'Ah, so you noticed!'

She laughed. 'What I meant was that men can father children until they're well into old age.'

Marcel grinned. 'Yes, but as you know I'm impatient. That's why I've already made a start with someone who looks as if she'll make the perfect mother.'

He stood up and drew her to her feet. 'Come on, let's go and get your bikini.'

They walked down one of the side streets that led to the beach, Debbie stopping to look into each of the shop windows as they passed. And then she saw it.

'That's the one!'

The white bikini was on a model in the centre of the window. It was two tiny scraps of material with gold rings at each side of the hips and through the centre of the bra.

'So long as you don't adopt that awful smug expression the model is wearing you'll look great in it.'

Debbie laughed. 'I promise I won't.'

Marcel followed her into the little boutique and sat on a chair in the corner feeling decidedly out of place in this very feminine shop. He stared studiously out of the window as Debbie told the saleswoman she'd like to try on the white bikini in the window. After she'd disappeared into a cubicle, Marcel thumbed his way through one of the magazines on the small wrought-iron table.

He was surprised to find a news magazine among the beauty and fashion magazines spread out for the female clientele. Probably meant for male escorts like himself. He hoped Debbie wouldn't take too long. He wanted to get out into the fresh air again. The cloying air freshener was tickling his nostrils.

Debbie emerged smiling, carrying the bikini. Marcel felt relieved that she'd made her mind up so quickly.

His credit card was already in his hand and he moved to the cash desk.

'*Merci, monsieur,*' the saleswoman said, handing over a receipt.

'It's perfect!' Debbie said as she watched the saleswoman placing it in a packet with the name of the boutique emblazoned on the outside.

'Thank you so much, Marcel,' she said, as they went outside. 'It's so lovely. I can't wait to put it on.'

'I can't wait to see you in it.'

He took hold of her hand and they walked back to the car.

Driving up the coast, Debbie lay back against her seat. Marcel had let down the hood of his silver sports car and the breeze was tumbling her long dark hair behind her as he increased his speed.

He took one hand off the wheel and reached for hers. 'I'm glad we took the day off, aren't you?'

'Mmm! This is the life! At times like this I can't think why I ever wanted to be a career-woman.'

'You could always give it all up and become a full-time mother.'

'Only if I had the money.'

'If that was what you wanted, I'm sure we could find a solution.'

'Don't even think about it,' she said, firmly, wishing she hadn't made her flippant remark about giving up her career. 'I'll never be a kept woman. I'll always work outside the home. I need to be fully independent for the rest of my life.'

'I know…and I admire you for it, but…'

He dropped the car down a gear as he drove round a narrow bend. He'd said too much already. Debbie was Debbie and would never change. He'd known that when they'd first agreed on their idea for a baby. He'd been lucky she'd agreed to the plan. But their plan of no commitment had to stand firm.

He turned off the main road and drove down a small lane that led to a quiet sandy cove. The beach was almost deserted. They found a quiet spot at the edge of the sand-hills and Marcel spread towels on the sand.

Debbie wrapped a towel round her as she changed into the white bikini.

'You look fantastic! It suits you much better than that miserable model in the window.'

Debbie smiled. 'Come on, I'll race you to the sea.'

They ran down. Marcel deliberately stayed beside her until the last few steps when he increased his pace and surged ahead. Watching his lithe, muscular body in the black swimming shorts streaking ahead of her made her feel excited. Excited in the knowledge that she was going to know this man all her life. He was going to be part of her child's life and she would always be able to contact him.

It wasn't ideal but it was all that was possible under the circumstances.

They swam out to a rock some way from the shore. Clambering up the warm surface, Debbie found she was breathless with the exertion. She clung to the stone surface as she lay down on her stomach, gazing down into the swirling waves. The sun was warm on her back.

'The sea's still quite cool,' she said, as Marcel lay down beside her, raising himself on one elbow so he could look down at her.

'It's a good thing the sun is warm.' Debbie said. 'My skin is cold.'

He bent down and covered her body with his. 'Are you feeling warmer now?'

She looked up into his eyes, so full of tenderness. 'I'm much warmer.'

She could feel herself relaxing against him. He was taking all his weight on his elbows but his skin, lightly touching hers was evocative of what had already passed between them.

He lowered his head and kissed her gently on the lips. She responded, parting her lips so that she could savour the moment.

Marcel pulled himself away. 'It's hardly an ideal spot for romance, perched on this precarious rock.'

She sat up, hugging her knees. 'Are we going to allow ourselves romance when we meet in the future?'

'I sincerely hope so! I would find it very hard to meet up with you and not feel romantic!'

'So we're going to have a platonic yet romantic relationship for the sake of our child—is that it?'

He smiled. 'Do you think that would work?'

'Sounds like you're hoping for the best of both worlds. Independence and occasional romantic liaisons.'

He shifted his position on the rock so that he was in a sitting position. 'That about sums it up. Would you agree to that?'

She smiled. 'Sounds like we're having a board meeting.'

Marcel laughed. 'Great place for a meeting, sitting on a rock surrounded by the sea with the summer sun warm on our bodies.'

He leaned forward and caressed her cheek. 'Years from now we'll remember this meeting when our child is growing up. The day we agreed on independence and occasional romance. You do think that would work, don't you, Debbie?'

She nodded. It was good to know that Marcel was

looking so far ahead. But their future plans were so nebulous. Would occasional romance satisfy her? In her heart of hearts she knew it wouldn't be enough, but she would have to go along with it.

Marcel stood up and drew her to her feet. 'Let's go back to shore. Careful on the edge of the rock here. It's very slippery. Keep hold of my hand and I'll help you down...'

They swam back to shore side by side, running up the beach to dry themselves and get dressed.

'Where are we going for lunch?' Debbie asked as she ran a comb through her tousled hair.

'I know a little restaurant on the edge of the sand-hills over on that side of the beach. Should take us about ten minutes to walk there. Very small, family-run place,' he said as they set off along the beach, 'and the food is excellent.'

The proprietor, Henri, and his wife, Antoinette, greeted Marcel like a long-lost friend.

'Oh, Dr De Lange, *quel plaisir*!' Antoinette said, bustling out of the kitchen, wiping her hands down her apron. 'Henri told me you were here. As soon as you telephoned this morning I reserved your favourite table for you.'

The plump dimpled cheeks were smiling as Antoinette shook hands with Marcel, turning to acknowledge Debbie with a polite '*Bonjour, madame.*'

They were quickly seated at a table by the window. In the centre of the red and white gingham cloth was a small glass vase containing a single red rose.

The proprietor leaned forward, pointing to the rose, and whispered something in Marcel's ear.

Marcel smiled. '*C'est parfait*, Henri!'

Their aperitifs were on the house. Debbie chose kir,

her favourite, made from white wine and *crème de cassis*. Marcel asked for a glass of Pernod. As he poured in the water he swirled his glass so that it turned cloudy. Raising his glass towards Debbie, he said, in English, 'Here's to the success of our plan.'

Debbie smiled. 'I'll drink to that.'

She felt a sudden qualm of anxiety. She glanced around the room. Two other couples were nearby but they were intent on their own conversations. She lowered her voice.

'I hope I'm going to be able to deliver the goods, so to speak. What will happen if we find problems in—?'

'Let's think positive!' He reached across the table and took hold of her hand. 'If there's a medical hitch, we'll face it together. We're both in good health. Let's just enjoy trying. That wasn't a problem, was it?'

She could feel herself blushing. Henri had arrived with their starters and was placing some *pâté de fois gras* in front of her. She took a piece of thin toast from the warmed napkin and spread some of the pâté on it.

'Delicious!' she said, looking across at Marcel. 'How's your *saumon fumé*?'

Marcel pronounced his smoked salmon superb.

'I love the rose in the centre of the table,' Debbie said. 'Was that your idea?'

He smiled. 'What makes you think that?'

'You're a romantic.'

'I'll take that as a compliment.'

'It was meant to be.'

As they looked at each other across the table Debbie felt her heart beating faster. She could imagine meeting up with Marcel in the future, enjoying lunch or dinner in a restaurant. Going to the theatre or a concert. During the course of their conversations during the past weeks,

they'd both discovered their mutual interest in the theatre and music. It could work out between them. Independence and romance.

She tried to convince herself that it was the only kind
of relationship for two independent people still suffering
from the scars of their previous relationships.

'You're looking very solemn all of a sudden,' Marcel
said.

'Am I? I was thinking about the future, our future.
What it will be like when we meet from time to time.'

Henri arrived with their main courses, and for a few
moments their conversation came to a standstill.

'I should imagine it will be something like this,'
Marcel said, picking up his steak knife. 'Except we'll
have our child with us.'

'In a high chair, throwing food on the floor,' Debbie
said lightly.

Marcel laughed. 'I can't wait to be a proper father.
That will be fun.'

Debbie was glad she'd eased the tension by making
an attempt at a joke. She reasoned she ought to stop
worrying about the future otherwise she would put a
damper on their day out together. It was no good constantly looking ahead to the problems they might encounter. Much better to live for the moment where her
relationship with Marcel was concerned. Simply take
each day as it came. Because each precious moment
with Marcel was worth savouring.

She enjoyed her pheasant cooked in Calvados, which
was a regional dish from Normandy. Marcel declared
that his steak was perfectly grilled, just as he liked it.

Debbie had decided to skip dessert, feeling replete,
but Antoinette hurried out of the kitchen carrying her
home-made *tarte maison* which she'd just taken from

the oven. The smell of the home-grown apples and shortcrust pastry was too tempting so Debbie changed her mind. After dessert they were served with coffee on the terrace facing the sea.

Marcel took hold of her hand. 'I think we've resolved a great deal today.'

Debbie looked up at him. 'Have we?'

'Yes, I feel more…er…comfortable with our relationship now.'

'Comfortable?'

'I think we've ironed out the creases. We know where we're going.'

She leaned forward. 'All I've got to do now is get pregnant.'

He drew closer and kissed the side of her cheek. 'Let's hope that's already been accomplished.'

'I'll let you know as soon as I'm sure.'

Marcel drove back slowly to the hospital. It was as if they were both winding down from what had been a memorable day together. Debbie knew she didn't want to get back. She wanted to prolong her time alone with Marcel. She began thinking about all the occasions in the future when their times alone would be so limited. Quickly she checked her thoughts again. No more looking into the future. Live for today and enjoy it while you could.

Everything was running smoothly when they got back at the hospital late in the afternoon. There had, however, been one car crash where two patients had been brought in, but they were both in Theatre. The only patients now in Urgences were being treated and the medical staff had everything under control.

Debbie went into the treatment room to help the plaster nurse fix a cast on a fractured ulna. The young woman patient had fallen from her bicycle, putting out her right hand to prevent her fall and cracking the bigger of the two bones in the forearm.

'I feel such an idiot,' the patient said, as she looked up at Debbie. 'One minute I'm cycling along and the next, just because a dog ran in front of my wheel, I'm stretched out on the road. Why on earth did I put my hand out like that? I should have simply rolled and then I would have been OK.'

'If it's any consolation, Susanne,' Debbie told the patient, 'this often happens to people who fall. It's a natural instinct to put out your hand as you go down.'

She pointed to the X-rays highlighted on the wall. 'Your injury is typical of the ones I've seen since I first began my training in orthopaedics. And the good news is that the majority of these injuries heal very quickly. In four or five weeks you'll have your cast off and your arm will be as good as new.'

'Thanks, Doctor. Will you be taking my cast off?'

'I'm referring you to our orthopaedic department now. You'll have an appointment to see the consultant and he'll take over your treatment.'

Debbie's next patient was a twelve-year-old boy who'd landed heavily on the side of a trampoline as he'd been bouncing up and down in the garden. His back was badly bruised. Debbie checked out his nerve responses. There didn't seem to be any serious neural damage, but she made a call to the neurology department, explaining the case history and asking that the boy be admitted for further neurological tests. You couldn't be too careful with back injuries, which were on the increase now since trampolines had become so popular.

Next she treated a small child who'd pushed a bead into his ear. When she investigated with an auriscope, she could see the bead wedged up against the eardrum. Very carefully, with a pair of long tapering forceps, she was able to dislodge the bead and pull it out of the outer ear.

'Your little boy has been very lucky that the bead didn't perforate the eardrum,' she told the mother as she handed her the bead. 'Do you want to keep this as a souvenir?'

The mother smiled. 'I don't think so. Put it in the bin, Doctor. I'm going to get rid of that box of beads when I get home. It's been such a terrible time for us. Thank you so much. You were brilliant. I thought he'd have to stay in and have an operation.'

As Debbie said goodbye, she didn't tell the mother that she herself had been extremely relieved when she'd successfully manoeuvred the bead out of the narrow external auditory meatus. It had needed a very steady hand not to damage the eardrum.

'It's time you were off duty,' Marcel said, standing in the doorway of the treatment room.

She glanced at the clock. 'So it is.' She began clearing up the instruments she'd used.

'Leave that. I'll finish off in here. You need to get home to Emma.'

'Thanks.'

She made for the door. He put one hand on the wall above her as she came through, effectively blocking the doorway. They were standing in a busy area, with doctors and nurses moving in every direction. Marcel knew there was no chance of kissing Debbie goodbye, but he could delay her for a few moments.

He looked down at her. 'It's been a great day,' he said quietly. 'Thank you.'

She smiled. 'I enjoyed it.'

He took his hand from the wall so that she could go through. He watched as she walked quickly away without looking back. She looked strong, self-assured, independent, the sort of woman who would always know her own mind, never wavering in her decisions. Especially the important decision never to commit herself to another man again.

He took a deep breath. He was going to honour their original plan but, after spending the day with Debbie, he was finding his resolve was decidedly wavering. But as he went over to the treatment trolley to check on the instruments, he told himself that when he'd first married Lisa he'd thought that his feelings would never change. And how wrong he'd been! He was lucky that he'd found someone like Debbie who was of the same mind as he was.

Debbie woke early on Saturday morning. She could tell at once that her period had arrived. She was always as regular as clockwork so she was totally prepared. Only this time she'd hoped that it might not happen. So she wasn't pregnant after all. Well, that would mean another pregnancy assignment, to give it the technical name she and Marcel had invented. Another night of making love was how she hoped it would be.

As she hurried out to the bathroom she realised how much she was looking forward to it. Later that morning she would phone Marcel and give him the news that he wasn't going to be a father—yet.

After her shower she went along to Emma's room. Her little daughter smiled as she opened her eyes and wriggled into a sitting position, holding her arms wide for a cuddle. She might be six years old but she was still Debbie's baby. She still had that definitive baby scent about her, kiddy jimjams, baby talcum powder, sleep. It was difficult to quantify but it was the scent of her own child. And, hopefully, she might have another baby within the foreseeable future.

Debbie pulled away and smoothed down her daughter's tousled blonde hair. She was still as fair-haired as her father was. She preferred to think that Emma took after her mother. She had Paul's high cheekbones and slightly pointed chin, but that was where the resemblance ended. Her personality was completely different—thank goodness!

Debbie busied herself putting out Emma's clothes.

'Would you like to wear your new shorts?'

'Ooh, yes, please.' Emma jumped out of bed and hurried over to stand beside her chest of drawers. 'And this T-shirt, the one with the fishes on that we got in that shop by the sea. Can we go to the sea today, Mummy? I want to swim and swim and swim!'

Emma was hopping on one foot now, happily singing a song she was making up as she went along, something she loved to do when she was happy.

'And the fishes will come up and tickle my toes and I will swim and swim and…'

'Put your clothes on and come down for breakfast, darling. I need to work out what's happening today. I expect we can fit in a trip to the beach for a couple of hours.'

Hurrying down the stairs a little later, Debbie knew she would have to make that phone call to Marcel. She'd promised to give him the news as soon as she knew.

In the kitchen she put the kettle on before picking up the phone.

He took the news in an objective sort of way. 'Oh, well, we'll have to try again. I'm disappointed, of course, but... Just a moment while I look in my diary. I worked out your next fertile period in case we needed another assignment, so now I have to see... Have you got your diary with you, Debbie?'

Her diary was always next to the phone when she was at home. She picked it up. Over the phone she could hear the sound of pages being turned.

'Yes, that would be excellent,' Marcel said.

'What would?' she asked.

'I've been thinking it would be fun to go to Paris for our next assignment. I know a wonderfully romantic little hotel in the sixteenth arrondissement. Right down by the Seine. You can sit on the balcony and watch the boats going past. How would you feel about that, Debbie? Don't you think it would be fantastic if you conceived our baby in Paris?'

She felt bowled over with excitement, but decided she should dampen down her enthusiasm. 'I...er...I don't know what to say.'

'Just say yes! And then we can sort out the most convenient date for you.'

She smiled. After a depressing start to her day it was good to hear Marcel enthusing about a trip to Paris. She felt her spirits lifting. A night in Paris with Marcel. What could be more romantic?

'Debbie, are you still there? You're probably thinking it's a mad idea, but we would always remember if our child was conceived in Paris, wouldn't we?'

'Marcel, I'm hooked on the idea already.'

'Great! I'll make the reservation. Now, there's the

little question of the exact date. I'll arrange for us to take two days off midweek, so if you could check your diary for the week beginning...'

'Just a moment, Marcel, I can't hear you above Emma's singing...'

Emma had come dancing into the kitchen, still singing loudly about the sea and the fishes and the sun.

'Mummy, Mummy, can we leave now?'

'I'll call you back, Marcel, when—'

'Mummy, is that the nice doctor who stitched my leg? Can I say hello to him?'

'Emma would like to speak to you, Marcel.'

'And I'd like to speak to Emma.'

Debbie thought he sounded pleased. She handed over the phone.

Emma beamed. 'Hello, Marcel. It's me, Emma.'

Debbie hovered close by, shamelessly eavesdropping on their conversation. She could only guess what Marcel was saying.

Emma was listening to Marcel's voice before volunteering the information that they were going to the beach.

'Would you like to come with us, Marcel?' Emma added. 'You'll have to bring your swimming costume and— Oh, no...'

She turned to look at Debbie. 'Marcel says he's on duty at the hospital today, but he'd love to come next weekend if that's OK with you.'

Debbie smiled. 'That would be lovely.'

Emma told Marcel what Debbie had said before she continued to chatter. It sounded as if Marcel was asking about her leg.

'Oh, it's fine now. Mummy took the stitches out and it tickled. But I've got a scar. Mummy says it will disappear in time but I don't want it to. It looks very cool. Do you know the word "cool"? I don't know how to say it in French... Oh, that's OK then.'

She turned to Debbie. 'Marcel says they now use the English word "cool" in France. Did you know that, Mummy?'

'Yes, I did. Emma, I think Marcel will be very busy as he's on duty.'

'Mummy says I've got to go now. OK, I'll get her. Bye.'

Emma handed over the phone.

'She's gorgeous, your daughter,' Marcel said. 'I'm glad you've given me permission to come with you to the beach next weekend. I'll look forward to it. And I'll look forward to our date in Paris. Give me a call this evening when you've sorted out your diary.'

She put down the phone and turned to hug her daughter. Emma would be so thrilled if she had a baby brother or sister. Since Emma had said she didn't want another daddy, she'd worried that Emma might consider Marcel, the baby's father, as having designs on becoming her father as well. She'd also worried about how Emma would feel about not having her own daddy around, too. But now that Emma and Marcel seemed to be bonding, with careful handling it might not be too much of a problem.

She reminded herself to stop looking too far ahead. She would take one step at a time. For the moment her priority was Emma, to make sure she had the happiest childhood possible.

'We'll go to the sea as soon as we've had breakfast, Emma. Would you carry this jar of jam to the table for me? That's a good girl. Careful, careful...'

CHAPTER SEVEN

THE following weekend, Debbie packed a picnic lunch in preparation for their day on the beach. Emma was tremendously excited about the fact that Marcel was going to pick them up in his sports car. When she heard the sound of a car pulling into the drive she was beside herself with excitement, jumping down from her place at the kitchen table and running out of the door to meet him.

Her eyes widened as she admired the silver sports car with the top down. 'Wow, are we really going to drive to the beach in that? Can I sit in the front?'

Marcel was smiling happily as he climbed out of the driver's seat. 'I don't think that would be a good idea, Emma. The seat at the back is better for you. It's too small for a grown-up so Mummy had better sit in the front with me. Hello, Debbie.'

'Hi, there!' Debbie hovered in the doorway. 'Did you have breakfast, Marcel? We had a late start and we're still finishing off.'

'I had some coffee.'

'Come and have some more. And maybe a croissant? I bought too many at the *boulangerie* this morning.'

Marcel followed Debbie into the kitchen.

'Come and sit next to me here, Marcel,' Emma said, grabbing his hand and directing him to his allotted place at the table.

It felt so right to be sitting round the kitchen table with her daughter chattering away to Marcel. He was working his way through a croissant, sipping his coffee and all the time listening intently to the story that Emma was telling him about her school.

'When I go back to school in September, I won't be in the baby class. I'll be in the bigger children's class and all the new children will be in the classroom I've just left. My teacher in my new classroom is very pretty. She's very young, much younger than Mummy, I think.'

'Your mummy's still young,' Marcel said solemnly, licking some apricot jam from his bottom lip.

Emma giggled as she took a sip of her orange juice. 'Mummy looks young but she's old really. She's nearly thirty. My new teacher's only about…er…sixteen, I think.'

Debbie smiled. 'She's twenty-two, actually. And, yes, she's very pretty.'

'Would I think she was pretty?' Marcel asked lightly.

'Oh, you'd think she was gorgeous!' Emma said. 'Because you're a man. Have you got a wife?'

'No.'

'Girlfriend?'

Marcel glanced across the kitchen to where Debbie was stacking the dishwasher. She turned to look at him.

'There's a woman I'm very fond of,' he said, slowly. 'But grown-up relationships are never as easy as you imagine when you're a child.'

'Well, have you got any children?' Emma wasn't going to let him get off the hook easily.

'Not yet,' he said quietly.

Emma pulled a wry face. 'It's a pity you haven't got any children. You could have brought them with you to play with me. I asked Mummy ages ago if I could have a baby sister like my friend Céline's got, but Mummy said she hasn't got a daddy to make a baby with. The daddy has to plant the seed in the mummy, you see. Did you know that, Marcel?'

Marcel nodded solemnly. 'Yes, I'm a doctor so I have to know about these things.'

Emma looked thoughtful. 'I suppose you do. Because you have to get the babies out of the mummies' tummies, don't you?'

'Yes, I do.' Marcel took a long drink from his coffee-cup while he prepared himself for the next question.

Emma fixed him with an intense look. 'Do you ever have any babies lying around that nobody wants to take home with them? I mean, if you did, could you bring one here? I'd look after it ever so well, take it out for walks and when it's bigger it could play with me, couldn't it?'

'I'm sorry, Emma, but I never have any babies to spare,' Marcel said solemnly.

Debbie closed the door of the dishwasher. 'I'm afraid you'll just have to make do with Marcel and me as playmates on the beach today, Emma. Have you packed your swimsuit in your rucksack? Let's go and check, shall we?'

She wasn't sure where Emma's questions would lead next, and she didn't feel she could handle any more explanations in front of Marcel.

As they walked out of the front door, he reached for her hand and squeezed it. Emma ran ahead excitedly and climbed into the back seat.

Debbie looked up at Marcel and whispered, 'I didn't think it was a good time to start explanations about the fact that I've found a man to father my child. It's not going to be easy to explain our complicated situation.'

He put an arm round her waist. 'If and when we find

a baby is on the way, will you let me help you with the answers to Emma's questions?'

'Absolutely! I'll need all the help I can get. At least I don't have to worry about whether she likes you or not. She seems besotted.'

Marcel smiled. 'The feeling's mutual. I wish she was my daughter.'

Debbie swallowed hard. So did she. She still couldn't be sure how Emma would react if Marcel became father to her second child.

As she climbed into the passenger seat she found herself fantasising about how wonderful it would be if they were a real family setting out for a day at the beach. The baby strapped into its special seat, their elder child sitting beside her baby sister—or would it be a brother? It didn't matter so long as it was their longed-for, much-cherished baby. And Marcel, the doting father, starting up the engine as he was doing now...

'Are you OK, Debbie?' Marcel asked, touching the back of her hand as he drove out. 'You look as if you're far away somewhere.'

'No, I'm right here with you. Just thinking, that's all.'

They found a quiet spot on the edge of the sand-hills at a nearby beach. There were a few families on the beach but it wasn't crowded. Emma spread the travel rug on the sand and began opening up the picnic basket.

'Not yet, darling,' Debbie said. 'We've only just had breakfast. The food will stay fresher if we leave it in the cool bag. Come and show Marcel what a good swimmer you are.'

Once Emma was in the water it was difficult to tempt her back on dry land again. She was an excellent little swimmer but she had to be supervised the whole time to ensure she didn't stray out of her depth.

Marcel stayed with her for the rest of the morning, teaching her how to improve her arm and leg movements and then simply having fun splashing around. Emma insisted on climbing on his back, pretending he was a big fish and she was a mermaid who wanted a lift. Debbie, who was now sitting on the sand with a towel wrapped round her shoulders, smiled as she watched the two of them playing together.

Marcel was so patient with Emma! And he had such energy! She wouldn't have the strength to keep going as long as he did in this game of make-believe. It looked as if Marcel had now been turned into a shark that was required to snap its jaws at Emma. She was screaming with delight as he began to chase her out of the shallow water towards the beach.

'Come on, Emma, I'll race you back to the shark's camp,' he said, winking at Debbie as the two of them streaked past her.

'Sharks don't have camps,' Emma said, puffing loudly as she tried to keep up with Marcel.

'This shark has a camp up near the sand-hills,' Marcel said, slowing his pace so that Emma would have no difficulty in running beside him. 'He's got lots of food that little girls like.'

Marcel turned his head as he heard Debbie running after them. 'What do little girls like to eat, Debbie?'

'Some of them like ice cream from my special container,' Debbie said.

'Yes, I love ice cream!' Emma said, shedding her mermaid role. 'Do you like ice cream, Marcel?'

'One of my favourite foods!'

Emma, with renewed energy, was now streaking ahead, shouting, 'I'm the winner! I'm the winner!'

Marcel turned to look at Debbie. 'I've got some ham baguettes in the cool box of my holdall. And a bottle of wine, some peaches, but no ice cream.'

'I've brought a cooked chicken and some salad so we've got everything we could possibly need.'

Marcel reached for her hand. 'We have indeed. I couldn't wish for anything more.' He lowered his voice. 'That must be the sexiest bikini I have ever seen. But it's what's in it that makes it look so stunning.'

'Thank you. It's a fabulous birthday present.'

'I'll buy you something else on your actual birthday in September. Maybe…I don't know, something significant. Perhaps there might be something significant to celebrate by then.'

'I hope there is,' she said, as they reached their camp near the sand-hills. Emma had already dried herself and put on a dry swimsuit just as Debbie had shown her so many times when she came out of the sea. Her little swimsuit was hung precariously over the branch of a gorse bush.

'What a good girl you are,' Debbie said, hugging her daughter. 'I do love you.'

Emma smiled happily. 'I love you, Mummy.'

Watching mother and daughter hugging each other, Marcel wanted to join them and tell them that he loved them both. But he held back. How often would he have to hold back in the future? This wasn't his family, however much he wished it was. He was hoping he would father Debbie's baby but he would have to be careful not to overstep the mark. It was going to be so difficult to define his role in this family.

He reached down into the holdall he'd carried from

the car. 'Ham roll, anyone?' he said, dispensing the baguettes from his cool bag.

Debbie cut pieces from the chicken and placed them on plastic plates. Marcel uncorked the wine and handed her a glass as she picked up the salad servers to toss the salad in the plastic bowl.

'Let me toss the salad, Mummy.' Emma took the salad servers from her mother, sloshing the prepared vinaigrette into the bowl.

'Not too much vinaigrette, Emma,' Debbie said, as she took a sip of her wine. 'Mmm, I love the wine.'

'It's another Bordeaux vintage. I remembered you enjoyed the one we drank at Henri and Antoinette's restaurant.'

He touched his plastic glass against hers. 'Tastes better when drunk from a real glass, but we're on a picnic and I didn't think the glasses would survive being bashed around on the beach.'

'Emma, I think you've tossed the salad enough now, darling. It's ready to be served.'

Emma grinned as she put down the wooden salad servers. 'What did my Grandpapa André say when he taught me to toss the salad, Mummy?'

Debbie smiled. 'Grandpapa André said that "*quand on est assez grand pour tourner la salade on est assez grand pour se marier.*"'

Emma looked up at Marcel. 'You know what that means, don't you, because you're French?'

Marcel smiled. 'It means when you're big enough to toss the salad you're big enough to get married.'

Emma giggled. 'I'm not going to get married. I'm going to be a doctor like mummy, and doctors don't have time to get married, do they?'

'Some of them do,' Marcel said quietly.

'Yes, but Mummy told me she's happy on her own, just looking after me, didn't you, Mummy?'

'Yes, I did, Emma. Would you like some ice cream now?'

'Oh, yes, please.'

After lunch Debbie and Marcel stretched out on the sand, enjoying the sun. Debbie rubbed a high-factor sun cream into Emma's skin as she curled up between them. Debbie closed her eyes. It was so peaceful, she found herself dropping off to sleep…

She became aware that Marcel was standing in front of her as she opened her eyes.

He leaned down, speaking softly so as not to wake Emma up. 'I've had a call from the hospital so I'd better get back. I promised to do some extra time if I was needed this weekend. I'm making up the time I'll be taking during our two days in Paris.'

'Do you want me to make up any time during this week?'

'No, I've taken your two days from your legitimate off-duty days. But as the boss I've got to put in a bit extra. Sorry to break up the beach party but I'd better run you home now.'

He put out a hand and drew her to her feet. Gently he slid his arms around her waist and held her close, touching her lips lightly with his own.

'I've enjoyed being part of your family for a few hours,' he said quietly as he pulled himself away.

Debbie held her breath. She wanted to say how she wished he really was part of her family, but she didn't dare.

'You've been wonderful with Emma. Worn her out!'

As if hearing her name, Emma opened her eyes.

'Emma, darling, we've got to go home now. Will you collect your swimsuit from over there and—?'

'Is Marcel coming with us?'

'I've got to go back to the hospital, but I'll drive you home first.'

'Can't you stay for supper?'

'Sorry, Emma, some other time perhaps.'

It was the end of a perfect day, Debbie thought as she tucked Emma into bed. In spite of the nap on the beach, her daughter was tired enough to go to bed early and fall asleep immediately. Debbie went downstairs and began clearing up the picnic things she'd dumped in the kitchen. The phone rang.

'Thanks, Debbie. It was a great picnic.'

Her spirits soared at the sound of Marcel's voice. 'We enjoyed it. Emma's asleep already. Where are you?'

'I'm at the hospital, having a break between patients. I found myself thinking about our trip to Paris. It's all fixed. They've promised to put us in a room overlooking the river.'

'Sounds wonderful!'

'It will be…' He broke off and she heard him talking to someone. She also heard the noise of a trolley being wheeled nearby, somebody coughing violently. 'I've got to go. See you on Monday.'

Debbie heard the click of his phone at the other end. Her spirits drooped again. Usually she enjoyed a quiet Saturday night after Emma had gone to sleep. Sometimes she watched a video she wanted to see, often she simply curled up with a good book and some background music on the radio.

But tonight she didn't want to be alone. She would have liked to phone Marcel and say that whatever time he finished she hoped he would come over and join her. Even better, he could stay all night, share breakfast with her in the morning.

She felt a tear pricking behind her eyelids. This independent yet romantic relationship wasn't going to work in its present form. But what was the alternative? Frighten Marcel away by saying that she wanted him to make a commitment to stay with her for the rest of their lives?

She couldn't do that to him. Couldn't risk shattering the delicate balance of the friendship they had. She had to go along with their agreement.

The day of their trip to Paris finally arrived. Debbie had been counting the days! She felt as childlike as Emma in her impatience. Her work at the hospital had helped to keep her thoughts fully occupied and Emma had needed her. But the thought of two whole days away with Marcel had kept popping into her head.

It hadn't been necessary to involve Francoise in the organisation of her two days away. Emma's friend Céline had been to stay with them for a sleepover and her mother had suggested that Emma go to stay with them one night soon when it would be convenient for Debbie. Debbie had said she had to go away for a couple of days and Céline's mother had agreed she would be happy to have Emma to sleep at their house and would collect and deliver her to school with her own daughter.

On the morning that Debbie was due to set off for Paris she took Emma to the place where the school bus stopped in the village. Emma was excited to be going to stay with Céline, and as soon as her little friend arrived with her mother she made a beeline for her.

'I've packed Emma's pyjamas, toothbrush, clean clothes for tomorrow and so on,' Debbie said, handing over Emma's bag to Sylvie, Céline's mother. 'I hope I haven't forgotten anything.'

'Oh, don't worry,' Sylvie said amiably, jiggling the handle of her baby's pram. 'We're well equipped at home for anything a child could possibly need.'

Debbie leaned over to peep into the pram. Wide blue eyes peered up at her and the baby gave a toothless smile.

'Oh, she's beautiful! And so good!'

'She's good now that I've just fed her. Takes up a lot of my time. I envy you, going out to work. Sometimes I think I'll never escape from the house and have time to myself. But I wouldn't be without my children. Such a blessing, aren't they?'

'Absolutely! It's nice for Céline to have a baby sister.'

'Oh, she adores Marianne! And she's so good with her. I look forward to Céline coming home at the end of the day to play with her. Oh, here's the bus. Céline!'

Emma came up for a hug before running off to climb up the steps to the bus. 'See you tomorrow, Mummy,' she called importantly, before turning to tell the assembled children on the bus that she was going to stay with Céline and wouldn't see her mummy that night.

Debbie swallowed the lump in her throat. Emma was growing up so quickly and soon wouldn't need her quite so much.

'My mobile will be switched on all the time if you need to speak to me, Sylvie,' Debbie said, as she prepared to leave. 'Thank you so much for having her.'

'My pleasure. Have a nice time in Paris!'

As she turned away and began walking back down

the street, Debbie was glad to be leaving Emma with someone like Sylvie who hadn't asked questions about the purpose of her visit to Paris. She probably thought it was something to do with her work at the hospital or else she was going to stay with her father. Or she may have sensed she was meeting a boyfriend and was discreet enough not to enquire. It would have been much more difficult to explain her absence to Francoise, although if she became pregnant she'd have to come clean.

Putting her key in the front door, she decided that she would be completely open with Francoise if or when the time came that she was pregnant. She was going to need Francoise's help if she was to continue working at the hospital before and after the baby was born. One possibility she'd thought of was that Francoise might agree to come and live with them. The extra money Debbie would give her would come in useful and Francoise loved babies.

But as she went back into the empty house and began clearing up the kitchen, she told herself not to count her chickens. Tonight was another step in the right direction. As she thought about it, she felt her body stirring sensually. She was going to spend the whole night with Marcel.

Her mobile rang almost as if on cue. 'Are you ready?'

She suppressed a sigh as she heard his voice. 'Almost.'

'I'll pick you up in half an hour.'

'I'll be ready.'

Debbie put her weekender bag down in the hall as she heard the car pulling into the drive. It had been difficult to decide what to wear, but in the end she'd chosen to travel in her denim trouser suit. And she'd packed her new, floaty chiffon summer dress for the evening. She could wear it again tomorrow during the day if the weather remained hot.

Marcel was getting out of the car as she opened the front door. He came across the drive, his feet crunching on the gravel, smiling broadly. He kissed her lightly on the lips before bending down to pick up her case.

'All set?'

She nodded, suddenly feeling nervous. She'd been looking forward to this day for so long but now it was actually here she wondered if her expectations were too high. Better to calm her excitement and pretend it was simply a day out with Marcel. And a night! At the thought of the night, she remembered that Marcel would be hoping so much that they would create a baby tonight. And so was she.

Marcel was holding open the passenger door for her. She looked up at him and he smiled down at her. He looked relaxed and happy in his casual lightweight suit. He removed his jacket and tossed it into the space behind their seats.

She settled herself in the passenger seat as Marcel started up the engine.

'In two hours we'll be in Paris,' he said as he headed for the autoroute.

As they slowed to take a ticket for the autoroute Marcel glanced sideways and put out a hand to touch her ruffled hair. 'Your hair looks so attractive when the wind ruffles it.'

She laughed. 'I wasted ages brushing it and now it feels like a bird's nest.'

'Leave it like that when you get to Paris. You look like a young girl going out on her first date.'

He handed her the ticket to keep until they got to the *péage* at the end of the motorway before moving swiftly away.

'I feel as if I'm on a first date,' Debbie said, as the car purred along the smooth road. 'I actually think I'm nervous about…well, about everything. Trying for a baby…'

'That wasn't a problem last time, was it?'

She shook her head. 'It was…' She searched for the right words.

'If you enjoyed our night together as much as I did you won't be able to find words to describe it,' he said huskily. 'Just relax, *chérie*. We're going to have a wonderful time in Paris.'

Debbie looked around her as Marcel put their bags on the luggage shelf in the bedroom. She immediately liked the ambience of the room. The décor was predominantly white and typically French. The long windows opened out onto a balcony overlooking the Seine. In spite of the late morning heat outside, the room was cool. She kicked off her shoes and padded out through the window.

'Mmm, what a view!' she said as she admired the gently flowing river, with its pleasure boats and busy launches drifting along in the sunshine. 'It's ages since I went on the river. My father's house is outside Paris and when I go to see him I never have time nowadays to indulge myself. I'd love to take a *bateau mouche* on the river. One like that one over there.'

Marcel came up behind her, putting his arms over her shoulders so that she would lean against him.

'If it's a *bateau mouche* trip you want, *chérie*, that's

what we'll do.' He hesitated. 'You mentioned your father just now. Does he know you're in Paris?'

Debbie shook her head. 'It takes so long to get out to his house. They live near St Germain en Laye. I've promised myself I'll make a special trip soon.'

'That's the other side of Paris from my parents',' Marcel said. 'I haven't told them I'm coming to Paris for the same reason. I feel guilty about it but we need time to ourselves today. We'll make a special journey here as soon as we can tell them about their forthcoming grandchild.'

'Do you think we should tell them as soon as we know? Perhaps we should wait a while. I mean, we're not exactly going to be conventional parents, are we?'

'Your father doesn't sound very conventional to me.'

Debbie smiled. 'I suppose not.'

'And my parents are completely unshockable. Besides, we're mature enough to be unconventional if it suits us.'

He took hold of her hand and drew her back into the bedroom. 'Let's go out quickly. If we stay here any longer, I'll be tempted to take you to bed and—'

She laughed. 'Later!'

Debbie was as excited as a young girl as they boarded the *bateau mouche*. She chose to sit on the top deck, enjoying the view as they floated past the spectacular sights she knew so well and yet couldn't admire often enough.

'The Eiffel Tower,' she said, pointing to the huge iron structure. 'My father helped me walk up the iron staircase to the first floor when I was very small. I remember he bought me some chocolate and after he'd pointed out lots of the Paris landmarks he carried me most of the way down again because my legs were aching so much.'

'You don't want to go up the Eiffel Tower today, do you?'

'No, but I'd like to go into Notre Dame. I feel that I'd like to...' She paused. 'I'd like to light a candle.'

After they'd left the *bateau mouche*, they walked along the bank of the river and crossed the bridge to the ancient cathedral. It was cool and quiet inside. Debbie paused to select a candle, putting some money in the box beside them. She lit the candle from the flame burning on the table and made a silent prayer.

Marcel watched her. He instinctively knew this had something to do with their baby and he felt a lump rising in his throat. He hoped it wouldn't be long before her prayers were answered.

They went out into the bright sunshine and walked across the bridge to the left bank of the river. Marcel succeeded in finding a small restaurant where he said he'd had an excellent lunch the last time he'd been in Paris. They chose to sit outside on the pavement, shaded from the sun by a large umbrella.

The waiter placed a carafe of house wine on their table, together with a basket of crusty rolls. Marcel chose oysters for his starter. Debbie decided she would have prawns.

'Oysters are very good for you, *monsieur*,' the waiter said as he gathered up the menus.

Marcel smiled. 'I know.'

After the waiter had gone, Debbie asked Marcel if he believed in the theory that oysters made a man more virile. 'I mean, from a medical point of view, is there any evidence to support the theory?'

Marcel gave her a rakish grin. 'I can feel the magic

working already and the oysters haven't even arrived yet.'

It was late afternoon when they left the restaurant. They drifted off through the narrow streets back to the river and crossed to the right bank so that they could walk up the Champs Élysées. By the time they'd window-shopped their way to the Arc de Triomphe Debbie's feet were throbbing with the heat of the pavement.

Marcel hailed a taxi and they returned to their hotel. The first thing Debbie wanted to do was soak herself in the huge old-fashioned bath. She emptied scented bath foam into the water and lay back to relax.

She'd left the door open, hoping that Marcel might join her. As he came in she looked up at him and smiled lazily. 'There's room for two,' she said.

'I thought there might be.'

As he stripped off his towelling robe and climbed in, Debbie felt the last vestige of her nervousness disappear. It felt so natural to be lying here together, their legs intertwined. Her body had stirred with excitement as she'd watched Marcel slipping into the water. It was going to be a fantastic night together. And she wasn't going to spoil it by thinking about the future implications.

Tonight, as they'd pretended last time, they were lovers intent only on making love with each other. The outcome, baby or otherwise, wasn't important. What was important was their love for each other. On her part she didn't need to pretend. Her love was one hundred per cent genuine.

And she would pretend that Marcel felt the same way…just for tonight…

CHAPTER EIGHT

WAKING up in the middle of the night, seeing Marcel sleeping peacefully beside her, Debbie remembered that she'd been determined to pretend he loved her while they'd made love. It hadn't been difficult to imagine that he felt the same way about her as she felt about him. Except, at the end of their love-making, as she'd curled up against him, he'd murmured that she needn't be afraid about the future. He wasn't going to take away her independence.

He'd whispered that even though it was so wonderful for him to have her with him for a whole night, he wouldn't try to change their plan. He knew how important it was to her to remain uncommitted.

Why hadn't she told him how she'd changed radically? There she was, her body tingling with erotic vibes, floating on cloud nine, wanting to stay up there in the clouds for ever... Ah, that was precisely why she hadn't put him wise about how she really felt! Her emotions had been out of control. Marcel was probably in a similar state. And in the emotional turbulence following their love-making she might have drawn him into saying something he would regret. He would feel trapped by a commitment he was trying to avoid.

No, it was far better they stick to the plan they'd made, when their emotions didn't come into the equation. If this was all she could hope for, she would go along with it.

She looked down at Marcel's dark, handsome head,

hair tousled out on the pillow beside her. She knew without a shadow of a doubt that she'd never loved anyone as she loved Marcel.

He stirred in his sleep, opened his eyes and reached out for her. She slid easily into his arms, gazing up at him as if trying to hold onto the memory of his features for the times she would be alone in the future.

'Mmm!' He nuzzled his face into her long dark hair. 'No regrets?'

'About what?'

'About trying for a baby with me?'

She smiled. 'So that's what this was all about, was it? And there was I thinking that maybe...'

He silenced her with a long, lingering kiss. 'I think we ought to make sure, don't you?'

He raised his head to look coaxingly into her eyes. She felt her body yearning to melt into his. He felt hard, erect, yet teasing, taking their love-making slowly this time...caressing her skin, exploring, driving her to distraction before the final ecstatic consummation...

Through the window she could hear the sound of revelry on the river. The bright lights of Paris were illuminating the dark night, reminding her that this was a city that never slept. And neither would she while she could stay awake and make love with Marcel...

Some time during the small hours, Marcel picked up the bedside phone and ordered champagne and smoked salmon sandwiches. The waiter who pushed in the trolley didn't blink an eyelid at the rumpled bed or the couple glowing in the aftermath of making love.

After he'd gone, Marcel raised himself and poured the champagne. Handing a glass to Debbie, he clinked the side of it with his own.

'Here's to our success,' he whispered. 'And if we don't succeed this time, we'll keep going until…'

'Until we're successful.' She hesitated. 'Marcel…'

She took a deep breath. She wanted so much to tell him how she really felt about their plan. How if they'd written it down as a contract on paper she would want to tear it into small pieces and…

'What is it, *chérie*?' He reached forward, caressing the side of her cheek, his eyes full of concern.

No, she had to hold back. She couldn't break up the rapport they had between them by demanding more than he was prepared to give.

She cleared her throat. 'Nothing. Just a little niggling worry about the future.'

He smiled. 'You're always worrying about the future. Take each day as it comes and it will all work out. You'll see.'

She sipped her champagne, telling herself that she would do just that. That was the secret. Take one day at a time and it would all work out easily. That was what she'd believed before she'd fallen in love, but now she knew the problems would always be there.

He reached forward and took her glass from her hand, placing it on the bedside table.

Drawing her against his hard body, he tried to reassure her that what they had between them was all she would ever need. She didn't want to voice her opinion that she knew she wanted their relationship to mean more to both of them.

But that would mean commitment, which she knew was totally out of the question where Marcel was concerned.

They were held up on the autoroute on the way back. A lorry had jackknifed and the police had had to close a large section of the road. After a slow crawl that took nearly four hours Marcel dropped her off at the house, saying that he needed to go to the hospital to check that everything was OK. No, he didn't need her to come in with him. She looked exhausted and should try to get some rest.

Climbing onto her bed, halfway through the afternoon, Debbie set the alarm for an hour ahead. She would wake up so that she could go to meet the school bus in the village. Yes, she did feel exhausted but she wanted very much to be reassured by the sight of her daughter.

Lying back on her bed, her mind became active again, reviewing the memorable events of her time away with Marcel. She would never forget how it had seemed as if they would be together for ever. She'd actively allowed herself to fantasise that their wonderful night was the precursor of many such liaisons. But when she came down to earth from her fantasy world, she knew that was all it was. Pure fantasy. The reality of her world was something quite different, and always would be while the man in her life was the totally un-committed Marcel.

Emma was delighted to see her as she got off the bus, rushing into Debbie's arms with a whoop of pure happiness. 'Mummy, Mummy, you're back! Sylvie said you might be late and I'd have to go home with her and Céline.'

Sylvie came forward, pushing the pram, smiling at Debbie. 'Did you have a good time in Paris?'

'Most enjoyable. Thank you for looking after Emma.

Perhaps Céline would like to come to stay with us again some time soon?'

Céline said she'd love to. Debbie and Sylvie agreed they'd fix a date over the phone when they had their diaries with them.

All through supper, Emma chattered happily about how she'd helped to look after the baby. She'd helped Sylvie to bathe her before they'd put her in her cot. The cot had a little pink quilt and lacy covers all round the side with tiny rosebuds embroidered on it.

'That's nice,' Debbie said, trying to concentrate on Emma's chatter but her mind still focusing on the events of the previous night and how wonderful it would be if she had her own baby. Wonderful...and yet so complicated.

She decided she needed some mature advice on the subject. Who better than her own father, who'd been through a very similar experience with her mother? Yes, as soon as Emma was asleep she would phone him.

She could hear Emma still enthusing about the baby's pretty bedroom. She really must concentrate and give Emma some feedback.

'The baby's bedroom sounds lovely,' Debbie said. 'And does she have many toys in her room?'

'Oh, lots of dolls and a big doll's house. She can't really play with them herself yet, so Céline and I helped her.' Emma paused, screwing up her little face into an enquiring expression. 'Mummy, there's one thing I don't understand. You know you told me the daddy planted a seed in the mummy to make a baby?'

'Yes, that's correct.' Debbie held her breath.

'Well, how does the daddy actually plant it? I mean, what does he have to...?'

Debbie took a deep breath. 'It's like this. The mummy and daddy lie close to each other and—'

'Sort of cuddling, are they?'

'Yes, it's a very special cuddle that mummies and daddies do.'

'So they must love each other, mustn't they?' Emma looked up at Debbie with innocent blue eyes. 'I mean, if they have to lie close to each other?'

'Yes, they have to love each other,' Debbie said slowly. Everything she was saying was simply reinforcing what she believed—in her own case anyway. She swallowed the lump in her throat before continuing.

'And because they love each other and lie very close, the daddy is able to put the seed that makes the baby in the mummy.'

'Wow! That's really clever! But, Mummy, does it hurt when the daddy puts the seed in the mummy?'

Debbie hesitated. She knew she had to tell her daughter the truth. No more prevarication.

'Actually, darling, it's rather nice.'

'Will I enjoy it when I'm a grown-up mummy and find a daddy to make a baby with?'

'I'm sure you will. Now, have you decided which story you want me to read tonight?'

Debbie spent longer than usual putting Emma to bed, giving her all the attention she craved. But as soon as she was asleep, Debbie remembered her earlier decision to ring her father. He was a wise man, with personal and professional medical experience that would help her sort out her problem.

She went downstairs into the sitting room, curled up on the sofa with a cup of coffee and dialled André Sabatier's mobile number. This was going to be a private conversation and she didn't want the whole of his household listening in.

'*Papa, c'est* Debbie.'

She spoke French with her father most of the time because her French was better than his English. In her younger days when he'd come over to England often, he'd been totally fluent. But now retired, André rarely needed to speak English except occasionally to his daughter and granddaughter.

'*Ah*, Debbie! *Comment ca va?*'

She told her father she was very well and asked how he was. He said the arthritis in his hip was still troubling him but he was playing tennis as much as he could so he didn't get stiff.

She'd never thought of her father as ever being anything but a young active man but he was now in his mid-sixties, although he didn't look it. The thought that his health wasn't good increased the guilt she'd been feeling at not visiting him while she'd been in Paris.

'I'm sorry to hear your arthritis is worse. Have you got a good orthopaedic consultant?'

'The best! He was a student of mine for a time when he was a youngster and thinking of specialising in general surgery. I keep him on his toes now, always asking awkward questions about what he's going to do with me.' André gave a little laugh before clearing his throat. 'So what's the news at your end, Debbie? Still enjoying your work in Urgences? What's the hospital at St Martin sur mer like? I've never been there. One of the purpose-built newer hospitals, isn't it?'

'Yes. It's a good hospital to work in. Excellent facilities. I've actually had a couple of days off.' She paused. 'Papa, I've been to Paris but I didn't have time to come out to see you and Louise while I was there.'

'That's perfectly all right, my dear. I know you're very busy. Was your visit to Paris something to do with your work at the hospital?'

'Not exactly…in fact, not at all! I was actually with a colleague, a male colleague. I'm very fond of him…' Her voice trailed away as she realised she didn't know how she was going to explain the situation.

'I see,' her father said in an easy tone. 'Sounds to me like you're more than fond of this man.'

'What makes you say that?'

She heard her father laughing on the end of the line. 'You forget I'm an expert diagnostician. From the sound of your breathy, excited voice I would say you were suffering from an acute or even chronic case of being in love. I'm intrigued. Do you want to tell me some more about your new boyfriend? Will I like him?'

She took a deep breath. 'I'm sure you would like him if you met him professionally. His name is Marcel De Lange and—'

'Yes, I know the man you mean. I met him at a conference once where I was speaking. He gave an excellent paper on…can't remember what at the moment. My memory isn't what it used to be. He was talking about some aspect of surgery he was keen to improve. He's working here in Paris at—'

'No, he's moved. He's working at the St Martin hospital as consultant in charge of Urgences. I'm sure you'll like him when—I mean if you meet him.' She hesitated. 'But there's a problem. You see…'

'He's not married, is he? He didn't have a wife with him when he was at the conference.'

'No, he's divorced, like me. And because we've both had such a terrible time with our previous partners, neither of us wants a committed relationship…but we would both like a baby. We thought that we might be able to find a solution to the problem if we got together.'

She'd spoken hurriedly in a matter-of-fact tone, as if the situation was perfectly natural.

There was silence at the other end as her father digested this information.

'*Papa, tu es toujours là?* Are you still there?'

'Yes, I'm still here, but I'm a bit confused. So you're planning to try for a baby together? Is that what you're leading up to, Debbie?'

'Yes, only it's not as simple as that…'

'Simple! Whoever said it was simple? Producing a child is certainly not simple.'

She drew in her breath. Her father's tone showed his disapproval.

'Well, it would be considerably simpler if I hadn't fallen in love with Marcel. That's the real problem. You see, when we decided we wanted to have a child together, neither of us wanted to make a commitment to a full-time relationship. We agreed that we'd do everything we could to give the child a good start in life but keep our own independent lives intact.'

'Ah! And now you want to change the rules, is that it?'

'Afraid so.'

A long pause. Debbie waited to hear if her father had any advice on this delicate situation. She waited. Eventually she heard him drawing in his breath, swirling a drink that had ice cubes in it. She could picture him now sunk deeply into the leather chair in his study, his brow furrowed as he gave all his attention to his daughter's problems, as he always had done.

'And how does Marcel feel about this?'

'That's the problem. I daren't tell him. I don't want to spoil the rapport we have between us. He wants to keep his freedom. He's such an independent sort of man and we both promised—'

'Debbie you're heading for trouble,' her father said quietly.

She felt a cold shiver running down her spine. 'But you and Mum managed to keep your independence and give me all the love I needed. You were always there for me, always...'

She was holding back tears now. How could her father say she was heading for trouble when he'd been through a similar experience? She'd phoned up for reassurance, not to be told that...

'I agree that both your mother and I gave you all the love you needed. But whereas your mother was adamant that she didn't want a committed relationship with me, I wanted everything with her. I wanted marriage, more children, a life devoted to each other. I wanted to show her all the love I felt for her but...'

He broke off and she heard him sighing deeply. 'I'm over it now because eventually I found Louise.' He lowered his voice. 'But it was your mother who was always the love of my life. She broke my heart and it was impossible to mend.'

Debbie swallowed hard. 'I had no idea! I mean, I knew that Mum was totally focused on her career but...' She broke off, feeling a great surge of pity for the strong, indomitable man who'd always been there for her, never realising how he'd suffered in the process.

'Debbie, don't go down that road. Pull out of this arrangement you've made with Marcel. He'll break your heart if you don't.'

'Papa, I'm too heavily committed.'

André drew in his breath. 'Are you already pregnant?'

'I may be.'

'If you're not pregnant, my advice is to give up the idea of having another child unless you're with someone who's going to live with you and love you for the rest of your life. I'm sorry I sound so negative, but my advice comes from bitter experience.'

'I can see that,' Debbie said quietly.

'Let me know…how things develop, won't you?'

'Of course. And thanks, Dad, for your advice.'

'I doubt you'll take it,' he said lightly. 'You'll probably decide to suffer as I did. But I sincerely hope you'll think long and hard about what you're taking on. A child is for life, and both parents need to be committed to the child…and to each other. My strongest piece of advice is to cool this relationship as soon as you can. And unless you find that you're pregnant, make a clean break and a fresh start.'

Her father hung up and Debbie cradled the phone in her hand for a few seconds, feeling terribly vulnerable. What had she taken on? The awful thing was that she wasn't sure that having another baby was worth paying the price of suffering like her father had done.

During the next couple of weeks at the hospital, she tried to remain as emotionally detached as possible from Marcel. But it was so difficult! They had to work together and being physically close as they struggled to save a patient's life or conferred about a difficult case was not conducive to cool, impersonal behaviour.

She saw the puzzled expression in Marcel's eyes when on a couple of occasions she said she couldn't go out with him that evening. She knew he wasn't fooled but was making the point that he had no hold on her. He respected her independence to live her own life.

Late one afternoon, as she was about to go off duty an unconscious patient was brought in. A witness testified that she'd seen a young woman falling from a car on the autoroute. Then another witness who'd been in a car close behind said they'd noticed the driver and the woman having an obviously heated argument. Shortly before the woman had fallen from the car, the driver had hit the woman. The door had then opened and the woman had fallen out before the driver had continued to leave the scene at speed.

The second witness was prepared to swear on oath that the driver had pushed the now badly injured woman out. Everything hinged on whether the woman could be revived to tell exactly what happened.

Marcel was dealing with another patient who'd sustained relatively minor burns when trying to put out a fire in the storeroom of the shop where he was working. Urgences was now swarming with policemen intent on getting at the truth. Marcel paged Debbie, asking her if she could take over his burns case. He needed to deal with the police and restore some order in Urgences so that his staff could concentrate on treating the unconscious woman.

'I don't like to ask you when you're supposed to be on your way home, but this is a real emergency and we're short-staffed this afternoon.'

'No problem,' Debbie said briskly. 'Francoise is collecting Emma.'

She hurried to the treatment room where Marcel had been treating the burns case. Marie was treating the burns on the patient's arms.

'First-degree burns,' she whispered. 'He's been very

lucky. Marcel has contacted the burns unit and we've got one of the team arriving shortly to take over.'

For a few minutes, Debbie helped with the preliminary treatment until the burns specialist arrived. As soon as she'd handed over she went to check on how Marcel was coping with the new emergency.

It was long past the time she should have gone off duty, but Urgences was still in a chaotic state. The press had now arrived and nobody seemed to be dealing with them. She found Marcel bending over his unconscious patient, shining a bright light into her eyes as he checked for her ophthalmic reaction. He looked up and smiled with relief as Debbie arrived.

'I've dealt with the police but now the press are asking for a statement. Apparently, the second witness is making a great fuss about what he saw. At this stage, whether she fell or whether she was pushed is of no interest to me. I'm a doctor, trying to save a patient's life. Will you deal with the press for me?'

'Of course.'

Debbie went out into the main reception area. The vociferous witness who had claimed that their patient had been pushed from the car was surrounded by several journalists, all keen to get a story.

Debbie moved into the middle of the crowd, politely requesting that they all leave as soon as possible.

'We have no further information to give you,' she said firmly. 'Later, when we have had time to assess the situation, a hospital spokesman will give you more details. But for the moment our only concern is that we should take care of our patients here in Urgences.'

'It's all gone quiet again out there,' Marcel said, looking up from his patient as Debbie returned to the cubicle where he was working. 'What did you do? Anaesthetise everybody?'

'They all went quietly. I think they thought I was more important than I am.'

'Oh, but you're very important, Debbie.' He lowered his voice. 'Especially to me.'

There was not as much as a flicker of an eyelid from the young houseman helping Marcel. But Debbie noticed that the two nurses who'd been assigned the job of handing over the instruments from the trolley were smiling with interest. The hospital grapevine had already picked up on the fact that she and Marcel had been seeing each other. She could tell that everyone was interested in where their relationship was heading.

If they only knew!

Marcel straightened up so that he could focus on what the CT scan had revealed. 'I'm going to transfer our patient to Theatre. It's essential that we relieve the intracranial pressure.'

Debbie looked across at the CT scan that Marcel was studying.

Marcel pointed to the trouble spot. 'See that great dark mass at the base of the skull?'

Debbie nodded. 'That looks like a sizeable haematoma, doesn't it?'

'Exactly!' Marcel peeled off his gloves.

The phone rang. 'It's the brain consultant, wanting to speak to you from Theatre,' one of the nurses said.

Marcel took the call. 'Fine. You're ready now? Yes, I'd like to be there. I agree, it's a complicated case.'

A junior doctor had arrived with a theatre nurse. The unconscious patient was carefully transferred to the trolley.

Debbie went out into the corridor. Marcel hurried after her. 'Thanks for staying on, Debbie.'

'Glad to be of help,' she said lightly.

He put his hand on her arm. 'Is everything OK with you?'

'Of course. Why do you ask?'

'Well, you've seemed a bit distant recently. Ever since we went to Paris you seem as if you're avoiding me.'

'Marcel!' Marie called. 'You're needed in Theatre.'

'I'm coming.' He leaned forward. 'We need to talk about…about whatever's worrying you.'

'We will,' she said quietly.

As soon as she began walking away from him she knew they would have to talk about how she was now feeling. Since her father had given her his advice to cool her relationship with Marcel, she'd been thrown into emotional confusion. Her head was telling her to take her father's advice. He'd been in the same situation and had suffered for the rest of his life because of his unrequited love for her mother. But her heart was telling her that because she loved Marcel she was prepared to suffer the hard times for the sake of the happy times in between.

As she walked down the corridor she reflected on what was uppermost in her mind at the moment. Her period was late. She would wait a few more days and then use the pregnancy kit she'd bought. And if she was pregnant, how was she going to deal with it? She should be overjoyed, but the initial scenario had changed. She'd changed so much since she and Marcel had first got together.

If only she could say the same for Marcel!

CHAPTER NINE

DEBBIE experienced feelings of extreme happiness mixed with alarm as she stared at the thin blue line. She'd half expected she would get a positive reaction with her pregnancy kit. When she'd first climbed out of bed this morning she'd felt decidedly queasy. A bit early in her pregnancy for that, but then she'd remembered how she'd felt for the first few months with Emma.

At the time she'd put some of her discomfort down to the fact that she'd had to contend with Paul moaning that he didn't think they could afford a baby. He'd asked her why she hadn't taken more care, insinuating that it had been all her fault.

It didn't seem to occur to Paul that he'd had anything to do with the conception. She'd had tonsillitis at the time and the antibiotics she'd been taking must have cancelled out the Pill. But she'd been thrilled when Emma had been born. She'd never for one second regretted having her daughter, though even with two salaries coming in, they had always seemed hard up. Paul had always been deliberately vague so, loving him unreservedly as she had, she hadn't realised at that point that he'd had a mistress.

She sat down on the stool in her bathroom and put her head in her hands as the unpleasant memories came flooding back. She'd thought that this time she would have been over the moon at the prospect of a much-wanted child, but the prospect of bringing up the child without Marcel there all the time suddenly seemed very daunting.

Her father's words had struck fear into her heart. He'd always kept up the pretence that all had been well when he'd visited them in London. But, looking back, she remembered her mother's cool manner on occasions. She'd always thought it had been because her mother had never had enough time to spend on the occasions when André had been in London.

Now that he'd explained the full story, it all fell into place. Her mother had been very focused on her career as a successful surgeon, one of few women to scale the heights that she had. But she'd also had fun in her private life, something which Debbie had accepted. Actually, she'd put it at the back of her mind and forgotten about it entirely!

Until her father had spoken about his broken heart. And now she'd got herself into exactly the same position. She mustn't be lulled into the idea that because she was the mother of Marcel's adored child he would feel under any obligation to be faithful to her. Her heart would be broken time after time in the future if she didn't pull herself together and hold onto her emotions.

Marcel was a handsome, sexy man who would undoubtedly have many girlfriends over the coming years. Their commitment to each other was to produce a child and go their separate independent ways. Marcel had said he wouldn't commit to any woman ever again. But that didn't preclude making love with women who were simply looking for a romantic liaison.

How naïve she had been when she'd agreed to try for a baby with Marcel! But love changed everything. Not necessarily for the better in her case.

She sat up and reached for a towel as she told herself

to snap out of it. She shouldn't have deliberately tried
for a baby if she'd had doubts about it. But she'd had
few doubts at the beginning of her big adventure with
Marcel. It will all work out, he'd told her constantly.
Think positively. Yes, that was what she had to do.
Concentrate on the main fact, that it would be wonderful to have another child in the house. A sister or brother
for Emma.

She stepped into her shower cubicle and turned the
taps full on. As the water cascaded down over her
shoulders she told herself that her little family would be
complete...wouldn't it? This was all she'd ever
wanted...wasn't it?

As she got dressed she decided that she would wait
until she was about three months pregnant before she
told Emma, make sure the pregnancy was fully established. The first three months was the period when most
miscarriages occurred and she would hate to disappoint
Emma.

But she would have to tell Marcel soon. She gathered
up some discarded clothes and ran with them downstairs
to load the washing machine. For the first time in her
life she felt she would like to stay at home and have a
completely domestic day. Spend her time mopping the
kitchen floor, doing some ironing. Anything but talk to
Marcel about the pregnancy.

OK, she told herself. A bit of early morning domestic
stuff and then off to the hospital. First priority after the
domestic bit...tell Marcel soon.

Soon as in that morning!

The reception area of Urgences was relatively quiet
when she arrived. The staff were going about their routine tasks. It was still early in the day. The overnight

emergencies had been treated and discharged or admitted. Time for the next set of emergencies to begin.

She asked Marie if Marcel was there yet. Marie said he was in his office. Debbie went along the corridor and tapped lightly on the door.

'*Entrez!*'

She took a deep breath, pushed open the door and walked purposefully across the carpet towards Marcel's desk.

Marcel looked up and smiled, pushing away the papers he was working on as he rose to his feet.

She took another deep breath. It would feel more natural if she told Marcel the news in English.

'Marcel, I've done a test this morning. I'm pregnant.'

'*Qu'est-ce que tu as dit?* What did you say?' Marcel ran round the desk to enfold her in his arms. 'Oh, Debbie, how wonderful! Come and sit down. We've got to make plans. I was hoping…I was praying… But now we need to make plans.'

Debbie smiled as she felt her tense body relaxing. Marcel's boyish enthusiasm was just what she needed to boost her morale.

'Hold on a moment, Marcel. We've got plenty of time. The baby's not due until next May. I'm going to carry on working as long as possible and—'

'Oh, no, you're not! I decided that when you fell pregnant I would arrange for the appointment of another doctor to replace you for at least the last three months of your pregnancy. It's better for you and the baby if you stop work, let's say in…January. That will give you plenty of time to prepare and—'

'Marcel!'

Debbie reached across and touched his arm. He was bending over her chair, his eyes shining with happiness.

This was the moment she'd longed for. The moment when she told Marcel that he was going to be a father. She didn't want to spoil the magic moment for him. Nothing had changed for him. This was all he'd wanted. To become a father. He was having no difficulty with accepting their original plan.

But her own feelings were now more complicated. She had to reaffirm her independence if she was going to save herself from having to mend her broken heart.

'Marcel, I'd like to be in charge of my pregnancy,' she said quietly. 'I'd like to organise my work schedule to suit me.'

He stared at her. 'It's your pregnancy but it's our baby, remember. I want only the best for the baby. And I don't want you to get tired so I'll set the wheels in motion so that we interview some doctors. We need another doctor who can speak good English. Your English has been so useful recently when we've had English tourists requiring treatment.'

He walked across to the window, pulling up the Venetian blinds so that the sun came streaming in.

'Oh, Debbie. I'm so happy! You've made me the happiest man in the world. I want to go around and shout the good news to everybody I meet.'

He turned round to face her again, his face radiant. 'I'm going to be a father! I'm going to—'

'Please, Marcel, let's keep it quiet for a while,' she said gently. 'I mean, it's early days and something might happen. You know as well as I do that from a medical point of view, until the pregnancy is firmly established it's better that...'

He walked back across the room and drew her gently to her feet, holding her tenderly as if she was very precious to him.

'Nothing is likely to happen, as you put it,' he said quietly. He hesitated, looking down at her with a quizzical expression. 'Is it that you simply don't want to announce the fact that you're having a baby with me?'

She looked up into his eyes and felt her body stirring with desire. But she was trying to remain focused on what she had to say. She had to establish the way that their relationship was to develop in the future, given that she wanted to limit the damage to her already bruised heart.

'Marcel, I'm going to tell everybody you're the father of my baby...but not yet. Give me a few weeks to think out what I'm going to say. I mean, it's not as if this was a conventional pregnancy, is it?'

He sighed. 'No, it's not. Is that what's been worrying you ever since we got back from Paris? You've been so quiet with me. Not at all like your usual self.'

She pulled herself away from his embrace so that she could think clearly. Whenever she was close to him it was difficult to remain objective.

'I've been feeling a bit queasy, that's all,' she said, hating herself for telling a white lie. It was half-true anyway. She had been feeling queasy. 'Now that I know for certain I'm pregnant, I'll be able to cope better.'

She lowered her voice, looking away so that she didn't have to watch the perplexed expression on his face. 'But, please, don't crowd me.'

He looked alarmed. 'Crowd you? What do you mean?'

She began again, in French this time. 'I need space. I need to come to terms with what's happening to my changing body...and to my changing life.'

Marcel took a step forward but seemed to check himself from reaching out towards her.

'Of course you need space, *chérie*,' he said. 'I shall respect your desire to remain independent even though you're carrying my child. So I'll contain my excitement and keep our secret for the first few weeks.'

'When my waistline starts to thicken at around four months, we'll make an announcement together but until then…'

'Four months! You want me to keep this to myself for four months? *C'est impossible, chérie!*'

'No it's not impossible. Please, Marcel.'

She knew she was playing for time. Time to come to terms with this new situation. The situation that they'd created and agreed on. But a situation that now filled her with apprehension about the future. Yes, she was thrilled that she was going to have another baby. She already loved the tiny life growing inside her.

But she couldn't help wishing that she and Marcel were fully committed to each other. That was never going to happen so she had to keep herself from being hurt too much and too often…as her father had been.

During the days that followed Marcel kept his promise not to reveal their news to anyone. They saw each other in their off-duty hours whenever they could. There was a small concert hall in the middle of St Martin sur mer, and Marcel was a member of the subscription ticket club. He asked Debbie to go with him on several occasions and she enjoyed the intimate atmosphere of the chamber music concerts.

The standard of playing by the instrumentalists was first class because good musicians came from other regions of France to supplement the long list of enthusiastic local players. She found herself looking forward to each concert she attended with him. And she enjoyed having supper with him afterwards in one of the small restaurants close by. The initial weeks of her pregnancy were passing by more easily than she'd anticipated on that first morning when she'd done the pregnancy test.

One evening, when she was three months pregnant, a string quartet came down from Paris and played music by Haydn and Brahms. As the haunting music of the strings wafted over her, she turned to glance at Marcel. He was looking so handsome this evening. His happiness at being a prospective father was palpable. Some of their colleagues had remarked on how well he looked during the last few weeks but he'd contained his secret with admirable restraint.

As if sensing she was looking at him, he turned towards her, smiled and reached for her hand. She felt a frisson of desire ripple through her. She knew that Marcel had wanted to make love with her during the past few weeks. Several times recently when they'd said goodnight, he'd held her very close. But she knew he'd been holding himself back because she'd indicated that she wanted to play safe in the crucial early stages of her pregnancy.

Tonight, she decided, if Marcel lingered over their goodnight kiss she would make it obvious that she still desired him. She could allow a little romance to creep into their relationship now and again if that was what they both wanted. In the future, when Marcel moved away from her, it wouldn't be so easy for her. She wouldn't be so sure that he wanted to make love with her. But now, when she knew it was what he wanted, she was determined to go for it.

She had no idea if Marcel had been seeing any other women during the past few weeks. That was one idea she would have to accept if she was to survive emotionally in the future.

She'd had no reason to suspect him of seeing someone else. She couldn't bear to think about it and banished it from her mind whenever the awful thought cropped up!

Going out into the cool evening after the concert, Marcel put an arm around her waist as he guided her to the car park.

'I thought it was a very good concert tonight,' he said, as he held open the passenger door for her. 'What did you think of it?'

Debbie smiled. 'I enjoyed it very much. I thought the first violinist was exceptionally good.'

'So did I. He's with us again in a week's time, playing the Bach violin concerto in A minor. If you're free that evening, I've got a couple of tickets.'

'Thank you. I'd love to come.'

Marcel started the engine. 'Which restaurant would you like to go to tonight? I phoned Au Bon Acceuil and they only had tables early in the evening. We could go to—'

'If you've got some eggs, I could make an omelette back at your place. I feel like relaxing tonight in a place where I can take my shoes off and loosen my belt.'

'What a good idea!'

Marcel drove out through the gates of the car park, looking each way before driving onto the seafront road.

'Except I'll make the omelette while you put your feet up and watch me, Debbie. No, I insist! You've been on your feet all day.'

In the kitchen, ensconced in the armchair near the cooker, Debbie felt cosseted as she sipped her glass of orange juice. This was the sort of intimacy she craved now that she was carrying Marcel's child. A family atmosphere. Whenever she managed to arrange this cosy kind of ambience in the future, she would savour every moment of the experience as she was doing now.

She was heading for heartbreak, allowing herself to get carried away as she intended to tonight, but she would hold back later! For one night she wanted to imagine that they were a real family. Emma had been invited to another sleepover at the house of one of her friends from school.

She hadn't yet told Marcel that she'd like to stay the night. She wouldn't blame him if he turned her down! He'd probably given up on her because of the way she'd tried to cool down their relationship. She'd better play it by ear, make sure it was what they both wanted. It wasn't too late to drive home.

Marcel was whisking the eggs now. He looked up and smiled at her.

'So you had to loosen your belt, did you? That's exciting news! I remember you said that when your waist thickened we would announce our secret to the world and in particular to our medical colleagues.'

Debbie smiled. 'My waist hasn't really thickened yet. It's pure imagination on my part. But my belt felt uncomfortable during the concert. I remember saying that it would thicken around four months. When baby begins to show, we'll make our announcement.'

Marcel tossed a sizeable slab of butter into the omelette pan and took a sip from his glass of wine as he waited for it to sizzle.

'Have you arranged to have a three-month scan?'

She hesitated, hoping that Marcel wouldn't suggest he would like to go with her.

'Actually, I've arranged to go tomorrow. I'll have a photograph taken and bring it to show you,' she added quickly.

Marcel put the whisked eggs into the prepared pan. 'I should hope you will.'

She felt relieved that he hadn't asked to come with her. It was impossible not to admire the way he'd stuck to his promise and allowed her to go it alone for these first few weeks. But she had no idea how he would behave when she was four months pregnant and their secret came out.

'That omelette was delicious!' Debbie said as she helped herself to salad from the large wooden bowl on the kitchen table.

'I'll drive you home tonight, Debbie,' Marcel said. 'I don't like the idea of you driving so late by yourself. If something happened to you on the way home…'

'Actually, Marcel, I'd like to stay the night if that's OK with you. Emma's away for the night with friends.'

Marcel's eyes flickered but his enigmatic expression didn't change. 'My *femme de ménage* always keeps the guest room ready. I'll make sure there's a dressing-gown in there for you when you go upstairs.'

Her frustration mounted. Well, she couldn't blame Marcel for interpreting her wishes in that way. He'd obviously come to terms with the cooler atmosphere in their relationship.

'Thank you,' she said politely, feeling a cold chill settling around her heart. She would have to get used to this sort of ambivalent situation in the future.

Looking across the table, she saw that Marcel was

smiling, his sexy lips parted as he studied her enquiringly. It was almost as if he was reading her thoughts. With swift fluid movements he rose to his feet and came round the table, putting his hands on her shoulders.

'Alternatively, you could share my bed,' he said huskily. 'It's a big bed and you won't even know I'm there...unless you invite me over to your side for a goodnight kiss or...'

'Marcel, I want you to hold me close tonight,' she whispered, looking up at him with a shy smile. 'I feel so...'

She checked herself before she could reveal her true feelings. He must never know how vulnerable she felt. She must continue to pretend that she loved her independence, her lack of commitment to him. Otherwise she would lose him completely and there would be no more romantic liaisons. If she could learn to enjoy the brief times of happiness she spent with Marcel, she wouldn't suffer as much from unrequited love as her father had done.

He held out his hand and drew her to her feet before holding her close. Gently he bent down and lifted her into his arms.

'You won't be able to do that much longer,' she joked as he carried her out through the kitchen door.

'You're still as light as a feather,' he whispered as he began to mount the stairs. 'I'm going to be very gentle with you tonight, Debbie, simply hold you in my arms, but...'

'Please, darling, let's make love.'

She looked up at him as he carried her up the stairs, wondering how she could so easily dismiss the small voice in her head that was telling her to get a grip on her emotions. Make love, yes, but don't lose your heart to him... Impossible! But would she think it was worth the inevitable heartache for one more heavenly night with Marcel?

He paused as they reached the bend in the staircase, lowering his head so that he could kiss her on the lips. She parted her lips, savouring the moment, intent on remembering this night for the rest of her life. It would be a long time before she allowed herself another night of bliss like this...

Waking up in Marcel's bed, Debbie stretched herself, feeling as lithe and supple as a kitten. It had been a totally different experience, making love with Marcel last night. She had never known such tenderness before...and yet the passion had still been there. He'd simply been so touchingly careful when he'd caressed her. And when he'd moved inside her he'd seemed conscious that he mustn't harm the baby. Their bodies had moved together as if performing a slow, leisurely, rhythmical dance.

As she'd given herself up to the steady rhythm it had seemed to Debbie a celebration of her pregnancy. As their bodies had fused, she'd felt the pace of the rhythm increasing and when the climax had come she'd called out Marcel's name, clutching his back so hard that she felt she may have bruised him.

She hadn't wanted him to leave her body. She'd wanted to stay like that, fused together, as if they would never be apart.

So different from reality! She watched Marcel as he stirred now in his sleep. It was time to tiptoe away. She didn't want to be here when he woke up. She couldn't bear to repeat the experience. Last night she'd allowed herself to imagine that they were a real family. Today she had to come back down to earth.

Quietly she followed the trail of her discarded clothes, picking up garments as she went out onto the landing.

'Debbie, what are you doing?'

As she heard Marcel's sleepy voice, she sighed. Too late! She poked her head round the bedroom door. 'I've got to get back home. I want to change my clothes and pick up some things I need for the scan this morning.'

'But it's so early. It's still dark. Come back to bed and I'll bring you a hot drink and something to eat. You shouldn't go out on an empty stomach in your condition.'

She went back across the room and leaned down to kiss Marcel's cheek. He looked so utterly desirable with his rumpled hair and little-boy expression as he rubbed his eyes.

'I have to go,' she said firmly.

Marcel groaned. 'I shall never understand you. Perhaps that's part of the fascination. You're such an enigma.'

He put out a hand to detain her, but she evaded his grasp. As she made for the door she was thinking that it was good to know he found her fascinating. But fascination would never be enough for him to make a life-long commitment to her.

'Don't forget to have a photo made of our baby,' he called as she went out onto the landing.

'I promise.'

She hurried down the stairs, anxious to be out of the house before she could change her mind and go back to snuggle up beside Marcel again.

Her body was still tingling with the aftermath of their

love-making. It had been a heavenly experience, spending the night with Marcel again. She had no regrets about letting down her guard. She planned to do this from time to time in the future—when she felt that it was what Marcel wanted, too.

But now it was time to listen to the rational sensible small voice in her head and stop following her heart. It seemed simple to her now that their romance should continue for as long as Marcel still wanted her. But she was storing up heartache for the future. Sooner or later he would tire of being part-time lover to the mother of his child.

And that was when he would cool their relationship—as her mother had done with her father—and Debbie knew her heart would break...

CHAPTER TEN

AS SHE lay on the examination couch, waiting for the scan to begin, Debbie looked up at the white ceiling above her, feeling decidedly nervous. She tried to focus on one spot on the ceiling. There was a hook with a light hanging down. There was no bulb in the light socket. She wondered why. She closed her eyes. Trying to distract herself by concentrating on her surroundings didn't help.

She'd scanned many pregnant women during her training in obstetrics but it was quite a different prospect when she was the patient. She was longing to see the fuzzy images of her baby on the monitor, but at the same time she was apprehensive.

She wanted her baby to be perfect in every way, for her own as well as for Marcel's sake. Having witnessed a full range of pregnancy complications during her medical training and work as a doctor, the slightest perceived abnormality that appeared on the screen would make her active brain go into overdrive.

'Madame Sabatier?'

A kindly middle-aged motherly-looking nurse came in and smiled down at her. *'Vous êtes prête, madame?'*

Debbie smiled back and said, yes, she was quite ready. As she watched the nurse massaging the greasy scanning cream over her abdomen she knew she was glad to have chosen a private obstetric clinic away from the hospital. It would have been impossible to keep the grapevine tongues from wagging if she'd simply gone along to the hospital obstetric department.

The clinic she'd chosen was several kilometres from the hospital, set in lovely, well-kept grounds, inland from St Martin sur mer. It was an old château that had been converted into a fully equipped obstetric and gynaecological clinic.

Her medical consultant had been utterly discreet when she'd first gone to see him. She'd told him that she was a single mother and this was her second child. He'd examined her and pronounced her in good health. He had asked if the father of the baby was healthy and she'd said he was. That was the only time the father had been mentioned. And she hadn't even told him she was a doctor.

At that point it hadn't seemed relevant and she'd been intent on keeping her anonymity. News travelled fast in medical circles!

A medical technician was switching on the screen. Debbie could feel the nurse moving the scanner over her abdomen. She focused her eyes on the screen set to one side of the examination couch.

'There, I can see him...or her!' she cried out excitedly.

The nurse turned her head to look at the screen as she continued to move the scanner over Debbie's abdomen.

'Do you want to know the sex of your baby, Madame Sabatier?'

'Yes, I think I do.'

'And the father, does he want to know?'

Debbie had no idea. It wasn't something they'd discussed. 'Probably,' she said vaguely. 'The image on the screen is very small. It's not always possible to discern the sex with a scan at three months, is it?'

'Sometimes it's possible,' the nurse said. 'If not, we can run the test on you afterwards to determine the sex of your baby.'

'There! Look just there, Nurse! I'm sure that's a boy, don't you think?'

The nurse smiled. 'I think you're right, but we'll run a test at the end to make sure. Were you hoping for a boy?'

Debbie smiled back. 'I'm just hoping for a healthy child. My daughter wants a baby sister but if it really is a boy I know she'll still be thrilled.'

'What did your daughter say when you told her you were pregnant?'

'I haven't told her yet.' Debbie hesitated. 'You know, first three months, wanting to make sure that everything's OK before...'

'Oh, you must tell her soon! Let her share in the excitement and wonder of Mummy having a baby. You've got a healthy baby and your own health is excellent, according to your case notes. I've got four children and each new baby was a wonderful shared experience for the others.'

'I'm sure it was. I'll tell her soon. Are you going to take a photo of my baby?'

'Of course! It's standard practice here. Your daughter will want to see it...and the baby's father, I expect.'

Driving along the road to St Martin, Debbie reflected on her morning as a patient. It had been a strange experience. She'd felt so vulnerable when she'd been in the hands of the capable nurse. She would have to let go and learn to trust again. Listen to advice from those who'd been through more childbirth experiences than herself. She was never going to have a cosy family unit, mother, father and children all in the same house, but she could make her unconventional family as happy as possible…under the circumstances.

She took one hand off the steering-wheel to touch her bag on the passenger seat. She'd got three pictures of her son. The test had confirmed she was carrying a boy. One copy for Emma, one copy for herself and one copy for Marcel.

She was nearing the village now. She'd taken the whole day off duty so had the whole of the afternoon to herself. Bliss! She went into the house, poured a glass of milk from the fridge, kicked off her shoes and lay down on the sofa.

Her mobile phone rang. She cursed silently as she reached into the depths of her bag.

'How did it go?' Marcel asked in English.

She smiled. 'The baby's fine. He's fine.'

'He?'

'Yes, I thought I could see he was a boy on the screen. It was a bit fuzzy so they tested me to make sure.'

'That's wonderful! And everything is OK with you?'

'I was pronounced perfectly fit.'

'Have you got a photo of the scan?'

'I've got three—one for you, one for me and one for Emma.'

'When will you give it to her?'

Debbie hesitated. 'I was going to wait another month until I started showing but maybe I'll tell her about the baby this evening. When I've finally decided how I'm going to explain the situation. She's only six but—'

'Would you like me to come over and help you out

with all the inevitable questions? You'll have to tell her I'm the father, won't you?'

Again she hesitated before relief flooded through her. The explanation would be complicated but with Marcel's help it would be easier.

'Yes, I think we're agreed you'd be with me when I tell Emma.'

'Why do you sound so apprehensive? Emma will be thrilled to know she's going to have a baby brother.'

Debbie sighed. 'I know. It's explaining that you're the father that's the difficult bit.' She paused. 'I believe I told you she doesn't want anyone to replace her own father.'

'I've no intention of trying to take his place! Emma's probably realised that by now. We get on very well when we see each other.'

'I know you do. But also Emma's idea of how babies are conceived is still a bit sketchy. I gave her a true version that a six-year-old would understand but there are gaps in her knowledge that could be a bit tricky.'

'Oh, don't worry about it. It's not rocket science, is it? She's an intelligent six-year-old. She'll be able to understand what happened.'

That's what I'm afraid of! Debbie thought anxiously. 'We'll see what she makes of it when we talk this evening.'

'I'll finish early if possible. *A tout à l'heure*, see you soon.'

She lay back against the cushions, her hands clasped over her abdomen. Yes, her tummy did feel a bit more rounded already. Well, her dear little baby boy was swimming around in his own private pool, getting bigger every day. She felt drowsy. She gave in as her eyelids drooped, falling quickly into a deep sleep.

*   *   *

It was late when she woke up. She glanced at the sitting-room clock. Only minutes now to get to the bus stop in the village and meet Emma! She'd told Francoise she would collect her today as she had a day off.

Jumping up, she reached for her warm jacket, which was still on a chair where she'd flung it when she'd come in. Hurrying out of the house, she slammed the door shut before checking for her keys.

Relief! The keys were in her jacket pocket. She was barely awake yet and it was difficult to concentrate. Thoughts about the baby were running through her head, mixed with thoughts about Marcel.

He was coming to see her this evening. That bit she remembered clearly. She turned up the hood of her jacket as a thin drizzle began. The sky was already becoming dark as the clouds loomed overhead.

Tonight was the big night when she would tell Emma about the coming baby, when she would have to explain somehow that Marcel was the baby's father. Her sharp-witted daughter with the ever-enquiring mind wouldn't let her off lightly about that situation! What she would make of it, Debbie had no idea.

There she was, already stepping off the bus with a purposeful step. For an instant Emma reminded Debbie of her mother. The long blonde hair, the determined self-confidence. Emma would need to be given all the facts this evening and the questions would be endless.

'Emma!'

'Mummy!' As she ran towards her Debbie realised she was still an innocent child. She would be receptive to everything that Debbie told her this evening. It was a big responsibility to teach her about the unconventional situation that she was going to be part of. It would have been so much more preferable if Debbie could have given her daughter a warm, loving, conventional family. She would have to work extra hard at smoothing the path ahead for both of them.

'What time is Marcel coming?' Emma asked as mother and daughter sat at the kitchen table.

'He's going to try and get here as soon as he can leave the hospital,' Debbie said, hoping it would be sooner rather than later. Since she'd told Emma that Marcel was going to come to the house that evening, she'd been full of impatience to see him. Debbie found more and more that she was glad she wasn't going to be alone when she gave Emma the news about the baby.

She spooned some pasta on to Emma's plate before adding some tuna.

Emma began eating hungrily before pausing. 'Aren't you going to have some, Mummy?'

'I'm not hungry yet, darling. I'll have something later.'

'Will Marcel be staying for supper?'

'He might be. It depends on whether he has to go back to the hospital or not.'

But most importantly, she thought, it depends on how things go between us after we've announced the news to you!

Emma finished everything on her plate before putting down her fork and taking a drink of milk. Halfway through the glass she stopped, pricking up her ears as she heard the sound of tyres crunching on the drive.

'That's Marcel. I recognise the sound of his car.' Putting down her glass, she jumped down from the table and ran out into the hall, yanking open the front door and shrieking with delight.

Debbie waited in the kitchen, trying to calm her nerves. She could hear her daughter's excited voice mingling with Marcel's deep tones.

Emma arrived back first. 'Look at the flowers Marcel has brought you, Mummy! Aren't they beautiful?'

Emma was completely dwarfed by the huge bouquet of roses she was carrying. 'Can I get that big vase to put them in? I'll be very careful and I won't break the stems like I did last time you let me do the flowers.'

'I'll help you,' Debbie said quietly, as she reached for the huge earthenware vase before placing it on the table.

She looked across at Marcel who was still standing in the doorway of the kitchen as if he was uncertain of his welcome. She smiled to reassure him.

'Thank you so much, Marcel,' she said. 'I love roses.'
'I know.'
'Would you like a drink?'
'Later perhaps. Shall we talk first?'

She nodded. 'I'll just help Emma with the roses and then— Ooh, careful, darling...'

Debbie reached out to catch hold of the huge vase before it toppled off the table. 'I'll put the water in and then you can help me to arrange them.'

'Let me snip off the ends of the roses, Emma,' Marcel said. 'Where do you keep your scissors?'

Emma pulled open the cutlery drawer and held the scissors towards Marcel, taking great care to hold them with the handles toward him.

'I can see you've been well trained how to handle instruments,' Marcel said as he took the scissors from Emma and began to snip at the stalks of the roses.

'Oh, yes. My mummy taught me how to handle knives and scissors. My French grandpa used to be a surgeon and my English grandmother was a surgeon as well. Like you are, Marcel. Did you know that?'

'Yes, your mummy told me.' Marcel said as he continued snipping.

Emma climbed up on a chair to watch, solemnly handing over each rose in turn. 'Grandma died before I was born but I've seen pictures of her. She was very beautiful. A bit like Mummy really, only with blonde hair. That's where my blonde hair came from. Mummy got her dark hair from Grandpa André.'

Emma watched Marcel closely. 'You're very clever at cutting, aren't you? Do you have to cut people open and then sew them up again?'

'Sometimes,' Marcel said solemnly. 'Not as much as I used to now that I work in Accident and Emergency.'

'I can't decide whether to be a surgeon or work in Accident and Emergency when I grow up. What do you think I should do, Marcel?'

'Well, you could do both. You could go through all your surgical training, work for a while as a surgeon and then go into Accident and Emergency, like I did. Everything's possible once you've finished all your training.'

He paused. 'I might go back to being a surgeon one day. Who knows what will happen in the future?'

He looked across at Debbie, his eyes giving nothing away. As their eyes met she felt a tremor of apprehension. It was so good to be here with Marcel behaving like a real father, as if he were part of the family. But for how long could she hope for this kind of cosy intimacy?

Emma began helping Debbie to arrange the prepared roses, taking great care as she put each one separately into the vase.

'Why did you change from being a surgeon?' Emma asked.

Marcel put the final rose into the vase. 'That's a long story. I'll tell you one day. But now I think Mummy has got something to tell you.'

Debbie picked up the vase and placed it on the kitchen dresser. 'Shall we all sit round the table?'

Emma looked at her quizzically. 'Is it an important something you're going to tell me? You look kind of…fierce. I haven't done something wrong, have I?'

Debbie smiled as she tried to adopt a more relaxed appearance. Years from now, Emma would remember the evening when the grown-ups explained how she would have a baby brother.

'No, you haven't done anything wrong, darling. Come and sit here next to me. I've got something really exciting to tell you…'

'Is Grandpa André coming to see us?'

'No, it's even more exciting.' She took a deep breath as her eyes locked with Marcel's across the table. 'I'm going to have a baby.'

Emma's eyes widened. 'Honestly? Mummy, that's wonderful!' She flung her arms around Debbie's neck, kissing her cheek enthusiastically. 'Oh, thank you! I knew you could get a baby if—'

She broke off and sat down on her chair, looking perplexed. 'But you can't be having a baby. You haven't got a daddy to help you, have you? Unless…'

She looked across the table at Marcel. 'Did you plant a baby seed in Mummy's tummy?'

Marcel nodded solemnly. 'Yes, I'm the baby's daddy.'

Emma digested this piece of information but still looked puzzled. 'I'm not sure I understand.'

'Marcel will be the new baby's daddy but not your daddy,' Debbie said.

Emma considered this for a few seconds. 'But he could be my second daddy, couldn't he?'

Marcel smiled with relief. 'I'd love to be your second daddy.'

Debbie swallowed the lump in her throat as she watched the two people she loved most in the world bonding.

'But, Mummy...' Emma turned to fix her puzzled eyes on Debbie. 'You said that when the daddy puts the seed in the mummy, they have to love each other so they can have a special cuddle. Does that mean that you love Marcel?'

Debbie looked across the table at Marcel. She could feel tears pricking behind her eyelids. She mustn't cry, but the situation was all too poignant. She would love to say that, yes, she loved Marcel, but...

As her eyes met Marcel's she saw an expression of deep tenderness. He stood up and came round the table to put an arm around her shoulders.

'I don't know whether Debbie loves me, but I certainly love her,' he said, his voice husky with emotion.

Debbie was still holding back the tears but now they were tears of happiness. She could feel Marcel's arm around her shoulders, so comforting, so reassuring. She couldn't believe he'd said he loved her.

'That's OK, then,' Emma said. 'Marcel planted the baby seed because he loves you, Mummy. Do you love him?'

'Yes, I do,' she whispered hoarsely.

She could feel his arm tighten on her shoulders.

He leaned down so that he could speak quietly to her.

'Does that mean we can negotiate new terms in our contract?'

She smiled. 'I think we'd better.'

'What does negotiate mean, Marcel?'

Marcel sat down on a chair and hoisted Emma onto his lap. 'It's what people do when they get together and talk over something that's a problem. Your mother and I had a problem but I think we've just solved it.'

'Oh, good! You don't need me to help you, do you? The teacher sets us problems at school and I'm quite good at getting them right.'

'It's kind of you to offer, Emma,' Marcel said gently, 'but I think your mummy and I can work this one out by ourselves.'

He reached across and took hold of Debbie's hand.

It was only a squeeze of his fingers but to Debbie it was a magic moment she would never forget.

Later, much later, when Emma was fast asleep, Debbie and Marcel sat on the sitting-room sofa, their hands locked together.

'I didn't dare to hope you'd changed,' Marcel said. 'You were so intent on remaining independent. And I thought you'd been hurt so badly before that you'd never be able to love again.'

'I tried so hard not to love you. But I couldn't help falling in love. And then I just kept on pretending nothing had changed because I thought you wanted to stick to our original plan. I thought that if I made my true feelings clear, I would frighten you away and we wouldn't even be friends.'

'I very soon realised that I wanted to be more than a part-time father. I wanted to be with you all the time.

But you were so unpredictable. Especially the last few weeks. I tried to put that down to your pregnancy but—'

'It was because I had a long conversation on the phone with my father. He told me that it had been very hard for him to keep up the pretence that all was well when I was a child. He'd always been in love with my mother. He wanted to marry her but she refused him. All his life while he was giving me so much love he suffered because his love for my mother was unrequited. When I told him about our baby plan and explained I'd fallen in love with you, he advised me to cool our relationship. He said he didn't want me to suffer as he had done.'

Marcel drew her against him. 'I'll never do anything to make you suffer, Debbie,' he whispered.

She snuggled against him. It felt so wonderful to be so sure that he loved her. She eased herself out of his arms and looked up at him.

'Thank you for letting me go it alone for the first three months of my pregnancy. Now that I know how you really feel about me, I'd like you to be in on every stage I go through.'

He smiled. 'That's a relief! I haven't felt like a real father until today.' He hesitated. 'Actually, I've set the wheels in motion to find a replacement for your maternity leave.'

She gave him a wry smile. 'That was one area we didn't agree on, wasn't it?'

'All we've got to agree on is when you stop working. The medical agency I've been dealing with in London has chosen the ideal candidate. She's working in Accident and Emergency in a hospital in the north of England but has agreed to spend a year working here at St Martin.'

'A year!'

Marcel grinned. 'I'm covering all eventualities. You might want to spend a few months at home with the baby. She can work alongside you if you do choose to come back soon after the birth. I've got to let her have the date she'll be required to start so that she can give in her notice.'

'I see. She's a doctor in A and E at the moment, you say?'

'Yes, her name's Jacqueline Manson. Likes to be called Jacky, I believe. She's got a French mother and an English father so she's totally bilingual, which will be useful. The question I need you to answer is when will you agree to give up work?'

'I know you suggested three months before due date, but how about two months?'

'OK. We could agree to compromise. I'll ensure that Dr Manson is here three months before.' He hurried on before Debbie could intervene. 'That way, she'll be there if you do decide to stop earlier. And if you actually do continue till two months before, you can help Jacky to settle into her new job and also she can take over from you any time you might be feeling tired.'

Debbie smiled and held her hand out. 'A good compromise. Let's shake on that. Now, is that the end of the negotiations?'

'There's one more question I have to ask you,' he said, his tone changing to one of deep tenderness.

She looked up into his eyes and a tremor of excitement ran through her.

'Darling, will you marry me?' he asked, his voice vibrant with emotion.

'Yes,' she whispered, her heart so full of love she could barely speak.

He lowered his head and kissed her gently on the mouth. She parted her lips to savour the wonderful moment. The moment when she knew that all her seemingly impossible dreams were coming true.

'I don't want to tire you,' he whispered. 'But it would be wonderful to cement our new agreement in the appropriate manner.'

'I'm not in the least bit tired…now.' She held out her arms towards him. 'If you were to help me negotiate the stairs…'

The ancient church of St Martin was completely full. Some people were standing at the back of the church, others had congregated in the churchyard. There was a brisk wind coming off the sea. Just five days to Christmas the weather was predictably chilly.

As Debbie walked up the path on her father's arm, she looked up at the sky. A few clouds floated overhead but no snow—yet. The odds of a white Christmas were shortening every day. For a moment she allowed herself to imagine how wonderful it would be to be marooned inside by the log fire on Christmas Day with Marcel and Emma, watching the snow drifting down outside the windows.

'You make a beautiful bride,' her father said quietly. 'I'm so glad everything's worked out for you. You're a very lucky girl.'

'I know,' Debbie said. 'I still can't believe that I'm living my perfect dream.'

She felt a little tug on the back of her white satin dress. Emma, looking like a little angel in her long fairy-tale bridesmaid's dress, was saying something in a loud stage whisper.

'Mummy, I just trod on my skirt and a bit of it got torn. Can you sew it up for me?'

The people standing on the edge of the path were admiring the feisty little bridesmaid who was in no way overawed by the occasion. Debbie smiled as she bent down to speak to her daughter.

'I'll mend your dress when we get home, darling. Oh, it doesn't look too bad. But you'll have to hold your skirt up so you don't trip.'

Jacky Manson, the new doctor who would be replacing Debbie at the hospital, stepped forward. 'I've got a couple of safety pins in my bag, Emma. Let me fix it for you. It won't take a moment.'

'Thanks, Jacky,' Debbie said, as her new friend bent down to pin Emma's dress up.

Debbie had become very fond of the new English doctor who she had been liaising with in the lead up to her taking her place while she was on maternity leave. But she was something of a mystery. Debbie wondered why a first-class doctor like Jacky, with an excellent job in England, would want to spend a year filling in for someone on maternity leave. It was her considered opinion that there was a man involved in Jacky's decision.

'You make a beautiful bridesmaid, Emma,' Jacky said as she hid the pins at the back of the torn dress. As she stepped back to the edge of the path she whispered, 'Good luck, Debbie!'

'Thank you.'

'Thanks, Jacky,' Emma said. 'Mummy, which home are we going back to? Can we go to Marcel's home?'

'Yes, we're going to live there all the time soon. That will be our home.'

'Ooh, lovely!'

André touched his daughter's arm. 'They're waiting for us in the church, *chérie*.'

'I'm ready, Papa,' Debbie said, taking his arm again. As she moved forward she could feel the rustle of the petticoat under her satin gown. Marcel had insisted on taking her to Paris to choose her wedding dress. She'd enlisted the help of Louise and had chosen a very simple beautifully cut gown at one of the designer boutiques her stepmother frequented.

Marcel had spent the morning with André as both men had been forbidden to see the gown until the wedding day. It had been a relief to find that the two most important men in her life got on together as if they were old friends. André had completely forgotten his misgivings about his future son-in-law now that he realised the situation was completely different to his own.

Despite her pregnancy, her shape had changed very little. The gown was her usual size but the seamstress in the boutique had let out a couple of seams at the waist. The sleeves were long and fitted closely to her arms. At the wrist of each sleeve was a strip of white faux mink, which helped to keep out the cold. A wider strip of the same faux fur adorned the hem of her fluted, exquisitely embroidered gown.

As she walked into the church she felt as if she was a princess going to meet her prince. The haunting music hung in the air as she went down the aisle. He was standing in front of the altar, her handsome prince. Her heart gave a little leap of excitement as he turned to look at her. His expression was one of love and admiration as she left her father's side to join him. The music ceased but her dream continued.

Looking up into Marcel's eyes, Debbie knew she would come down to earth one day soon. And there would be times ahead when they might have to face difficult problems. But the most important thing that would help them through any problem was knowing that they both loved each other.

And love changed everything…

EPILOGUE

DEBBIE put baby Thiery back in his cot on her side of the bed. She lingered a while, her fingers gently caressing the soft downy hair on his tiny head. The hair was still baby blond but it would probably change. He had long legs already like Marcel. And she could tell already that he was going to be handsome just like his father.

Marcel stirred in his sleep and opened his eyes.

'Did you just feed Thiery?'

Debbie smiled. 'Yes, and you slept through it. You didn't hear him crying out at the beginning when I changed his nappy?'

Marcel raised himself on one elbow so that he could look down at his beautiful wife.

'I didn't hear a thing.'

'That's what you always say!'

'Well, I'd be no good at breastfeeding, would I? For a six-week-old baby, Thiery is a hungry little man. Would you like me to bring you something to drink, hot, cold from the fridge or…?'

'No, thanks, I'm working my way through this flask of water to replace the fluids I'm giving out.'

'You know, motherhood suits you.' He leaned forward and caressed her cheek lovingly. You always look so radiant now…even in the middle of the night.'

'I'm happy, that's the reason. I've got everything I ever wanted. Emma's happy as well. Have you noticed?'

Marcel nodded. 'She adores her little brother. She told me today she didn't mind he was a boy, but next time could we try for a sister for her.'

Debbie laughed. 'Did you explain that we don't get a choice in the matter?'

'No, I changed the subject quickly. I thought we could deal with that one together some time.'

'And the fact that mummies like to have a breathing space between babies,' Debbie said.

'But not too much of a space,' Marcel said.

She smiled. 'Of course not. When I had my six-week check-up today I was declared completely fit. Everything's back in place.' She hesitated. 'So all the signs are that we could make the space between Thiery and the next baby quite small.'

Marcel kissed the side of her cheek. 'You're wonderful! So you've really decided not to go back to work for a while? I'm so glad!'

'I think Jacky will be, too. She's enjoying her work at the hospital. I was right about her, wasn't I?'

'Oh, you mean about a man being involved with her decision to come over to France? Yes, you were, but it's all a bit complicated, isn't it? I wouldn't like to speculate how...'

'Well, I think it's terribly romantic!'

'And you love a good romance, don't you?'

'Of course I do. Especially ours. I think our life here is so romantic. Listen, can you hear the waves out there?'

Marcel nodded. He drew her into his arms.

'And can you smell the scent of the roses in the garden?'

He nuzzled his lips against her hair. 'Yes, I can.'

'Marcel, let's go and walk in the garden for a few

minutes. It's still warm out there. I want to walk with my bare feet on the grass and look at the moon. We'll leave the windows wide open so we can hear if Thiery cries…'

'Sounds good to me.'

She held out her hand towards him. 'And when we come back, now that I've been given a clean bill of health, will you hold me close and…?'

Marcel gave her a rakish grin. 'You mean we could have one of those special cuddles that mummies and daddies have when they want to make a baby?'

Debbie laughed. 'That's exactly what I mean!'

Marcel took hold of her hand and brought it to his lips. He knew he would always love his beautiful, fascinating wife. She seemed to make everyday situations into an adventure. It was early days in the big adventure of their marriage, but each day seemed to be better than the one that had gone before…

HIS UNEXPECTED CHILD

JOSIE METCALFE

CHAPTER ONE

LEAH'S hand was shaking violently as she tried to put the telephone back on its cradle and she was only successful on the second attempt.

For just a moment she was blazingly angry that she'd been treated so cavalierly, but then her brain returned to its usual logical processes.

Still, she was sorely tempted to drop her head to the desk and howl her disappointment but the last thing she wanted was for the whole department to know what had just happened—at least, not until she'd had time to come to terms with it.

For a moment she glanced around the cramped room, focusing on all the things she hated about it—the shabby, boring paintwork, the limp, sun-bleached curtains and the institutional furniture piled high with the overflow of case files—and mourned the fact that she wouldn't have time to finish her self-imposed task of rearranging the chaotic filing system into something more streamlined and efficient.

'Problem?' queried a voice from the doorway, and she realised that her trembling hands could not have been the only outward sign of her feelings. She drew in a swift bracing breath before she turned to face the department's most senior nurse, knowing that the time for licking her wounds was already over.

'No problem that I know of, Kelly,' she said brightly, hoping her smile didn't look as false as it felt.

'So you got the lab results at last!' A smile lit her gamine face as she entered the room eagerly.   ·

Lab results? Leah blinked, having to force her mind back to her first phone call of the recent session, the one before disappointment had descended over her.

'Ah… Yes! Here they are. I got Stanley to read them out for me over the phone and jotted them down.' She handed the piece of paper to Kelly. 'They've promised to follow up with written confirmation, a.s.a.p., and *I* promised to come up there personally and extract them with the most painful methods at my disposal if they didn't keep *their* promise!'

Kelly laughed at the empty threat. They both knew exactly how important it was that the labs were meticulous, especially in the work of this department, and Stanley was one of the best.

'Well, we'll see what happens, won't we,' Kelly said with a doubting shake of her dark head. 'They promised me the same, hours ago, and nothing happened. Still, I'm not the head of St Luke's Assisted Reproduction department, so perhaps that'll make all the difference.'

A swift pang of renewed disappointment tightened around Leah's heart, but she couldn't avoid breaking the news any longer. Soon everyone would know.

'Only *acting* head,' she reminded Kelly, hoping she didn't sound as bitter as she felt. She'd been carrying the full load for months while Donald had avoided coming to terms with his need for heart-bypass surgery. Due to her willingness to work herself to a standstill, her superior's sudden death had hardly registered in the smooth running of the department, and she'd hoped that it would be little more than a formality for her unofficial position as head of the AR department to be given the stamp of approval.

'That's just administrative claptrap,' Kelly declared supportively. 'We all know you're the best one for the position, especially as you've been doing it for so many weeks—'

'Apparently, not everyone agrees with you, Kelly,' Leah interrupted, her voice a little sharper than usual with restrained emotion. 'The board has appointed a new head of department from outside the hospital. He's supposed to be joining us in a matter of days.'

'Oh, Leah,' Kelly murmured, clearly stricken. At least that was some kind of sop to Leah's ego. 'Oh, damn, I'm sorry. Why didn't you say something? When did you find out?'

'Just a moment ago.' She gestured towards the phone. 'Apparently someone was supposed to have informed me of the board's decision before the weekend, but in the excitement of snagging someone as eminent as David ffrench…' She shrugged, trying to appear philosophical about hospital management's total lack of courtesy.

'David ffrench?' Kelly frowned.

'The name doesn't ring a bell with me either,' Leah agreed. 'But, then, I just grabbed the minimum time necessary from the department to attend the interview. There just wasn't time to hang around to meet the competition so I don't even know where he's been working.'

'Well, if he's such hot stuff, how come he's free to take up a position here at the drop of a hat?' Kelly demanded.

'All I know is that he's apparently been at a top-

flight IVF centre in New Zealand and he's come to
Britain for family reasons.'

'Is he a New Zealander?' There was a definite spark
of interest in Kelly's dark eyes and Leah actually had
to subdue a grin at the predictability of her colleague's
reaction. 'Oh, tell me he's one of those gorgeous
seven-foot rugby-playing Maoris, please! That's what
this department could do with—a few really sexy
hunky single men!'

'Sorry I can't oblige,' said a dry voice behind them,
and they both whirled in surprise to face the man who
had arrived unannounced at the office doorway. 'I'm
not a New Zealander and it's years since I played any
rugby.'

That didn't mean he was lacking in the looks department, Leah registered with an unexpected surge of
awareness, something that hadn't happened since…for
ever.

At five feet seven, she wasn't short, but she had to
look up some way to meet his uncomfortably direct
greeny blue gaze, in spite of the fact that she hadn't
had time to change out of her heeled shoes this morning. His bronzed skin was a testament to the fact that
he'd just returned from a summer in New Zealand but
his face was all planes and angles as though he'd recently lost more weight than was good for him. He
certainly didn't look as though he was carrying enough
muscle bulk to be a rugby player now.

'You're English!' Kelly's gurgle of laughter startled
her and Leah felt a wash of heat surge up into her
cheeks. Had she really been standing there admiring
the man's physique, for heaven's sake? Had he noticed?

'Through and through,' their new boss agreed with

a slight smile, but Leah noted that, for all his pleasant manner, the smile hadn't reached his eyes. 'In fact, I did part of my training at this very hospital.'

And *that* would account for his appointment, Leah thought waspishly, then had to stifle a grimace.

She knew she was being illogical. No hospital would appoint a head of department without being certain that they were the best for the position, especially when they had several to choose from. She would just have to learn to console herself with the idea that it had probably been her age—or lack of it—and a lack of seniority in this particular discipline that had lost her the headship this time. David ffrench looked to be several years older at least, and had already headed a similar department in New Zealand. Added to that, her experience of holding the department together over the last few months had gone largely unnoticed by the hospital hierarchy as her head of department had been covering his tracks to conceal how badly his health had been hampering him. While the extra burden had been exhausting, Leah hadn't really blamed Donald for wanting to hang on to the job he loved as long as possible. She knew what it was like to build your whole life around a special profession.

'I'm Kelly Argent,' Kelly was saying with the sort of blinding smile that would tell even the slowest-witted man that she was interested. 'I'm Senior Sister in the department.'

'David ffrench,' he said, accepting her handshake but, as far as Leah could tell, not even registering any other offers. 'I'm not actually starting till the beginning of next week but I was hoping to meet up with my second in command so that we could compare notes about the department and the case load. Is he here at the moment?'

'He?' Leah repeated in shock, her thoughts a whirling maelstrom. Had she lost out completely? Had she been so shocked by the announcement of his appointment over her that she'd missed a vital second part to that phone call? Had there been *another* appointment, replacing her without her knowledge? Was she now relegated to third in the pecking order, or even bounced out of the department altogether?

'Lee Dawson,' he said with a hint of impatience. 'The chap who's been holding everything together since my predecessor—'

'Lee!' Kelly giggled, clearly delighted with his mistake. 'You mean Leah!' She sketched a sweeping gesture in her direction. 'And I bet the panel didn't tell you that if it weren't for her working twenty-six hours a day, there wouldn't be a department for you to take charge of.'

Leah cringed with embarrassment when he turned the full force of those striking eyes on her. It had been for the sake of her—*their*—patients that she'd worked so long and hard, not to have fulsome praise heaped on her shoulders. She would far rather have had the position of head of department instead.

'Loyal staff,' her new boss said quietly, his eyes giving nothing away. 'That speaks well of a department. I hope I can earn the same sort of loyalty as my predecessor.'

'Oh, *he* wasn't the one—' Kelly began, but Leah quelled her with a glare. She might be disappointed to have lost the plum job but there was no way she wanted to start off a new working relationship with the rest of the staff taking sides.

A frown briefly pleated the smooth skin of his forehead, as though he'd suddenly become aware of unanticipated undercurrents, but with her deliberately noncommittal expression, Leah hoped that there was nothing for him to glean.

'Well, then, Leah, if it's convenient, I'd like to spend some time in the department today to see how things are run at the moment. I expect you've got everything ready for my arrival on Monday, but have you got time this morning to go over the current patient files?'

To see how things are run at the moment? Leah's heart sank. That certainly sounded as if he intended making changes before he'd even seen how things were organised. Not that there weren't changes that she'd had in mind should she have been given the job, but she already knew what needed changing because she'd been running the department for months.

'Actually, there's *nothing* ready for your arrival on Monday because we had no idea that you were coming,' she said bluntly, unable to stop her frustration coating her words. 'In fact, we'd never even heard of you until five minutes before you turned up, and we certainly didn't know that you'd been appointed head of department.'

To say that he looked taken aback was putting it mildly, Leah thought, and, in spite of her own feelings of disappointment, she suddenly found herself having to fight laughter. Was it hysteria? Perhaps. But it certainly wasn't a good example of professional courtesy, especially when she was going to have to work with the man.

'Of course, the patients' notes are completely up to date,' she assured him with a touch of justifiable pride.

He obviously didn't think so and she could hardly blame him, given the fact that there were piles of files dotted around as a result of her ongoing reorganisation. 'And the computer system the hospital uses is very quick to master so you shouldn't have any trouble accessing any other details you may need.'

'I see.' He was silent for a nerve-stretching moment as his eyes roved the apparent chaos surrounding them, the dubious expression on his face saying everything. 'And *will* you have any time free this morning?'

There was something in the tone of his voice that she couldn't put her finger on, but it made Leah feel uncomfortable. She had no idea whether he was pleased to hear that all the paperwork was in order or whether he seriously doubted it and was wondering how soon he could find a way to replace her.

Just the thought of having to leave her beloved department was enough to send a chill down her spine and she instantly resolved to be less prickly. After all, she may have applied for the post but she hadn't got it. It certainly wasn't the first disappointment she'd suffered. Life went on.

She slid back behind the desk, leaning forward to press a combination of keys on the computer keyboard until the relevant diary page flashed up onto the screen. She always arrived at least an hour before she was due to start and she may as well get their initial meeting over as soon as possible. The situation wasn't going to change even if she put him off until the end of the day, and she'd have it hanging over her, too.

'I'm free for the next three-quarters of an hour,' she began briskly, then realised that she'd automatically treated the room as her own domain, sitting at the desk as if it was her right. 'That is, I'll be free as soon as

I've had time to take my belongings out of your room…although where I'll be able to put them…' she finished under her breath, completely unable to think of anywhere in the department that she could set up as her own space. She'd been doing so much of the day-to-day running of the department for so long that there was very little in the room to remind her that it had actually been her former head of department's office.

'That's not important for the moment,' he said dismissively. 'We'll just have to share the office if there isn't anywhere else.'

Leah nearly choked at the impossibility of the idea. The room was far too small for a second desk to be shoehorned into the cramped space and they certainly couldn't share the existing one. What was he proposing? That she should sit on his lap?

'The important thing,' he continued while she fought to rid her brain of that seductive image, 'is that I need to be up to speed before I start work properly on Monday. Where we do it or whose name is on the door is immaterial.'

'So, what do you think of him?' Kelly demanded eagerly, her coat over her arm, at the end of her shift.

'Who?' Leah asked weakly, knowing it was a forlorn hope that the topic of conversation would be anything other than their new head of department.

'David ffrench, of course,' Kelly said impatiently, almost as though she doubted Leah's sanity. 'Remember? The man you've spent ages closeted with in that cosy little office, you lucky girl.'

'He's very different to Donald,' Leah said blandly, hoping that Kelly hadn't picked up on the fact that her heart had just performed a sudden jig at the mention of his name. It had been bad enough when he'd been standing in the office doorway and she'd been able to put the width of the desk between them, but sitting side by side with their elbows and knees in almost constant contact had quickly become torture. She'd never been this aware of *any* man, not even...

'Duh!' Kelly mocked, halting that particular train of thought before it could hit the buffers. 'Tell me something I *haven't* noticed! David ffrench is absolutely nothing like Donald, thank God. Tell me...while you were in here, what have you managed to find out about his private life? Is he married, engaged, living with a significant other or is he gloriously, wonderfully free to fall instantly in love with yours truly?'

'I haven't got a clue,' Leah replied honestly, but felt the tide of warmth seeping up her face with the silent admission that for the first time in a long time she'd actually found herself thinking exactly the same questions. 'All I can tell you is that he doesn't wear a ring—not that *that* is any indication of anything these days, especially for a surgeon.'

'Ah, so you were looking!' Kelly pounced.

'Not really, but I couldn't help noticing as we were working our way through the current case files.' And couldn't help noticing what nice hands he had either. They were all lean and long fingered and looked as if they had the sort of sinewy strength that any surgeon needed, combined with the delicacy of touch and fine control that was essential for their exacting specialty.

'So, do you think he'll be good for the department?' Kelly asked, suddenly reverting to a more serious frame of mind. 'Do you think you'll be able to work with him?'

'Time will tell,' Leah said noncommittally. 'He certainly seems to know his stuff.'

'And the fact that he's so easy on the eyes is a big help, too,' Kelly joked archly. 'Not that he seems very interested in playing the flirting game. I think nearly every female in the entire obs and gyn section perked up as he's gone by, but he didn't even seem to notice. Oh!' She gasped as a sudden thought struck her. 'You don't think he's...you know, batting for the other team?'

'You mean, homosexual?' Leah fought a grin, determined to at least appear to take the suggestion seriously. 'I suppose he could be. Once again, though, only time will tell.'

She was grinning openly as a scowling Kelly made her way out of the unit, muttering darkly that all the good-looking men were either married or gay, absolutely certain in her own mind that, married or not, David ffrench was a hundred per cent pure functioning male.

'Hey, big brother! How did it go today? Did you get a chance to look around your new domain?'

'Hi, Moggy! How are you doing?' David felt a wide smile spread over his face at the sound of his sister's voice at the other end of the phone, grateful for the chance to stop unpacking boxes. He lowered himself into his borrowed armchair and suddenly realised why it had been so eagerly donated when it nearly swallowed him whole. He might have to call for help just to escape from its smothering clutches. 'Is that new husband of yours treating you right?'

'Like a fragile piece of priceless china,' she grumbled, but he could hear the happiness underlying the complaint. It was so good to know that she'd finally found what she'd always wanted—a man who loved her every bit as much as she loved him—and if it left *him* feeling pea green with envy, that was his own problem. He'd thought he'd had it all once, and look where he was now.

'Perhaps that's because you're not only newly-weds but you're also pregnant with his baby,' he pointed out. 'And you know you wouldn't want it any other way.'

'True,' she conceded cheerfully and with a definite hint of smugness. 'Hey! No sidetracking! You didn't answer my question. What *did* you think of your new department? Are you glad I twisted your arm to apply for the post? Did you have a chance to meet Leah Dawson? What did you think of her? Don't you think she's just—?'

'Hey, Moggy! Give me a chance to answer the first half-dozen questions before you pile on the next dozen!' He chuckled, glad that she'd never grown out of that habit. He'd been teasing her about it ever since she'd learned to talk.

'Not so much of the Moggy!' she complained, as she always did. 'I'm not ten any more. So, start answering. Isn't Leah just great?'

For some reason that was the last question David felt like answering, and he couldn't think of a single logical reason why—at least, not one he cared to contemplate with his nosy little sister on the other end of the phone.

Hurriedly, he reverted to an earlier question.

'Yes, Moggy, I freely admit that I'm absolutely delighted that you brought the AR vacancy to my attention. It has the makings of an excellent department.'

'The makings? You mean, once you've done your new-broom bit and completely reorganised it?' she teased, but he knew there was more than a hint of the truth in her words. He did like to put his own stamp on the way his department was run, but he certainly didn't want to start off by alienating the existing staff.

He wondered just how well his sister knew Leah. Maggie and Jake hadn't needed the assistance of his new department to start her pregnancy, but she might have met his new colleague when they'd had to call for someone to take a look at a potential admission down in A and E. She might also have met her when she'd accompanied an emergency patient up to the department at some time.

Had she also noticed the chaotic disarray in his predecessor's office, with files on every available surface? It certainly wasn't the way he liked to run a department and he'd been amazed that Leah had apparently had no trouble putting her hand on everything he'd requested.

And there she was, back inside his head again, no matter how hard he tried to keep her out. He had far more important things to think about than a pair of serious grey eyes and a wealth of honey-blonde hair tied tightly back to reveal the delicate bone structure of her face.

He shook his head, glad that Maggie couldn't see him. What did it matter that his new colleague was tall and slender and filled with almost incandescent nervous energy? It certainly hadn't helped her to keep on top of a simple job like keeping the office straight. Come Monday, he dreaded discovering that her attention to other things, like the important details that should have been recorded in each of those case notes since her superior died, was equally slap-dash. In the short time she'd had free, he hadn't been able to do much more than get an idea of the scope of patients currently under investigation and treatment, and the general routine of the department on a daily and weekly basis.

'Would Jake be happy working in a disorganised department?' he challenged gently. 'I bet the first thing he did when he got his consultancy was go over every tiny detail in person.'

'And you'd win, you rat!' Maggie grumbled. 'Just promise me something—don't ruffle too many feathers on your first day. Take it gently until you've had a chance to get to know the people you'll be working with. They're a good tight-knit team.'

'Yes, Mother,' he said in a singsong voice. 'I'll play nicely with the other boys and girls.'

'Oh, you're impossible!' she spluttered. 'Sometimes I don't know why I bother.'

'Because I'm your lovable big brother?' he suggested, tongue in cheek.

'Exactly,' she said, heaving a theatrical put-upon sigh. 'But, seriously, David…'

'Uh-oh! When she uses those dreaded words…!' he teased. 'It's OK, Moggy. You can stop worrying about me, I'm a big boy now.'

'I know that, but I don't just want you to be successful, I want you to be happy, too,' she said plaintively.

The words hung in the air between them for several seconds.

David knew exactly what she meant. Since she'd found happiness with Jake, she wanted everyone to be equally happy, but he knew that wasn't possible for him. He'd had his chance and it had all gone horribly wrong.

'It wasn't your fault, David,' she said softly in his ear, and he shivered at the accuracy of the way she'd followed his thoughts. Was he really that transparent?

'That didn't make any difference to the pain,' he said gruffly, startled that he'd even admitted that much. In fact, it was probably the most he'd said to anyone about the loss that would haunt him for ever, and it would be the last. 'So, if you don't mind, little sister, I'll concentrate on my new job and making the department second to none. That'll make me happy.'

'But you can't take the department to bed for a cuddle,' she retorted stubbornly. 'David, you can't cut yourself off from people like that. If you don't want to talk to me, you could phone Mum and Dad. Calls to New Zealand may be expensive, but on your salary—'

'No way!' he exploded a second before he could put a guard on his tongue.

'What?' Maggie sounded startled. 'But, David, you've always been so close to them—they moved halfway round the world to be near you, for heaven's sake. Surely they'd be willing to listen if you wanted to talk?'

'Too damn close!' he muttered under his breath, then realised that he needed to make some sort of explanation.

'Mum and Dad—at least, *Mum*—is one of the reasons why I *left* New Zealand. I had to get away, Maggie. She was still trying to smother me, the way she did when I was a kid. I'm thirty-four, for heaven's sake! I don't need my mother to bandage my grazed knees and kiss them better!'

Maggie giggled. 'That's an image to conjure with!'

'Well, it's not so funny when you're on the receiving end of it,' he pointed out grimly.

'But, David—' she began persuasively, but he'd had enough.

'And you'd better watch your step,' he warned. 'If you're going to start nagging, I'll set Jake on you. I'll tell him that he needs to keep a closer eye on you.'

'Don't you dare!' she squealed in dismay. 'I can hardly breathe as it is. If somebody from Obs and Gyn told him I needed watching he'd never let me out of his sight.'

'That's because you and the baby mean that much to him,' he pointed out softly, the pain of memories tightening its grip around his throat and his heart. 'Enjoy every precious minute of it, Moggy. Sleep tight.'

'This isn't working,' Leah muttered as she stepped back from her little workbench in disgust.

Usually she could lose herself in the timeless art of repotting, trimming and training her precious bonsai trees, the cares of the day simply melting away as she put her concentration to each measured task. Tonight it just wasn't happening and it was all *his* fault.

'I might just as well be doing something useful, rather than risking spoiling one of you,' she muttered as she collected and cleaned her tools and put them away. 'And I know just the job.'

Decision made, it took mere moments before her hands were washed and she was reaching for her keys with a wry grimace. It would always seem wasteful to drive such a short distance, but it would be a very foolish woman who would wander about in the deep shadows between her flat and the hospital buildings in the dark.

Not long after that, she'd shut herself in the night-time seclusion of the untidy office and was rolling up her sleeves in preparation for the final stage in her reorganisation of Donald's filing system. The audit of all his files had been long overdue and a surprising number should already have been sent to the hospital archives. The remaining stacks were a far more manageable number for the available space in the filing cabinets.

She pulled open the first empty drawer and couldn't help chuckling when she remembered the horrified expression on David ffrench's face when he'd seen the chaos in the room. It had been sheer stubbornness mixed with her disappointment at losing out on the head of department job that had stopped her from explaining what was going on, and she felt a bit guilty about it now.

'Guilty enough to lose some sleep to finish the job, but as I've already checked the contents of each one of these and put them all into alphabetical order, at least this part should be a breeze,' she muttered as she prepared to slot each file into position. In a relatively short space of time she could have every last piece of paper filed neatly out of sight and she could push the last drawer shut with a warm feeling of achievement.

Suddenly she paused and threw a disparaging glare around the room.

'The trouble is, when there are none of Donald's piles of filing to distract the eye, it will be even more obvious just how shabby everything has become.'

The walls, in particular, could do with a fresh coat of paint—something rather more welcoming than dingy Institution Beige. 'But fresher walls will make the curtains look worse than ever,' she muttered in defeat, until an image of the spare pair of curtains lurking back at her flat leapt into her head. She'd bought them for her last flat and, while they didn't fit any of the windows in her new one, they were still nearly new.

'And if I can corner one of the maintenance men some time tomorrow... Even if he can't do something about it, perhaps I could get him to beg a can of paint from the stores. Then I could come back again tomorrow evening...'

Course of action decided, she put the pile of files back where she'd got them from, switched off the light and locked the door behind her, a tiny smile betraying the thought that she was actually looking forward to David ffrench starting work on Monday. She could hardly wait to see the expression on his face when he saw the finished transformation.

'And it'll be every bit as good as any of the makeovers he'd see on the television,' she vowed, a fresh spring in her step in spite of the time.

David ffrench stepped back into the shadow of the stairwell with a frown.

'What on earth is Leah Dawson doing here at this time of night?' he muttered into the darkness, his eyes following her swiftly moving figure as she made her way to the lifts. She'd obviously been home since the end of her shift because she'd changed from her neatly tailored trousers into a pair of decidedly disreputable jeans, jeans that revealed a figure every bit as neat and slender as he'd imagined.

And that smile! It was the first one he'd seen that

didn't look as if it had been forced out of her by well-drilled manners, and it had instantly intrigued him.

What had she been doing in his office at this time of night…? Well, it would be his office when he took it over on Monday morning. His frown deepened as he considered the possibilities. She must be in her late twenties or early thirties, so far too old for juvenile pranks such as whoopee cushions, and he hoped that she was far too professional to do something as stupid as to mess about with patient files.

'As if I'd be able to tell,' he groaned softly, remembering the chaos littering every surface. 'As it is, it's going to take me a month of Sundays just to get things organised. How I'm going to be able to run the department at the same time…'

He couldn't imagine what the patients must think when they were shown into the room for the first time. It certainly wasn't confidence-inspiring, and the frustration was that he couldn't do anything about the situation until he officially started work.

'Unless…' he mused as he turned and made his way back down the stairs, then shook his head. The possibility of enlisting Leah in some overtime to sort through the mess had briefly flashed through his mind, but it wasn't a good idea.

'No,' he conceded. 'I've got enough to do in the next twenty-four hours with organising my living space. And I really don't need to get off on the wrong foot with Leah before we've even started to work together.'

As he left, he smiled absently at the security guard who'd earlier verified his identity before admitting him to the building, then lengthened his stride as he set off towards the nearby block of flats, wondering why the woman seemed to have taken up permanent residence inside his head when he'd only met her this morning.

'The last thing I need is getting tangled up with some woman,' he said aloud, startling an elderly gentleman taking his equally elderly dog out for its late-night constitutional. 'Been there, done that,' he muttered more quietly. 'I've got the scars to prove it.'

CHAPTER TWO

'THAT looks better!' Leah exclaimed aloud as she clambered down from her perch on the window-sill and stepped back to admire her handiwork.

In the distance, she heard the chimes of the church clock striking two, a reassuring sound that couldn't be heard at all when the department was busy during the day, but now only served to remind her of just how late it was.

'If I'm going to be awake enough to work a full shift, I'd better get home to bed,' she muttered. 'I wouldn't want to oversleep and miss out on seeing his reaction.'

She'd already deposited the decorating equipment in a nearby storage cupboard, as arranged with the helpful maintenance man. Now that she'd hung the curtains, she was going to leave the window open for the rest of the night to help to dispel the last of the paint fumes.

'Now *I'm* the messiest thing in the room,' she said with a grimace for her paint-splattered clothing, but the results were certainly well worthwhile.

In spite of her need to get home, get cleaned up and get some sleep, she couldn't help pausing by the door for a little gloat at all she'd achieved.

She'd barely had time to rejoice over the improvement—the calm, professional appearance of the 'business' end of the room, with not a stray piece of paper to be seen, compared to the softer, more welcoming area where prospective parents would be invited to sit—when her pager shrilled its imperative summons, startling her out of her wits.

'I hope it's a misdialled code,' she muttered even as she was reaching for the receiver to answer the call.

'Leah? How long will it take you to get here?' demanded the familiar voice of one of the midwives.

'Is there a problem?' Leah made a sound of disgust. 'Ignore the stupid question, Sally. Blame it on the time of night and change it to "What's the problem?"'

'Major, *major* problem,' she said grimly. 'An IVF patient in advanced labour, multiple birth, malpresentation.'

Already Leah's head was reeling with the staccato presentation of facts. One part of her brain was sifting through 'their' patients, but she couldn't think of any of the sets of twins who were anywhere near due yet.

'Which one? Is she miscarrying?' Unfortunately, there was a high rate of loss and all its attendant heartaches in their vulnerable group of patients.

'Not one of ours,' Sally reassured her succinctly. 'She's in a bad way. How soon can you get here? I think the only way we're going to save any of them is an emergency Caesarean, pronto, and Chas is already fully occupied.'

For just a fleeting second she wondered if she was about to bite off more than she could chew. This would be her first really complicated case since Donald had died, and although he hadn't delivered a baby for several years, there had been a certain sense of security in knowing that such an experienced man had been nearby.

'How long will it take you to get her into Theatre?' She glanced across at the clock on the wall above the filing cabinets to confirm the time while she contemplated her course of action. 'I'll go straight there and start to scrub.'

'Ten minutes, tops. I've already warned Theatre to get ready,' Sally informed her, then added, 'Leah, make it as fast as you can, please. I've got a really bad feeling about this one.'

The butterflies in Leah's stomach became helicopters with those parting words. Sally was an experienced midwife not prone to panicking at the slightest hitch. If she was worried, then there was something to worry about and even though she could have taken the case on herself, Leah knew what she had to do. With mother and babies' lives at stake, this was no time for egos or hospital politics.

'Hello, Switchboard, I need to contact one of the consultants urgently, and I don't have his home number,' she announced briskly, her fingers crossed that the computer had already been updated ready for David ffrench's commencement today at a more civilised time. It only briefly crossed her mind that his insurance cover might not start until he was officially on duty. 'It's David ffrench...two f's. He's the new appointment to Obs and Gyn.'

It took several more precious minutes to persuade the person on the other end that if *they* made the connection to the outside line, they wouldn't actually be breaking his right to confidentiality.

'H'lo?' said a husky voice right in her ear, and every nerve quivered with the knowledge that she'd just woken him up, that he was probably lying in his bed—totally naked?—with his dark hair all rumpled and...

'Mr ffrench?' she squeaked, and had to clear her throat before she could continue, gabbling in her embarrassment at her unruly imagination. 'I'm sorry to disturb you when you haven't officially begun working here, but could you possibly come over to the hospital? There's an emergency Caesarean...multiple birth... And I think I'm going to need you. Oh, this is Leah Dawson.'

'Foetal distress?' he demanded, already obviously firing on all cylinders, much to Leah's envy. She still hated being woken in the middle of the night, even after all these years in the profession. 'How many weeks gestation and how long has the mother been in labour?'

'I don't know much more than I've told you,' she admitted. 'But it was Sally Ling, one of the most experienced midwives in the department, who called me, and she knows what she's talking about. Chas— Charles Westmoreland—isn't available because he's already dealing with a problem delivery,' she added, anticipating his next question.

'I can be there in ten minutes. Get her into Theatre,' he said tersely, and before she could utter a word of thanks, he'd broken the connection.

Leah could have wasted energy feeling snubbed by his abruptness, but all she was conscious of was relief that he was on his way. Now it was time to get moving.

'Have you got any more details for me?' she demanded over her shoulder as she began the scrubbing ritual, the cotton of the theatre greens feeling very thin and insubstantial after her jeans.

Sally's head appeared round the corner, her dark curls already trying to escape from the disposable cap.

'Mum tried to tell me that she's thirty-eight, but I'd say she's much closer to sixty.'

'What?' Leah gaped at her, hands suspended in mid-scrub. 'You're joking! She probably just looks a bit…shattered after carrying a double load around for so many months.'

'You could be right,' Sally said dubiously. 'See what you think when you see her. Ashraf's not too happy about any of it. We've got absolutely no previous notes and she's being extremely cagey about where she had her treatment, and he's in charge of her anaesthesia.'

'Not another one!' exclaimed David as he joined Leah at the sink. He'd obviously heard enough of the conversation as he'd come in to pick up on what was happening. 'We had one like this at my last post. Apparently she'd had extensive cosmetic surgery so that she could use her niece's passport for identification as she was well beyond the age limits for properly regulated IVF. We never did find out where she'd been treated and we nearly lost her to eclampsia.'

'Oh, boy, am I glad I invited you to this little party,' Leah groaned. 'By the way, should I make the introductions? David ffrench, new head of our little domain, meet Sally Ling, midwife *extraordinaire*.'

'I take it this is what's called being thrown in at the deep end,' David commented as he took his turn at having the ties fastened at the back of his gown, then held his hands out for gloves.

'We wouldn't like you to think you were going to be bored here, so we thought we'd lay on a bit of entertainment,' Sally quipped, taking another look into the room behind her. 'I think Ashraf's nearly ready for you to begin, but he doesn't look happy.'

'Too right, Ashraf's not happy!' exclaimed the man in question, his dark eyes firmly fixed on the array of monitors grouped at his end of the table. 'Some things are just not right.'

'Is there a problem with her anaesthesia?' Leah heard the sharp edge of concern in David's voice.

'You mean, apart from the fact that her blood pressure's too high and her lungs aren't the best?' he said wryly. 'No, what I meant was that I reckon we can add at least twenty years to the age the patient's given us, and a woman in her fifties or sixties should be looking forward to grandchildren, the way nature intended. There are sound physiological reasons why there should be age limits for IVF. *And* it's a multiple birth!' he finished, the words almost completely incomprehensible as his accent became stronger and stronger in his passion.

'You'll get no argument from me,' David said grimly as he painted the grossly swollen abdomen preparatory to the incision. 'And to turn up obviously *intending* to leave us completely in the dark about the details of her pregnancy...!'

He didn't bother finishing the sentence, but Leah knew he didn't need to when everyone in the room knew just how much that omission could affect the outcome of what they were doing.

'Is everybody ready?' he asked, and Leah threw one last look around the assembled staff. Apart from those grouped around the operating table, there were two teams waiting in the background with the high-tech Perspex incubators for the other two tiny individuals who would hopefully be joining them in the room soon. What they were going to do if both babies needed high-dependency nursing was another problem entirely. There were never enough beds or specially trained staff to cope, and they would need to do some serious juggling with the babies already in the unit to cope with just one seriously sick preemie. A second one would probably have to face a life-threatening dash to whichever NICU had the nearest free HDU bed. She'd probably have to spend several hours on the phone begging and pleading...

But that was in the future. First they had to deliver the babies.

'Ready,' she confirmed as she turned back to the table. Those striking eyes were waiting for her, somehow all the more potent for the fact that they were all she could see of him above his disposable mask. For just a second it almost felt as if the two of them had made some sort of silent connection but then he had his hand out ready to receive the scalpel, and when he immediately applied it to their patient's skin in an expert arc she knew she must have been mistaken.

It was lovely to watch him work, she thought, admiring the efficient way he'd exposed the uterus. Without a word needing to be spoken, she was ready to zap the inevitable bleeders then stood poised with suction as he carefully chose the site for the second incision. The last thing they needed was to injure one of the babies with an injudicious cut.

Amniotic fluid gushed out of the widening aperture and he had to pause for a moment before he could insert two fingers into the gap as a guide, positioning them between the wall of the uterus and the babies it contained to enable him to continue cutting.

'It's all arms and legs in here,' he muttered as he inserted one long-fingered hand through the incision. 'Ah! Gotcha! Leah?' he nodded towards the exposed belly above the incision.

She placed one hand on the strangely brown flesh

and waited for his signal, but he hardly needed her assistance, the baby's head emerging cradled in his palm and the rest of the spindly body following in a rapid slither.

'It's a girl!' Leah announced as the cord was cut and she immediately turned to place the wriggling infant into the waiting warmed blanket held out by Sally just as she let out her first wail.

'One down, one to go,' David said as he inserted his hand again, this time emerging with a tiny foot and going back to find the other one of the pair. 'Come on, sunshine,' he said encouragingly. 'There's a lot of people out here waiting to meet you.'

Leah smiled behind her mask, once more poised for the nod that would come if he needed help to get the baby's head out into the world.

'It's another girl,' she said, the sex of the baby all too obvious in such an undignified position, then it was time to cut the cord and hand her little charge over to the second waiting team.

She turned back, expecting to find David dealing with the clean removal of two placentas, but found him scowling darkly.

'I don't believe it!' he exclaimed. 'There's a third one in here!'

'What!' Leah gasped, unable to believe her ears.

For a second nobody moved, then they all spoke at once.

'You're joking!'

'We'll need another team with an incubator. Hurry.'

'Her blood pressure's dropping.'

It was the final voice that silenced them all, and while Leah knew that there was frantic activity behind her as extra help was summoned from the NICU, she was focusing solely on David.

If she hadn't been so close to him for the last half-hour she probably wouldn't have noticed the new urgency in his movements, but, as it was, she could almost feel the tension emanating from him.

'Come on, come on!' she heard him mutter under his breath, almost growling with frustration.

Perhaps his hands were too large for the job, even though they were relatively slender for a man. Perhaps her smaller ones would help—anything to bring the unexpected third baby out successfully.

'Do you want me to—?'

'Got it!' he exclaimed, interrupting her offer before it had been made. 'It was a transverse lie and the poor little thing had been squashed by its sisters trying to get out.'

Even as he was speaking he was lifting the tiny scrap out of its mother's body, and Leah's heart clenched when she saw the state the infant was in.

'He's terribly floppy!' she exclaimed, already reaching out to take the precious burden. 'Is he breathing?'

She didn't really want to pass the tiny being over, all her protective instincts demanding she take care of it herself, but with Ashraf's renewed warning that they needed to finish the operation as soon as possible, all she could do was relinquish her into Sally's waiting hands, knowing that her colleague would do everything she could.

In the meantime, there were now three placentas to remove and check for completeness before the incisions in both uterus and skin could be closed—and all with the clock ticking ominously.

'Damn! Where is all that blood coming from?'

David swore suddenly. 'Leah, suction! I can't see what's going on…'

'Hurry up, guys,' Ashraf warned. 'We're going to lose her.'

'Not without a fight,' David countered fiercely. 'Get some more fluids into her as fast as you can,' he directed as he peered into the gaping wound. 'Damn it, the uterus is paper thin. It's almost shredding as we look at it.'

'You'll have to do a hysterectomy,' Leah said, hoping she sounded calmer than she felt. 'With blood loss this rapid there isn't time for any sort of repair, not if she's going to be around for those babies.'

David met her eyes for the briefest moment and she knew that they'd both come to that same decision.

She'd thought she'd seen him working quickly before, but it was nothing to the speed at which he excised the life-threatening tissue in a room filled with the din of shrilling monitors warning of imminent disaster.

'She's going to crash!' Ashraf called, and out of the corner of her eye Leah could see his hands flying from one control to another as he tried his best to support their failing patient.

'Thirty seconds, Ashraf!' David growled, without pausing for a single one of them in his determination to cheat death. 'Just keep her going for another thirty seconds.'

'I'll do my best, but I can't promise you've got even that long,' the anaesthetist warned as the monitor told them that their patient's heart was beating almost out of control in an attempt to circulate the remaining blood, but David didn't even falter.

Leah was aware of a strange feeling that was almost

exhilaration as she assisted in one of the most frantic operations she'd ever witnessed. For the first time ever in an operation, the lead surgeon didn't even need to say what he wanted. Somehow she just knew and was there ready with the next clamp or the diathermy to seal off another bleeding blood vessel.

'Bowl,' David said, even as Leah was holding it out to him. He finally glanced towards Ashraf. 'How is she doing?'

'Holding her own—just,' he said cautiously, and checked all his monitors again. 'We're actually managing to get some volume into her, now that she's not leaking like a sieve. Her heart rate is coming down and her blood pressure's coming up.'

'In that case, Leah, would you like to close?' He raised one dark eyebrow but she was more interested in the expression of relief she detected in those beautiful eyes.

'Oh, yes. Of course,' she floundered, feeling like a fool for standing gazing at him like that. What on earth was going on? She'd never behaved like this before. Imagine—standing in the operating theatre in the middle of a procedure and thinking that the new consultant had beautiful eyes!

Whatever next? she demanded silently as she did a final check to make sure that nothing was bleeding any more, then carefully sutured the abdominal musculature layer by layer.

'Nice neat job,' David murmured at her elbow, but she'd known that he was watching, every nerve seeming to recognise his proximity even though she couldn't see him.

'Thank you, sir,' she said with a mock curtsey, then stepped back to allow others to take over the application of protective dressings before their patient was taken through to Recovery.

'And may I return the compliment, in spades,' she continued, when they'd made their way out of Theatre to divest themselves of their liberally splattered clothing. Sudden nervousness at the thought that he was about to see her in nothing more than her underwear made her chatter. 'I've never seen anyone work that fast or that accurately, and I'll be eternally grateful that you agreed to come in tonight. I know I could have delivered the babies, but I doubt whether I'd have been able to save the mother when it all went pear-shaped so quickly.'

Suddenly confronted by the tanned width of his naked chest, her tongue stopped working, her jaw all but hanging open. Had she thought he was too thin? She could obviously blame his tailor because there was nothing wrong with the body she was seeing in front of her...close enough to touch if she just reached out...

'You'll be surprised what you can manage to do when there aren't any other options,' he said quietly, jerking her out of that dangerous line of thought, then a glint of mischief lit his eyes. 'And I like the sound of *eternally grateful*. Does that translate into fetching cups of coffee?'

'In your dreams!' she retorted, grateful that he hadn't noticed the way she was eyeing him and surprised that he felt at ease enough to tease. The rather solemn man she'd met the other day hadn't looked as if he had a single joke in him.

'But you'd join me in one?'

She glanced up at the clock and pulled a face.

'I may as well,' she agreed. 'It certainly isn't worth

going back to bed now, and I'm going to need plenty
of it, strong and sweet, if I'm going to stay awake
today.'

'Well, shall we agree that the first one out of the
shower pours the coffee?' he suggested. 'How do you
like yours, exactly?'

'You're making the assumption that you'll finish
first,' she pointed out sweetly. 'I like mine strong but
white with just a dash of sugar—how do you take
yours?'

'White. Without,' he said, then grinned. 'I'll see you
in a few minutes, then. Your coffee should have cooled
enough to drink by the time you get there,' he added
in what was clearly a challenge.

David tensed when he heard the door open behind him,
wondering how he could possibly know that it was
Leah who had just entered.

He was surprised to see that there was a slight
tremor to the hand that was pouring the coffee when
it had been perfectly steady in the life-and-death situation just a few minutes ago in Theatre.

'Drat!' he heard her say, and knew that it was in
response to the fact that he'd beaten her.

He quickly stretched a triumphant smile over his
face and turned to face her with a coffee in each hand,
and nearly dropped both of them.

He certainly wouldn't have expected her hair to be
that long, and to see it hanging all the way to the
middle of her back, still dripping with water, sent his
imagination into overdrive...until he hastily put the
brakes on it. He was still having difficulty trying to
forget the sight of her elegant curves clothed in noth-

ing more than creamy lace underwear as she'd stripped off after surgery.

Now was not the time for mental images of Leah in the shower, slick, wet hair flowing over her naked body, not while she was standing in front of him with her hand held out for the coffee he was clutching like a lifeline.

'All right, I concede,' she said. 'But under duress. If I cut my hair as short as yours I'd be able to—'

'Don't!' he exclaimed in horror at the idea. It was only when he saw the surprise on her face that he realised he'd spoken aloud and was abashed to feel the slow crawl of heat up his face. Was he blushing like a gauche teenager, for heaven's sake? What was this woman doing to him? 'I mean, it must have taken you years to grow it that long. It would be such a shame to just...' He was making it worse, he realised when he saw her fighting a grin.

'It would grow again,' she said with a shrug, apparently totally unconcerned by the prospect of destroying what used to be called a woman's crowning glory. 'I'd even thought of getting people to sponsor me to have my head shaved, to raise money for charity.'

'*Shaved!*' He was definitely horrified. 'Well, would you take offers *not* to cut it?' he countered, while a tiny voice inside his head tried hard to remind him that this woman was little more than a stranger and there was absolutely no reason why she should take any notice of his wishes.

'Now, that's another possibility,' she said as she put her cup down and casually twisted the length of her hair into a thick rope and wound it neatly against the back of her head, securing it with a giant clip. 'But sometimes I think it's not worth the bother and all the time it takes. After all, with a shaven head, I would easily have beaten you to the coffee.'

She took a careful sip to test the temperature then a larger mouthful when she found it bearable. He nearly groaned aloud when she closed her eyes and moaned in ecstasy.

'Why does the first cup of the day taste so good?' she demanded.

He didn't reply. The memory of waking up to other activities, and the realisation of just how long ago that had been, reminded him with a jolt of all the reasons why he shouldn't be indulging in this sparring with her. It wasn't right, not when he had absolutely no intention of following through. His days on the relationship merry-go-round were over, and he was glad of it. He wouldn't willingly go through that pain again for anything.

'I stuck my head round the door to check up on the babies,' he announced, needing to get his thoughts onto more professional matters. As that was the only sort of relationship the two of them could have, he might just as well set the boundaries right from the start. 'Baby three—the little boy who got squashed—wasn't doing very well, but his big sisters were doing amazingly well, in spite of their size and prematurity.'

'And Mum?'

'Still in Recovery. Ashraf's hovering over her. All her vital signs seem to be slowly coming good but she hasn't really shaken off the anaesthetic yet.' He frowned briefly. 'She's certainly not compos mentis enough to be told what happened on the table.'

'Well, that's certainly going to be an interesting set

of notes to write up. Perhaps you could make a presentation of the case at the monthly meeting.'

'A presentation?' He was startled by the suggestion.
At his last post he'd barely had time to breathe, let
alone prepare presentations, then he realised how logical the suggestion was when she continued.

'Not only would it serve as a cautionary tale for
those who weren't involved today, but it would also
scotch the rumours that are bound to grow with every
telling.'

'Ah, yes. The hospital grapevine,' he said ruefully.
'That's one aspect of our job that's the same wherever
we go—a hairline crack becomes multiple fractures and
a Caesarean delivery and hysterectomy becomes—'

'A life-saving procedure performed superbly to give
mother and all three babies the best chance possible,'
she interrupted, and for the first time in a long time,
in spite of his embarrassment, he allowed himself a
brief moment to bask in the warmth of her praise.

'Which I couldn't have attempted without a damn
good team to back me up,' he added, giving them their
due, too. 'Ashraf's definitely one of the best anaesthe-
tists I've worked with. That woman was emptying out
so fast...' He shook his head at the scary memory. 'I
honestly don't know how he kept her going long
enough for me to tie everything off. And as for you...'

It was her turn to blush, but he wasn't giving her
empty words—he wouldn't waste his time on anything
but the truth.

'I admit that I was quite surprised to hear that you
were one of the applicants for the AR head of department. I couldn't believe that someone so young could
possibly have the necessary skills.' He bowed briefly

towards her. 'Suffice it to say that since I've witnessed your skill and intuition, albeit assisting this time rather than leading, I'm no longer surprised. You knew exactly what I was going to do and how to make it easy for me—proof, in spite of your own doubts, that you would have been equally able to do the job.'

She was obviously trying to bury her embarrassment in her coffee-cup but he could tell that she was pleased with his recognition of her skills. He had a brief image of the chaos that awaited him in his office and suppressed a shudder that it had been allowed to get into such a state. Was it just that organisation was not one of her skills? He supposed he had to make allowances for the fact that she'd been trying to run the department short-handed, but just in case her weakness *was* paperwork, he was going to offer to write up this morning's case notes himself.

'Are you sure?' she said doubtfully. 'Donald hated doing them—said he'd rather have his teeth pulled.'

'I'm sure,' he said with an even deeper sense of foreboding. Had he been unlucky enough to take over a department that hadn't had anyone willing to take on the essentials? 'I've brought everything with me and I shall have another cup or three of coffee while I get it done.'

'In that case, I'm going to check up on Mum then sneak in for a peep at the babies. I wonder if anyone's been able to contact their father yet.'

'I'll leave you to check up on that and I'll see you in my office at, say, eight?' he suggested.

For just a moment there was a strange expression on her face but it was gone too quickly for him to decipher it. Was it chagrin that it was now *his* office rather than hers, or was it the fact that she was handing it over in such a disastrous state? Well, either way, there was nothing she could do about it now. The job was his, and, providing there wasn't a run of emergencies like this morning's, it really shouldn't take him long to get everything organised, even if he had to ask Personnel for the temporary loan of some sort of specialist filing clerk.

In the meantime, he had a complicated surgery to document, right down to the last suture and cc of drugs. At least *that* ought to push Leah out of his mind until he saw her again at eight.

CHAPTER THREE

'HELLO... Ah, g-good morning, sir,' Leah ended up stammering, suddenly unaccountably uncertain as to what she should call her new boss.

Working together in Theatre in such fraught conditions had definitely given her a feeling of connection with him, but perhaps he preferred a little more formality from the more junior members of his...

'Sir?' he queried with a blink, then ostentatiously looked over his shoulder as if looking for someone else she might be addressing.

Leah couldn't help the brief giggle that escaped her. It was probably the result of the nerves that had built up while she was trying not to look as if she was hovering around in the corridor, waiting for him to arrive. She'd even unlocked the door in preparation for his arrival, in case he hadn't been given his own set of keys yet.

Then he'd swept open the door at the other end of the corridor and begun striding towards her, all long lean legs and broad shoulders, and all her rational thought processes had ceased.

'That's better,' he said with an answering smile as he reached for the door handle. 'Obviously, there has to be a degree of formality when there are patients present, but at all other times you're free to call me... God! What on earth happened here?'

He took a step back to look at the name-plate on the door, as though doubting that he'd come to the right room, but even *that* had been changed after she'd chased Maintenance to install his name in place of Donald's—just one of the last-minute things she'd done while he'd been occupied writing up the post-op notes.

His reaction was everything she could have hoped for, but it was his slip of the tongue that actually made her laugh aloud. It was a struggle to speak for several seconds.

'So, let me get this right,' she said, smiling in the face of his frown of puzzlement. 'You don't want formality but I'm free to call you… *God*?' she teased.

He was walking warily towards the miraculously clear desk.

'You know I didn't mean that,' he objected distractedly as he turned in a circle. 'When did all this happen and who did it?' he demanded, then she saw panic take over from approval. 'What happened to all the files, Leah? Where are they? They haven't been taken away, have they?'

'They're all here,' she soothed, taking the bunch of keys out of her pocket and selecting the correct one to open the first filing cabinet. 'And all in their proper alphabetical order, too.'

'But…I only saw this room on Friday…'

'And you've been having nightmares about it ever since,' Leah finished for him. 'The walls were dingy, the curtains were limp, drab and sun-bleached and there was paperwork on every horizontal surface.'

'Exactly!' he agreed. 'So…who, what, when, why and how? Obviously when I saw it before you must have known that the room was due for a visit from Maintenance for some overdue redecoration.'

'Not exactly.' She knew it was time to come clean.

His surprise had been everything she'd hoped for, but she wanted him to know the real reason for the chaos he'd stumbled into on his first visit. The last thing she wanted was for her new boss to think that had been the way she'd been happy to run the department. That impression might linger and could affect what he wrote about her when she needed a reference when another AR department headship came up.

She refused to let herself ponder the fact that the idea of leaving St Luke's had suddenly become much less attractive than it had been when she'd been told about David's appointment. She needed to concentrate on making her explanation.

'Maintenance were here this morning to install your name-plate and they also supplied the paint and brushes over the weekend.'

'And?' he prompted. 'Am I to take it that *you* provided the labour? When on earth did you find the time with all the hours you've been putting in on keeping the department running?'

'Well, it only took a couple of hours one evening to give everything a once-over.' And another couple for a second coat when the dinginess refused to disappear the first time, she added silently, but he didn't need to know that. Anyway, she wasn't into blowing her own trumpet. 'And the curtains were a spare set I had at home. They've hardly been used but they don't fit any of the windows in my new flat.'

'OK, so that's how the décor changed, but what about all the piles of paperwork? You certainly couldn't have sorted through all that and filed it away in a couple of hours one evening.'

'Actually, that's almost exactly how long it took,' she said giving him a smug smile, forgiving herself again for exaggerating a bit. After all, a doctor was well used to late nights, whether it was to deliver triplets or to sort out patient case notes. 'I'd already completed an audit of all the files, so some of the piles you saw on Friday were ready for collection to be archived. As for the rest, the only reason why I hadn't returned them to the filing cabinets was because that would have made them too heavy to move when I decorated.'

'And you achieved the whole thing in a weekend!' he marveled, and she didn't correct him with details of the many weeks it had taken to do the audit in the first place. She'd been horrified to find that Donald had probably avoided auditing his files ever since he'd come to the department, and the overfilled cabinets were the reason why the current patients' files had permanently littered the room, albeit in relatively tidy piles.

She'd actually believed that she'd been doing the tedious job for her own benefit, hoping that *she'd* get the appointment, but as it turned out...

'Well, I can't tell you how grateful I am that you went to all this trouble.' He spread his arms to indicate the whole pristine room. 'Not only will it be nicer—and more efficient—to work in, but it will look far more welcoming to the patients. And...' He drew the word out, suddenly pacing across the room and back again with a determined expression on his face.

'Yes! I thought so,' he announced. 'Now that you've removed all those boxes and piles, you've made enough room—if my desk is moved just a little further across—to juggle another desk in here, so you won't have to be served with an eviction order after all.'

That was the *last* thing she'd expected him to say,

and while her heart had suddenly taken up a faster beat
at the thought of sharing this room with him on a daily
basis, her reason was telling her that he would probably be such a distraction that she'd never get any
work done. She'd have to do some careful juggling of
her own to make sure that she only came in here when
he was otherwise occupied.

'I'll contact Maintenance and find out how to get
hold of another desk,' she said, bowing to the inevitable. It wasn't as if she'd been able to think of anywhere else to park herself. As one of the newer dis-
ciplines, the AR department had been forced to carve
itself a niche at one end of the obs and gyn department,
and space was at a premium.

'Great!' he said, clearly satisfied with finding a solution to her problem so swiftly. Equally obviously, he
was totally undisturbed by the fact they would end up
all but joined at the hip. 'Now, show me again how to
get this beast to let me know what's in the diary.' He
gestured towards the computer.

'Make sure it's switched on first,' she began with a
straight face. 'And then—'

'Smart alec!' he scowled. 'You do it this time. Come
here and sit down at the desk.'

Leah sat in what had so recently been *her* chair to
switch the computer on, and as David leaned over her
shoulder to watch what she was doing, she rued her
unruly tongue. It was actually very simple to access
the program and she could easily have explained without having him get so close.

Unfortunately, the fact that she was surrounded by
a mixture of soap, shampoo and something that could
only be David's skin, must have short-circuited a few

brain cells because it took her two unnecessary attempts to bring up that day's diary.

'So, according to this, starting at nine we have back-to-back appointments with new patients referred by their GPs. Is that usual?'

'What? That they're referred or that they're back-to-back?' Had his meaning been clear and it was his proximity that was muddling her?

'Both, I suppose.' He straightened up from his position leaning over her shoulder and she silently sighed in relief, but then he perched one hip on the corner of the desk, so she was no better off, her eyes drawn to the firm muscles in the thigh just inches from her hand. 'And why are they all new patients?'

Leah forced herself to look away, concentrating on the list of names on the screen while she gathered her thoughts.

'Donald set it up so he saw the new ones all on the same day, but there's no reason why you can't change the system if you want to. It was just *his* preference.' She chanced a glance in his direction and, when she found his intent gaze fixed unwaveringly on her, hurriedly looked away again. 'As for the referrals, as you know, this AR department is a centre of excellence and that means all the GPs within our catchment area are free to refer. That also includes obs and gyn departments in other hospitals that don't have a specialist AR department like ours.'

'And how does the lab cope with such a sudden influx? Do you have to give them special warning?'

'Yes and no,' Leah said with a smile. 'As referrals, most of the patients have already undergone the most basic tests through their GPs, so we only have to do the more specialised stuff. All our samples are sent direct to Stanley, who wouldn't hear of anyone else in the labs handling them.' She smiled as she digressed. 'Do you know, he actually resents having to take his annual leave because someone else has to do them while he's away? He says it takes him weeks to get everything running smoothly again.'

'A bit obsessive, is he?'

'No, just very grateful for the twins the department helped him and his wife to have after years of disappointment,' she explained with a reminiscent smile for the photos that Stanley always carried with him. 'He actually took himself off to learn the specific techniques he'd need for our work.'

'Well, when we've finished with this morning's list, you'll have to take me down and introduce me. He's someone I need to stay on the right side of, by the sound of it,' he said with a brief chuckle.

It was a sound that could even warm her deep inside where she'd thought the ice of disappointment would live for ever. The sensation that things were changing was more than a little frightening.

She didn't want anything to change. She'd already made the decision on the direction her life was going to take because it couldn't be any other way. She had no option.

Her profession. That was what mattered. That was all that mattered in her life now.

'The afternoon is a little more fluid,' she continued, hurriedly dragging her thoughts back to the screen in front of her. 'What you'll be doing then depends on the results of the blood tests and the ultrasounds—whether there'll be any mums ready to have their eggs harvested. There may be any number from none to eleven today.'

'And Stanley could cope if it was eleven?' David sounded very doubtful. That sort of lab work was painstaking and time-consuming, to say nothing of the strain on the eyes and the back from gazing down a microscope.

'If it meant a childless couple had their chance of parenthood, yes, he would, even if he had to work all night,' Leah confirmed quietly. 'Sometimes none of us get much sleep, especially when we have a group of mums whose cycles synchronise the way these seem to have done.'

She was prevented from saying any more by the imperious summons of the telephone. Without thinking, she reached out to pick it up, only to have David's long fingers land on top of hers.

'Oops! Sorry!' She jerked her tingling hand back. 'Force of habit. Let me—' She tried to relinquish her seat to him.

'It's all right. Stay put,' he said with one hand now on her shoulder as he lifted the receiver.

'Obstetrics and Gynaecology,' he announced, and then listened to the speaker on the other end, but Leah wasn't interested in eavesdropping on his conversation. She was far more interested in the discovery that he had inordinately long eyelashes, their existence disguised by the fact that the tip of each one had been lightened to gold by the New Zealand sun.

'Yes, this is David ffrench speaking. How can I help you?' he was saying, just as there was the sound of impatient knocking at the door.

He glanced across, then stepped away from Leah, finally releasing her from her position in the chair.

In response to his silently mouthed request, she set off towards the door, but before she could get there it

was flung open and a florid-faced man stormed into
the room.

'Are you Dr Dawson?' he demanded abruptly.

'I am,' she confirmed, quite taken aback. 'And you
are?'

'*I* am one of the hospital's senior administrators,' he
announced grandly, then totally ignored her, turning
his fulminating gaze on the man just putting down the
telephone. 'And you, I suppose, are Dr ffrench.'

'*Mr* ffrench,' Leah corrected swiftly.

He ignored her, directing his words solely to her
new head of department.

'Well, I hope your slapdash behaviour today isn't
an indication of how you intend to run this department—or do good manners not mean anything to you
once you become a consultant?'

'I *beg* your pardon!' David said with enough ice in
his voice to reverse a century of global warming.

'Well, I should think so, too,' the man continued,
completely missing his meaning. 'Half an hour ago
you were supposed to attend a brief reception to welcome you to St Luke's...'

'So your secretary has just informed me,' he interrupted frostily with a gesture towards the phone, '*and
without a single word of apology.*'

Leah could remember the woman's self-righteous
voice all too well. She'd actually tried to make it sound
as if it was *Leah's* fault that she hadn't been informed
earlier that the head of department position had gone
to someone else.

'Don't talk rubbish, man,' scoffed the administrator.
'The press were all there—with photographers—and
you wasted everybody's time and money! The least
you could have done is informed us that you couldn't

be bothered to attend, although why you would refuse,
I can't—'

'Excuse me!' Leah interrupted sharply, stepping
right in front of the obnoxious little man. For just a
second she was inordinately glad that her smart heels
meant that he had to crane his jowly head back to look
up at her. Her blood was boiling that a jumped-up,
overweight pencil-pusher should be so rude to such a
skilful doctor. Without David's willingness to help this
morning, regardless of the possibility of a court case
if his insurance wasn't yet in force, there would be
three babies without a mother.

'Didn't you listen to what Mr ffrench said?' she demanded heatedly. 'He *couldn't* go to your little party
because your secretary *forgot* to send him his invitation, exactly the same as she *forgot* to inform me that
I was going to be getting a new head of department
until five minutes before he arrived.'

Out of the corner of her eye she saw David's hand
go up to cover his mouth, but whether it was to prevent
himself speaking or to warn her not to say any more
she didn't know. It didn't make any difference anyway. There were things she needed to get off her chest.

'You claim you're worried about the waste of
money?' she continued while the administrator was
still gaping at her. 'Well, I've got a *wonderful* money-
saving suggestion for you. I don't know how much
you pay your secretary, but if you sack her, you'll save
the hospital thousands because she's got the memory
span of a geriatric goldfish and she's totally useless at
her job.'

Even while the obnoxious man was gobbling
speechlessly, David took over, grasping him by the
elbow and directing him firmly out of the door.

'Thank you for your visit, but my colleague and I have a busy department to run and our first patients will be arriving any minute,' he announced gruffly, and closed the door in the administrator's purple face.

Leah was shaking with a combination of shock that she'd actually said all those things and nervousness at David's reaction. And she'd so wanted to get off on the right foot with him, especially as they were going to be working together so closely.

Then he turned round and she realised that his gruffness hadn't been displeasure at her lack of courtesy towards the administrator—no matter how pompous— but a cover for the urge to laugh.

'A geriatric goldfish?'

There was nothing stopping him now, and the rich sound filling the room sent a sudden wave of warmth through her as she joined in helplessly.

They were both wiping tears of mirth from their eyes when they finally managed to catch their breath.

'Oh, dear. How often am I likely to meet up with that delightful gentleman?' David said with a grimace.

'Never again, if you're lucky. I've certainly never met him before, so either he's new to the post and desperate to make his mark, or—as I was only caretaking your position—he never thought me worthy of a visit.'

'Well, going on first impressions, I wouldn't—'

'Oh, *please*, don't go on first impressions!' she exclaimed. 'I've explained why everything was in such a mess on Friday.'

'In that case, I shall take the blame for turning up early and seeing the work in progress, and I shall rephrase that.' He gestured around the immaculate room. 'Going on first impressions—and Kelly Argent's spirited defence of you—what you've been doing is far more than mere caretaking.'

The compliment fell sweetly on her bruised self-esteem. It wasn't his fault that she still harboured a degree of resentment that she hadn't been appointed to the position.

'As far as that's concerned, you won't really know how well or how badly I've been doing the job until you've been here a week or two,' she cautioned. 'Apart from anything else, you've probably got your own way of organising things and it's not necessarily the way we've got it set up here.'

'We'll just have to wait and see, then, won't we?' he said easily, then visibly switched into work mode. 'Now, what happens about setting up the case notes for the new patients this morning? Who's responsible for collating their previous histories and test results?' He settled himself against the edge of the blessedly clear desk and crossed his long legs at the ankle, and she had to drag her eyes away from all the lean power on display before she could get her mouth to form sensible words.

'Well, you have a very able secretarial team—'

'Team?' he queried with a blink. 'How many, exactly?'

'Job-sharing,' Leah said with a grin, realising that he was imagining a whole squad of people waiting with fingers poised over computer keys. 'As you know, there's a lot of routine correspondence between the department and the patients' respective GPs and-or referring hospital, all needing to be kept in the loop.'

'A lot?' he echoed with a grimace. 'Make that a mountain of the stuff.'

'Quite!' she agreed with feeling. 'And while it's important that it's all kept up to date, we learned that there was no reason why it had to be done strictly nine to five when there were plenty of people wanting jobs at different times of day—mums with preschoolers who prefer to spend the day with them and work a shift when their partner comes home after work, or mums with school-age children who want to finish in time to be there at the end of school, for example. It was just a matter of putting the pieces of jigsaw together to have enough man-…and woman-power to get the job done.'

He nodded thoughtfully, his eyes never leaving her face.

'And I don't suppose I need to ask who worked the jigsaw out, do I? So, where does this jigsaw live? There certainly isn't room in here.'

'No, and it wouldn't have been workable with patient consultations going on either.' Her sense of the ridiculous kicked in. 'To maintain patient confidentiality, they'd have had to spend a fair amount of time standing outside the door, waiting until it was appropriate to come back in.'

'So?' he prompted, the slight quirk at the corner of his mouth apparently all the humour he was going to allow himself now he was in an 'on duty' frame of mind.

'So there's a small office immediately behind the reception desk as you come into the department,' Leah explained, disappointed that the connection she'd felt between them seemed to have been deliberately severed. Or had she imagined it? 'When you want whoever's on duty to come to your office, you can either pick up the phone to call them in, or stretch your legs with a quick stroll along the corridor. I printed up a list of the various contact codes and taped it to the computer monitor—the side closest to the phone.'

'And are they responsible for organising the patient files each day?' he queried, returning to his original question.

'Yes, and no,' Leah admitted, feeling a twinge of disloyalty towards her old boss, even though she'd despaired of his slapdash methods with paperwork. 'Donald hated anyone "*messing*" with the files. He liked keeping the current ones "to hand" as he called it, but he didn't really have a system.'

'Hmm. At a guess, the only reason why he could find the file he was looking for was because you'd put it right under his hand,' he suggested wryly. 'So, what system had you devised for yourself over the last few months?'

'A simple one,' she said, and couldn't help the grin that went with the announcement, especially when it made that fugitive smile reappear on his face. She had to deliberately ignore the increase in her pulse rate that it caused, silently reminding herself that he was her new boss and they were here to work.

'Because I was doing the audit, I've been getting out each day's files myself, but there's no reason why they can't be got ready for you at the start of the day now. Here, let me show you,' she offered, and proceeded to unlock the rest of the cabinets and the deceptive cupboard door behind which was hidden a handbasin and shelves neatly stacked with disposable supplies.

Because she'd devised the system, it didn't take long for her to point out the way she'd organised everything, including her favourite drawers—the ones with the files of the department's most recent successes, many with photographs of those precious successes.

'Actually,' she began hesitantly, 'I was thinking of putting up a board somewhere in the department with all the photos on it—a sort of positive reinforcement for the parents going through the mill at the moment.'

'You haven't already got one?' he said with a frown, settling himself back against the desk and endangering her concentration again. 'I'm sure I've seen some photos…'

'Oh, there *are* photos around,' she agreed quickly, wondering what on earth was the matter with her. She'd never been one to ogle men's bodies, yet here she was, hardly able to drag her eyes away from him. 'Some mums and dads send us photos, and others actually come back to visit and then we get Kelly's instant camera out. The results are scattered on various walls, but I thought it might be a good idea if we could—'

'Of course we should!' he exclaimed. 'I can't imagine why there isn't one already.'

'I don't think Donald could see the point of spending the time on it. He wasn't really interested in his surroundings.' Leah didn't know why she felt it necessary to explain. His successor already had the memory of the drab room he'd inherited to go on.

'So where were you suggesting we put this photo collection? In here?' He straightened up from the desk and turned around in a circle. 'There's a stretch of blank wall there, over the filing cabinets.'

'Either that, or the big wall that confronts you as you come into the AR department,' she suggested.

'Or both?' he countered. 'This wall for our patients to see during their consultations, but the other one can be seen by everyone who visits Obs and Gyn when they get a glimpse of it through the glass doors. There's nothing like a display of baby photos to put a smile on your face.'

'Except when you're one of those who *can't* have one of their own, no matter how sophisticated the technology,' Leah pointed out sombrely. 'Then it can just be another source of heartbreak.'

'It can be devastating,' he agreed quietly, 'Especially when they've pinned all their hopes on us helping them. Too many think that IVF is the absolute answer—that they're guaranteed success just by coming here and going through the system. They don't realise just how many women...and men...there are for whom we can do nothing.'

Leah knew the statistics only too well, having been a part of them. 'It's especially hard when there's absolutely no apparent reason for the failure,' she added, and when he sharpened his gaze on her, she wondered if her own devastation had been evident in her voice.

She held her breath for a second, hoping that he wouldn't ask. There was no way she could talk to him about it—no way she could talk to anyone without becoming emotional about her failure.

'All we can do is keep trying to find reasons and means to get around them and, in the meantime, do our best for as many as we can,' he said, and she started breathing again.

'Now!' he said briskly, standing and gesturing towards the door. 'If you would like to lead the way, I think it would be a good idea if you introduced me to the first pieces of my jigsaw puzzle before the patients start arriving.'

'What about the nursing and ancillary staff?' she

suggested. 'Do you want me to get everybody together so you can have a quick word?'

'No, thank you!' he said with a definite shudder. 'The last thing I want to do is the "rally the troops" scene. I'd far rather meet them a few at a time so that we can get to know each other. I want them to know that I'm approachable—in fact, I insist on it. If there's something a member of my staff wants to tell me, or ask me, the last thing they need is a remote figurehead.'

'Message received and understood!' Leah feigned a salute but her heart was growing lighter by the minute when she realised just how different the department was going to be under its new head. Obviously, it wasn't as satisfying as if she'd been appointed, but the situation could have been much worse. Now all she needed was an hour or three to work out what went wrong with her pulse every time he looked at her with those stunning blue-green eyes. 'I'll certainly pass the word around that you're happy for people to—'

'What do you mean, *pass the word*?' he interrupted, stopping and turning back so suddenly that she nearly ended up with her nose pressed to his pristine white shirt...and the broad chest beneath it... Her unruly pulse went into overdrive again.

She took a hasty step back, but it still wasn't far enough to escape the enticing mixture of soap and man that surrounded them.

'You're going to be coming with me,' he continued, apparently completely oblivious to her turmoil, thank goodness. 'I'm going to be relying on you to perform the introductions as we go.'

So much for getting a chance to catch my breath, she thought as she directed him along the corridor with a wave of one shaky hand. It sounded as if she was going to be working all too closely with the man for at least the next few days. There certainly wasn't going to be time to analyse the effect he was having on her.

CHAPTER FOUR

'LEAH? Can I have a word?' queried a hesitant voice.

Leah looked up from the mountain of paperwork on her newly acquired desk and saw the petite figure of one of the department's team of secretaries hovering in the evening shadows outside the doorway.

'Of course you can, Sue. Come in.' She groaned as she straightened her back. 'Anything to take a break from this. I swear I'm going to end up hunchbacked before my next birthday. Is there a problem?'

'My husband just rang. He said that my daughter—Mandy, she's three—has just been very sick and she's crying for me. I wondered if you wouldn't mind...'

'Of course you should go home to her,' Leah said immediately. 'Apart from the fact that Mandy needs her mum, you've often worked on when we've needed you to in the past so it's only fair.'

'Are you sure? It won't cause problems with David that I haven't finished all the typing, will it?'

'I'm positive. Now, scoot! And give her a cuddle for me.'

Sue thanked her breathlessly then hurried away, home to the husband and child waiting for her.

'While *I* might just as well stay here all night,' Leah muttered with a burst of uncharacteristic despondency. 'My bonsai certainly aren't waiting to be tucked up for the night.'

The echo of her words came back to her and when

she realised just how self-pitying and downright silly
they sounded, she shook her head and got back to work.

She didn't know how long she'd been concentrating
and hadn't really registered the fact that she was totally
alone at this far end of the department. It happened so
often and had never mattered before...until she heard
the sound of footsteps coming along the corridor towards the office.

She froze with her hands suspended over the computer keyboard, every hair on her body lifting as her
skin tightened with fear.

There was someone else in the department with her
and there shouldn't be, not now that Sue had gone
home. Had she been in such a hurry to get to her
daughter that she hadn't checked that the door had shut
properly behind her?

The only time this department was humming with
noise and movement was when their patients arrived
for consultations. Any procedures—and the babies that
hopefully resulted from them—took place at the other
end of the obs and gyn floor. *That* was staffed twenty-
four hours a day, and as she was first on call tonight,
if they'd needed her to assist with a difficult delivery,
someone would have paged her rather than wasting
time coming for her on foot.

Now it was almost eerily silent except for the owner
of those feet, and whoever it was definitely shouldn't
be here.

A flurry of scenarios whirled through her head like
autumn leaves in a high wind...

Had someone broken into the department in search
of drugs?

Was it a stalker, seeing her lonely light and picking
her out as an easy, isolated target?

It couldn't be Sue returning to work. She wouldn't be back until her next scheduled shift and, anyway, these footsteps sounded far more like a man's.

Even as she concentrated on the way they were drawing ever closer to her door, their pace slowed and grew ominously quiet.

Her heartbeat didn't. It was working so hard to pump the adrenaline around her system that she was surprised the walls weren't vibrating in time with its mad gallop.

Then the door was flung open so suddenly that she gave a shriek of shock, her knees trembling too much for her to get out of her chair, never mind running.

'Leah! I thought you were an intruder. What on earth are *you* doing here?' David demanded harshly as he stalked into the room.

'I work here,' she snapped back, too shaken to say more.

'Not at this time of night,' he declared, abruptly leaning over her shoulder to press buttons on the keyboard.

With a blink of amazement she watched him save what she'd been doing and shut the programme down as efficiently as if he'd been using the system for years rather than a single day.

'You've done too much overtime in the last weeks and months,' he continued, taking a scant step back before swivelling her chair to face him. 'You've essentially been running the department single-handedly, and then you threw in a marathon decorating spree. You should be home, catching up on some sleep.'

He reached out both hands and her thoughts were so jumbled that she automatically put her own in them. Effortlessly, he pulled her to her feet, only to have to grab her and pull her against him for support when her shaky knees refused to bear her weight.

'Hey! Are you all right? Are you ill?' he demanded, peering down at her face, and those stunning eyes met hers at close quarters, robbing her of what little breath she had left.

She'd forgotten just how good this could feel, she thought as she registered the supporting way he'd wrapped his arms around her, surrounding her with his strength and his warmth. She felt safe, here…almost cherished.

But that was crazy!

She'd only known the man a matter of days, and now that she thought about it…

She stiffened and pushed herself away from him, refusing to acknowledge that she missed the physical contact.

'No thanks to you!' she snapped. 'What are you doing, stomping around at this time of night? Storming in here like that could have given me a heart attack.'

'Only if you had a serious heart problem to begin with,' he pointed out far too rationally. He folded his arms across his chest and leant back against the desk in an increasingly familiar stance. 'And the reason why I came in like that was to surprise whoever was in here, interfering with the medical records.'

'Interfering with records?'

'Well, it's not as if there's anything else of value in here. The computer's hardly top of the line and for all your hard work redecorating, the fixtures and fittings certainly aren't worth risking a gaol sentence to steal. In fact,' he said, warming to his theme, '*you're* probably the most valuable item in the room, *and* the most at risk if there were an intruder.'

'Oh, that's crazy,' she protested.

'It's not crazy at all, when you think of all the statistics about hospital staff being attacked. In fact, I don't want you staying on your own in the department at night. When you're in this office, you're far too far away for anyone to hear if you needed help.'

Leah wasn't feeling frightened any more. In fact, her blood was boiling that he thought he could hand out such high-handed commands.

'And how am I supposed to do my job if I'm banned from the department?' she demanded heatedly. 'How am I supposed to keep all my paperwork up to date? What am I supposed to do with myself if I'm on call— sit and twiddle my thumbs and drink too much coffee instead of getting on with things?' She planted one fist on each hip, determined to stand her ground. 'This is nothing more than blatant sex discrimination. We wouldn't even be having this discussion if I were a man.'

'You're partly right about that,' he agreed calmly, his level voice only infuriating her more. 'But until Maintenance has been around the department beefing up security, that's the way it's going to be. I will not be responsible for putting members of staff at risk.'

'You *wouldn't* be responsible,' she snapped. 'It's *my* choice to work on in the evening and I've been responsible for my own actions for a good few years now. My decisions and my safety are my own responsibility.'

'Fine!' he agreed abruptly, but before she could savour the fact that he'd backed down he added, 'As long as you realise that you'd also be responsible for blowing a hole in the AR department's meagre budget. If you insist on staying, I'll have to pay for someone from Security to sit outside the door until you go home.'

'What! That's ridiculous!' There was absolutely nothing wrong with her knees as she stomped across the limited space in the room to stand almost nose to nose with him, conscious that she must sound like a fishwife. 'There's no reason to have anyone sitting outside the door. I've been working alone in the department for months and there's never been any problem. I don't see why—'

'Because I said so,' he cut in brutally, then paused and groaned. 'Did you hear what I just said? You've got me using those dreadful phrases my parents used to say, and I always swore I'd never do it.'

'And it's hardly appropriate as I'm not your child,' she pointed out stiffly. 'You can't tell me what I can—'

'I'm head of department,' he broke in very softly, not a trace of levity in his voice this time. He was obviously deadly serious. 'I had a look around the department earlier today and discovered just how many roundabout routes there are to access this particular floor, so until Maintenance have sorted out the security, I will be making an absolute rule that *no one* stays here on their own.'

Leah had never really thought about the fact that there was more than one staircase and more than one bank of lifts accessing the obs and gyn floor. If she was honest, she could remember hearing the sound of approaching feet just a few minutes ago and the way her heart had pounded while she'd wondered if Sue had forgotten to shut the door properly on her way out. If it *hadn't* been David...

'How long is it all going to take?' she demanded,

finally conceding that this was a battle she wasn't going to win. 'I hope you realise that it can take months to get even simple repairs done.'

She dreaded the thought of getting behind with her work. It had nearly killed her to have to spend so many hours sorting out Donald's neglected filing. She certainly didn't want to have to do it all over again. She also couldn't bear the idea that someone might miss their last window of opportunity for having a family of their own if she didn't keep on top of every detail.

'They promised that it would be done before the end of the week,' he announced, and she blinked in surprise.

'Did they say *which* week?' she asked skeptically, and surprised half a grin out of him. She was taken aback to discover that it actually felt good to make him smile, sending an unexpected warmth spiralling through her.

'*This* week,' he confirmed with a roll of his eyes. 'Now, is there anything you need to pick up before I see you home?'

'See me home?' It was her turn to smile. It was years since anyone had offered to see her home. It was almost a shame that she didn't need him to. 'I came by car.'

'In that case, I'll see you to your car.'

'Phil or Den usually do that,' she pointed out, and at his frown explained, 'The night security men on the main door. They take it in turn to keep an eye on the female staff until they're safely in their cars.'

She paused in the hallway while he checked that the office door had closed properly behind them then had to hurry to keep up with his much longer strides.

'Sorry,' he muttered when he realised what was happening. 'I forgot you're small.'

'I'm not small for a woman,' she objected as the lift doors opened and he gestured for her to enter. 'In fact, if I'd been an inch taller I could have been a model.'

'Did you want to be a model?' He seemed intrigued by the idea but the way his eyes gleamed as they roamed over her from head to toe suddenly made the steel-walled lift feel more like a sauna.

'I've heard it's exhausting and boring but I've heard that the pay is fantastic for the most successful, and, no, I'd never want to be a model even if I did have the height.'

The doors slid open again on the ground floor, partly masking his muttered comment. It had actually sounded as if he'd said, 'You've got all the rest of the equipment.' But that couldn't be right. She'd never had the right equipment—at least, not in working order.

She threw him a frowning glance and instantly knew she must have been mistaken. His thoughts were clearly elsewhere than on her dubious charms, especially when the first thing he spoke about when the lift doors closed was the work she'd been doing on the computer.

'I take it you were entering the details of the latest batch of new patients?'

'And starting all the new cross-checks to verify their identities,' she confirmed. 'Although I can't say I feel very comfortable with the process.'

'Neither am I,' he said grimly. 'When you're dealing with people desperate to have a child, it doesn't seem right to waste precious time playing the policeman to check up that they're telling the truth.

Unfortunately there are sound reasons why the rules and regulations are set down.'

'Not least the fact that multiple births have a far higher incidence of birth defects, with fewer surviving, and that older mums have a pitifully low rate of success with a greater chance of complications. Yes, I know all that, but it still feels…wrong, somehow, to have to pry into every nook and cranny before we can make a final decision.'

'You'll find it feels much less *wrong*—' he deliberately stressed her own word '—if you think of it from the other direction. You're doing the checks to make absolutely sure that you're giving any babies the best possible chance. After all, they're the reason why we're doing all this.'

'At least we don't have to make the final decisions all by ourselves,' she muttered as she watched the numbers change above the doors. 'We can blame "the committee" if we have to pass on bad news.'

David was just waving a signal to the security man on duty—Den tonight, Leah registered—indicating that he was going to escort Leah to her car, when both their pagers started to shrill.

'Oops!' Leah performed her about-face a second faster than David did and ended up ploughing into him…again!

For just a fraction of a second she forgot to be embarrassed and simply enjoyed the feel of such a solidly male body against hers. Then his long legs were taking him rapidly in the direction of the lifts and there was no time for such nonsensical imaginings.

'Can you tell Obs and Gyn we're on our way?' Leah called over her shoulder, and Den waved a hand in acknowledgement, his other hand already reaching for the phone.

This time she was still filled with a strange awareness of every breath David took as they stood watching the numbers above the door, but there was an overriding impatience to reach their destination and find out what emergency necessitated both of them to attend.

Yin Bo Chan was waiting for them when the lift doors swished open and blinked, apparently surprised to see the two of them arrive together.

'What's the problem?' David demanded as he strode towards her, already taking the cufflinks out of his shirt ready to don protective clothing. Leah was left to hurry in his wake.

'Oh, dear! You're both here!' exclaimed the petite midwife. 'I only asked for whoever was on call.'

'That's me,' Leah announced. 'How can I help?'

'Actually,' David interrupted, 'I replaced your name on the board tonight. I put myself as first on call, so you could catch up on some sleep.'

'Well, as you forgot to tell me…' Leah said ominously, her anger at his high-handedness returning in full force. She turned back to the increasingly uncomfortable midwife. 'Did you have a problem?'

'One of your IVF patients, Mrs Joliffe, has presented with antepartum haemorrhage and pain.'

Leah's heart sank at the news. After years of misery, Pam Joliffe was finally, ecstatically pregnant.

'How many weeks is she?' David demanded, just beating Leah to the punch. In spite of the fact that she'd been so recently updating all the patient files, she couldn't immediately recall the stage the pregnancy had reached. If it was too soon for viability…

'She's thirty-three weeks gestation with twins,' Yin

said succinctly. 'She's in pain but there's no rigidity to the belly. No apparent contractions, but the cervix is slightly dilated—less than one centimetre.'

'Yin...?' called a panic-stricken voice in the nearby room, swiftly followed by a head appearing round the door.

Leah fought a sympathetic grin when she recognised Greg Martin, one of the newest recruits to the department, a junior doctor in his first week of a six-month obs and gyn rotation. He looked distinctly green around the gills and was almost quivering with apprehension.

'Oh, hello, sir,' he said over a nervous gulp when he saw who was standing there. He visibly braced himself to make a report. 'We've put Mrs Joliffe on oxygen and put two large-bore cannulae in. So far, she's only on Ringer's solution for hydration. I've taken...' He paused, then corrected himself. 'Actually, *Yin* has taken blood and ordered U and E, FBC, blood glucose, cross-match, rhesus and antibody status, Kleihauer test and clotting screen. We've also got cardiotocography running to monitor the baby and we were just going to do an ultrasound scan to see if the blood loss was part of a much larger haemorrhage retained behind the placenta.'

He was completely out of breath by the time he came to the end of his recitation, and also, rather obviously, feeling totally out of his depth, but Leah couldn't fault any of it.

'Well, done, Greg,' David said quietly, and Leah wasn't surprised to see the steadying effect the praise had on the young man's nerves. Somehow the sincerity of his tone was far more potent than any amount of gushing praise.

'You've made a good start,' he continued, automatically reaching to the nearby dispenser to tip soap into his hands to wash them before he joined their patient. 'Now, what would your next steps be?'

'My next steps?' he repeated faintly.

Leah had to duck her head over her own hand-washing when she heard Greg's loud gulp of apprehension, but she was impressed with David's teaching style. Some consultants were far too quick to take over without giving their juniors a chance to test themselves, even with a verbal run-through of possible courses of action.

'Ah, well… It would partly depend on blood loss and the degree of separation we see on the scan…?' he suggested hesitantly, and at David's encouraging nod expanded on his theme. 'If it shows placental abruption, we'll need to do a Caesarean before the babies get into difficulty, in spite of the fact their lungs aren't mature enough yet. If there's no major abruption, we continue support and see if things settle down enough to go closer to term.'

'Well, then, let's go in and see our patient. When we see what's on the scan, we can make our decision,' David said with a smile and a gesture for Greg to lead the way.

Our patient…and *we* can make a decision, he'd said, and as she followed the two of them into the room, Leah couldn't help noticing that, thanks to David's careful choice of words and his encouraging manner, the young man seemed to have grown at least an inch taller in the last few minutes and he wasn't nearly as pale and shaky any more.

'Oh, no!' exclaimed Pam Joliffe fearfully when she

saw the three of them arriving. 'What's happened to my babies?'

'Nothing, as far as we know,' soothed David. 'Whatever makes you think something's wrong?'

'So many of you arriving at once,' she said anxiously. 'It *must* be bad news.'

David laughed easily, as if he hadn't a care in the world.

'No,' he said. 'That's just called bad planning on our part. I'm David ffrench, the new head of department, and Dr Dawson and I had just finished a meeting when our pagers went off. Dr Martin knew that one of us would want to see you as you're one of our special patients. Anyway, we decided that it was far too undignified to have an argument in the middle of Reception about whose turn it was to come up, so we both came to see you together.'

His apparently light-hearted manner took some of the panic out of Pam's expression and her tension eased still further when he perched himself on the edge of her bed.

Leah wondered if she was the only one who noticed that he started to reach for her hand, only to cover the gesture by curling his own into a loose fist and resting it on his thigh.

Was it the new politically correct regulations about unnecessary physical contact between patient and caregiver that had prompted the withdrawal? Leah didn't know, but the fact that he'd had to consciously stop himself from automatically offering the comfort of human touch told her a great deal about the type of doctor he was, and her chagrin about losing the job to him faded a little more.

'Now, what have you been up to?' he asked gently.

'I think you're in too much of a hurry to meet these little people. I'd rather they stayed where they are to cook a little longer.'

'I wasn't doing anything silly, I promise, especially with my husband away,' she said, suddenly tearful as she threw a pleading glance towards Leah. '*You* know how long it's taken me to get this far in a pregnancy. I wouldn't do *anything* to jeopardise...' She couldn't finish.

'We know you wouldn't,' Leah said soothingly. 'But if you remember, I did warn you that twins often try to arrive early, probably because carrying two is an extra burden on the mother's reserves. What Dr Martin's going to do now is run a few checks to see whether the two of them really mean it, or if we can persuade them to stay put a bit longer.'

Out of the corner of her eye she could see the ultrasound trolley being wheeled into position and she stepped aside, carefully positioning herself so that she'd be able to see the screen without getting in the way.

It was a relief to see the shadowy images of first one and then the other baby, and she was nearly as relieved as the mother when those images showed both strongly beating hearts much in evidence.

The rest of the news wasn't quite as rosy, as the screen displayed images of a definite area of separation of one placenta from the uterus.

Pam was unaware of the problem and was now sobbing with relief that her precious babies were still alive and well. She was delighted when she was offered printed copies of the clearest images of their faces.

Leah was loath to puncture her euphoria but a glance at the concerned frown pleating David's forehead confirmed the necessity. He looked up to meet her waiting gaze and without a word needing to be spoken, she knew what the decision had to be.

She had a horrible feeling about this one, but it was the strange sensation of connection she'd had when their eyes had met that was worrying her more. She barely knew the man and there was absolutely no point in developing any sort of relationship between them apart from a professional one.

'Pam, I want to start you on some steroid injections,' David announced calmly, dragging her besotted eyes away from the pictures and Leah's attention back to the job in hand.

'Steroids?' she echoed, clearly puzzled. 'What for? Aren't they what athletes use to cheat in their races...or is it what body-builders take to pump up their muscles?'

'Both, unfortunately,' David confirmed. 'They take anabolic steroids and, because they take them in excess, they can do untold long-term damage to their bodies. In your case, we want to give you corticosteroids—just a short course over a couple of days—to help the babies' lungs to mature.'

'Why do you need to do that?' Panic was creeping in again and she briefly clutched the pictures protectively to her chest before gazing at them with renewed fear. 'The pictures show that they're all right...don't they?'

'Your babies are beautiful and strong, but the pictures also showed us that there's an area of one of the placentas that's coming ''unglued'' from your uterus,' he explained gently. 'That's why you were bleeding.'

'But the bleeding's stopped now, hasn't it?' she implored. 'Everything's going to be all right, isn't it?'

'We hope so,' he agreed. 'But we don't want to leave anything to chance, either with the babies' health or with yours. That's why we want to give you the steroids.'

'But what will they do?' she demanded. 'Glue the placenta back again?'

'We wish it was that easy,' Leah said with a chuckle that she hoped would lighten the fraught atmosphere a little. It failed.

'We're hoping that everything will settle down,' David continued, 'but just in case we have to deliver the babies early, the steroids help to make their lungs stronger, so it isn't quite so much of a shock when they have to start breathing much earlier than they should.'

'Oh, God!' she wailed. 'Why is this all happening when Jonty's so far away? When they're submerged, I can't even phone him and get him to come home.'

'Submerged?' Greg echoed, clearly puzzled.

'He's a Royal Navy submariner,' Leah explained in a succinct aside, leaving the younger man to work out the logistics of getting a man out of a vessel deep under one of the world's oceans at short notice and transporting him to his wife's bedside.

'He'd already organised to take some leave so he could be with me when the babies are due,' Pam continued tearfully. 'If anything happens *now*, it could take *days* before they could get him here.'

'Well, that gives us time to make sure that this pair are in the best possible health when he does finally make it,' Leah said, deliberately upbeat.

'On the plus side, there's the fact that you've only had a bleed,' Greg offered.

'Only? What do you mean, *only*?' The panic was back in full measure and Leah had to stifle a groan.

'Oh...well...' *Now* Greg realised his mistake and glanced across in a mute appeal for help out of the hole he'd just dug under his own feet.

'You really don't want to have to listen to a long and boring lecture on obstetrics and gynaecology,' Leah said quickly, hoping to distract Pam, 'especially when we already know that your babies aren't growing two heads apiece, have all the right number of arms and legs and have fully functioning circulatory systems.'

Above all, she didn't want Greg to mention the fact that they were all crossing their fingers that she wouldn't start having contractions. Ritodrine would be their drug of choice to halt labour and could buy them a little more time, but it wasn't suitable in every case and certainly wouldn't be a guarantee of success.

'How long will I have to be on the steroids?' Pam asked as she watched the intramuscular injection being prepared.

'Just four doses at twelve-hourly intervals,' Yin Bo Chan confirmed soothingly as she smoothed the covers back into position.

'So I have to come back in twelve hours for the next one?' she said with a glance at her watch.

'No, we'll be keeping you in for a while, so that we can keep a close eye on you...and the babies,' David added quickly, certain that concern for her precious children would override any objections. 'It will give you a couple of days to catch up on your sleep and do a bit of reading while someone else does the cooking.'

'But there's still so much left to do to get ready before they arrive,' Pam fretted, still close to tears.

'I've still got the last pieces of furniture to get for the nursery and I haven't finished half of the knitting I was going to do.'

'Well, you can do all the knitting you want in here,' he pointed out. 'And I'm certain your babies won't be critical if their nursery isn't perfectly kitted out. They wouldn't be the first to have to go to sleep in a padded drawer.'

'Well, no, but—'

'But nothing, Pam.' This time David *did* touch her, resting a reassuring hand over hers where her fingers worried the sheet into a series of crumpled pleats. 'No worrying allowed. Leave that to us. All *you* have to do is concentrate on relaxing and getting that knitting done. Sister will be able to ring a friend or neighbour to fetch whatever you need from home.'

Whether it was his touch or his words of reassurance that finally got through to her, Leah didn't know, but he'd achieved his purpose as Pam finally relaxed her head on the pillow.

CHAPTER FIVE

'LET me give you a lift home,' Leah offered when they finally made it to her car an hour later, their patient resigned to spending at least the next few days in hospital for the sake of her babies.

Once more, David had insisted on walking her across the car park, their shadows impossibly long under the security lights, but all Leah had been able to think about was how good it felt to have his company for the short walk.

It definitely didn't feel the same when Phil or Den accompanied her. There wasn't the same awareness of the scant inches between David's arm and hers as they'd crossed the reception area, or her reaction to his brief touch at the small of her back as he'd ushered her through the door into the chill of the night outside.

'Thanks for the offer, but there's no need. I don't live far enough away to warrant it,' he said, nodding in the direction of the block of flats just outside the hospital grounds. 'I've just moved into Cedars.'

'Cedars,' she echoed stupidly, as if she didn't know the name of her own address, then several half-forgotten facts suddenly connected. '*You're* the person who moved into the top-floor flat the other day.' She'd been working when the removals company had delivered his belongings but until this moment had had no idea whether the new owner had moved in with them. No wonder she hadn't caught sight of her new neighbour if he'd been spending all his time at the hospital.

'How could you know where I…?' He didn't bother finishing his question, so something in her face must have told him the answer. 'You live in the same block,' he said with a wry smile. 'In that case, it makes sense to accept your offer…although I'm surprised you thought it worthwhile to drive such a short distance.' He strode round to the passenger side and opened the door as soon as she activated the key fob to release the locks, and she had to grit her teeth to prevent the heated words spilling out before she'd had time to temper them.

She managed to wait until he'd fastened his safety belt before she refuted what she saw as an unwarranted criticism.

'I drove for exactly the same reason that you escorted me across the car park tonight—because it's safer than walking at this time of the year,' she said sharply, resenting that he seemed to see her as both lazy and wasteful. 'As the evenings grow lighter, I won't bother.'

'Oops!' he said ruefully. 'That was obviously a case of open mouth and insert foot, especially after I'd made such a point of escorting you. And I'm sorry for impugning your conservational tendencies.'

'You're forgiven,' she said with a decidedly gracious nod, surprised that he'd been so quick to admit his mistake and once more fighting the urge to grin. She really didn't want to find the man so…humorous… self-deprecating…appealing. It was bad enough that they were going to be working together, but to discover that they were going to be living together…

No! Not living together!

Just the thought of the words filled her imagination with forbidden images.

What she'd meant was that they were going to be living in the same building, and the fact that there was going to be nothing more than a single, far-from-soundproof wall separating their flats made it doubly important that she stamped hard on any feelings of attraction towards him. That would be a certain recipe for disaster.

It wasn't a long journey around the hospital's perimeter road and out of the main gates and then it was just a matter of yards before she turned into the parking area attached to the small block of flats, but Leah clamped her mouth shut, determined not to allow any further conversation to build between the two of them. If she was going to react so strongly to the man after such a short acquaintance—it was just the fact that she'd discovered that he was going to be living in the same block of flats, for heaven's sake—then she was going to have to work harder than ever to stop her emotions becoming involved.

So, having made that decision, why did she find herself pausing outside her front door, the key already in her hand, ready to make her escape behind the safety of solid wood?

'Would you like something to drink?' she heard herself say, and nearly groaned aloud. That certainly wasn't the way to maintain some distance between the two of them. 'Not coffee, of course…not if we want to get to sleep…'

If we want to get to sleep? As she realised that she'd made it sound as if the two of them would be sleeping together, her face flamed with embarrassment and she tried to cover her gaffe with hurried words. 'I've got tea or fruit juice or bottled water or—'

'I'm still unpacking,' David said, and she breathed a sigh of relief that he was actually going to let her off the hook, then he dashed her hopes when he added, 'and I didn't manage to get to the shops today either, so I'd love a cup of tea.'

Silently damning her unruly tongue she slid the key into the lock and swung the door open then led the way inside.

This was the last thing she'd needed, she thought as she flipped on each light as she passed on her way to the tiny kitchen, overwhelmingly aware of the steady footsteps behind her that told her he was following her.

She had to see him at the hospital every day and now that she knew he lived in the same building she could expect to run into him here from time to time, but at least her flat could have been a ffrench-free zone.

Not any more. With her invitation, she now wouldn't be able to relax without seeing the way he propped one shoulder against the door-frame while he watched her fill the kettle, those stunning blue-green eyes seeming to follow her every move as she hovered over the choice between proper cups or her usual mugs.

'A mug is fine for me,' he murmured. 'I don't take sugar, so I won't need a saucer to put the spoon in.'

Leah wasn't certain if she was comfortable with the way he seemed to be able to read her mind. She hadn't realised that she was that transparent, she thought as she retrieved the milk from the fridge, then paused as she caught sight of the food neatly stacked in her fridge.

She might have been busy, but she hadn't been trying to move house at the same time, she argued silently as she justified the urge to give the man something to eat. She certainly hadn't seen him leave the department for anything as mundane as a trip to the canteen and she'd be surprised if he'd had anything more than coffee all day. He must be starving.

'Do you subscribe to the theory that real men don't eat quiche?' she challenged as she withdrew a thick wedge filled to the brim with bacon and cheese and topped with colourful circles of tomato and placed it on the work surface in full sight.

For a second he seemed startled into silence as his eyes travelled from the food to her almost combative stance, then his face creased into a grin that completely stole her breath.

'Actually, I subscribe to the theory that real men will eat anything they can get their hands on if they want to keep body and soul together,' he admitted. 'Especially something that looks as good as that. Anything's better than chicken ping.'

'Chicken *ping*?' she echoed, sidetracked by the unfamiliar phrase.

'Anything heated in the microwave,' he explained with a grimace. 'It doesn't seem to matter what fancy name they give it on the packet, it all tastes the same.'

'As well as being woefully short on protein and massively overloaded with salt and artificial colourings and flavourings,' she agreed. 'Well, give me a second to pour your tea and then you can take your mug into the other room while I get some salad out to go with the quiche.'

'If I sit down, I'll probably be asleep before you can get it on a plate,' he admitted wryly, then began to roll up his sleeves. 'Put me to work instead. Which would you rather I did—pour the tea or make the salad?'

'Oh, but…' That had backfired with a vengeance, she thought with a silent groan. She'd suggested he wait in the other room to put a bit of distance between them and give her a chance to get her galloping pulse to settle down. Now they were going to be in closer proximity than ever in her tiny kitchen.

'If you pour the tea, then,' she conceded weakly as she busied herself at the fridge again, retrieving a selection from the salad drawer in the bottom.

Over the next few minutes she was still very aware of every move he made but there was that strange feeling of companionship and uniformity of purpose as they prepared the meal together that she'd had right from the first time they'd worked together to deliver that unexpected set of IVF triplets.

That reminded her…

'Did you hear that the last of the Masson triplets is breathing on his own?' she asked over the muted clatter of cutlery being added to the tray.

'Yes. Isn't it great? If he continues to do this well, his sister will soon be able to come back to join them,' David said with a smile. 'I must say, I was horrified when I realised she was going to have to be sent halfway across the country to another unit because we didn't have room for her.'

'It doesn't happen often,' Leah said defensively, even though she knew the system was indefensible and one that she'd railed against herself. 'It's only when we have an unexpected multiple birth when we're already full of highly dependent babies, or when we have an urgent referral from one of the hospitals that doesn't have a specialist unit like ours. Then we have to free up a bed by sending the strongest one here to the nearest bed that can cope with their needs.'

'It just seems crazy to me,' he said heatedly. 'We've got all the equipment and the expertise of a centre of excellence but we're having to turn away babies from other hospitals and even send away babies that are already here—risking their lives in unnecessary ambulance journeys—just because there aren't enough qualified staff available for that level of high-dependence nursing.'

'Well, if you can think of some way to get the bone-heads at the top to realise that unless you pay them a proper wage, love of the job alone won't keep staff in the department...' Leah knew she didn't have to complete the sentence. It seemed as if it was an almost worldwide complaint that dedication to a profession was no guarantee of appreciation by the paymasters. 'Still, now that you've been appointed, perhaps you can do some cage rattling,' she suggested over her shoulder. 'Donald hated all the politics involved. He just liked getting on with the job.'

She turned to face him with a plate in each hand. 'I hope you like potato salad, as well as green. I had some leftovers to use up.'

It made her feel good to see the way his eyes lit up at the colourful display on the plate she held out to him.

For just a moment she allowed herself to remember how much she'd enjoyed the daily rituals of being half of a couple—all the little companionable gestures and intimacies, the caring—then quickly pushed the memories away. There was no point in yearning after them because there was no chance of ever experiencing them again, not when she knew how it would inevitably end.

'You didn't have to do this,' he demurred, then added hastily, 'not that I don't appreciate it, because I do. How on earth did you manage to whip all this up so quickly?'

It was flattering how eagerly he settled himself at the table to take the first mouthful and the appreciative groans that followed were almost sexual.

Don't go there! she told herself sternly when her atrophied hormones began to sit up and take notice.

'The green salad doesn't take more than a minute,' she said, hastily dragging her thoughts back to his question—anything to get them away from the possibility of putting her boss and sex in the same image. 'And I cheated with the potato salad because I used bought mayonnaise rather than making my own.'

'And the quiche?' he managed between hearty bites. 'This certainly doesn't look like a commercial product, neither does it taste like it.'

His praise spread a warm glow through her. How long had it been since someone had appreciated her for anything other than her medical skills?

'Thank you for the compliment.' She hoped she wasn't grinning like an idiot. 'I've always enjoyed cooking. I find it's a good way to unwind after a difficult shift.'

'I'm surprised you've had the time since Donald died.' He held up a hand when she would have interrupted. 'I know you aren't the only member of staff—we've got a couple of excellent junior registrars on board and the nursing staff is the equal of any I've worked with—but you were the most senior and by all accounts you'd essentially been running the department for months before Donald went. That was an enormous load, especially when you were short of senior staff.'

Leah was sure her face must be glowing with the heat that poured into it, and it wasn't just David's words. The expression in his eyes told of his sincerity, too, and was there also a hint of personal appreciation, or was that just wishful thinking on her part?

Wishful thinking? Now wait a minute! She pulled her thoughts up short, angry with where they were straying. She didn't want…didn't *need* a man's approval to know she was doing a good job. And she certainly didn't need a man in her life, no matter how tall dark and handsome he was, and certainly not when his eyes held as many shadows as David's did.

With that stern reminder she applied herself to her own meal, using the food as an excuse for ending any attempt at conversation. And the sooner they finished, the sooner he'd stop invading her privacy.

Except when he'd cleared his plate he sat back and started looking at his surroundings and her discomfort increased.

She knew what her flat looked like—almost bereft of furniture since she'd come out of her divorce with little more than her clothing. Since then she'd put all her energies into her career, not bothering with any of the trendy decorating knick-knacks that would make the flat look more homely or more elegant or even more lived in.

'I like this,' he pronounced after a minute, much to her surprise. 'It's totally uncluttered and…peaceful.'

'That's a polite way of saying empty,' she said with a wry grimace. 'Ever since I moved in here, I don't seem to have had time to do anything with it.' Or the inclination, she realised. After all, it was nothing more than somewhere to lay her head at the end of the day. It was never going to be the family home she'd once looked forward to.

'No. I mean it,' he insisted. 'So many of these designer make-overs seem more interested in the high-priced labels they can stuff into a room rather than the…the feeling you get when you're in it. Oh…!' He made a dismissive noise. 'I'm not explaining myself very well, but…look at what you've done in here. There's the minimum of comfortable-looking furniture with enough storage to hide any clutter, and instead of fussy floral arrangements that drop all their petals the day after you buy them, you've got a single plant.'

'Bonsai,' she murmured distractedly as she gazed around at the room anew. Seeing it through his eyes was a revelation because it did look good, far better than she'd realised.

'Bonsai?' he echoed. 'One of those Japanese miniature trees? Didn't I read somewhere that they don't make very good house-plants?'

'You're quite right. The majority only do well outdoors, where they belong, but most will put up with limited stays inside, provided their requirements for light and water are met. Of course, there are some varieties—the ones native to more tropical regions—that can be kept indoors, but their life span is far more precarious because they're prone to… Oh, I'm sorry for rabbiting on like that. Information overload?'

'It's obviously something that interests you.' Those beautiful eyes looked more blue than green this evening and he was watching her as though fascinated by this new facet of her life.

'I visited a Japanese garden several years ago, during a particularly…difficult time.' A time when she'd actually been wondering whether to abandon her career and retrain for something else entirely. 'I was walking through a little bamboo grove and sat down on a bench and an elderly Japanese gentleman started talking to me about listening to the sound of the wind…' She still went back to visit Itsuo Sugiyama whenever she could, especially when the chaos in her life started to overwhelm her. There was something about his timeless view of life that calmed both her mind and spirit.

In between those visits, she had her precious trees to keep her feet on the ground and soothe her heart— not that she would be telling David that. That was something strictly between herself and her trees.

'Well, my place is still half-full of boxes, but if I'm lucky, the washing machine will be connected tomorrow so I'll at least be able to have clean clothes for the next week. All I've got to do is remember to do some grocery shopping tomorrow and I stand a fighting chance of surviving.'

As he was speaking he stood up from the table and she was surprised to feel a sudden pang at the realisation that he was going to leave.

'You did the cooking, so let me help with the washing-up,' he offered, beginning to stack their plates.

'You'd do better to go home and unpack another box or two before you grab some sleep,' she suggested, taking the dirty dishes from him. 'These won't take me a moment, and we've both got a frantically busy day tomorrow. There are thirty patients booked into the morning clinic alone.'

He groaned theatrically. 'And that's without the interruptions we'll get if there are any problem deliveries or transfers from other units.' He paused a moment, just inches away from her. His gaze was warm and steady on her as she waited for him to speak and her heart suddenly performed an improvised quickstep. 'Thank you for the meal tonight,' he said seriously. 'I can't tell you how much I appreciate it…and the company.'

For just a moment it looked as if he was going to reach out to her, and her pulse kicked into a rumba beat, but then he turned away.

'I've put myself as first on call,' he announced as he reached the door, holding up a hand to forestall her objection. 'I've put you on for tomorrow, so catch up on your sleep tonight. You might need it if Mrs Joliffe doesn't settle down as we hope.'

'Don't even think it!' Leah exclaimed. 'Those babies need to stay in there as long as possible…but you already know that as well as I do.'

'If we manage to keep them in there long enough to get the course of steroids into them, that'll be one hurdle crossed, but all I allow myself to do is take things one day at a time,' he said quietly, and for some reason she didn't think he was talking solely about his approach to his work.

'How much longer is it likely to be?' Jonty Joliffe asked when he buttonholed Leah on her way down to a consult in A and E a week later.

He'd arrived just over forty-eight hours after his wife had been admitted and had looked completely shattered as he'd been unaware whether their babies had arrived or not. The fact that the course of steroids had been completed meant that the babies' lungs were now better prepared to deal with the outside world, but after a couple of contractions Pam had needed to be put on ritodrine to prevent her going into labour. The possible side-effects of tachycardia and hypotension meant that she was having to stay in hospital.

While Leah knew that the two of them were ecstatic that their babies were still safe, she also knew that neither of them was dealing well with the boredom of Pam's enforced hospital stay.

'Well, the longer they stay put, the better,' Leah began, not wanting to fob the man off but very aware that there was a patient needing her urgent attention on the ground floor. 'She's not thirty-five weeks yet, and while multiple births usually arrive early, she's still some way from—'

'I know all that,' he said impatiently, then closed his eyes and sighed heavily, shaking his head. 'I apologise, Dr Dawson. That was rude, but...well, I was flown home at enormous expense from the other side of the world because the hospital told us that it was an emergency situation and the babies could be born at any minute, and my leave isn't indefinite.'

'I do understand,' Leah assured him. 'But I'm afraid I don't have any answers for you. This is just a case of taking it one day at a time and hoping that the babies will stay where they are until they're as big and as strong as possible and her body is ready for them to be born.'

'But this drug Pam's on—the ritodrine—couldn't that be stopping the labour when she's already reached that point? She had the steroids to help their lungs so—'

'We're monitoring both Pam and the babies to try to get the optimum moment—the moment when the babies have the best chance of survival without the

risks of brain damage and all the other problems pree-
mies can suffer. If there's the slightest chance that
Pam's body has reached the limits of its tolerance,
we'll have those babies out of there so fast that it'll
make your head swim—and that's a promise!' she
added.

She glanced down at her watch and realised that
time was passing too quickly for her to spend any more
time debating the issue with him. Her unknown patient
was more of a priority at the moment.

'I'm sorry… I'm not trying to fob you off, but I've
been called down to Accident and Emergency to have
a look at a pregnant mum who's been injured. If you
need to speak to me again, I'll be back as soon as I
can.'

She paused only long enough to throw him an apol-
ogetic smile before she hurried out of the department
and took to the stairs at a run.

'Leah Dawson, Obs and Gyn,' she panted as she
arrived in A and E seriously out of breath a few moments later. She took a steadying breath, knowing it
wouldn't do the patient any good to think that her condition warranted doctors sprinting to her side. 'You
want me to take a look at a pregnant mum?'

The charge nurse swung round to consult the ubiq-
uitous white board dominating the wall behind him. It
was covered in colour-coded names allocated to the
various treatment areas, and Leah could remember
only too clearly a very similar board during her rotation in A and E during her training…and the fact that
she didn't think there'd been a single day when she'd
seen it empty.

'Yes. She's in…er, no,' he corrected himself apologetically. 'I'm sorry, we did need you, but Mr ffrench is here so he's seeing her.'

Leah swallowed a sudden flash of anger at the realisation that not only had she just wasted her time and energy hurrying all the way down those dozens of stairs, but David hadn't even had the courtesy of letting her know he was going to take over the call.

With a murmured word and resigned shrug of her shoulders, she set off to retrace her steps. There was no point taking her resentment out on the A and E staff. It wasn't their fault that this had happened again. They weren't to know that over the past few days it didn't matter how hard she worked, every time she turned round, her boss was doing her job as well as his own.

She didn't know what his problem was, she thought as she slogged up the next flight of stairs, torturing herself with the unnecessary exercise to give herself a few minutes to try to work out what had gone wrong between them.

It certainly couldn't be the standard of her work. If anything, having someone with his clinical skills around was lifting the whole department to greater heights. There was almost a buzz in the very air— something that had been sadly lacking in Donald's time.

All she knew was that his strange behaviour seemed to have started the day after she'd invited him into her flat and given him an impromptu meal.

Had he had second thoughts about the implied intimacy of it?

Did he think she'd been chasing after him?

Was he trying to send her a signal that he didn't

want any sort of a relationship between them beyond a professional one?

If that was the case, all he had to do was tell her, and she could reassure him in no uncertain terms that he certainly wasn't so much of a catch that she was willing to change her plans for him. Her plans for her own life couldn't be changed because she didn't have a choice.

She'd more or less talked herself into a more equable frame of mind by the time she pushed open the door at the top of the stairwell, but the first thing she saw as she entered the department was David ffrench exiting the lift and her ire returned full force.

'If you need me, I'll be in Theatre with an emergency Caesarean,' he said brusquely, and was just beginning to stride away from her when Sally Ling appeared in the doorway of Pam Joliffe's room.

'David, the ritodrine's not working any more,' she announced. 'Pam's starting to dilate. Is it worth trying terbutaline?'

If the situation hadn't been so serious, Leah would have laughed at the expression on the head of department's face. For all that he'd been working as hard as a one-armed paper-hanger, he'd finally come up against a situation that he couldn't solve just by working himself harder. There was no way that he could perform an emergency Caesarean at the same time as monitor the state of premature IVF twins.

'David?' she prompted, and for the first time in days he actually met her gaze. What she hadn't expected was to see the fleeting expression of misery in their blue-green depths.

In spite of the rigid control she kept over her own emotions, her heart went out to him. Although he did his best to hide it, this wasn't the first time she'd caught a glimpse of the evidence that something was making him very unhappy.

At the moment there wasn't time to do more than promise herself that she would corner him and demand some answers before too long. Their patients came first.

'Shall I check on Pam while you get started in Theatre?' she suggested. 'As soon as I see what's happening, I'll come through and tell you. If the twins need to be delivered, they can follow your emergency patient through.'

'That should give us sufficient time to organise enough humidicribs,' Sally said briskly, and turned back into Pam's room, clearly believing that the decision had been made.

For several tense seconds David held Leah's gaze, almost as if he was finding it difficult to make a decision.

'Trust me,' Leah said softly, and for a moment it felt as if her heart was beating louder than the words. She hadn't realised just how much it mattered to her, and not just on a professional level.

He must have heard her because she saw the second when his tension eased and the single nod that followed.

'I'll see you in Theatre as soon as you can get there,' he agreed, and swung round to stride away again, then paused to look back over his shoulder. 'I do, you know,' he said cryptically.

'You do...what?' There was something almost fierce in his eyes now and it was scrambling her own logical thought processes so that she couldn't follow what he was talking about.

'I trust you,' he said seriously, and left her open-mouthed with surprise as she watched his long legs take him out of sight.

CHAPTER SIX

LEAH reversed her way through the doors, her scrubbed and gloved hands held carefully away from her body to prevent contamination.

'What's the score, Leah?' David demanded, and she was convinced that he must have eyes in the top of his head because she could swear that he hadn't looked up from his task.

She joined him on the opposite side of the table and saw that the patient was draped and ready for the word from the anaesthetist, her hand twined in a white-knuckled grip with her equally pale husband's.

She paused just long enough to give them both an encouraging smile before she answered David's question.

'There's no point trying terbutaline,' she said briefly. 'I left Sally getting her ready to come into Theatre.'

'Right.' He glanced up and met her eyes for a fraction of a second and when he didn't ask a single further question, she realised that he *did* trust her judgement.

'This is Rosalie Taylor,' he announced quietly, dragging her thoughts back from the quiet glow his confidence had given her.

'We know Dr Dawson,' Mike Taylor assured him in a voice made jerky by nerves. 'She's been monitoring Rosalie ever since the scan showed that the placenta was in the wrong place. We knew it was going to have to be a Caesarean birth because it was completely covering the cervix, but the baby isn't due for three weeks yet and then, suddenly, she went into labour and when she started to bleed...'

'It's all right, Mike,' Leah interrupted softly, understanding just how terrifying this must be for both of them. 'You got the three of you here safely before too much damage could be done. We're just waiting for the epidural to take effect, so all you need to do is make yourself comfortable so you're ready to give Rosalie the ringside commentary while we do our job. OK?'

He blew out a shaky breath then gave a nod and a strained smile. 'OK. One ringside commentary coming up.'

'Will I still be able to see the baby being born?' Rosalie asked anxiously, her glance going from Leah to David and back again. 'You did promise...'

David raised a dark eyebrow and those beautiful eyes spoke volumes without saying a word.

'As soon as we've done the gory bits,' Leah confirmed with a hint of challenge in her voice, hoping that David wouldn't object the way Donald had done. Her previous head of department hadn't liked anything to interfere with his work, but while she'd been running the department she'd discovered just how many of their new parents welcomed the opportunity to see their precious offspring's arrival, even though it couldn't be part of a normal delivery. 'If you still want to, we can drop the screen so you can see Baby Taylor's grand entrance into the world—*and* finally discover whether it's a boy or a girl!'

Even though half of his face was covered by a disposable mask, Leah saw a smile of approval light

David's eyes and welcomed the revelation that they were on the same wavelength on yet another topic.

'Just one word of caution,' he said to the parents-in-waiting, the serious tone completely at odds with his suddenly playful expression. 'Just because my face is the first one you see when the screen goes down, that doesn't mean you have to bond with me and take me home for the next eighteen years.'

'Ready when you are,' the anaesthetist announced over the startled burst of laughter, letting them know that the epidural had taken effect, and then there was no time for anything but concentrating on the mechanics of trying to deliver a healthy baby before the mother suffered serious blood loss.

'May I present the new Miss Taylor?' David announced just a few minutes later, as he lifted a squirming bundle out of the gaping incision and held her tenderly in both hands.

He'd long ago lost count of the number of times he'd performed this little ritual, but it never failed to lift his heart or bring a smile of satisfaction. It made all the years of study worthwhile when a risky delivery could be turned into a resounding success—especially one with such healthy lungs.

Without a word being spoken, Leah had clamped and cut the cord so that he could pass the squalling infant to Sally, and a moment later, wrapped in a warm blanket, their new daughter was placed in Rosalie's arms.

'Hello, precious,' she murmured, the words barely audible over the strident cries, then looked across at Leah. 'You wouldn't mind if we call her Leah, would you?' she asked. 'After all your help and understanding, we'd like to name her after you, but if you were saving that for your own daughter...'

If David hadn't been watching Leah's face he wouldn't have seen the flash of agony that crossed her face, but it was gone so fast, hidden behind smiling eyes, that he wondered if he'd imagined it.

Not that he had time to ponder the question, he thought as he concentrated on delivering the problematical placenta. He had to make certain that the cervix was undamaged if this young couple was going to be able to contemplate having more children without intervention. That didn't mean that his ears weren't listening for his pretty colleague's response.

'I would be honoured to have her named after me,' she said softly, sounding quite choked by the idea.

A quick glance in her direction told him that her soft grey eyes were glittering with the suspicion of tears and he was almost taken aback at the sight. Although he'd quickly realised that Leah cared deeply about all the aspects of the work she did, he'd had her pegged as too clinically involved with the processes to allow her emotions to become involved.

Those hastily hidden tears told another story completely. Inside the almost frighteningly efficient doctor who had not only managed to keep the department together but had also taken on extra duties such as conducting an overdue audit, there was a much softer person. And in spite of his determination to keep the rest of the world at bay, one bright glance from those grave grey eyes was enough to attract his attention, and when they gleamed with humour or sparkled with the threat of tears, it was all he could do to remind himself why he couldn't allow himself to weaken.

It wasn't until he was signing off on the paperwork

after the successful delivery of the Joliffes' twins and had to add the date that the most important of all those reasons was brought home to him full force.

'It's the seventeenth tomorrow,' he whispered around the sudden lump in his throat, the image of a laughing face and the memories of childish giggles searing his heart with the white heat of loss.

That was why he couldn't allow himself to weaken. There was no point in starting any sort of relationship with Leah, no matter how much he liked her as a doctor and a woman, because he couldn't bear to go through that sort of pain ever again.

In the meantime, there was the never-ending mountain of paperwork to climb...when he could fit it in between consultations, case reviews and the daily essentials of lab results. Sometimes it seemed as if the adrenaline-inducing trauma of an emergency Caesarean was the least stressful part of his day, especially when it resulted in healthy babies like the Joliffes' twins and little Leah Taylor.

Inside his head he carried the image of one Leah cradling the other and he was struck by a sudden painful desire to see her face soften at the sight of her own child...and his.

'*No!*' he exclaimed sharply, the agony in the single word echoing around his office just as her scrub-suited figure appeared in his open doorway.

He could have groaned aloud when he saw the way her ready smile disappeared.

'If you don't want to be disturbed, you should have shut your door,' she said crisply, and turned to stalk off.

'No!' he called again. 'Don't go, Leah. I wasn't talking to you.'

She paused just long enough to glare at him over her shoulder and her expression told him he would have to speak fast if he was to retrieve the situation. It wasn't her fault that his mood had been ruined by the realisation that it was the seventeenth tomorrow.

'I was having an argument with myself,' he said lamely, knowing that he couldn't tell her the real reason for his outburst. Perhaps his decision to run an open-door department needed a little refining. He'd believed that it would signal the fact that he was approachable, but if his private stresses were going to make him upset his staff...

He hadn't realised he was holding his breath until he saw her shoulders relax and a faint grin lift the corners of her mouth.

'Who won?' she teased, surprising an answering smile out of him.

That's when he knew he was in trouble, even though he didn't know how it had happened.

What was it about Leah that attracted him so much?

Granted, she was a beautiful woman, even in faded green scrubs. The crumpled baggy garb couldn't completely disguise her slender curves, and now it wasn't hidden under a disposable paper cap, her honey-coloured hair gleamed, but her heart-shaped face was dominated by the keen intelligence of those silvery grey eyes. She'd been all cool efficiency at first glance, but it hadn't taken long until he'd discovered the warmth and caring that were hidden just underneath.

But he'd known other women just as beautiful, just as intelligent and efficient and just as warm and caring. What was it about this particular combination that had started the revival of his long-dead emotions, the unwanted revival of emotions that he'd believed he'd buried for ever?

Whatever it was, it didn't matter. As the saying went, he'd been there, done that, seen the film, got the T-shirt and collected the broken heart. He couldn't go down that road again. It hurt too much.

Professional detachment…*that* was what he needed to concentrate on, not the fact that nothing more then the thought of Leah had his blood pumping faster, or the fact that the seventeenth was going to gut his emotions like a blunt knife.

'What on earth is the matter with the man?' Leah demanded in exasperation as she stripped off and climbed under the pelting spray of the shower at the end of a particularly gruelling afternoon.

It was a fact of life, working at the cutting edge of medical technology, that there were no guarantees, and today's disaster certainly proved it.

'I don't like it any better than he does,' she muttered, desperately trying to convince herself that the sting in her eyes was caused by her shampoo rather than the image of the tiny boy who hadn't stood a chance. 'Every time a baby dies it feels like a failure…for *all* of us.'

So why had David given her the silent treatment? He'd been glowering at her under dark brows as though it was *her* fault that India Smythe had lost her baby, but had that been nothing more than the final straw after a grim day?

Yesterday she'd thought that they were working really well together, especially when he'd let her know that he trusted her judgement over Pam Joliffe's treatment, but the last twenty-four hours had been dreadful.

'In fact, it's been going on ever since I caught him arguing with himself,' she mused, the urge to howl her eyes out diminishing as she remembered the welter of expressions that had crossed his face in a matter of moments.

She didn't think that it was a problem within the department, otherwise she was certain that he would have told her about it. He'd long since revised his initial impression that the department had descended into chaos with Donald's death. In fact, they'd even laughed together about the state of the office when he'd seen it in the final stages of her audit.

No, this was something else...something personal and private.

She grimaced, wondering if he was hiding a secret, too. Did he have a similar reason to her own as to why the department was such an all-important part of his life? There was certainly something putting that desolation in his eyes, even though he managed to keep it hidden most of the time.

'Whatever it is, it's none of your business unless it has an effect on the department,' she told herself firmly as she gave up on her determination to take the stairs to the top floor. After the day she'd had today, she really didn't need the exercise of climbing up to her flat, she rationalised as she watched the doors of the lift swish shut and the claustrophobic box lurched into action.

'And I'm definitely too tired to knock on his door and ask him what's been bugging him,' she muttered when the doors opened again, deliberately refusing to let her eyes stray towards that door.

She was just putting her key in the lock when she heard the sound of a thud and a crash just feet away from where she stood, closely followed by a very clear profanity.

Without another thought for what she could or should do, she was knocking sharply on the one door she'd been determined to avoid.

'David? Are you all right?' she demanded urgently. The visions of burglars attacking him that filled her head should have had her running in the opposite direction, but the possibility that he needed her help had her hammering on the unresponsive wood again. 'David! Do you need help?'

The sound of the lock being released made her step back a pace, suddenly aware that she couldn't be sure what she was going to be confronting.

A blood-spattered David ffrench was not one of the better scenarios she'd imagined, but it was exactly what was standing in the doorway.

That wasn't the only thing different about him either.

She'd grown so accustomed to seeing him in one of his smart suits when he was working at his desk or meeting patients for the first time that she actually managed to keep her eyes on her own work most of the time. His other persona, dressed in thin cotton scrubs that concealed nothing of his lean muscular body, was more difficult to ignore, especially when she was looking at him from the other side of the operating table and was treated to intimate glimpses of the pattern of dark hair that spread across his chest when he leaned forward.

This David ffrench, with rumpled hair and a bad-boy shadow on his chin and dressed in a paint-splattered polo shirt and a disreputable pair of jeans that were worn white in some very interesting places, was another person altogether.

Unfortunately, he was someone that made every one of her dormant hormones burst into life, no matter that any sort of relationship between them would be impossible, and the fact that her hands itched to touch that tousled hair and smooth it back from…the rivulets of blood trickling down his forehead?

'What on earth happened to you? Were you attacked?' she demanded, her heart inexplicably clenching in her chest at the thought that he was in pain. She peered uncertainly around his shoulders into the room beyond. Surely a burglar wouldn't just have allowed him to open the door like that.

'In a manner of speaking…if you count assault with a deadly picture frame,' he said with a pained chuckle, taking a crimson-streaked hand from a decidedly bloody head with a grimace. 'You might as well come in. I might need a hand to sort this mess out.'

As she reached for his arm, Leah's pulse was racing so hard it was making her feel quite light-headed.

'How badly have you damaged your hand?' she demanded, concerned for a moment about its effect on his professional life. Like many surgeons, he was adept with both hands, but to have the dexterity of one of them seriously impaired…

'Apart from a black nail where I hit it with the hammer, there's nothing wrong with my hand,' he said, leaning forward so that the top of his head was visible. 'All the blood's coming from my head.'

'Your head? How on earth did you manage that?' There was quite a gash hidden in the thick darkness of his hair and as was the usual case with head wounds, it was pouring blood in a steady stream.

'All too easily,' he said wryly as he led the way across his lounge. 'I'd been putting up a picture on the wall—the last of the unpacking in this room, thank goodness—but when I sat down to celebrate with a glass of wine while catching the news, the wretched thing fell down on my head.'

For a moment Leah had to fight the urge to chuckle at the image that painted, but then she saw him stoop to pick up some of the scattered glass.

'Hang on! Leave that till I've sorted your head out,' she ordered, grabbing for his arm. 'You'll be dripping gore all over the carpet and giving yourself another job to do. I presume you've got some sort of first-aid kit?'

He threw her an old-fashioned look and she couldn't help grinning.

'Well, you'd be surprised how many people don't,' she said. 'Now, let's get you to the bathroom and get you cleaned up.'

He muttered something indecipherable under his breath but did lead the way into the little room that was the mirror image of her own.

Except that hers felt bigger than David's, with plenty of room to move around, and there was the scent of a different brand of soap and shampoo in the air that made it seem as if the room was filled with his existence.

Her awareness of their proximity was made worse by the way she seemed to be bumping into him at every turn as he reached into the cupboard to take out a white tin with a prominent red cross on the top, then settled himself on the cork-topped stool beside the basin.

It was almost as if his presence sucked the oxygen

out of the room and she had to fight to stop her breathing growing shallow in response. And it was going to get worse.

'First of all, will you look at me so I can check your pupils?' she asked, hoping that he was more concerned with what he was seeing than in noticing her reaction to those beautiful blue-green eyes.

This close, the colour was even more stunning, reminding her of the changeability of light playing through water, and with those gold-tipped eyelashes and pupils large enough and dark enough to lose herself in their depths...

'Is there a problem?' he demanded, and she suddenly realised that she'd barely registered that both pupils were equal, neither had she checked that they were reactive to light. All she'd been doing had been gazing at them in admiration.

'No problem that I can see,' she reported briskly. 'It looks as if you escaped concussion, but if you start being sick or feeling nauseous—'

'I know the drill,' he interrupted, 'although how I'm supposed to be able to tell the difference between concussion-induced drowsiness and normal tiredness at the end of a hard week, I don't know.'

Glad that he didn't seem to have noticed her lapse in concentration, she busied herself with drawing some water in the basin then turned with one of his dark blue towels in her hands, knowing there was no way she was going to be able to put any distance between them while she tended his injury.

She wasn't going to allow herself to think about the fact that there was something...something magnetically attractive about the man that made her *want* to be close to him.

'If you lean your head over the edge of the basin, I'll be able to irrigate the cut and see just how bad it is.'

He perched the first-aid kit on one thigh, anchoring it there with his hand before resting his head on the towelling pad she'd fashioned to soften the edge of the white porcelain.

His hair was very thick and silky, with just enough natural curl to make it cling to her fingers as she sifted through it to expose his injury.

'It's bigger than I thought,' she said with a grimace. 'The edges are fairly clean but you should probably go into A and E for a couple of stitches if it's going to heal neatly.'

'I think I can trust you to do that for me,' he said as he straightened up far enough to show her just how well stocked his emergency kit was. Apart from the usual supplies, his contained several extras, including saline solution and sterile packs of swabs and needles, and while she was swiftly cataloguing them, he continued speaking. 'I'd rather not spend the rest of the evening waiting for attention while the staff deals with heart attacks and broken limbs. That's if you don't mind?'

Leah was glad he couldn't see the colour sweeping into her cheeks when he spoke of trust. It was just such a juvenile response for a woman already in her early thirties but she couldn't deny the warmth that spread through her.

'I can understand that you don't want to wait your turn for such a minor injury to be treated,' she murmured as she selected the things she'd need. 'Oh, dear. There's everything here except anaesthesia. It looks as if you're going to have to go in after all.'

'I've got a fairly high pain threshold, and it'll only be a couple of stitches,' he said stoically, and laid his head down again.

'It didn't sound like a high pain threshold from outside,' she pointed out, needing to keep up a distracting conversation—anything to steady the sudden tremor in her hand at the thought that she might hurt him. 'That was definitely more than a yelp I heard and the air in here was still distinctly blue around the edges when you opened the door.'

'Oops! Sorry about that, but it was the unexpectedness of having it land on my head like that,' he apologised, and she could have sworn that it was his turn to flush with embarrassment this time. 'I haven't been here long enough to find out how soundproof the walls are.'

'They're pretty good, unless someone's got the TV or stereo turned up loud,' she said as she trimmed the minimum amount of hair from either side of the gash so as not to leave the wound obvious after stitching. 'I just happened to be standing out on the landing at my door, or I probably wouldn't have heard a thing.'

'And I'd have been left here all on my own, bleeding to death,' he said in a pathetic little voice that had her chuckling at the whimsy of it even as she pierced his skin with the first suture.

She froze when she heard his sudden intake of breath.

'Are you sure about this?' she demanded, certain she could never allow anyone to do this to her without anything less than a full shot of local. 'We're only minutes away from A and E and I'm sure they would make an exception to the usual triage as you're a member of staff.'

'I'm OK. Let's just get it over with,' he said, but even though his voice was slightly muffled by his position, she was certain it sounded as if he was gritting his teeth.

Still, it was his body and his decision.

'Well, this is something we can never say to our patients when they're in labour, but…if you change your mind…!'

He gave a short huff of laughter then fell silent as she bent to her task again, determined to get it over with as quickly as possible for both their sakes.

'I washed the blood out of your hair so you don't need to get it wet again tonight, but it took three stitches to make a good job of it,' she announced as she straightened up a little later and began collecting the debris.

'I know. I was counting,' he said gruffly as he sent an exploratory hand up towards his head.

'Uh-uh! Don't touch!' She smacked his hand away. 'If you want to inspect my handiwork, I'll get a mirror.'

'Yes, Doctor. Thank you, Doctor,' he said, pretending meekness as he stood up to his full height.

She took a hasty step backwards, then another when he still seemed to be too close. Unfortunately, too many of her receptors were telling her brain that he wasn't nearly close enough.

'Can I make you a drink or would you like to join me in a glass of wine?' he offered. 'Luckily I only had white or I'd have made even more of a mess when I spilt it.'

Common sense told her it would be best for her peace of mind if she left straight away but when she opened her mouth to refuse, she found herself hesitating instead.

'Just a small glass,' he pressed persuasively as he led the way back into the lounge. 'I'm not having much myself after a knock on the head, but it does help the unwinding process before we go to bed.'

Before we go to bed?

Leah's brain stalled completely, filled not with thoughts of sharing a pleasant drink but with images of the two of them…naked…sharing his bed.

'Hang on a minute,' he said, and came to a halt so suddenly that she only just avoided ploughing right into his back. 'I've still got this mess to clear up. Would you like to pour the wine while I get rid of the glass?'

'Why don't you pour the wine while I do the clean-up?' she countered. 'You won't be very comfortable bending forward after you've had a knock on the head. It'll probably make it thump.'

They both reached for the picture that had caused all the problem, jostling for possession, and it was only when David's longer reach allowed him to swing it up from behind the chair that he revealed the other object that had been dislodged.

'No!' he exclaimed hoarsely, discarding the picture in his hand without a care for its survival as he stretched for the much smaller frame it had hidden. 'Oh, no!'

It almost sounded like despair in his voice and Leah felt a chill raise the hairs on her arms.

'What is it? Is it broken?' she asked as she angled her head to try to see what he was cradling so tenderly.

'Yes, it's shattered, and the glass has damaged the picture,' he added in a voice full of misery.

'What is it?' she repeated. 'Was it very valuable?'

There was desolation in his eyes when they finally met hers.

'It's precious, rather than valuable,' he said, and finally turned it around to show her a photograph of a chubby baby boy with an expression of absolute joy on his beaming face as he waved a brightly coloured toy at the camera. 'It's a photo of my…' He hesitated just long enough to draw in a jagged breath before he finished in a heart-breaking whisper. 'He was my son and he would have been one year old today.'

CHAPTER SEVEN

DAVID stifled a groan.

What on earth had possessed him to tell Leah about Simon?

That had been one of the reasons why he'd moved back to England—the fact that no one would know anything about his recent past.

Well, no one except his sister Maggie, and she was too deeply involved in her precious husband and equally precious new baby to do anything as crass as gossip about his failures.

Even Maggie knew nothing more than the bare bones of the facts. He hadn't been able to bring himself to admit to the sister who'd idolised him throughout their childhood that he'd been an utter fool, and the thought of baring his soul to a comparative stranger... Well, until a moment ago he would have said it was anathema.

Then he saw the empathy in Leah's soft grey eyes and knew why.

The two of them might not have been working together for very long, and she'd actually been antagonistic towards him at the beginning for being appointed to the post she'd wanted, but they'd soon overcome that with the discovery that they shared similar goals for the department.

Almost immediately, he'd realised that her professionalism was paramount, but over the time they'd been working together he'd also seen many examples of the way she related to their patients' feelings.

There were also the glimpses he'd had of the shadows that lurked behind her smiles, the hints that there had been tragedy in her life as well. Were these, too, the reasons why he'd known instinctively that Leah would understand?

And now she was looking at him with those big intelligent eyes and he knew that her sharp brain was busily cataloguing everything he'd said and matching it against his tone of voice and the expressions on his face.

He could only imagine what she'd seen when he'd caught sight of that precious photo lying in the shattered debris. The thought that it had been destroyed...that he had lost the last tangible proof that Simon had existed...

Emotion caught at his throat, making breathing difficult, and the hot press of tears threatened to overwhelm the stoic face he'd made a habit of showing to the rest of the world.

Afraid he was going to lose control and disgrace himself in front of her, he started to turn away but a single gentle hand on his arm stopped him in his tracks.

'Oh, David, I'm so sorry,' she murmured, and for the first time he felt as if someone wasn't just mouthing the usual social platitudes. Leah really meant the words because somehow she knew how much Simon had meant to him and how badly his loss had hurt.

After an almost totally trouble-free childhood—even he would have to admit that everything he'd attempted had come easily to him, whether it was sports or study—it had seemed that his adulthood was progressing the same way, with the job of his dreams and a beautiful wife and baby son.

From the first moment he'd known of the baby's existence, just weeks after he and Ann had met, he'd willingly planned a speedy marriage to legitimise his birth. Then, just weeks after his son was born, Ann had thrown the fact that he wasn't Simon's genetic father in his face.

He'd been devastated, but after the initial shock he'd discovered that it really hadn't mattered whose sperm had created the baby. Simon had been *his*.

Then Ann had taken Simon and just disappeared one day while he was at work, to go to join the man who'd fathered his precious son, and his bright plans for his future had died.

He'd built up so many pictures in his head of the things they'd do together as Simon grew older...helping him to walk and talk, ride a bike, play football...

'Even *that* I was able to rationalise,' he muttered, shocked to realise that the torrent of words hadn't just been running through his head but that he'd actually been voicing them to the slender woman sitting beside him on his settee, her grey eyes shimmering with sympathetic tears. 'I was able to tell myself that it didn't really matter who was his father as long as he had someone who would do all those things with him, but most of all who would love him...'

He bit his lip, but it didn't stop the first betraying tear sliding down his cheek. Suddenly he knew that nothing would stop the tears now. They had been dammed up for too long.

'But he didn't want him,' he forced out in a choked voice, feeling as if a vice was tightening around his chest. 'He didn't want my precious little boy and he sent Ann away... And she was driving when she shouldn't have been... And when the car came off the road...'

He couldn't go on, and then he didn't need to go on as Leah's arms slid around him to hold him close.

His last thread of restraint snapped and with a mixture of horror and utter relief he heard himself give in to the tears that felt as if they came direct from his heart.

'I'm...s-sorry,' he groaned into her shoulder, unable to stop the harsh sobs now that he'd started.

'Shh. It's not a problem,' she soothed, and he felt her hand begin to stroke him rhythmically—his back, his shoulder, his arm. 'Let it all out,' she whispered as she rocked him like a little child. 'Let all the poison out.'

And that was what it felt like, he realised with a distant sense of surprise. As he poured out his grief it was like the lancing of a hidden abscess that had been growing for month after month until there had been no room for anything else inside him.

He'd been doing his job and doing it well because that was all there was left for him. After the exposure of such a betrayal, followed so closely by the loss of his precious, loving child, he'd known that he would never be able to allow any woman close enough to hurt him again. The less a man had, he'd decided, the less he had to lose.

He'd just been lucky that when Maggie heard what had happened, she'd told him about the obs and gyn post being advertised at her hospital. With all his dreams shattered, he'd jumped at the chance to escape the wrenching memories to travel to the other side of the world again.

And he would probably have been able to keep working without the heartbreak overwhelming him— frantically busy for enough hours each day to ensure he was exhausted enough to sleep without dreams—if it hadn't been for the damage to the photo.

That precious image had been his lifeline back to the few blissfully happy memories of his disastrous marriage, the days when he'd revelled in the simple joys of fatherhood and believed that having Simon would be enough compensation for any amount of marital discord. To have lost that photo…

He lifted his head, uncomfortably aware that Leah must be regretting the day she'd ever met him. He was just so grateful that she had been there for him when the dam had burst, but what on earth must she be thinking about him for collapsing in such a way over nothing more than a photograph? Would he find one of the hospital's psychiatrists waiting to make an assessment of his mental competence when he arrived at work tomorrow?

But there was no condemnation in her eyes, not even a trace of discomfort that she'd seen him at his nadir. All he could see in those soft grey eyes was sympathy and acceptance and something more—understanding.

He'd guessed that there had been sadness in her life from the shadows he'd seen in her eyes and the special sensitivity she displayed when she dealt with patients who had spent years hopelessly longing to have a child.

For a fleeting moment he wondered if this was the right moment to ask her about the demons that lurked in her past, but then she lifted a hand to cup his cheek, her thumb gently stroking away the evidence of the last of his tears.

He would probably have felt nothing more than a lingering embarrassment at this evidence of his loss of control but then her gaze met his and, that quickly, the mood between them changed.

In the blink of an eye her protective embrace felt like something very different, her curves and hollows fitting him as though the two of them had been made to go together, and her soft mouth... Had he only just noticed how sweetly her lips curved? He couldn't imagine waiting another moment to know if her mouth was as soft and as sweet as it looked.

And it was, every bit as soft and sweet, but it was also hotter than he could have imagined and more inviting, and when she welcomed him inside, he found the one place in the world where all the pain and misery couldn't follow.

Between one breath and the next they were wrapped in each other's arms, not one offering comfort while the other accepted but both giving and receiving pleasure equally while desire rose to twine about them.

'Leah! Oh, Leah!' he groaned when their naked bodies met for the first time. Without a word being spoken they had each known instinctively what the other had wanted and the best way to achieve it, their minds and bodies every bit as closely attuned in their passion as they were in the operating theatre.

But this was no clinical procedure. This was two eager bodies cleaving together in a maelstrom of emotions, need and compassion and desire and acceptance and even absolution.

At the last moment, with his last shred of sanity, he paused long enough to demand, 'Are you protected?'

'What?' she panted, dragging her gaze up from the point where his body had been about to disappear inside hers.

Her pupils were huge and dark with arousal and he nearly ignored the warning voice inside his head, but the memories of Simon were too close and too painful. He wouldn't risk going through any of that again.

'I'm clean—I haven't been with anybody for more than a year—but I haven't got anything with me and I don't want to get you pregnant,' he said gruffly. 'Are you protected?'

A spasm of despair crossed her face but her voice only wavered slightly when she answered.

'You don't have to worry,' she whispered, but her pain was as clear to him as if she'd shouted, and he suddenly knew what was coming. 'I can't have children.'

He closed his eyes and when he pressed his forehead to hers he could feel the quiver of tension that thrummed through her, could feel her pain.

'I'm sorry,' he said, even as he knew how inadequate the words were. At least he'd had Simon for a little while, whereas Leah… No wonder she could empathise with the women they treated. She'd obviously walked at least a mile in their shoes.

He lifted his head and forced himself to meet her gaze, every nerve screaming with the knowledge that in his caution he'd probably ruined any chance of ever making love with this beautiful, complex, loving woman, but he was honour-bound to give her the choice, even though they had come this close.

'Leah, would you rather not…?'

He heard her draw in a sharp breath and as her

mouth tightened into a narrow line he saw the spark of indignation in her eyes.

'Don't you find me attractive enough to desire me now you know I'm a barren woman?' she demanded, and he laughed aloud. Surely she knew how ridiculous that was? Didn't she look in a mirror?

'Not find you attractive?' He directed her gaze down their bodies, his own still blatantly poised to take full advantage of her body's silent invitation. He deliberately ignored the little voice in a tiny corner of his mind. The fact that she was the first woman since Ann's betrayal to have any effect on his hormones was perfect since her inability to have a child probably made her the ideal woman for him. 'You must be joking!'

'That's just biology,' she said dismissively. 'It doesn't mean that it's *me* that you—'

He cut her off by the quickest and easiest route, his mouth stopping her lips and tongue from voicing any more words, then persuading them to speak another language entirely.

Long seconds later he lifted his head again, pleased to see she was every bit as short of breath as he was.

'In case you didn't get the message, let me say it in words of one syllable,' he growled, teasing both of them by brushing his body lightly over hers and having the satisfaction of feeling her instinctively arch up in response to deepen the contact. 'It's never happened to me like this before, and I don't know what sorcery you've used to make it happen now but, *yes*, I want you. Here and now, I want you. Any way I can have you, I want you. Now, please, woman, will you put me out of my agony?'

It took a second for his words to register but the

smile that bloomed across her face warmed him right to his bones, and then she raised a single quizzical eyebrow.

'Put you out of your *agony*?' she questioned with a hint of bravado in her voice as she deliberately wrapped first one slender leg and then the other around his hips. 'You don't know what agony is...*yet*!' she promised as she tightened her grip and drew him into the hot dark depths of her body for the first time.

For a moment Leah lay with her eyes closed, wondering why she felt so exhausted, then she felt the heavy weight of David's possessive arm around her waist and she *knew* why.

Her face heated with the memory of how brazen she'd been during the night, taunting him into that first blazing inferno on his settee then inviting him to join her in the bathroom for the most sensual bubble bath of her life...or had that been *after* he'd carried her to his bed and made slow delicious love to her until she'd barely been able to breathe, let alone even the score?

Her brain was on emotional overload, whirling with so many images from the hours they'd spent together that it was almost impossible to single one out from the rest. But that didn't stop her logic from posing the important question—where did they go from here?

Last night had been something special, she admitted silently, and that wasn't just the starry-eyed opinion of an innocent. She'd been married and had known the early days of excitement and experimentation. She'd also charted their decline into desperation and disillusionment when she and Gordon had been trying to have a baby. But even at its best, it had been nothing like this and she didn't know why.

Was it the novelty of a different partner? After all, Gordon had been the first and only man she'd slept with until last night. Or had it been the element of catharsis that had made everything seem so much *more* than it had ever been before? More exciting, more erotic, more tender, more intimate, but most of all more fulfilling.

Or had it been the fact that, until David had let her inside his protective shell and shown her his wounded soul, she hadn't been able to admit to herself that she'd been slowly falling in love with him from the first time he'd looked at her with those beautiful but wary blue-green eyes?

Where did they go from here, now that the night was over?

What would happen when he woke up this morning?

Logic told her that he was unlikely to declare his undying love for her as soon as he opened his eyes. If he'd been going to do that, there had been plenty of opportunities during the night, and he hadn't taken one of them.

Would he actually resent the fact that she was still in his bed, an unwelcome reminder of the fact that she'd been a witness to the moment when he'd lost his tight control on his emotions?

With a feeling akin to dread she silently acknowledged that a night that had been nothing less than a magical revelation for her could turn out to be a disaster where their working relationship was concerned. And they'd been working so well together, sharing the burdens of running a busy department with more than the average levels of stress as seamlessly as if they'd been colleagues for years.

Panic began to flood through her as she imagined

how difficult it would be to do something as simple as share their office if there was a barrier of embarrassment between them, and as for the strained atmosphere when they shared an operating theatre, with patients' lives and happiness in their hands... It didn't bear thinking about.

So, what was she going to do about it?

She didn't have enough experience to be able to carry off a blasé morning-after-the-night-before scene with any degree of believability, and without knowing what he felt about their time together she could hardly wait around expecting some hearts-and-flowers scene where they fell into each other's arms and vowed eternal fidelity.

No, by far the best answer was to leave as quickly and as quietly as she could, before he had a chance to wake, and keep her fingers crossed that the first time they met each other today would be in the middle of a throng of other people. Once that first meeting was over, she would know just how much damage their encounter had done to their working relationship and would have to decide what she was going to do about it.

As for the damage to her heart, that was another matter and something she definitely didn't have time to think about yet.

David silently berated himself for a coward as Leah slid surreptitiously out of his bed.

For a moment he was tempted to tighten his arm around her, suddenly struck by a ridiculous fear that he was about to let something infinitely precious out of his grasp, but he resisted the urge.

Hoping that she wouldn't realise that he was already

awake, he kept his eyes closed but he didn't need to be able to see her setting off in search of her scattered clothing to imagine how perfect her slender body would look in the subdued light of his bedroom clothed only in that lustrous fall of honey-blonde hair. He'd spent hours admiring it during the night, and exploring it and enjoying every sweet, giving, enticing, welcoming inch. In fact, he didn't know how he was going to be able to meet those soft grey eyes again without picturing her in all her naked glory.

And that was going to be a problem.

Thus far he'd had no trouble treating her as just another colleague, even when the scent of her shampoo wreathed its way around their office. The heartbreak he'd been through had armoured him against even the most attractive of women...until she'd appeared on his doorstep last night just as he'd reached the limits of his endurance.

The soft click of his front door closing sounded as clearly as a rifle shot through the silent flat, and he bolted to his feet.

'What a stupid thing to have done!' he snarled as he began to pace, uncaring that he was still stark naked. 'At the very least you could have ruined a very satisfactory working relationship, and at the worst...' For a moment he couldn't decide whether it would be more of a disaster to be hauled over the coals for sexual harassment of a female junior member of staff or if that member of staff should take it into her head that she'd fallen madly in love with him and expect an ongoing relationship.

'Any of those would be a disaster!' he groaned as he set off for the bathroom then groaned a second time when he realised he was never going to be able to enter the room again without seeing Leah in there with him…surrounded by bubbles in the bath, or with her curves outlined by rivulets of water under the shower, or with her face halfway between agony and ecstasy as he lifted her onto the edge of the vanity unit and buried himself in her depths.

'Mrs Thompson…Julia…I can't tell you how sorry I am, but as you've seen on the ultrasound, the baby's heart isn't beating any more,' David said to their sobbing patient, and just from the rough edge to his voice, Leah knew he meant every word.

It was the first time she'd seen him since she'd slipped out of his bed that morning but there was no time to even think about their personal lives. They were facing a situation that, out of all the scenarios she came across in her work, was guaranteed to put a dark cloud over the department—a full-term baby that, for some inexplicable reason, had simply died before the mother had gone into labour.

It was bad enough when patients lost their precious babies in the first few weeks of gestation, but to have come so close to success…to have spent all those weeks and months nurturing and loving and anticipating, only to have it snatched away without warning…

'So, what happens now?' asked an ashen-faced Trevor Thompson. 'Do you have to operate to…?' He couldn't finish.

'A Caesarean is major surgery, with all the risks that entails, and because it also permanently damages the uterus, we only use it if the life of the mother or the baby is at risk.'

This was another important point on which she and David were in complete agreement—that their department would not condone the use of surgery just for convenience. Much to the disgust of some staff and patients who wanted to avoid the uncertain timetable of natural birth, it was now only used as a last resort. Those who wanted Caesareans on demand to suit their social lives now had to pay to go elsewhere.

'In a little while we'll be putting up a drip to induce labour,' he went on gently. 'Sally, your midwife, will explain it all to you and give you the option of having an epidural to make things less painful.'

'*Nothing* could make it less painful!' Julie said vehemently, losing her fight with the next flood of tears. 'I'm going to have to go all the way through labour *knowing* that my baby's d-dead! I'm never going to be able to h-hold it or—'

'Of course you can hold your baby!' Leah exclaimed, her own eyes stinging with the threat of tears. 'You'll finally find out if it's a girl or a boy and you'll name it and spend time with it…as much time as you need so you can start to grieve for what you've lost.'

'But I thought…' Trevor shrugged. 'I remember something about babies being taken away before the mothers saw them.'

'Unfortunately, that used to happen a lot in the mistaken belief that if it was out of sight it was out of mind,' Sally admitted. 'Some mothers went the whole of their lives convinced that their babies hadn't died at all but had been stolen and were still alive somewhere. Once we realised what a dreadful effect it could have on the mother's mental well-being, we made certain that we changed our policies. Now it's very much centred on what the *parents* want. I can promise you that you won't be rushed into anything, and if either of you want to speak to someone—a counsellor, a priest, your parents or even one of us—all you have to do is ask.'

For some reason Leah was reluctant to leave the room, but unless there were unexpected complications, she wasn't needed any more. Sally was very good at her job and had obviously formed a good relationship with the couple during their antenatal visits. Leah had confidence that the experienced midwife would do everything she could to make such an awful event a little more bearable.

'What is the protocol here?' David asked quietly as they walked back towards the office, all awkwardness over their night together apparently pushed to one side by the sadness of more recent events. 'Does Sally inform the coroner once the baby's born or do we? And how long does it take to get the results of post-mortem examinations?'

She gave him the information by rote, wondering if he was waiting until they reached the privacy of their shared space before he said anything, but almost as soon as they entered the room the phone rang.

From then on it seemed as if there was hardly time to breathe before they were hurrying towards Theatre to start a busy list.

The first patient, undergoing her first cycle of IVF, should have been gently relaxed by her pre-meds, but the adrenaline of knowing that they were going to be harvesting her eggs today still had her bouncing off the walls with a mixture of fear and excitement.

'I don't need to ask if you want Peter to come in with you,' Leah teased gently, gesturing towards their tightly entwined hands. Her husband was already decked out in scrubs and looking rather self-conscious but with a determined air about him.

'Well, I'm going to be out for the count so I need him to keep score while you're collecting them,' Carol Stanford said. 'My grandmother used to keep chickens, and when I stayed with her I used to collect the eggs. If I managed to find more than a dozen, she used to scramble the extra ones and we had them for breakfast on a piece of toast.'

'Well, I'm not sure whether you'll need much toast for these eggs,' Leah warned as she gave Ashraf a nod to commence anaesthesia. 'They *are* going to be rather small.'

'I don't mind how small they are…just as long as there's…lots…' She only just managed to finish the sentence before the anaesthetic claimed her.

'Ready, Peter?' Leah invited as she kicked the lock off the trolley wheels and helped to aim it towards the theatre. 'One of the nurses will give you a stool to sit on by Carol's head. You'll be able to hold her hand while you're watching the screen to keep an eye on what we're doing.'

Once in the theatre, professionalism took over as she and David manipulated the microscopic camera through the neat incision to examine the swollen ovaries and then, one by one, aspirated each egg that had been triggered into ripening by the cocktail of hormones.

It was delicate and time-consuming work, especially at the start of the procedure. Sometimes weeks of nasal sprays and painful injections only resulted in three or four eggs, but as today's tally mounted, the atmosphere in the room became almost giddy with relief at their success.

By the time Stanley had checked the count under

the microscope in the lab, Carol was in Recovery and already surfacing from the anaesthetic.

'Hello, Carol…Peter. How are you doing?' Leah greeted them, one hand hidden behind her back.

'Great!' Carol said. 'Groggy but great! Peter said there were lots of eggs but he didn't know how many.'

'What *was* the final count when you got them to the lab?' Peter demanded eagerly. 'Was it more than six in the end?'

'Six babies!' Carol exclaimed euphorically before Leah could answer, and she hurried to caution both of them in case they had unrealistic expectations. She knew only too well that there were absolutely no guarantees with IVF.

'Remember what we said about not counting your chickens?' she warned. 'There's no guarantee that they'll all fertilise successfully, or that they'll go on to develop properly for implantation. And even if they *are* successfully implanted, there's still only an average of—'

'A one in five chance of success,' they chorused, the statistics clearly doing nothing to dampen their elation at having got this far.

'We know all that,' Peter reassured her more soberly, then his eyes brightened. 'But just for a little while it's nice to terrify ourselves with the prospect of every one of those eggs becoming a real live baby. So, tell us. How many did you harvest in the end?'

'Does this give you a clue, Carol?' Leah said with a broad grin as she took the plate of toast out from its hiding place behind her. 'Didn't your grandmother give you toast for the extra eggs if you collected more than a dozen?'

CHAPTER EIGHT

IF LEAH had thought that there would be time to talk at the end of their list, she'd been wrong.

That evening, she'd sat at her desk in their shared office for several hours battling with a pile of post-operative paperwork and then completed a mountain of routine form-filling with her ears straining for the familiar sound of David's footsteps coming towards her along the corridor. To boost her courage she was freshly showered and had donned the smart trousers and shirt she kept as a standby in her locker. She knew that outwardly she looked cool and professional, but inside her heart was still beating so fast she could almost hear the sound echoing off the freshly painted walls…but he'd never arrived.

At first, she'd put the fact that she hardly saw him, let alone spoke to him, down to coincidence. It had actually taken several days of missed opportunities before the penny had dropped and she'd realised that he must be deliberately avoiding her.

'Well, that tells me how much that night meant to him!' she'd muttered as he'd disappeared around the corner yet again, murmuring something almost incomprehensible about a meeting he needed to attend, leaving her feeling a complete fool.

It was bad enough that, in spite of all her determination, she'd fallen in love with the man. She'd quickly discovered that it was even worse to have him treating her as if she were carrying a plague.

Had he guessed at her feelings? Had she somehow given herself away? Or was it just that she'd become so besotted with the man that she'd simply misunderstood his motives? Perhaps he hadn't seen that precious night as anything more than a single night of comfort…a time out of time to take his mind off the fact that it should have been Simon's first birthday? With the brutal honesty of hindsight, she realised that she didn't really know what he'd wanted from her. Perhaps he was even afraid that she might try to trap him into a more permanent relationship.

Was that why he seemed to be afraid of spending any time with her? Did he think that she was going to grab him and demand a wedding ring if he spent a single minute in her company that wasn't strictly work-orientated?

'Well, I've got two choices,' she announced to the empty room, glad that she'd closed the door to signal that she wanted to be left undisturbed for a while. She really didn't want to have her private conversations with herself broadcast right through the department. It was bad enough that they happened in the first place.

'I can either confront the man—and risk making the atmosphere between us even worse—or I can just ignore him the way he's ignoring me and continue to give all my attention to the job.'

Neither option made her very happy.

The two of them had been working so well together right up until that night, the workload seeming far less onerous when they were tackling it together.

Still, in spite of the fact that it had made her working life less pleasant, she had to admit that there was no way she would have missed the magic of that night. It had given her memories that would last for ever and had been worth every bit of the continuing tension between them.

It was up to her to get over her longing for more of the same. Obviously David didn't feel the same way.

This was killing him, David thought as the scent of Leah's soap reached him from her position just inches away—or was it her shampoo? In spite of the hours they'd spent in each other's arms he hadn't been able to work it out, not when the underlying scent of warm woman had been enticing him to madness. And now that he was trying to put a bit of distance between the two of them, he couldn't even make an excuse to ask.

Anyway, he needed to concentrate on something, *anything* but the scent of Leah's body. He was supposed to be working. He had a worried couple sitting on the settee in front of him who had been waiting for the results of the last lot of tests they'd had done. After all their years of heartbreak, the Whittiers wouldn't appreciate the fact that his mind wasn't on his work because all he could think about was what he'd rather be doing...

He cleared his throat and had to shuffle the sheaf of papers on his lap to hide his body's all too obvious reaction to his thoughts, wondering for a mad moment why he didn't just change his mind and mix a little pleasure into their business relationship.

It would be such a blissful relief from unremitting nights of misery if he could just sink into the welcoming depths of her body, and if he was reading Leah's eyes in her unguarded moments, it wouldn't take much persuasion for her to agree to a repeat performance.

One part of his brain was following the conversation as Leah did her best to put the anxious couple at their ease, but the other part was trying to talk some sense into himself.

Yes, he would welcome the chance to burn up the sheets again with Leah, but even though it would ease his immediate obsession with her it wouldn't be fair to either of them. In spite of his attraction to her, he certainly didn't want any sort of permanent relationship, not after his disastrous attempt with Ann. And, anyway, unless his instincts were off the mark, Leah wasn't the sort of woman to settle for an affair and that was all he could offer.

The bit of office gossip he'd picked up since he'd come to St Luke's had confirmed that her colleagues knew virtually nothing about her private life—just the fact that she didn't date anyone from the hospital. He wouldn't allow himself to think about why that thought pleased him.

His own observations of the long hours she spent in the department had told him that she had time for little besides her work. One of the younger midwives had even hinted that she might be a lesbian and he'd nearly laughed in her face. He knew only too well that Leah was definitely heterosexual...a fact that was replayed in graphic detail every night whether he was awake or dreaming.

She'd revelled in everything they'd done together, quickly getting over her initial reticence to be the most sensual lover he'd ever had... And here she was, perfectly poised and so very professional in her charcoal-grey pinstripe trouser suit with not a honey hair out of place—unlike that night when it had been spread across his pillow or draped over his naked body or...

Suddenly he realised that all three of the other people in the room were throwing him some strange glances and with a flash of horror for whatever his unguarded expression might have revealed, he had to force his thoughts back to the meeting in progress.

What on earth was the matter with him?

He'd never had a problem with his thoughts wandering like this before. He wouldn't have risen so far, so fast in his profession if he hadn't been able to keep his mind on what he was doing. What had happened to his concentration?

As it was, he'd barely noticed that Leah had started going through the results of the battery of tests the couple had undergone, from the blood test on the woman to determine whether she was ovulating to the swim test on the man's sperm to confirm their number and whether they had sufficient motility to reach their goal once they'd been released.

'So,' she was summarising with another uneasy glance in his direction, before she returned to the anxious husband, 'we now know that there's nothing wrong with your sperm. It has the same proportion of non-swimmers and swimmers with absolutely no sense of direction as the majority of the male population, and also the same proportion of really determined ones that know exactly where they're going and why.' She turned to the wife next. 'And we now know that there's nothing wrong with your system either. All your plumbing is in normal working order and you're ovulating regularly, too. We've also established that there's no chemical incompatibility between the two of you that prevents conception.'

'So, you're saying that everything's working properly?' James Whittier summarised with an entirely male expression of relief on his face that their problems weren't his 'fault'.

'Exactly,' Leah said.

'But I'm still not getting pregnant, so…where do we go from here?' demanded Sonia, obviously frustrated by the ultimate lack of answers after all the weeks of poking and prying and waiting. 'Can we have IVF?'

'Before we make that decision, we'd like you to have a meeting or two with one of our staff psychologists,' David interrupted, even though he knew Leah didn't really need him jumping in. She'd been successfully conducting these interviews for months before he'd been appointed, but he had a feeling that the only way for him to keep his mind on the right track was to actually take part in the conversation.

'A psychologist!' James exclaimed, clearly disgusted by the suggestion. 'Don't tell me you think it's all in our minds! What's he going to do—hypnotise us into getting pregnant?'

'You'd be surprised the lengths that some couples will go in their attempts to have a baby,' David said in a calming voice. 'Changing their diets to cut out all junk food, aromatherapy, Australian bush flower she-oak essence, changing their underwear if they wear thongs…all sorts of things. And you'd also be amazed at how successful some of them are—but that's not why we want you to go.' He leaned forward to add weight to his words.

'The two of you already know just how frustrating and stressful it's been while you've been going through all the various tests,' he continued, waiting just long enough for them to nod their agreement before he went on. 'We want you to have a word with the psychologist because she'll be taking you through the implications of embarking on an IVF programme.'

'I hope the implications are that we'll end up with a baby,' James interrupted gruffly.

'We hope so,' David agreed evenly. 'It would be wonderful if you were one of the one in four couples who are successful, but there are also risks beyond the physical stresses on Sonia that you'll need to consider.'

'Such as?' his petite wife prompted with a frown.

'Such as the fact that IVF is a long hard road without any guarantee of success, and that there's a definite possibility that having to undergo repeated unsuccessful cycles could have serious effects on your marriage.'

'But if it's our only option…' James said, his tone a cross between belligerence and despair.

'There's also adoption,' Leah suggested gently. 'Have you considered that?'

'Not until we've tried all the other options,' James said firmly. 'If there's a possibility that we can have our own child—one that's a part of each of us—then we'd rather do that first. For me, adoption would be much further down the road. A last resort, if everything else had failed.'

'That's a decision for the two of you to make, of course, but first give yourselves a little time to come to terms with what you've found out today.'

'No!' Sonia exclaimed urgently. 'I want to make the appointment straight away.' Her pale blue eyes flicked from Leah to David and back again as though fearful that they might try to stop her putting her argument. 'Every day that goes by I'm getting older and my chances of getting pregnant go down and the chance of IVF working gets less. I don't want to waste any more time, especially if it takes several cycles before I get pregnant. We want to be young enough to be able to do all the usual things with our child that other parents do. It wouldn't be any fun for him or her if the two of us need Zimmer frames just to go the park to feed the ducks.'

David joined in the laughter then joined in the fare-wells as Leah escorted the couple out to organise their first appointment with the psychologist. He nearly groaned aloud when he realised that his eyes were greedily following every gentle sway of Leah's slender hips as she walked away.

'When am I going to be able to forget what she looks like under those smart business clothes?' he growled, but if he was honest, he already knew the answer. Never.

Leah buried her face in her hands and sighed heavily.

It seemed impossible that everything had changed so much in the last month or so.

She thought back to the morning she'd learnt of David ffrench's imminent arrival and her sharp dis-appointment that he was to take up the position as AR department head that she'd set her heart on. She'd be less than honest if she didn't admit that it had been a blow to her ego and a setback to her ambitions. It would also be dishonest if she didn't admit that the longer she'd worked with David, the more she appre-ciated his clinical skills and his surgical ability. And as for the man himself…

The heat that seeped through her with nothing more than a passing thought about him said more than enough about the way she felt about him, and that was in spite of the fact that he'd turned into a taciturn por-cupine since that night they'd spent together. Well, it wasn't his fault that he hadn't fallen in love with her, too, and if his avoidance tactics were the result of embarrassment that he'd let his guard down on the anniversary of his son's birthday, she could soon put his mind at rest if only he'd give her a couple of minutes to speak to him in private. It would only take that long to promise him that she'd keep his confidences to herself.

Her intermittent lack of concentration was bad enough, but the air of misery that had descended over the department during the last week or so was something else entirely.

'I bet I know what you're thinking about,' said Sally's voice from the doorway. 'You've got the same expression on your face as David.'

Leah hoped her expression hadn't also betrayed the sudden leap her pulse had taken at his name, but she beckoned the midwife in, smiling her thanks for the second mug of coffee she'd brought with her.

'It was bad enough when one of the Masson triplets went down with necrotising enterocolitis,' Leah said grimly before trying to take a sip of liquid that was still far too hot to drink.

'Well, he was the smallest and weakest but until then he'd seemed to be managing to hold his own,' Sally agreed, perching her own mug on the corner of the desk and peering into a paper bag that rustled enticingly. 'The onset was so insidious that we'd only just worked out what was wrong with him, so when it suddenly flared out of control...' The progression to generalised sepsis had been so virulent that there had been little anyone could do, and within hours he'd been dead.

'Then there was the shoulder dystocia,' Leah continued, feeling sick all over again as she remembered the moment during that delivery when she'd thought they were going to lose that baby, too. At the last moment one twin had interfered with the safe delivery of the other, and in trying to deliver both without risking oxygen starvation and brain damage, one had ended up with a broken clavicle.

She put her coffee aside untasted, suddenly finding the smell of it too rich.

'At least it turned out reasonably well in the end. Both babies arrived with good Apgar scores, but Mum isn't at all happy with the size of her episiotomy or the number of stitches you had to put in,' Sally said with a grimace.

They both knew that an abnormally large cut was unavoidable with some of the complications of mal-presentation, but they could hardly ask a woman in pain whether she would rather her babies had been put at risk for the sake of fewer stitches.

'And that's just down at your end of the department,' Leah said. 'You'll have heard about the run of heartbreak cases up at this end, too. The last few days we've had more than our share of patients with diagnoses that...well, with the best will in the world, all we could do was tell them that there was nothing we could do for them.'

They were the cases that Leah thought about in the middle of the night, wondering how the couples were coming to terms with the verdict that they would never be able to conceive and carry the baby they longed for. Some were stunned into silence by the conclusion while others were furious, convinced that the media-hyped miracle of IVF was being unfairly withheld from them.

'Then we've had several patients who only managed

to produce four or five eggs to harvest after all those weeks of hormone therapy, and a higher than usual failure rate for implantations,' Leah finished, completing the litany of disasters.

'So, what do you think we should do to perk everyone up?' Sally demanded, silently offering to share the second half of her onion-laden hot dog with Leah. 'It can't be good for the department to have everyone going around with long faces. We'll be frightening all the customers away.'

Leah shook her head at the offered food, her stomach turning over queasily at the greasiness of it, but before she could make any suggestions about raising department morale, Sally's pager shrilled.

'Cross your fingers that this is going to be a delivery that goes as easily as shelling peas,' she said, then stuffed the last of the hot dog into her mouth in one huge bite even as she was snagging her coffee and making for the door.

Was that all it was? Leah wondered. Was it just a run of sad cases that had her feeling so down and out of sorts, or was it more than that? Was it also because she was angry that David's change of attitude towards her had robbed her of part of her enjoyment of her job?

There had always been patients they couldn't help and, given the nature of the work they did, there would always be more failures per IVF cycle than there were successes. Even those successes weren't immune to the occasional tragedy during labour, but the birth of each normal, healthy baby was a comforting reward for all their efforts.

She wasn't just fascinated by the mechanics of monitoring hormone levels, harvesting eggs, fertilising them and then returning them to the mother's body, hopefully to have them implant and develop normally for an uneventful nine months. She also took great satisfaction from the intellectual side—the puzzle-solving involved as they tried to identify and isolate the reasons why each individual patient wasn't able to conceive the baby they so desperately wanted or maintain a pregnancy for a viable length of time.

Once they'd overcome their initial wariness of each other, she'd enjoyed sharing her philosophy with David and had felt a growing bond with him when she'd discovered how many goals they shared—a bond that had apparently been severed for ever by that night.

Determined to break the interminable circular track of her thoughts, she reached for the mug of rapidly cooling coffee, but before the liquid even touched her lips, nausea rose up in her throat and cold perspiration covered her body.

On shaky legs she took the mug across to the basin and tipped it out. Holding her breath, she rinsed every trace of it away then abolished even a hint of the smell with a swish of the antiseptic tea-tree soap the department used on their hands to help prevent the spread of infection.

'So...' she whispered when she sat down again, still feeling sick and out of sorts but with a quiver of something electric, too. 'What's *this* all about? I haven't heard anything about a bug doing the rounds, so is this just an emotional reaction because I'm angry with David for building that wall, or because...?'

She couldn't even give voice to the possibility that she was pregnant. The whole idea was impossible...unthinkable.

It had taken so long for her to get even that far when

she'd been married. Month after month she'd cried when her body had produced the bright evidence that once more she'd failed to conceive. Surely fate wouldn't be so cruel as to make it happen so easily as the result of a one-night stand.

Her eyes were burning with the threat of tears when she'd thought she had none left. She'd cried a whole lifetime's supply of them in the years when she'd been married to Gordon, her hopes alternately raised and then dashed by each failure.

Knowing how much it had hurt her in the past— how close the failure had come to destroying her—she had sworn that she wouldn't ever go through it again. But here she was—one second her heart soaring as she imagined the tiny fragile beginnings of a new life deep inside her and the next plummeting to earth, knowing that even if she *had* conceived, the child would never live long enough for her to hold it in her arms.

She scrubbed her hands over her face and straightened her shoulders, drawing in a deep breath to steady the nerves still quivering in her stomach.

'There's one sure way to put my mind at ease,' she muttered, getting to her feet with a return to her usual determination. 'I'll send a sample up to the lab. Stanley will soon let me know that it's all in my imagination.' And then she could start coming to terms with yet another hope dashed. She already knew that it was futile to wish that it could actually be true—that she really *was* pregnant with David's child and that this time she would actually be able to carry it to term.

David allowed himself a silent sigh of relief that he had the office to himself for a few minutes, then found himself unable to make a start on the everlasting paperwork.

Even though he reminded himself at intervals that it was none of his business, he was worried about Leah.

When he'd first arrived at St Luke's, she'd been a live wire with enough energy and determination for at least three grown men.

'Talk about multi-tasking!' he muttered. For heaven's sake, she'd been doing her own job and Donald's as well...and she'd *still* found time to conduct a major audit and redecorate the office.

She certainly didn't seem to be the same person any more. Oh, she was still brilliant at her job, but she was so quiet and self-effacing these days, almost as though she didn't want him to notice she was there.

It was killing him by inches!

For a start, he wasn't sleeping worth a damn, and when he did finally drop off, his dreams were every bit as hot as his memories of that night, and left him wanting more, too.

As for work... He groaned aloud and rammed his fingers through his hair, knowing that the problems they were having were all of his own making. He'd been so worried that she might get the wrong idea about his intentions after they'd spent the night together that he'd completely stonewalled her, and now he was reaping the results. She barely spoke to him any more, and that couldn't continue. In such a busy department, there were things about which he desperately needed her input.

Last night, he'd actually started thinking about his options. He'd even got as far as thinking about moving house or changing jobs before he had some sort of a breakdown, until he realised how ridiculous he was being. He didn't want to change his job, and, even though it was playing havoc with his sleep patterns and the fit of his trousers, he didn't want to move away from Leah.

In the meantime, there was a paper he'd been asked to present at an IVF symposium—if he ever got any time to prepare it—and an interminable Mount Everest of paperwork to do.

'Why are there never enough hours in the day?' he growled in frustration, and picked up the latest batch of test results. He'd been toying with some ideas for streamlining the system and now that he needed another informed point of view as to whether they were workable, it wasn't available. Leah was the obvious person to ask—the one person in the department who would understand what he was trying to achieve and whose opinion he would trust to be logical and unbiased—and he'd totally alienated her.

Well, that situation couldn't go on or the department would start to suffer. Something was going to have to change and it was up to him to change it, even if he had to make a grovelling apology for his inappropriate behaviour.

Surprised that his burden seemed to have lightened fractionally just by the fact that he'd decided to take action, he reached for the first set of test results back from the lab and tried to access the patient's file on the computer.

'Not found? Check spelling and reference number,' he groaned aloud as the message appeared on the screen. 'How many ways can you spell Jane Smith, for heaven's sake?'

Impatiently, he tried again, with the same result.

With a frown, he read the brief details on the result sheet and realised that he didn't recognise the patient. Had the result been sent to the wrong department? That was unlikely, knowing what a tight ship Stanley ran.

'Anyway, it was a check for the level of pregnancy hormones, so that means it *must* be one of our patients,' he muttered.

With a frustrated sigh he set it to one side. With her signature on the request form Leah would definitely know which patient it was. For all that she looked permanently exhausted, she took such a personal interest in each of their patients that she probably knew the details of every one of their current cases, right down to the name of the family pet. He would just have to ask her about it when she came in.

As if he'd conjured her up by thinking about her, Leah came in at that precise moment and she looked so white and strained that his guilt nearly buried him. The way she avoided looking at him made him more certain than ever that their problems all dated back to that night.

Remembering his decision to clear the air he cast about for a moment, trying to find a subtle way of bringing up the topic. He came up blank. It was so long since their conversation had covered anything other than work that he hadn't a clue how to start.

His eye fell on the mystery patient's results and, like a drowning man clutching at the nearest object, he seized on them as a way of starting some sort of communication going.

'Leah, what do you know about this?' he asked, lifting up the piece of paper.

She'd been about to settle herself at her desk but at

his words turned to approach him, as warily as a timid animal.

Silently cursing himself and afraid of scaring her away with a sudden move, he didn't move a muscle—at least, not intentionally. A certain part of his anatomy had other ideas as he slid his gaze over her elegant body and remembered…

He gritted his teeth when he saw how gingerly she took the piece of paper from him, obviously avoiding even the most accidental contact between the two of them, and knew he had an uphill climb in front of him if he was going to rebuild a good working relationship between them.

'We seem to have a phantom patient in the department,' he said, trying for a light-hearted approach. 'Stanley's sent through some results but I can't find her in the computer system. What do you know about Jane Smith?'

To his horror, what little colour she had in her face disappeared completely. For a moment she looked so ill that he was seriously concerned that she was going to keel over. He leapt up from his chair to look after her but when he reached out to take her arm he was shocked to have her flinch away from him as though even his touch was now abhorrent to her.

He was completely stunned by her reaction. Was this how bad it had become? Was she actually afraid of him now?

He felt sick at the thought. He would never raise a hand against her or any woman, no matter what the provocation. Surely she knew that much about him, even if she didn't like him any more.

The mystery patient was completely forgotten as he tried to find the words to reassure her. He couldn't promise not to touch her again. That would be totally impractical when the two of them worked together in an operating theatre. All he could do was promise her that any contact between them would be strictly work-orientated.

'Look, Leah, can you forget about those test results for a moment? I need to...' Where were the words when he wanted them? He'd never had a problem communicating before.

'Look,' he began again, his brain tangled in too many threads to be able to follow any of them properly, what with phantom patients, the desolate expression that had appeared in Leah's eyes and his need to clear the air between them. 'I'm sorry about what happened the other night... Well, not for what happened but the fact that it happened... Well, not even that, if I'm honest, but the fact that I've been like a bear with a sore head and avoiding you... Well, we've both been avoiding each other...' Oh, for heaven's sake! Why on earth was he rambling like this? He hadn't been this incoherent even when he'd been a tongue-tied teenager asking for his first date.

He snatched a steadying breath and forced himself to meet her eyes, suddenly struck by the fact that it almost looked as if she was about to cry. 'Leah, I promise you don't need to worry that I'll... What's the current term? Jump your bones? I promise that it won't happen again.'

He'd been right about the tears.

Even as he waited to see relief at his assurance, the first droplet fell, swiftly followed by a second and then a third.

'It's too late,' she whispered through trembling lips and turned the piece of paper she held so that it faced him. 'I'm pregnant.'

CHAPTER NINE

'WHAT do you mean, it's too late?'

David barely glanced at the lab result, more concerned with Leah's tears until she thrust the sheet towards him. Then he forced himself to read the words again and the bottom dropped out of his stomach.

Not again! a voice inside his head screamed, even as he was trying to come to terms with what she was telling him.

He could remember Ann saying exactly the same thing just a couple of weeks after he'd ended up in her bed in a moment of complete stupidity. She'd been beautiful and she'd been so flatteringly eager to be with him and had sworn that she was protected when he'd confessed that he wasn't in the habit of carrying condoms with him. Well, he'd been focusing so hard on his career that he'd had too little time to even *think* about having a social life, let alone commit himself to an intimate relationship.

He couldn't bear it, not if history really was going to repeat itself.

'You told me you couldn't get pregnant!' he accused, the betrayal gripping him in fierce talons and shredding the first green shoots of his growing trust. He wouldn't allow himself to remember the flash of guilty relief he'd felt when she'd told him that there was nothing stopping him from selfishly burying himself inside her body over and over again. Whether her inability to conceive was deliberate or a malfunction of her own reproductive system hadn't mattered in his desperation to forget the loss of the child he'd loved as his own.

'No, I didn't!' she argued fiercely, her knuckles white with tension as she crumpled the paper in her hand. 'I told you I couldn't have children, and we know better than most that it's not the same thing.'

'Well, however you want to split hairs, it was obviously a lie, if that result is to be believed.' He gestured towards the result sheet then rammed his fingers through his hair in disbelief. 'Dammit, what is it about me?' he demanded. 'Have I got "sucker" tattooed across my forehead or something?'

If he hadn't seen it happen, he wouldn't have believed how swiftly Leah's expression went from distraught to icy disdain.

With a single swipe of both hands she cleared all trace of her tears from her cheeks, then her chin tilted up and her shoulders went back.

'Don't worry about it, Mr ffrench. It's not your problem. Now, if you'll excuse me, I'd like to go home.' And without another word she strode swiftly out of the room and vanished from sight.

Leah had never been so glad that she used her car to get to the hospital. She'd barely held herself together long enough to shut the door before her tears began again, and they were still welling up in an inexhaustible supply when she finally locked herself into her flat.

The only thing she couldn't decide as she sobbed out her misery in the privacy of her bedroom was whether she was more unhappy about the unexpected pregnancy or about David's reaction to it.

Still, remembering his devastation about the loss of little Simon, any pleasure he might have felt at the prospect of another child had probably been overshadowed by memories of his double loss.

'Not that it would do him any good to get excited about it,' she murmured several hours later when she'd finally been able to control her immediate misery. At least her bonsai wouldn't take any notice of her swollen red eyes and blocked nose and they might even be able to help her reach some kind of equilibrium in advance of the misery still to come.

She tried to concentrate on repotting a young beech tree into a new pottery container, knowing that it would be difficult to empty her mind of the contempt she'd seen in David's eyes when he'd thought she'd tricked him. Even focusing on the exacting task of spreading the roots out so that they could support the tree's eventual height couldn't stop her remembering the reason why she'd begun raising bonsai in the first place, especially as she'd deliberately chosen a specimen from a different variety for each of the children she'd lost.

How *could* she forget when she would be choosing another one, sooner or later, to commemorate this latest doomed foetus?

The strident summons on her front doorbell was so unexpected that she nearly knocked the tree, pot and all, onto the floor of the balcony.

'Who on earth is that?' she muttered, not in the mood for company. With the level of security in this block of flats, any visitor should have been contacting her by the entry-phone at the entrance to the building, not at her own front door...unless they already had a key to the building.

With a sense of inevitability she brushed the loose soil off her hands and the front of her shirt and jeans and then walked towards the door with all the alacrity of a victim on the way to the gallows. Even though David usually stayed at the hospital much later than this, she didn't doubt for one minute that *he* was the one standing outside in their shared hallway.

'This is not going to be pleasant,' she whispered, with her hand hovering over the latch. At least she had to give him credit for the fact that it was going to take place out of earshot of their colleagues. Since she'd already been divorced before she'd moved to St Luke's, none of them knew about that part of her life.

She'd rather they didn't learn of her night of stupidity with David either, but that might become unavoidable if her condition...

Her train of thought was derailed by another peal of the bell, louder and longer than the last, and she resigned herself to the inevitable.

'Come in, David,' she invited quietly, already turning away as the door swung open with the sudden memory of her blotchy face. 'Can I offer you anything to drink?' A moment alone with a cold tap wouldn't do much, but...

'I don't need a drink, Leah. I need some answers,' he said, his voice much closer than she'd expected. Even so, his touch on her arm was unexpected as was its gentleness when he silently insisted that she turn and face him.

Just one glance at his beautiful eyes and the expression of concern in them was enough to have her fighting tears again. Even to the most casual observer it would be obvious that he was more worried about her now than angry...and she wasn't a casual observer.

'Sit down,' he said, leading her across to her settee and sitting down far too close to her for her peace of mind. If he was going to lambaste her again for misleading him, she needed him to be further away. How could she even think clearly let alone speak when she could breathe in the mixture of soap and man that was his alone, and could feel the warmth radiating from his body?

'First, I need to apologise,' he said abruptly and, as though wiped by the flick of a switch, her mind was clear.

'Apologise?' Just because her mind was working again, it didn't mean that she wasn't confused, especially when she'd expected his anger to have grown since she'd left him seething in the office.

'I tried to take advantage of my position as head of department to have a look at your medical records,' he admitted. 'Not that it did me much good.'

For a moment Leah didn't know whether she was annoyed that he'd tried or amused at his chagrin that he'd failed.

'It wouldn't,' she said wryly, easily able to see how much that had frustrated him. 'I left my records with my old obs and gyn department as the professor was the one who was treating me. I didn't move here until after my divorce and decided I wanted to come with a clean sheet. Donald was the only one who knew anything about my reproductive history.'

'So you only appear in St Luke's records as Jane Smith, patient of Dr Dawson?'

'Exactly. The last thing I wanted was for my private business to become public knowledge—not that Stanley would have breathed a word, of course. He's

the soul of discretion. But somehow the hospital grapevine…'

He nodded his understanding and was silent for a
moment before he spoke again. 'They're going to find
out sooner or later, you know. A pregnancy isn't something you can keep secret for ever.'

'Not necessarily,' she whispered, having to force the
words out through a rapidly tightening throat.

'You've already decided to have an abortion?' She
couldn't tell whether he sounded shocked or dismayed
and her eyes were too full of tears to see his face
clearly enough to tell.

'An abortion won't be necessary,' she said bitterly,
years of disappointment and despair forcing her to continue. 'In seven attempts, I never even got to eight
weeks before I lost the baby.'

'Oh, Leah,' he murmured, and suddenly, without
knowing how it happened, she found herself cradled
in his arms and sobbing her heart out on his shoulder.

It seemed like for ever before the tears finally abated
and only the knowledge that she needed to tell him
the rest of the story helped her to pull herself together.
Even then, he wouldn't let her put any distance between them and somehow she found it easier than
she'd feared to talk with his arm wrapped securely
around her.

'Start at the beginning,' he prompted when she hesitated at the last minute, trying to decide where to begin the sorry tale. 'Were you married?'

'I was,' she confirmed, and it wasn't until she felt
some of the tension leave his body that she realised
that he hadn't been certain whether there had been
another man in her life. If history had been repeating
itself, he must have been afraid that he could lose this

child, too. 'Ironically, we got married when I realised I was pregnant, just before finals. I lost the baby the day the results came out.'

Her story was no different than dozens of the women they saw, the special category who actually managed to conceive naturally over and over again, only to lose the baby before it had the slightest chance of survival. It was heartbreaking enough for those who discovered that their inability to conceive was due to a low sperm count or damaged Fallopian tubes or any one of the dozens of other combinations that prevented sperm and egg from meeting and combining to form that longed-for child.

For years she'd lived in that special hell where each time she became pregnant the baby stayed with her just long enough for her to know it was there and feel that precious protective connection before the onset of wrenching pain told her that it wasn't to be. And it hadn't mattered what tests the professor had performed. They'd never been able to find any reason why, or discover any treatment to stop it happening.

'In the end, Gordon got fed up with waiting for me to carry his son and heir and moved on to someone who could.' She knew there was little humour in her laughter; the ever-present pain wrapped tightly around her heart made it far closer to hysteria. 'Irony struck again—she had twins just four months after he left me, so he even managed to make up a bit of lost time. They were expecting their fourth the last time I heard.'

'I take it the two of you had all the tests,' he said and she could almost hear his brain switch into diagnosis mode.

'With the prof as my head of department, what do you think?' she challenged, knowing that the man's reputation for thoroughness was legendary and world-wide. 'Just like the Whittiers, there was regular ovulation and a normal supply of sperm but, unlike them, the two elements actually got together, achieved fertilisation and went on to implantation. Mind you,' she mused aloud, remembering the months it had taken the two of them to get that far each time, 'it's never happened after just one night before.'

'Should I take that as a backhanded compliment?' he asked, and surprised her into an unexpected chuckle. She would never have believed she could find any part of this situation in the least bit funny. David had managed the impossible...in more ways than one. If only...

No. She wouldn't allow herself to wish for the moon. He might have managed to get her pregnant, but so had Gordon, over and over again. It was carrying the baby to term that was impossible.

'Anyway,' she said briskly, knowing their conversation had nearly run its course and just wanting to get the painful bit over and done with, 'I didn't know whether I was pregnant and even though I know that I'll lose it before I get to eight weeks, I know you had a right to know about it. I was just waiting for Stanley to let me know one way or the other and then I would have told you, but you saw the results first.'

The hot press of tears threatened to overflow and she really didn't want to start crying all over him again. The only thing she could latch on to in an attempt to control her shaky emotional control was her trees.

'I'll have to choose another tree,' she said, wondering which species would best commemorate David's child.

'Tree?' he echoed, sounding as though he was wondering whether she'd fallen out of one and landed on her head at some time.

'A bonsai,' she exclaimed, deliberately upbeat. She welcomed the chance to put a little distance between them as she got up to lead the way to her balcony even as she mourned the loss of his closeness. 'These are my babies now,' she said with a gesture towards the display she'd set up on slatted wooden shelving, glad that there was still just enough daylight for him to see them.

None of the seven trees was taller than knee-height and each was a perfect miniature, down to the smallest detail, of their cousins growing naturally in the countryside.

He was silent for a long moment while he looked at them one by one.

'You've grown these?' he murmured, and the admiration in his voice was balm for her soul. 'They're beautiful. Perfect.' He leant closer to touch a tiny leaf of the silver birch and she could see in his eyes the same fascination that had come over her with her first close encounter.

'Tell me about them,' he invited with a glance over his shoulder, and she knew it wasn't an idle request.

Pleased by his interest, she began by describing the tiny oak that had been her first choice, not knowing at the time that it was one of the more difficult species to develop a natural appearance in miniature form, given its habit of carrying the leaves in small bunches at the end of twigs. As ever, when she was thinking about the trees, her thoughts went to the babies they commemorated, and she barely realised until it was far too late to stop that she'd slipped into talking about the qualities of the trees—strength, resilience, grace, longevity—that she hoped her children would have shared...if they'd survived.

'Do they really help?' he asked with a touch of desperation in his voice as he straightened up and turned to face her, and she knew he was thinking of little Simon.

'To a certain extent, yes, because I can switch my thoughts off while I'm taking care of them.' She hated to destroy the glimmer of hope that appeared in his eyes, but it wouldn't be honest to tell less than the whole truth. 'But if you're asking if they can replace a lost child, then, no. Nothing can...ever.'

David wondered as he lay staring up at the ceiling in the darkness if Leah realised just how much those words had told him about her.

There had been a world of sadness and loss in them, but also a measure of anger at the cruel fate that had thwarted her so often.

She probably hadn't realised that, even as she'd wept at her impending loss, she'd had one hand spread protectively over the place where her child—*their* child—was nestled.

His heart had gone out to her in that moment. Any hint of anger at the fact that she'd told him less than the truth about her fertility had completely gone once he'd understood the reason.

He had seen this heartbreaking situation so many times in his work that it shouldn't have been able to affect him so strongly, but this time everything was different... What he couldn't work out was why. There were only two possibilities really. Either it was be-

cause the doomed child was his…this time, unequiv-
ocally his…or because it was Leah's child.

'But that raises other questions,' he murmured. Why
should he care so much that Leah was going to go
through such a devastating loss all over again? After
all, he'd made a firm decision not to allow himself to
become involved any more, so it couldn't be because
he cared about her.

He snorted. 'And if you believe that…' he scoffed,
silently admitting that, in spite of his determination, he
did care about Leah. 'And not just as a colleague either,' he said aloud, feeling a measure of relief to hear
the words spoken. He didn't know when she'd got under his skin—had it been that first day they'd met
when she'd stood her ground so defiantly in the middle
of a room full of chaos? He certainly wasn't ready to
explore just how important she'd become to him, but
that didn't mean he wouldn't move heaven and earth
to do everything he could to spare her the heartache
of another lost baby.

It would be a long shot, hoping he could succeed
where others had failed especially as she'd spent years
under the professor. He certainly wouldn't have left
any stone unturned while Leah had been in his care,
but how long ago had her last pregnancy been? Had
the latest research about unexplained miscarriage
emerged since then?

What was more to the point, how was he going to
persuade her to let him do any tests? After seven miscarriages, she was clearly resigned to the prospect of
losing this baby too. How was he going to find out if
there was anything he could do to avert that without
putting her emotions through a wringer all over again?
He didn't want to raise her hopes, only to squash them.

Perhaps he should wait...not mention what he had in mind until he saw her notes. He still had to get her permission for that, and there was also the delicate ethical position, with him as her departmental superior, her one-time lover and the father of the child she carried. What would the hospital authorities think of the fact that he also wanted to take on the role of her obs and gyn specialist?

'But I can't pass her over to someone else!' he exclaimed, taking less than a second to dismiss every possible candidate in the department. As good as his young team was, the only other person to whom he would entrust such a case would be Leah herself.

'No. *I'm* dealing with this. If there's the slightest chance of saving her baby's life...' Even as he said the words, a lightning bolt of realisation shocked him into silence.

It wasn't just Leah's baby. It was his baby, too, and the idea that it might not survive long enough to draw its first breath suddenly terrified him.

He was finally drifting off to sleep when the shrilling of a distant telephone dragged him back to full wakefulness.

He was already halfway across the room before he realised that it wasn't even his phone ringing, but his brain hadn't yet learned to ignore all the sounds from the other flats.

'Not mine,' he muttered, while his pulse gradually slowed towards a more normal rate, then it speeded up again with the realisation that it was most likely Leah's phone he'd heard.

With the thought that it was probably the hospital ringing her to attend an emergency patient, all his protective instincts immediately leapt out from behind the concrete wall he'd erected around his feelings.

'If someone just wants a word with her, that's one thing, but if they're calling her back to the hospital...' He reached for his clothes, grabbing his off-duty jeans rather than bothering to find a suit at this time of night. 'If she's needed, then I'm going in, too,' he muttered, knowing he was being ridiculous but unable to quash the urge to keep an eye on her. Until he'd had a chance to talk to her and find out whether there was anything he could do to preserve their baby's life, he didn't want her put in any stressful situations.

The familiar sound of Leah's front door being unlocked told him he had guessed right and he stepped out of his door just seconds later.

'Shall I give you a lift?' he offered casually, with all the appearance of having been summoned to the hospital, too.

'Oh! Yes, thank you.' He'd startled her and she was endearingly flustered and still a little red-eyed after her emotional outpouring earlier that evening, but no less beautiful with her honey-coloured hair pulled back into a hasty ponytail and her grey eyes wide and soft. She nibbled her lip as they took the lift for speed and he imagined himself taking that plump flesh into his own mouth and...

Enough! he chastised himself silently, deliberately dragging his eyes away before his body's reaction became too obvious. *You haven't got time to go back for a cold shower.*

It's just my luck, he continued inside his head as she tucked her slender legs into the car with a smile of thanks. *My sex drive is all but invisible for years then I meet Leah and it appears with a vengeance.*

Knowing that his sex drive was the last thing he should be thinking about on his way in to St Luke's, even if he was sharing a car with Leah, he fought for some way to take his mind off the warm scent of a woman who had just climbed out of bed.

He couldn't talk about the patient they were going to see because he had no idea who it was. That just left his plan to persuade her to let him take another blood test, but perhaps that would be better if he waited until her notes arrived... *if* she gave her permission for him to request them from the professor.

There was only one way to find out, and he'd rather do it before they were surrounded by other members of staff.

'Will you be returning to the professor or are you happy for me to take care of you?' he asked, hoping he sounded as calm as if hers were no more complicated a case than that of any ordinary mother. She didn't need to know that his pulse rate was at least triple what it should be for a man of his age and state of health, and it was getting faster with each second that she made him wait for her answer.

'I suppose there's no real point in travelling all that way just for him to tell me that nothing's changed from the previous seven times,' she said eventually, her tone totally devoid of the happy lilt that her condition should have given her. It was every mother-to-be's right to feel excited about the miracle that was taking place inside her, and with everything inside him he wanted to be able to give that to Leah.

'Fine,' he said quietly, hoping his voice didn't betray his delight that he'd overcome the first hurdle so easily. 'I'll get you to sign the release form when we get to the office.'

'There's no hurry,' she said. 'It's not as if there's anything you can—'

'Leah, I won't be doing any less for you than I would for any other patient,' he said sharply. 'In fact, as my right-hand man…or woman, in your case…you should receive the best treatment the department can offer.'

'David, please…' As he parked the car in his assigned slot she struggled in silence for a moment before finding the words she wanted. 'In the circumstances, I really don't want a lot of fuss. I'd rather no one else in the department knew unless absolutely necessary.'

'If that's what you want,' he agreed, then had a brainwave of a suggestion that he was sure would instantly ease her tension. 'How about sticking to your Jane Smith alter ego for the time being?'

'Can I do that? Is it legal?' she demanded eagerly. 'I wasn't sure when I sent my sample up to Stanley whether I could end up being dismissed for…I don't know…falsifying an identity or something.'

'I haven't a clue,' he said as he released his seat belt. 'And I have no intention of finding out, so long as it's just the two of us in the know…'

'Thank you, David,' she said, with the first real smile he'd seen from her in far too long, a smile that dimmed all too quickly when she continued. 'It's not as if the deception will go on very long—another four to six weeks if previous episodes are anything to go on.'

'In the meantime, we have a patient waiting for us,' he said as he waved to Den on security duty and set off briskly for the bank of lifts. 'How much do you know?' he asked as the doors swept open to admit them, hoping that would prompt her into letting him know why she'd been called in at all.

'Nothing more than that Mrs Masson was making herself thoroughly objectionable, *again*, and upsetting the other mums and dads,' she said. 'Do you know any more than I do?'

The lift arrived at their floor and the noise that they could hear even before the doors opened was enough to make any evasive reply superfluous on his part.

'What on earth is going on here?' he demanded in an icy voice, barely needing to raise it to cut through the cacophony. 'You seem to have forgotten that this is a hospital. If you can't keep your voices down, I shall call Security and have everybody escorted out of the department.'

For just a second it worked like a charm, but he should have known that nothing could keep the objectionable Mrs Masson quiet for long. She seemed to have been determined to make their lives difficult from the first moment she'd arrived at St Luke's

'It's all very well threatening us, but what I'd like to know is where the two of you were while my babies are dying,' she demanded stridently. 'Why aren't you here doing the jobs you're paid to do?'

'Mrs Masson, I've warned you once,' David said coldly. It was difficult to keep control when he was suddenly furiously angry that the objectionable woman should have dared to attack his dedicated staff. As if Leah didn't have the right to her precious off-duty hours. She already worked horrendously long hours, and with an unexpected pregnancy of her own taking its emotional toll...

Enough! He couldn't afford to think about that, not

with a dozen or more pairs of eyes on him, waiting for him to resolve this unwelcome disturbance.

He fixed baleful eyes on the woman and gestured briefly along the corridor. 'If you have something you want to say to me, would you kindly join me in my office?'

Out of the corner of his eye he saw Sally grab Leah's arm and mutter furiously in her ear, but he couldn't stop to find out what that was about, not with Mrs Masson on his heels.

He'd barely got her settled and was preparing himself for the onslaught when Leah slipped quietly into the room and closed the door behind her.

Instantly, he felt better…calmer…as though a missing part of the picture had been replaced, although why he should feel all that just because Leah had joined them… He would have to think about that later.

'So, why are you letting *my* babies die?' Sylvia Masson demanded. 'Everyone else's are getting better, but mine…'

She broke off but in spite of the emotional tone of her words, David had the strangest feeling that there wasn't any real feeling for the babies in the accusation. But how could that be when—if their suspicions were correct—she'd perjured herself and risked her life to go through all the rigours of IVF to achieve the pregnancy? How could she not care desperately that the fact that she'd been implanted with triplets had significantly reduced the likelihood that any of the babies would survive?

'Mrs Masson, would you like me to call your husband?' Leah offered gently.

The angry woman turned to snap at Leah and David found himself tensing, ready to intervene, but then their eyes met, Leah's soft cool grey and Sylvia Masson's china-doll blue, and he saw a connection being formed although he didn't understand how or why.

Discretion kept him silent as the older woman's shoulders slumped in defeat, her attention all on Leah, now.

'You know, don't you?' she murmured, and gave a slightly hysterical laugh. 'It was probably obvious to everyone that I'm nothing more than mutton dressed up as lamb, trying desperately to hang on to the man I love when all he really wants is a son.'

Tears started to roll down her cheeks, eroding their way through the dark eye-liner to leave trails of despair.

'You *couldn't* understand,' she sobbed, grabbing the handful of paper tissues Leah offered as she rocked backwards and forwards in her misery. 'You've got your whole life ahead of you and I'm afraid he's going to leave me because I've already lost my son, and because you did the hysterectomy, I can't ever have another and...and my daughters will be dead any day now and then I'll be alone...all alone...'

'Shh, Mrs Masson...Sylvia...' Leah soothed, wrapping an arm round the woman's shoulders. 'I do understand.' She glanced up at David and he felt the connection sear the air between them as their gazes met. 'We *both* understand because we've both lost children and...and my husband left me to have a family with someone else.'

It was several minutes before the distraught woman could control her tears and a lot more than that before they could both reassure her that her two tiny daughters were having the best possible treatment during the roller-coaster ride of their fight for life.

'We're only minutes away,' David pointed out gently. 'Both of us live within sight of the hospital and even when we're off duty, the on-duty staff know we'll come in as soon as they call us—like we did tonight.'

Finally, Sylvia left to spend some time sitting between her daughters' high-tech cots and it was just the two of them in their shared office.

David was guiltily aware that he was probably taking advantage of the high emotions that had filled the room in the last hour, but he knew that he was unlikely to find a better opportunity to persuade Leah to agree to his request.

'Leah, before you leave…could I ask you to do something for me?'

'As long as it doesn't involve using my brain,' she said with a tired smile that made him feel guiltier than ever. 'The tension of that little encounter turned it to mush.'

'It's that little encounter that…well, partly anyway… But that woman's desperation to have a child…well…' Oh, for heaven's sake, he was making a complete hash of this. He'd never persuade her at this rate, so he might just as well… 'Will you let me do the tests?' he demanded bluntly, and when he saw her blink and take a step backwards he was certain he'd been too blunt.

But this meant so much to him. Far more than he'd ever believed it would, and the last time he'd lost a child it had nearly destroyed him.

'Tests?' she repeated warily. 'But, David, I've already told you that nothing does any good, so what use would double-checking what the professor has already—?'

'Humour me?' he begged with an attempt at a smile

that failed dismally. He was actually reduced to crossing his fingers in the secrecy of his pockets. 'If you think about it, this pregnancy is different to all the others because it's a different mix of genes, and if there's the slightest chance of a different outcome... Leah, I couldn't bear to lose another child just because I didn't do some blood tests.' Even as he was saying it he knew it was deplorable to play on her emotions that way, but if his suspicions proved correct...

'Oh, David. After seven failures for no apparent reason, we both *know* what's going to happen.'

She was refusing, he realised, feeling sick at his failure. Even after he'd shamelessly tugged on her heartstrings. Now he had nothing left in his armoury to persuade her, other than telling her his suspicions and raising her hopes unforgivably high.

If she *had* allowed him to do the blood test he wanted and he'd found that—as he suspected—her immune system was mistaking her pregnancies for an invader and sending in armies of NK cells to destroy them, he could have put her on powerful steroids to calm down her immune system enough for the baby to survive. Not the stilboestrol that had caused so many problems several decades ago when it had been used for a similar purpose but other—

'All right,' she said suddenly, interrupting his distracted thoughts and taking him completely by surprise. He was so jubilant that he almost missed her following words. 'But it has to be first thing tomorrow, before I have time to come to my senses, and on condition that this is strictly between the two of us.'

'And Jane Smith,' he added, hoping to end on a lighter note, but already he was filled with foreboding.

He could see that in spite of those seven lost pregnancies she was actually beginning to let herself hope.

Regret followed him like his own personal black cloud as he drove the two of them back to their flats.

He was almost certain that she hadn't already had her immune system investigated. Surely she would have mentioned it earlier when she'd been telling him about the tests she'd undergone, but he couldn't ask her directly without tipping his hand, and he didn't want to do that.

After all, what were the chances that he was guessing right? Was he just setting her up for more heartbreak? And, more importantly, what would it do to her if she lost another child after allowing herself to hope?

CHAPTER TEN

'COME on, Stanley. Ring me, now!' David muttered, his eyes fixed on the telephone while he waited for Leah's results.

He was desperately hoping they would come through before she returned to the office. At least then he would have a few minutes to assimilate the significance so that he could speak to her without his own emotions getting in the way.

He closed his eyes and shook his head, wondering where his detachment had gone. He'd been so determined that he wouldn't allow himself to get involved again, determined not to put himself through the agony of loving and losing. After a lifetime spent coping with his mother's suffocating love, he'd been wary about the very idea of marriage and family...until Ann had told him she was expecting his baby.

He'd honestly believed that when he'd lost Simon, something had died inside him...something that could never be revived.

'And what happened?' he muttered, hoping no one was out in the corridor listening to him talking to himself. 'Leah happened, that's what.'

Leah, the hard-working, talented, intuitive, compassionate, beautiful woman who made every molecule in his body sit up and take notice and had made his life a much brighter place. Leah, who was carrying the tiny foetus that—if his guess was right and the treatment worked—would become his son or daughter. Leah who in one night had gifted him with the most sensual and erotic memories of his life and who…was standing in front of him with a concerned frown on her face.

'Are you feeling all right, David?' she asked, and only someone who knew her well would have seen how tense she was under her calm exterior. Had she slept as little as he had after her decision to have the tests done? At least she'd had a morning of face-to-face appointments to occupy her mind after the sample had been delivered to the lab, while he'd sat here trying to concentrate on paperwork…and failing miserably.

'I'm fine,' he began, just as the phone rang. He pounced on it, desperate for the relief of hearing Stanley's voice on the other end. 'David ffrench,' he announced, and when it *was* Stanley, he found the tension only increased.

'Your guess was spot on,' the older man confirmed, bringing the hot threat of tears to his eyes. 'Jane Smith's system is reacting exactly as if it's rejecting an organ transplant, rather than to a pregnancy. I'll send the figures down with the rest of the batch, unless you want me to send it down straight away?'

'No hurry,' David said gruffly, only just remembering to thank the man for putting the test through as a priority before he fumbled putting the receiver back in the cradle.

'Was that Stanley?' Leah demanded with a mixture of dread and eagerness. She sank into the chair behind her desk as though her knees wouldn't hold her any more. 'What was the result?'

Unable to bear so much distance between them as he gave her the news, David came round to perch one hip on the corner of her desk then wondered if he'd done the right thing when her soft feminine scent twined distractingly around him. The pleading expression in her eyes brought him to his senses.

'While you were carrying Donald's work as well as your own, it might have slipped your notice that there's been some research going on for a couple of years now, trying to prove a link between an overreaction of a woman's immune system and repeated unexplained miscarriages,' he began as soberly as any medical school lecturer when what he really wanted to do was dance and sing that at least their baby now had a chance of life. 'Your tests showed that your white blood cell count is very high, similar to a patient with organ rejection after a transplant.'

The dawning comprehension on her face told him that he didn't need to explain that this could be a sign that her NK cells had been alerted to hunt out the foreign tissue inside her to kill it and get rid of it.

'What I propose is that we put you on steroids in the hope that it will damp your body's reaction down until the baby's well enough established to survive the rest of the pregnancy.'

'How long?' she demanded faintly, as though she was having trouble taking it all in. 'How far has the research gone? Have the researchers found a workable treatment protocol yet?'

'It's ongoing, but so far the optimum appears to be to the end of the first trimester, with a gradual withdrawal after that. They also suggest backing the steroids up with aspirin to prevent the NK cells from attacking the foetus through the blood-clotting mechanisms.'

It was heartbreaking to see the way she was teetering between disbelief and hope. David wished he could give her guarantees but…

'What's the success rate?' she whispered shakily, her thoughts obviously following a parallel route. 'Has the study been going on long enough for them to have any figures?'

'It's still very much in the experimental stage and relatively unproven, and the numbers are small, but so far it looks as if there's a twenty per cent success rate.' He knew he was playing devil's advocate, but he didn't want to get either of their hopes up too far.

'A one in five chance isn't very good odds,' she said soberly, then she took his breath away with a beatific smile. 'But it's so much better than no chance at all, David. So, when do I start taking the tablets?'

Three months had never gone so slowly, or been so exhausting, David thought with a heavy sigh.

In a way, it had felt as if he was holding his breath the whole time, and even now that Leah was coming off the steroids, David didn't feel that he could relax.

He should have been able to. After all, it looked as if the pregnancy was well established now, and in spite of her understandable caution, Leah was absolutely bubbling over with joy.

Especially today.

They'd deliberately come in to work early so that they could have the antenatal department to themselves. Feeling almost like giddy teenagers on a prank, they'd let themselves into the silent room that held the ultrasound equipment. She'd climbed up onto the table as he'd switched everything on, and as he'd run the probe over the gentle swell of her belly to reveal visible evidence that the baby was growing normally, his heart had swelled inside his chest and he'd wanted to crow from the rooftop.

It was a scary feeling after everything he'd gone through with Ann and Simon. He'd been so determined not to get involved, and it was only the fact that Leah's expression was similarly awed and fearful that made the whole thing bearable.

Except…

Except she was still determined to keep her condition a secret from their colleagues and she was definitely keeping him at arm's length, too. It was almost as if she felt she had to concentrate all her spare energy on the baby and had nothing left for even the most casual of social contacts. She certainly didn't seem to be willing to spend any time with him.

Even so, she seemed to have appreciated the cake he'd brought over to her flat to celebrate the fact that she'd finally managed to carry a baby past the heart-breaking eighth week. She'd clearly been touched that he'd even thought of it, but…

'Has she forgotten that it's my baby, too?' he demanded of the empty room, frustration at the limbo he'd been cast into finally exploding into words. 'Doesn't she realise that I'm every bit as concerned about the result of every test, terrified that something might go wrong?'

She'd certainly been terrified when she'd reached the end of the third month of the pregnancy and they'd started to wean her system off the steroids. She'd been convinced that it was too soon and that it would allow her immune system to turn on the baby and kill it.

Not that she'd said as much to him. She didn't say anything much at all to him and it was killing him, especially when he wanted to know everything—what

she was thinking, what she was feeling… But to someone trained to observe, it had been easy to see the
increased strain that gave a tense edge to her usually
elegant movements, and as for the shadows around her
eyes and the way she wouldn't meet his gaze…

'Dammit! She'll be halfway through the pregnancy
soon,' he exclaimed, remembering his last glimpse of
the curve of her belly before she'd pulled the loose top
of her theatre scrubs down to hide the evidence, and
the way his hands had itched to explore. 'That won't
leave me long before the baby's born…'

The sound of the unfinished sentence hung in the
air for a moment as the significance struck him. Leave
him long enough for what? What *did* he want? What
did he need to accomplish before the baby arrived?
And why?

Before he could find any answers the phone interrupted his scrambled thoughts.

'David? I'm down in A and E,' Leah announced,
overwhelming stress clear in her voice, and as his heart
leapt straight into his mouth, he had all his answers.

How could he not have seen it before when it had
been staring him in the face for weeks…months, probably?

All this time he'd been concerned on a professional
level to try to ensure that Leah didn't lose her
baby…*their* baby. He'd known how much it would
hurt if he were to lose another child and could only
imagine how devastating it would be for Leah.

What he hadn't realised until just this minute was
that—baby or no baby—his life wouldn't be worth living if anything happened to Leah.

And she was at the other end of the phone, telling
him she was in A and E.

Was she losing the baby? Haemorrhaging? Dying?

He couldn't lose her. Not now. Not before he'd held her in his arms again and told her that he loved her.

'I'm on my way, Leah. Hang on,' he said, cutting through her words and already half out of his seat, his heart trying to beat its way out of his chest.

Leah looked down at the blood and her heart rate doubled.

There was so much of it and it was so bright under the glare of the lights. Nobody could survive very long if they were losing blood at that rate, and everybody in the room knew it. They were running out of time and they couldn't afford to wait until David arrived. There was a baby at risk and that was all that mattered.

'He's on his way,' she said, although whether it was to let the rest of the team know or to reassure herself, she wasn't sure. She held her freshly gloved hands clear of contamination as she approached the patient, having to raise her voice to be heard over the cacophony of shrilling monitors. She didn't need all that noise to tell her that Ela Dahsani was in trouble. Under the natural golden hue of her skin she was already ashen with blood loss. 'We need to get on with it,' she muttered impatiently under her breath, waiting for the anaesthetist's nod before she could begin the emergency Caesarean.

'Please, Doctor, save my wife!' pleaded the distraught man clinging to her limp hand at the other side of the table, his dark eyes desperate in a face nearly as pale as the unconscious woman's. 'I nearly lost her when she had the cancer and we thought we would never be able to have this baby but…if you have to choose between the two of them, save my Ela!'

'She's under!' announced the anaesthetist. 'And her BP's already on the floor, so get moving!'

Even as she grasped the scalpel and prepared to make her incision, Leah knew how important it was to reassure the poor man.

'I'm going to do my best to save *both* of them, Arif,' she said firmly. 'So get ready for some sleepless nights when Ela makes you take your turn at walking the floor!'

Behind her, she heard the swing door slap open under a forceful hand and knew that David had arrived, but she was already preparing for the second stage of the incision, knowing that she didn't even have time to glance in his direction.

'Leah!' he exclaimed. 'What's going on? On the telephone you said—'

'You hung up before I could give you any details, but thanks for getting here so quickly... Suction! Oh, Lord, there's far too much blood,' she muttered under her breath, hoping Arif couldn't hear her. 'I think her uterus has ruptured. It's as thin as tissue paper...*wet* tissue paper!'

She reached a hand into the gaping incision and found the familiar shape of the baby's head then managed to hook a finger under a slippery little arm.

'Can you...?' She didn't even need to complete the sentence. David was already providing the steady pressure that would help her to lift the tiny being out of his dangerous abode.

'Clamp and scissors,' he offered, even as she supported the ominously limp form in both hands. She ached to do something to stimulate the baby into life but the paediatrician was ready at her elbow and Ela's life hung in the balance.

It didn't take more than a few seconds' examination and a sharing of professional glances with David to know what had to be done.

'Arif, we need to do an emergency hysterectomy if we're to have a chance of saving Ela. That means she'll never be able to have any more children. Do we have your permission?'

'Do whatever you have to!' he exclaimed, clearly overwhelmed by the speed of events. 'Just save my Ela!'

He'd barely spared his tiny son a glance, Leah marvelled as she and David worked as swiftly and as accurately as they'd ever done in the race against disaster. Even as they located the site of the haemorrhage and brought the blood loss under control, she was wondering what it would feel like to have a man love her that much.

She had no doubt that if all went well, Arif would be as loving a father as any child would want, but at the moment every atom of his being was concentrated on the woman he loved and willing her to stay with him. How could she herself do any less than her best to try to make it happen?

Even as she concentrated on her task, she was aware of a strange tension in David. It wasn't that he was any less proficient, but she now knew him well enough to know that there was definitely something else on his mind.

Something to do with her?

Probably, if it was anything to do with that last frowning glance he'd thrown in her direction before he'd left her to finish closing up their now stable patient. And in that case, it was something that needed sorting out, and the sooner the better.

*   *   *

Leah was about to shoulder her way out of the room, determined to track David down, when someone caught her sleeve.

'Will she *really* be all right?' pleaded the young woman who'd accosted her. 'Only I've never seen anyone lose that much blood before.'

For a moment Leah was taken aback, and it wasn't only by the young registrar's intensity. She'd only ever seen two people with eyes of that particular mixture of green and blue and as far as she knew, David and Maggie didn't have any other siblings or cousins.

'New to A and E?' she asked, even as she noted that the name on her tag was Libby Cornish.

'Painfully! Does it show?' she asked with a self-deprecating grin. 'How many of *those* am I going to be seeing in a day?'

'Hopefully, that's your quota for months!' Leah exclaimed. 'We really don't like performing emergency obs and gyn surgery in A and E. We'd rather take it at a more sedate pace up in our own department.' A department where she wanted to be *now*, confronting David ffrench with the fact that she was in love with him and...

Whoa! She was really getting ahead of herself here. She wasn't really going to put everything on the line like that. She wasn't brave enough to risk that sort of heartache again...or was she?

'I'm sorry, but I need to...' She gestured wordlessly towards the bank of lifts, then found herself adding, 'If you want to come up later and check on the Dahsanis, you're welcome.'

'Mr ffrench wouldn't mind?' she asked, almost eagerly, and Leah felt an unaccustomed twinge of possessiveness at the thought that the young woman was attracted to the man she loved.

'Not at all. He'd probably show you around the department himself, and spend the whole time trying to persuade you to change your specialty,' she joked, and made her farewells, suddenly eager to see David again.

'The Massons have disappeared,' Kelly Argent announced almost as soon as she arrived inside the department.

Leah stifled a groan, wondering how long it would be before she finally came face to face with David.

'What do you mean, disappeared?' she asked, trying to be patient. 'Have they gone back home?'

'That's just it!' the senior nurse exclaimed. 'This is the first time that we've actually had to phone them to come in—Sylvia Masson left late last night but both babies are very poorly again today and we thought they'd want to be here in case...' She didn't need to finish the thought. These tiny babies had such a fragile hold on life that their condition sometimes seemed to change every hour.

'Anyway,' Kelly continued, 'we've found out that they've been living in an hotel. Only they're not there any more. They've checked out without leaving a forwarding address.'

'How are the babies?' Leah asked as she turned towards the unit, taking the problem one step at a time and starting with the things that were marginally under her control. Tracking down parents was another thing entirely.

'They both looked very poorly when I started my shift—cranial bleeds,' she said sombrely. 'David's organising for an MRI to see how extensive the bleeds

were, then we'll have a better idea how badly their
brains have been damaged. Isn't it strange that both of
them should have suffered at the same time…?'

A gasp somewhere behind Leah had them both
twisting to face a shocked-looking Sylvia Masson.

'Are you talking about *my* babies?' she demanded
faintly, reaching out one shaking hand to support herself against the wall. 'What's happened to them?
They're not…?'

Leah and Kelly reached for her at the same moment,
both thinking she was going to collapse.

'They're alive,' Kelly reassured her as Leah
wrapped an arm around her and led her towards the
unit, guessing that she would want to see for herself.
'Come and sit with them.'

For a moment the older woman held back, her expression torn as tears started to trickle down her pallid
cheeks.

'I wasn't going to come back,' she whispered finally, confirming their suspicions. 'Marcus just wanted
a son. He didn't want the girls, especially if they're
going to be…brain damaged, and I didn't think I'd be
able to cope by myself.'

'We don't know, yet, how much damage they've
suffered. We'll have some idea after the scan, but we
won't know for certain until—'

'It doesn't matter,' Sylvia interrupted fiercely, shaking off their supporting hold and suddenly straightening her shoulders. 'It doesn't matter if they can't…
can't do all the things other children can do. They're
mine. My precious babies. And however long they've
got…whatever they can do…' She dashed her tears
away and continued. 'I'm their mother and I'm

going to be there with them, fighting for them... fighting with them...'

She turned and with a quiet sort of dignity made her way to the sink to scrub her hands and don the required protective clothing then sat herself in the seat she usually occupied, positioned between the two high-tech cots that monitored her daughters' shaky condition.

Leah's eyes burned as she watched Sylvia put one hand on each of the tiny babies, and although she couldn't hear anything through the glass, she could see Sylvia's lips moving and knew she was talking to them.

'Well, that's another problem solved,' she murmured, halfway between joy and tears as she finally made her way to the office she shared with David. Now she just had to find some way of tracking the man down and...

There he was!

She paused in the doorway, silent while she filled her eyes with the sight of him and her heart swelled with emotion. It was such a relief to be able to admit that she loved him, if only to herself so far. And she didn't only love his integrity and his commitment to his work; she loved everything about him, including those amazing eyes.

He wasn't working, for a change. His gaze was apparently fixed on something outside the window, but from the expression on his face it was what was going on inside his head that had all his attention.

Suddenly he raked his fingers through his hair and groaned aloud before he caught sight of her and leapt to his feet.

'David?' she said uncertainly as he strode towards her, but it was the last thing she said before he swept her into his arms and kicked the door closed behind her.

'Don't you *ever* do anything like that to me again!' he groaned with his forehead pressed against hers.

'What?' she squeaked breathlessly as he tightened his grip still further, almost as if he wanted to absorb her into his body. Her toes barely reached the floor but she didn't care. She'd never felt safer in her life.

'My blood ran cold when you rang from A and E,' he said, the words sounding almost painful as he forced them out. 'I thought you were losing the baby.'

The baby...?

Her heart sank. Was *that* what it was all about? Was that why he'd had such a stony face and why he'd put up such a barrier between them?

But what had she expected? He'd already lost one child. Of course he'd be gutted if he thought that he was losing another. She knew only too well what it was like to cope with the possibility of loving and losing a child again, even if she'd never actually held one of her babies.

But if she was lucky this time...became part of a set, mother and child...would that make it impossible for him to accept...?

'Then...' he grated, dragging her out of her despairing thoughts with a hand cradling each side of her face, tilting it up until her eyes met his. That blue-green gaze was so intent that there was no way she could mistake his sincerity, even as her heart stumbled with uncertainty. 'Then I realised that *you* matter more to me than the fear of losing a baby...

'Oh, don't get me wrong,' he continued hastily when she tried to interrupt. 'I know it would have broken your heart if *you* had been the patient down in A and E and it was *your* baby that…'

'Me?' she questioned, momentarily silencing him with one set of fingertips across his mouth while her heart stuttered and leapt with dawning joy. '*I* matter more than…' Her other hand caressed the soft swell of her growing child.

'Yes, *you*.' He covered her hand with one of his own. 'That's not to say that I don't want this little person, because I do…in spite of…'

'In spite of the fact that you're afraid of something going wrong?' she challenged when he faltered, suddenly determined to get everything out in the open. There was no chance of any sort of lasting relationship between them if they didn't.

'In spite of the fact that I was absolutely determined not to let anyone get close to me, because I knew I wouldn't survive that sort of pain again,' he admitted quietly. 'I thought we could have a purely professional relationship until that night. Even then I tried to stay away from you, but I should have known I was wasting my time. As soon as I met you, life seemed…brighter. I felt more…hopeful…more optimistic than I had since I lost Simon. Dammit, woman!' he exclaimed. 'I fell in love with you and you seemed ideal for me—a career woman who couldn't have children.'

'Then I found out I was pregnant…'

'And I panicked,' he admitted grimly. 'But even while I was scared to death that history was going to repeat itself, I was slowly coming to realise that I didn't just want a cordial professional relationship with you. If I'm honest, that would never have been enough for me either.'

'And now?' The joy dawning inside her was almost too much for her to contain.

'Now I know exactly what I want,' he declared. 'I want it all—you, the baby and the whole story-book happily-ever-after...if you'll have me?'

'What are you suggesting? That we move in together for the sake of the baby—so you can be there while he or she is growing up?' She didn't want to be presumptuous. If that was all he was offering, she'd take it, even though she wanted so much more. But he'd married once for the sake of a baby and he wouldn't necessarily want to...

'What do you think I'm suggesting?' Suddenly he dropped to one knee in front of her, one hand held tightly in his as he looked up at her. 'I'll say it in words of one syllable so that there's no confusion. Leah, I love you and the unexpected miracle we managed to create. Will you do me the honour of becoming my wife?'

'Your *wife*?' she whispered in disbelief, and with the realisation that everything she'd ever wanted was within her grasp, her knees refused to hold her any longer. 'Oh, David, yes! I'd love to be your wife. I love you,' she said, and threw her arms around him as they knelt together on the floor.

His mouth went from gentle to hot and hungry in an instant and she responded as she had that night—passionately, with her own hunger leaping up to meet his.

It was several minutes before either of them realised that someone was knocking on the door and at least that long before they were on their feet and calm enough to be able to invite their visitor in.

'I'm sorry. Is this an inconvenient time?' Libby

Cornish asked when she stuck her head around the door. 'Dr Dawson said I could come up to see the Dahsanis' baby.'

For a moment, Leah didn't dare look at David or she knew she would have laughed aloud. If the young registrar with the beautiful blue-green eyes had knocked a couple of minutes earlier she would have interrupted David's proposal, and a couple of minutes later...

'It's not inconvenient at all,' David said, and looked down at Leah with a smile that showed her she'd finally banished the last of the shadows in his eyes. 'In fact, you can be the first to congratulate me. Dr Dawson...Leah...has just agreed to marry me.'